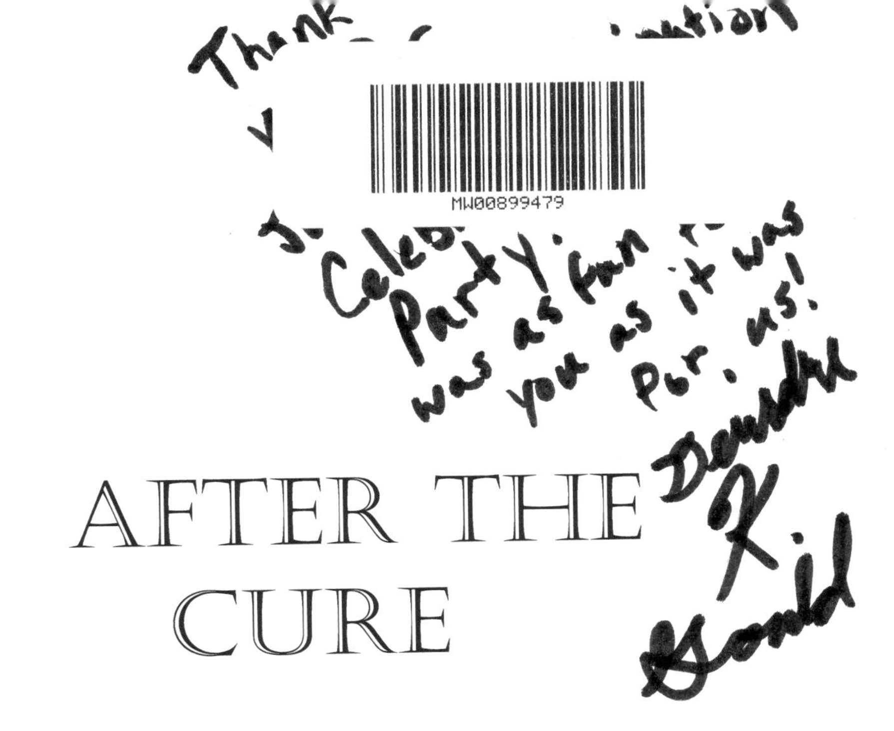

AFTER THE CURE

DEIRDRE GOULD

After the Cure

This is a work of fiction. Names, character, places and incidents are either the product of the author's imagination or are used fictitiously, and any resemblance to actual persons, living or dead, business establishments, events or locales is entirely coincidental.

For Dad for helping me get it all right and Tim for not minding when I get it all wrong

AFTER THE CURE

<<<<>>>>

THE CURE

Nella tried not to think about the hundreds of people nearby, all rotting in their sleep, but the raspy hum of the flies was almost overwhelming. The heat trebled the intensity of the rotting sewage smell that hung in a cloud over them. It would be worse when they woke up and began moving around. What would they think of each other? Of themselves?

"Be ready to take notes," Professor Taylor told his small crew, "Remember to stay back from the Infected- er *Cured* until the soldiers say it's safe and then I want you to try to observe them as closely as possible. We don't know if they will remember anything after infection, but for many that will have been traumatic. They may be exhibiting confusion, fear or even mild aggression. You are the only people left in the world that are trained to deal with this. History is depending on your faithful recollections and hard work on this day."

Nella tapped a pencil on her legal pad nervously and walked down the slope where the soldiers had their weapons aimed squarely at the sleeping Infected. There was no breeze and she could clearly hear Rick Framden orating his broadcast from fifty yards away, even over the insistent buzz of the insects.

"This is it ladies and gentlemen. In just a few moments the sleeping darts should wear off and the whole world will be able to see whether the Cure has worked. This could be the beginning of the end of this terrible plague . . ."

"No pressure right?" sighed an attractive Indian girl at Nella's elbow.

Nella grinned in spite of the situation. "Hey, aren't you supposed to be over with the film crew?"

she asked.

"Nah, the Great Rick Framden sent me to shoot b-roll. I'm not much more than an intern. And I'm stuck behind these louts. I'm barely going to get a shot of anything except uniformed backs."

Nella liked her already. "We can't let someone like Rick Framden dictate what gets recorded for history. No offense."

"Believe me, none taken. Sevita Das by the way."

"Dr. Nella Rider. Stick close to me and get ready."

Slow movement on the field caught her eye and her smile faded. It was happening. One of the Infected was stirring. Nella looked around as a restless shuffle traveled through the soldiers. These weren't hardened veterans. They were kids and homemakers and retirees. All that was left that could prop up a weapon. She thought to herself that they were going to be as desperate for psychiatric care as the Cured after today. If they didn't accidentally shoot each other first. Nella pushed her way forward.

"Hey, I wouldn't do that if I were you-" began a young soldier next to her, but suddenly he stopped. One of the Infected, a man, began to stand, rising from the crushed whorl of long grasses. Sevita pushed in next to Nella and began filming. "Hold still!" shouted the young soldier. The Infected man held his hands up. The nails were long and jagged and his hands and cheeks were black and scaly with old blood. He was shaking.

"Identify yourself!" yelled the soldier and Nella felt him tighten like a guitar string stretched too far.

"Isaac- my name's Isaac Green." His voice was stronger and clearer than Nella had expected. The man caught sight of the blood on his arms and brought them in front of his face. He was shaking more now.

"Mr. Green," Nella broke in, "Isaac. Listen to me, you've been ill for a long time, but it's going to be okay now." She took a few steps toward him and the still slumbering mass of Infected behind him.

"Don't-" the soldier said, but Nella kept walking. Sevita followed her, camera focused on Mr. Green.

"Ill?" said Mr. Green, "was it all a dream, was I just delirious?" He held his hands out in front of him as if he would drop them from his body if he could. He turned around slowly, his eyes widening at the sight of hundreds of people lying motionless on the field. He turned back and sought Nella's face. "Where is my family? I need to find them. In my dream, I- I did terrible things- I need to find my wife-" Mr. Green began to weep, his face cracking into a deep grimace.

"It's okay, Mr. Green," said Nella, "We'll help you find your family just as soon as we can. If you'll come with me we'll have a physician check you over and then we can add your name to the Found List-" she reached him and suppressing a shudder, placed a warm hand on his back. The rag that had once been his shirt was stiff and rough like sandpaper, caked with blood and dirt. He turned suddenly toward her and she jumped slightly. The soldier called, "Steady there!" and she watched the entire line of military personnel clench their weapons tighter. Nella held up her hand. "It's okay," she said.

But Mr. Green was staring at her. "What do you mean the 'Found List'?"

Nella's response was slow and deliberate, "Mr. Green, there have been some changes in the world while you have been ill . . ." She got no further.

"Oh my God!" screamed Mr. Green, "Oh my God! It was all real! It was all real! I killed them, I killed my own babies- my neighbors, it wasn't a dream? Tell me it was a dream!" he grabbed her arm, but weakly. He was crying so hard that she physically had to help him stay standing for a moment.

"It's over now," she said helplessly, "It's going to be okay for everyone now." But even as she said it, she knew it was a blatant lie and she blushed with shame. Mr. Green dropped her arm.

He started shaking his head, "It wasn't a dream." He whispered and then he started running toward the soldiers.

"Stop!" they shouted, but Mr. Green didn't listen. He limped in an awkward sprint toward them, his ankle or foot broken some time long before. The soldiers were unused to an Infected that could speak and weep. They hesitated to fire, and Mr. Green reached the young man Nella had pushed past. Isaac threw himself on the outstretched bayonet. The soldier had tears streaming down his face as he pulled the trigger. Nella was dumbstruck. She looked at Sevita who was still filming as the soldier dropped his gun and fled up the hill. Nella heard movement behind her. She turned and saw the mass of people slowly sitting up, stretching limbs and shaking their heads as if they could clear away the memory of the past two years. She looked back at Sevita who was still shaking and saw the pretty Indian girl turn the camera on herself. She tried to concentrate on the Cured woman beside her who was trying to stand and heard Sevita begin her broadcast in a dreadfully calm voice.

"Good afternoon Ladies and Gentlemen. This is Sevita Das reporting live from the Cure facility. It has finally happened, the Cure has worked. And the Infected remember. They remember everything. The madness has cleared. As you have just seen, this will be a massive burden of guilt for the Cured to bear, and many, no doubt, will not survive. Remaining family members and friends are urged to make contact with the doctors here, who will be able to help with the intense therapy that will be necessary to repair relationships and rebuild not only the Cured, but everyone affected by this terrible disease . . ."

THE PRISON

Six Years Later . . .

"You're Ms. Rider?"

The man squinted at her through thick sleet as he held the heavy glass door open for her. Nella tried not to slip as she trotted inside. She flicked cool gray slush from her leather briefcase with one hand. She suppressed a shiver, desperate to appear older and harder than she felt. The man next to her was almost unnaturally tall and she had to look almost straight up to see his face.

"You must be Mr. Courtlen." She smiled pleasantly, then immediately felt foolish. Nella coughed lightly to cover her embarrassment and said, "And it's *Dr.* Rider please."

Mr. Courtlen smiled, crinkling a thick raised scar on his cheek. "Of course, my apologies Dr. Rider. It's nice to meet you."

Nella was surprised. "Really?" she asked before she could stop herself. Mr. Courtlen's smile was warmer, more genuine this time.

"Really," he said, "We know you're here at the judge's request, but whichever way this trial turns out, it's important that history can show all the participants were completely sane. If the judge hadn't ordered these evaluations, I would have requested them." He extended a hand toward her. Nella shook it, but felt more rough scar tissue on his palm. She fought a sympathetic wince.

"So you aren't intending to go with an insanity defense?" she asked.

"Well," he laughed, "that's not really for me to decide is it? But I don't think we'll need to." Mr.Courtlen held a hand out toward the long blue corridor. "This way please. Dr. Pazzo is expecting us."

She quickly fell a few paces behind him, no match for his lengthy stride. Nella marveled again at his height. *Imagine how fast he must have been,* she thought, *I doubt anyone could have outrun him. And then those long skinny arms would wrap around you and yank you in toward snapping teeth.* She shuddered and tried to think of something else. They had reached the metal detector and Mr. Courtlen was removing his watch and car keys.

"Where's Stan?" he asked a nervous looking soldier.

"Uh . . . He went to get coffee," the kid managed to squeak, "He'll be back in a minute." Mr. Courtlen nodded. *At least I'm not the only one scared to death of this place,* thought Nella as she watched the young guard bouncing his knee. He gripped his weapon so hard that his knuckles glinted like bone. Dr. Rider flashed him a kind smile when he glanced at her and she could see his grip relax as he responded. Mr. Courtlen waved at a middle aged officer coming toward them.

"Hey Stan," he said, "Is it any good today?"

"Hi Frank. I made it myself, still have a can or two of the good stuff kicking around. I'll be glad when someone can figure out how to grow coffee beans in the populated zone again though. There's still half a pot in the break room, help yourself." Stan passed through the detector and set two full mugs on the table. "Who is our visitor?"

Mr. Courtlen said, "This is Dr. Rider. She is the court appointed psychiatrist for both Dr. Pazzo and Miss Connelly. She'll be a regular here for the duration."

She saw Officer Kembrey raise an eyebrow at Mr. Courtlen. He obviously thought she wasn't going to last. She brushed it off. Nella stuck her hand out and Stan shook it heartily. "Pleased to meet you. I'm Stan Kembrey but everyone just calls me Stan. Terry and I will be here every day shift. If you come at night you'll see Wanda Treim. Dr. Pazzo and Miss Connelly are the only detainees at this facility, so the rules are a little more relaxed. For now, at least, until and unless Miss Connelly becomes violent, you can bring pens or pencils into the cell to make notes with. Of course, if it were me in that cell, I think I'd rely on my memory instead. Dr. Pazzo seems to be in a calm state of mind. However, since the Cure doesn't seem to have worked as well on some of the earlier cases, there are big green buttons in the hallway in case either of them 'reverts.' Press one and all the guards will come running. If you have any questions about how things are supposed to work you can usually find the Warden in his office. If you have questions about how things *actually* work, well, Terry and I are here to serve." Officer Kembrey flashed her a smile and a wink. Mr. Courtlen rolled his eyes dramatically and walked through the detector, immediately setting it off. The younger soldier leapt forward, pointing his weapon at the lawyer. But Mr. Courtlen simply waited and Stan's only reaction was to the junior soldier's zeal.

"Relax Terry, Frank isn't going to stage a jailbreak. Just wand him. Should be near the right shoulder." He handed a gray wand to Robert who looked torn between taking it and maintaining his grip on the weapon.

"You know Frank, you should really have that taken out one of these days."

Mr. Courtlen laughed and rubbed the side of his bald head in embarrassment. "The doctor said it would be worse to take it out than leave it in for now. At least until someone starts producing antibiotics again. Besides-" he looked toward his feet, avoiding their gaze, "My wife gave me this one. Before- well, you know."

The back of Nella's neck prickled and her mind drew back, rejecting the picture that tried to grow there.

"Jesus, Frank, I'm sorry." Stan shook his head and then snapped at Terry, "Get on with it soldier! These folks have places to be."

Mr. Courtlen took off his sleek gray jacket and spread his long arms across the hall. Nella's mind flashed another picture of his hands turned into claws, long black nails ragged and stained and thin arms coated in dried black blood to his elbows. Her neck felt pinched and cold and she noticed her breathing had become rapid and shallow. *Be professional*, she thought, and forced her aching fingers to relax on the handle of her briefcase. Terry swiped the wand over Mr. Courtlen and was satisfied when it only screeched near the lawyer's shoulder. Officer Kembrey held his hand out for Nella's briefcase.

"I'll scan that for you Dr. Rider."

She handed him the case with a smile and walked through the detector. Mr. Courtlen was calmly buttoning his jacket as Terry looked nervously on. Stan handed Nella her briefcase.

"You're all clear," he said, "Have a nice day."

"You too," Nella mumbled.

Mr. Courtlen touched her shoulder and she jumped. "This way, Dr. Rider."

They walked the rest of the way down the hallway and paused before a dented metal door. The lawyer reached for a large button to be buzzed in but Nella stopped him. "Mr. Courtlen, wait," she said, "The best way for me to get an accurate picture of the defendants' mental health is for me to build a rapport with them first. I know you don't have to discuss this, but if you are willing I would be grateful. Is there anything I should steer clear of during these first few sessions?"

He frowned slightly in concentration. "Well, I think you'll find Dr. Pazzo is not what the press had made him out to be. He's actually been remarkably patient with answering questions, and I think you'll find him polite, if a bit on the cool side. Of course, I assume you are intelligent enough to not ask very stupid questions, like: 'What does it taste like?' or 'Are you invulnerable except if you get shot in the head?' And for the love of all things sacred, don't call him a zombie." Mr. Courtlen threw up his arms and then gave her a conspiratorial smile. He pressed the buzzer.

"And Miss Connelly?"

Nella watched the smile drop from his face. "I'm- I'm not Miss Connelly's counsel. I don't think I could really say."

"Of course," said Nella as the dented door swung open. She managed a bright smile at him as she stepped toward the door. Mr. Courtlen held it open but gently caught her wrist to stop her. Nella flinched as the rigid bones of his hand closed around her. He ignored her revulsion.

"But what Stan said about pens? I think I would trust him if it were me. Just to be safe." He let her go and straightened his jacket but the color was high in his face.

"Thanks," she said, though he had only made her more nervous. Mr. Courtlen cleared his throat.

"Dr. Pazzo is in the common room, if you'll follow me." He appeared unruffled as he strode through the door that separated the world from its most notorious living villain.

ROBERT PAZZO

Nella recognized Dr. Pazzo's face from the case files and the television news, but only barely. She'd been shown the pictures that were available and they were of a doctor still fresh from grad school. He had looked young, slightly bewildered, but happy and eager. She hated to admit it, but his picture had even been *attractive.* She tried to equate it with the man in coveralls standing near the plastic table in the most secure prison on earth. *It has been eight years since the Cure and probably ten since the photo was taken,* Nella thought to herself. Still, this man looked closer to the father of the boy in the pictures. Unlike the other Infected he had no visible scars, since he had secluded himself before the madness overcame him. But the other signs were there. He was underweight even all these years later and his hair was bright white and thinning in places. His shoulders curled around him like a dried rind. His face though, his face held the most marked changes. His eyes had sunk into his skull as if they were too ashamed to look upon the world. His cheeks and chin were jagged peaks that closed off any expression in their tight shadows. Nella glanced back at Mr. Courtlen. She had thought him too lean for his height and that his bald head made him look sickly, but compared to Dr. Pazzo, the lawyer was a model of health and vigor.

Mr. Courtlen saw her glance at him and noticed her shock. He stepped quickly toward her and touched the back of her elbow to steady her. "Dr. Pazzo, this is Dr. Rider, the court appointed psychiatrist. She'll be evaluating you and Miss Connelly throughout the trial. This is not a private relationship, so it isn't privileged. This means anything you say-"

"Yes, yes, Frank, I know. We don't have anything to hide. Dr. Rider, a pleasure to meet you." He offered her a hand that was little more than a rake with a thin covering of skin. Nella took it, intending to be gentle, but his grip was surprisingly strong. "Please, have a seat," he said, indicating the plastic picnic table. Mr. Courtlen sat beside him. Nella chose to sit on the opposite side, facing them. She placed her briefcase on the seat next to her.

"I just want to clarify what I'm here for. Judge Hawkins has asked me to monitor you and Miss Connelly to insure that you are competent to stand trial and that you remain so during the trial. It's important, no matter the verdict, that you are a healthy and active member of your defense and that this tribunal gets a reliable version of the events which caused the December Pandemic. Do you understand?"

Dr. Pazzo looked amused. He leaned back slightly and crossed his arms. "Well, aren't you the perfect reincarnation of Gustave Gilbert?"

Nella smiled, but it never reached her eyes. "I don't think the world is going to fall for another Albert Speer, Dr. Pazzo."

Mr. Courtlen frowned at the reference, his scar stretching and blanching. Nella felt a pang of remorse for having said it. Dr. Pazzo just laughed.

"I think I'm going to like you," he said, "But I have a few rules myself, if you want full access to me."

Nella straightened her posture and stared intently at him.

"Relax doctor. They're nothing unexpected. First, my lawyer, Mr. Courtlen must be present during our interactions. If he isn't here, our conversations will be limited to the current state of the weather. Second, I will answer any question you have *and* I will answer them truthfully," said Dr. Pazzo with a beatific smile, "But you need to make sure you have recording equipment or are taking notes," his voice began to become strident, "My answers will not change with repetition. So don't ask me over and over and over." Dr. Pazzo was shouting at her and had risen from his seat. His cuffed hands were two balls of shaking bone. Mr. Courtlen looked alarmed and helped his client sit back down as the guards moved nervously closer around them. Nella remained calm and motionless. "I understand," she said as Dr. Pazzo rearranged himself and softly cleared his throat. He smiled again.

"Very good doctor, very good indeed. Third, we will get to all of your questions. We're probably going to become very tired of each other. We have time. So if I say we are done for the day, I don't want to hear any whining or see any fits. You'll get your answers, just be patient. As unpleasant as these visits will be for you, I guarantee they will be ten times more unpleasant for me. But I've resolved to do this." Dr. Pazzo was serious and quiet. Nella sensed that she was now seeing the real man that Dr. Pazzo was. The one that had destroyed the world. And then lived to regret it.

"Very well, Dr. Pazzo," she said, "Is there anything else?"

He straightened his shoulders and looked up at her brightly. "Well, not as a requirement, but maybe a favor? I'd really love some books."

Nella shot a confused look at Mr. Courtlen but his face was impassive. "They won't let you have books?" she asked, surprised.

"I'm allowed to have them, but I don't exactly have people racing to the library to borrow books for me." Dr. Pazzo tapped his foot restlessly. "Look, you may have already decided that you don't like me.

Hell, I think even Mr. Courtlen doesn't like me and I'm *paying* for his company. But right now, and for the forseeable future- probably until my death, you are the only two who are willing to talk to me. And that makes you the closest thing I have to friends.

If you want me to stay sane enough to be tried, I need to do something besides pace my tiny cell. A few more weeks of this and I'll be as mad as poor old Ann next door. I've already been mad once in this lifetime. I have no wish to do that again."

Nella pulled a notepad and pen from her briefcase. "What kind of books do you like?" she asked. Dr. Pazzo gave her a list of a few dozen books, pretty evenly mixed between novels and scientific journals, but nothing jumped out as suspicious or even as a reliable pattern of tastes to Nella. She looked up from her list just in time to see Dr. Pazzo discreetly nod at Mr. Courtlen. The lawyer looked uncomfortable, his scar pulsing an ugly dark brown across his cheek.

"What is it? What did I miss?" she asked sharply.

Dr. Pazzo gave her a slow, sly smile that she didn't much care for. I'm sure they didn't tell you in court, but you are the fifth psychiatrist to enjoy my hospitality," he said, the smile still growing in his skull face. Nella felt the painful prick of her neck hair again. "I had to refuse to speak to them. They were more interested in maintaining their power by denying simple requests than in discovering the truth. I was just indicating to Mr. Courtlen that we can work with you. Oh yes, I think you'll do nicely. It's a good thing too, I was beginning to wonder if they'd find someone suitable before time ran out."

She saw Mr. Courtlen start and glance quickly at his client. Nella knit her brows and slightly shook her head. "Before time runs out for *what*?" she asked.

Still smiling, Dr. Pazzo rose and backed away from the plastic table. "That's enough for today, I think. I'll see you both tomorrow." And he walked back to his cell leaving Mr. Courtlen and Dr. Rider still sitting in shock.

Nella coolly placed the booklist and pen back in the briefcase. "What did he mean by that?" wondered Mr. Courtlen aloud. Nella snapped the case latch closed. She stood, smoothing wrinkles from her lap.

"If he hasn't told you," she said, "I wouldn't worry about it. This is just narcissistic posturing, the same as his rules. Dr. Pazzo knows that we have more power than he does right now and it irritates him. He is simply trying to find a way to gain the upper hand by pretending to magically have information that no one could possibly have found in eight long years. There is no such information. Hundreds of investigators have meticulously examined that lab and his home."

Mr. Courtlen shook his head. "Doctor, my client may seem arrogant and controlling right now, but I assure you, he is not truly that way. This is something more."

"I know this is my first meeting with Dr. Pazzo, but it is also the first time he has had to engage with someone who has more power than he does. No offense, but up to this point, he's seen you as his employee, his subordinate. This may have been the first time that he realized that you and I can truly influence his fate and that he doesn't have any real control over either of us. This is just an attempt to manipulate us, to 'indebt' us if you will, by waving this secret in front of us and hoping we'll jump."

Mr. Courtlen still looked troubled. Nella sighed. "Look, if you really want to know what he seems to think is so important, take my advice and don't ask him anything about it. If you do, he'll just keep stringing you along. If you wait, he'll become desperate and tell you quickly in hopes of bargaining."

Nella walked toward the soldier at the end of the room. "I'd like to visit Ann Connelly, could you show me the way?" she asked.

"Of course," said the soldier and led the way down a narrow hall lined with small solitary cells. "We'd sure appreciate your help, Doc," the soldier said casually, "See, we don't want to keep her locked in a tiny, windowless cell, not when there is all this room to roam around in." He waved his hand back toward the large community room. "And considering what's likely to happen at the end of the trial- well, begging your pardon, Doc, but we can't really begrudge her what freedom she has left can we? It's just not human, you see. And some of us ... well, some us just got back to *being* human after all." The soldier blushed deeply and rubbed the back of his neck. Nella touched his elbow.

"Your compassion does you credit. And it's a rare thing to find even these days."

The soldier cleared his throat. They had reached the cell and a female soldier was watching the tiny slot of glass in the door.

"Well, you see Doc, we're afraid she'll hurt herself if we let her out. She chews everything-"

"Pica," said the female guard.

"Yeah, like Johnson says, she's got pica. And she shakes and trips a lot. She's not like any other zom- I mean Cured, I've ever seen."

Officer Johnson stepped away from the window for a moment. "The other prisoner says it's because she got a concentrated dose of the early prototype. Her brain is like swiss cheese now. The Cure won't help her."

"The kicker is that she did it on *purpose*," the male officer said, shaking his head, "Some sort of high pressure internship. Thought the bacteria would give her enough endorphins and adrenaline to stay up through exams. She did it without telling the others until it was too late."

Johnson spat. "Then that bastard Pazzo locked her in with the dead animals. I don't know how she survived as long as she did."

"They say you're the best at helping folks who didn't get all the way Cured. What do you think Doc, is there a way we can fix it so we can let her out for some exercise once in a while?"

Nella puffed out her cheeks in a slow breath. "I'm not sure," she said at last, "I'll have to examine her. But if there is permanent physical damage I'm afraid there's not much that *anyone* can do. Does she have a regular physician?"

"Sure," said Johnson, "But he basically just changes the bandages anywhere she's bitten herself and tells us to keep her clean. I think he's scared of her, he always leaves in a hurry."

"Well," said Nella, "I should probably get in there. Do you mind if I leave my briefcase here?"

"That's probably for the best."

Nella set the case down. Johnson held out a bag of carrots. "For the pica," she said, "just give them to her one at a time. It takes her a little while to get through them. Otherwise she'll try to bite you. But she can't help it." Dr. Rider took the bag of carrots and the pair of rubber gloves Johnson held out next. "She's no longer got the disease of course, but human bites can cause nasty infections, so you might want these just in case."

"Thanks," said Nella, snapping them on.

"She's really quite docile," said Johnson, "but Wells and I will be watching the whole time, so things won't get out of control."

"I appreciate that," said Nella. She took a deep breath with her hand on the door and prepared to meet patient zero in the greatest plague that ever befell mankind.

The room was lit erratically by a dull florescent bulb, its mate long burnt out and the drop-in shade littered with insect carcasses. Nella noticed the room itself was clean and utterly free of both furniture and debris. All the surfaces were padded and covered with vinyl, but they were blank, and endless cube of dull green.

Ann Connelly was wandering the edge of the room, her arms in a permanent self embrace inside a blindingly white straitjacket. Someone was taking care of her. Her face was clean and the little cuts she had somehow managed to inflict upon herself were freshly bandaged. Someone had taken the time to brush her hair and fix it securely so that it would not hang in her eyes. Still, with one glance at her stumbling movement and her constantly snapping teeth, Dr. Rider knew that there was something wrong. Ann's eyes slid over everything alike, not stopping even when Nella held out a carrot. However brilliant Ann Connelly had been before, might still be in some deep place, she offered no sign of it now. She kept wandering the perimeter, stumbling every now and then, though there was nothing to trip on.

"Miss Connelly," said Nella.

The prisoner stopped walking but didn't turn her head toward Nella. "Ann, I'm Dr. Rider. I'm just here to talk with you."

Ann started fighting the straitjacket. Her arms whipped up and down, giant worms writhing around the woman's thin chest.

"The teeth must gnash," mumbled Ann.

"I'm sorry, what did you say?" asked Nella.

"The teeth must GNASH," Ann's voice was hoarse and toneless, a quality Nella recognized. When she had helped in administering the Cure, she had known many of the Infected to wake up from the drugged sleep screaming. Some of them took hours to stop. Some of them never did, their voice boxes losing the music that had once flowed through them.

"THE TEETH MUST GNASH!" Ann turned toward Nella and her jaw clicked together with a snap.

"THE TEETH MUST GNASH!" Ann lurched toward Dr. Rider, stumbling as if pushed from behind. She continued to shout in her broken voice, "THE TEETH MUST GNASH!"

"Okay, Ann, okay. Here-" Nella guided a carrot between Ann's rapidly clicking teeth. Ann chewed it immediately but began to choke. Johnson opened the door and calmly walked up to Ann. She untied the straitjacket releasing Ann's arms. "We only keep her in this so she won't chew her hands or claw at her face anymore. She'll be okay as long as you are giving her the carrots."

"Is she ever sedated?"

"She has to be to sleep, otherwise she just wanders all night until she collapses. But Mr. Green, her lawyer, said he doesn't want her drugged for the trial, so we only administer a very small dose of sedative at night."

"Thanks," said Nella as Johnson left the cell. Ann was holding the carrot with hands so thickly bandaged that they were no more articulated than wool mittens.

"Ann, do you know why you are in here?"

"Because the teeth must gnash. Because Dr. Schneider made all the teeth gnash. But I didn't know! I only wanted to feel better. I didn't know the teeth would want more!" Ann became frantic, smashing her hands into her face. Nella gently held Ann's hands for a moment and then handed her another carrot. She tried not to think of how similar the crunch of bone and the damp snap, snap, snap of the carrot between Ann's tireless teeth sounded.

"Can you tell me what happened? Do you remember how this started?"

Ann's teeth stopped. "So tired, so tired. But the eyes must see, they cannot close. They can *never* close! Dr. Schneider says so, she says to stay and to see. Always the eyes must see."

Ann paused to chew on the carrot and Nella winced without meaning to. "But then, they are so heavy, the eyes. Like glass marbles, rolling and rolling and scratching. They ache to close and Ann has mist inside her head. So Dr. Schneider gives her a key. It's the special key for the beast door. Dr. Schneider tells her the beast room will turn her eyes to flesh again. Her eyes will see without closing and the mist will drain from Ann's head, but only if Ann stays in the beast room. Only if Ann breathes what the beasts breathe. So Ann goes into the beast room many times. And she makes the teeth that gnash. She makes them everywhere but does not know. No, not even when they fill her own mouth." Ann stuck her bandaged hand between her teeth and before Nella could jump up to stop her, Ann's jaws snap around it. Ann's eyes streamed with tears as her mouth ground down upon the thick pads of gauze near her fingertips. Nella gently pulled Ann's hand away from her mouth and replaced it with another carrot.

"Okay Ann, okay. We don't have to talk more about it today."

Nella checked Ann's hand and rebandaged it. Ann became calm again, her gaze again like oil, sliding over the room and Dr. Rider without pause. Nella gently replaced the arms of the straitjacket but Ann didn't even seem to notice.

"Goodbye Ann. I'll come and see you again soon. Maybe we can get you out of this room for a while. Would you like that?"

But Ann just resumed her restless stumbling around the perimeter of the cell. She didn't even turn her head to look at the doctor. Nella left the cell profoundly depressed.

SEVITA DAS

Nella made her way back toward the entrance of the prison. She felt drained and uneasy, as if she'd forgotten something important or as if she had exhausted every possibility to an unsolvable problem. She groaned inwardly when she reached the heavy glass doors and saw that the sleet had changed over to snow and was already thick on the pavement. Nella hated this in between time of year. As if the old wheezing world couldn't decide whether to finally die or rally itself for one more spring.

She pushed open the door and slipped into the slimy, chilled evening. Her car was the only one in visitor parking. It wasn't unusual. Most people were used to being alone now. Gas was reserved for critical purposes at least until the Farm could produce enough ethanol or the Cure spread far enough south to recover countries with oil fields. Nella doubted either would happen in her lifetime. Only the counsel for the defendants and herself would have vehicles here. The loneliness seeped in everywhere these days, part of the atmosphere and only rarely noticeable. Now, with the small circles of streetlight hovering over her and the extra silence of the snow, she felt it again, like a sudden stumble on a forgotten stair. Nella walked toward her car and suddenly realized that the vehicle had been cleared of snow. She smiled and looked around as if her helper would suddenly pop out. She drove home feeling a little better about the world.

Her good mood lasted until she saw the envelope from the Department of Human Reproductive Services in her mail box. Nella swore under her breath, but didn't bother to open it. Instead, she dropped it on her kitchen table and went to call Sevita.

The two had remained together after the first administration of the Cure. Sevita had been offered a position on the World News Broadcast as soon as her report with Dr. Rider had been aired, but she had refused the job. Sevita was drawn to the stories of the Cured as they looked for relatives or tried to come to terms with the violence they remembered committing. She documented the work of Nella's team for six years as they pushed farther and farther into the infection zones along with the military. As a result, both women had become best friends. Sevita had been selected to document the Plague Trial just months before Judge Hawkins had appointed Nella the chief psychiatric adviser.

The phone only rang for a second before Sevita answered.

"Guess what I got in the mail today?" said Nella, before they had even exchanged greetings.

"You too huh? Seems our friendly neighborhood matchmakers have been busy. Our entire unit got them today."

"What are you going to do? Have you told Chris yet?"

Sevita sighed. "Yeah, she knows. She's excited. I think she sees it as the final blow in the marriage argument. She doesn't know I was going to ask her after the trial anyway."

"Sure you were."

"I was! I just wanted to have all this behind us. I don't want to remember the year our baby was born as the year the first public executions took place."

"You don't know that's what will happen."

"Come on Nella, I know *you* aren't that naive. Whether this Dr. Pazzo and his assistant are guilty or not doesn't really make much difference, does it? They were *there*. The survivors of the Plague think they've seen the worst. But you and I, we're the ones who know how much damage has really been done. You've talked with the Cured, been with them from the moment they realized the weight of what they had done. You know the suicide rates. You were the one that compiled the report. Once all that comes out in court, the world is not going to be able to let go. Maybe just being there is close enough to guilty."

"Then what's the point of even having the trial Sevita? Why didn't the military just shoot them when they found them? They wouldn't have bothered appointing you to document it if we weren't going to try to have real justice."

"We're just pretenses, you and I, to make it *seem* like a fair trial. Whatever you find, the trial will still move forward. Whatever I record will be rewritten. And Pazzo and Connelly will burn. I just hope for our sakes that they really are guilty."

Nella was quiet. "I don't want to talk about it anymore," she said at last.

"Neither do I. There's nothing you or I can do to change it. So come over for dinner. We'll talk about baby clothes and nursery designs with Christine. She'll be ecstatic. She brought home a case of beer from her last scav mission as part of her pay."

"Mmm eight year old beer."

Sevita laughed. "We have to drink it tonight, she wants to have the fertilization done this week."

"You aren't going to adopt an orphan?"

"No, Christine is set on the pregnancy. She says we all have a 'genetic responsibility' now. I think she's been reading too many DHRS pamphlets. But this is what she wants. And you know I can never resist it when she sets her heart on something. Come on, come over. I know you'll fall asleep over your notes without eating if you don't. No trial talk, I promise."

"Okay," said Nella, grinning, "I'll be over in a few."

Sevita and Christine had met during the worst part of the Plague, long before either knew Nella. Christine had been an EMT when the outbreak began. She found out quickly that she was immune to the December Plague, though her partner was not so lucky. So Christine drove her ambulance alone, ferrying the Infected to local hospitals until the military took over management and burned them all to the ground. After that, Christine ran a mobile triage out of her ambulance for those who had been bitten or injured. The world quickly emptied of sanity and Christine had to routinely defend herself both from Infected and desperate people. But she never thought about quitting. She kept her radio on at every hour and kept her ambulance clean, running and well-stocked when she had time. The military tolerated her, even supplied her with fuel and medical supplies but warned her that she was on her own. And that was just fine with Christine. But when she heard repeated distress calls from Sevita's office, she followed a military unit in to help. The entire building had been surrounded by Infected. But because it was one of the few remaining stations still capable of broadcasting, the military decided it was a worthwhile target to retake. It was a massacre. When they finally escaped, the building was overrun and most of the military unit had been eaten alive. Only four people remained, huddled in Christine's ambulance as they sped away. Sevita was one of them.

Sevita had been wounded in several places trying to defend her coworkers. Christine had stopped driving her ambulance in order to care for the dying girl and eventually nursed her back to health.

But Sevita clung to Chris long after she had healed, uncharacteristically afraid of the strange city and mistrusting of its thinly manned safety barriers. Nella never understood how two such opposite people could be so madly in love with each other, but there it was. They'd been inseparable as long as she had known them- since Sevita's arrival in the City. Though Sevita regained her bold, friendly nature, neither she nor Christine ever felt the need to look any farther for their happiness.

Most of the remaining humans had kept to themselves after the Cure. Everyone had witnessed or participated in the death of almost every person that they knew. Even eight years after the Plague, almost no one had any real urge to build new ties. Especially after the old ones had been so brutally broken. In the beginning, people had avoided each other as much as possible for their own safety. Now though, it had become habit. Love like Sevita and Chris had just didn't happen anymore. Because of her work, Nella had more contact with other people than was the norm. But Nella didn't have many friends, or even very many colleagues. Sevita and Chris were her new family and she spent almost every evening walking to or from their small apartment.

Warm and slightly buzzed on skunky beer, Nella listened with her eyes half closed as the couple had the same good natured argument that they had for years.

"You have a fear of commitment. Tell her Nella."

Sevita scowled. "No I don't. You are just having a reaction to the disaster around us. It's natural. People after the Black Death bred like rabbits. And again after the last world war. I just want to make sure this isn't some short term shack up. You'll get cold feet in six months, I know it."

Chris smacked Sevita lightly on the knee. "It's been eight years!"

Nella snorted and almost dropped her beer.

"What are you laughing at?" grumbled Sevita, "You're supposed to be on my side. You should be telling Christine that she's just bowing to peer pressure and she should strive to make up her own mind."

"Oh no," laughed Nella, "I know better than to get in the middle of this mess. I'm going to get dessert while you two duke it out." She winked at Sevita and went into the tiny kitchen. Nella pulled out Sevita's enamel canister. It still smelled warm and sweet like the tea it had held so long ago. Now it was the temporary home for Christine's engagement ring. Nella had known it was there for years, a warm sparking star waiting for Sevita to grow some courage. Nella smiled. She remembered the day Sevita had bought it. The two of them had stood in front of the scavenger's shop window and debated for hours. Nella placed it on the plate next to Christine's apple crisp. She sighed. It should have been chocolate cake and champagne, not fruit jumble and stale beer. But Nella had checked, both had been far, far out of reach. She wondered if any of them would ever taste chocolate again. It didn't matter, of course, she decided. She looked around the tiny kitchen, its warm yellow paint and cluttered cupboards peeking through pictures and tiny glittering ornaments that Christine collected like a magpie. This place pushed out the empty world. How much this little home would change in the next year! Nella could almost forgive the DHRS for forcing people into parenthood if it could put the world back together like this.

"Garcon!" called Sevita, laughing.

"Oh! Coming!" yelled Nella, picking up the

dessert tray.

THE MAINTENANCE MAN AT THE END OF THE WORLD

Nella arrived at the prison early the next morning. The happiness of her friends still sat like a warm stone in her chest and she barely even noticed the clammy drizzle. She pulled into visitor parking and noticed Mr. Courtlen arguing with a short, portly, middle aged man. Nella got out of the car but paused in the open doorway when she heard their raised voices.

"Your client is a *monster* Frank!" shouted the older man, "He locked her in a room full of infected animals and abandoned her for months."

"She was already infected! What should he have done?" Mr. Courtlen's long arms were stretched toward the other man, almost pleading.

"I can't believe you are going to blame this all on Ann. She was an overworked, practically abused intern that was then exposed to a vile plague that *your* client cooked up." The fat little man was jabbing a finger toward Mr. Courtlen's face. "And you have the gall to try to weasel out of this by pointing to *her*?"

"No, that's not what-"

"Listen Frank," the little man talked over Mr. Courtlen, "I know you are court appointed to defend Robert Pazzo but how could you live with yourself if you destroy an innocent person? She's already incapable of ever leading a normal life because of what your client did. If you make a deal with the prosecutors claiming that Ann was responsible, she'll be completely at the mercy of the court. She can't even coherently defend herself. Can you live with yourself knowing that?" The little man walked a step past Mr. Courtlen.

"But we're not-"

The lawyer spun around and interrupted him again. "Oh, that's right. I forgot who I was dealing with. You're already comfortable destroying a defenseless woman." The little man sneered and Nella thought Mr. Courtlen would hit him. But Frank's shoulders sagged and he leaned his back against his car as if he were the one who had been punched. She watched the older lawyer trot into the prison and though she didn't even know his name and she knew she was supposed to be a neutral party, in that moment Nella truly hated the nasty, strident little man.

She was utterly still, not knowing whether to pretend she had seen nothing or check to see if Frank were okay. He put a hand to his forehead but didn't move. Nella closed her car door and watched him start. He hadn't even seen her drive in. He turned around and his face was dark red. The ragged scar on his cheek pulsed purple. Nella thought he was angry but he managed a small, tight smile and she realized he was only surprised and embarrassed.

"Good morning, Dr. Rider," he said, and his voice was smooth and calm.

"Are you okay?" she asked, circling her car towards him. He rubbed the back of his neck and his smile loosened and grew.

"I'm fine. It's not like I've never been called a monster before. I've even called myself worse on occasion. Mr. Grant just doesn't understand that we're not practicing law from Before. He wants things to work the same as they used to. He thinks that the world just has this out of order sign temporarily tacked to it. Any minute a maintenance guy is going to come along and plug the world back in and everything will go back to what it was."

Nella sighed. "I doubt he's the only one that

thinks that."

"He can't believe that this trial is about anything other than getting his client released. He thinks that's my goal too. Mr. Grant is expecting me to make some kind of deal with the prosecution by sacrificing Ann Connelly in return for a lighter sentence for Dr. Pazzo."

Mr. Courtlen walked to his trunk and waved his keys as he talked. "I'm not stupid," he said, "I know my client is never going to walk out of here. Hell, I probably won't even be able to stall his execution. But that was never the point of all this."

Nella heard Sevita's words echo in her head as he disappeared behind the opening trunk lid.

"What *is* your goal Mr. Courtlen?" she asked.

He slammed the trunk. "Well, it's to help my client to have his say and to find out about what really happened. Dr. Pazzo has promised to tell the world the truth. So I have promised to defend him as well as I could. We both understand that he is not likely to escape this."

"And you believe him?" Nella kept her voice neutral.

Frank opened a black umbrella and walked up to her. "Please," he said, holding it out for her, "It's cold out here."

Instead of reaching for it, Nella stepped underneath the umbrella with him. He smelled almost impossibly clean, like fresh shaving foam and wind dried linen. Nella was dismayed to realize that she had expected him to smell like the other Infected she had met during the Cure. They had been putrid and coppery with rotten meat and dried blood. She tried to put the memory from her head and scolded herself for her prejudice.

"Yes, I believe he's going to tell the truth," continued Frank, "I also believe he's guilty of at least *helping* to start this whole thing, because he admits it, as you will see. But everyone deserves to say their piece. Mr. Grant has this delusion that because I was Infected I have some affinity for Robert Pazzo. But I have more reason to hate my client than many." He watched her face as he spoke, "The things I've done, what I have lost- what we *all* have lost because of this terrible plague. How could I be his friend?"

He shook his head as if to clear it. "I'm sorry. It's cold and wet and I've kept you here complaining about unimportant things." He touched her elbow and this time she didn't shudder. "We should go in," he said.

"I think it *is* important," replied Nella as they walked toward the prison, "How can you defend him if you are convinced he is guilty?"

Mr. Courtlen laughed. "I'm hardly the first lawyer to ever believe his client is guilty."

"No, I suppose not. But if you hold him responsible for all of your loss-"

"Who is left in the world who doesn't hold him responsible for their losses? Besides, it's far, far more complicated than it seems. I believe he plans to start telling you the story today."

They reached the heavy glass door and Nella held it open for him as he shook the chill out of the umbrella.

"We didn't expect you this early though," he said.

"I was told that this was the best time to speak with Miss Connelly's council." Nella felt guilty saying it, but pushed the feeling aside.

"Ah, I see," said Mr. Courtlen with a small smile, "Well, I'll see you later this morning then."

"Will ten o'clock be alright?"

"I think that will be fine. I'll see you then, Dr. Rider."

And because he still seemed shrunken somehow, still red with embarrassment, she added, "I look forward to it."

His smile warmed and he stood a little straighter. Nella walked down the hall to the metal detector without looking back at him.

THE TEETH MUST GNASH

Mr. Grant was pacing the hall in front of Ann Connelly's cell. When he saw Nella, a grin split his round face so quickly that Nella felt queasy. He quickly smothered the grin, but Nella was too distracted by the dull thuds coming from Ann's cell to notice.

She opened the cell door and saw Ann much changed from what she had been the day before. Wells was trying to hold her back from flinging herself into the walls and Johnson was speaking calmly to her and holding a gloved hand between the prisoner's head and the wall as Ann whipped back and forth in frantic wriggles. Both guards looked exhausted.

"What has happened?" asked Nella.

"Oh, thank goodness, Doc," sighed Wells, "We didn't think anyone was coming to help."

Nella gently but firmly held Ann's chin so she could make an examination of her. "How long has she been like this?"

"Well, she started doing this sometime overnight. The night shift said she seemed to be building up to it all evening." Johnson ran a soothing hand over Ann's hair, trying to smooth it back into place. Ann had slammed herself against the padded wall hard enough to bruise her left cheek and her lip had been bitten until it bled. Ann's eyes skittered and leapt over everything.

"Has her physician been called? Did he prescribe a sedative at all?"

Mr. Grant trotted into the doorway as Nella asked. She looked up from Ann's face in time to see Wells and Johnson exchange a disgusted glance at the lawyer's entrance.

"The doctor says he can't do anything for her since we've all been told she is not to have sedatives during the trial," Johnson mumbled.

"Did her physician order that?" Nella knew it was the lawyer that had told them not to sedate Ann, but she wanted to make a point.

"No, Dr. Rider, it was me. I need Ann to be aware and able to assist in her own defense," a slow oily smile oozed over Mr. Grant's face, "Unless, of course, you determine that she is incapable of doing that."

"With all due respect, Mr. Grant, you are not a physician," Ann whipped her head forward and Nella struggled to keep her from smacking her forehead on the wall, "Regardless of what I find, Miss Connelly cannot continue to live with these kinds of episodes without relief. Being in a state of such extreme anxiety isn't helping her *or* your defense case."

"How am I supposed to put together a defense with a catatonic doll?"

Nella tried to control her anger, but her voice was louder than she meant it to be. "Mr. Grant, this conversation is over. As her doctor, for Miss Connelly's safety and the safety of her guards I am recommending immediate sedation with lorazepam. If you have an issue with this, take it up with Judge Hawkins. But this *is* happening for now. As for your case, Mr. Grant, I recommend you take the day off. Your assistance is not needed today." Nella turned back toward Johnson. "Do you have a supply on hand or should I request some doses from the military liaison?" Nella could hear Mr. Grant spluttering with anger and without looking could picture his round face deep red and puffed with rage, but she didn't turn around to look. Wells, though, was trying not to smile and failing. Johnson shot him a warning look. "Yeah, we've got it," she said, "Wells, go up to the

Warden's office and tell him we need a dose of lorazepam."

"You sure?" asked Wells as he struggled to hold a thrashing Ann.

"The Doc and I can handle it. Just hurry."

Johnson held Ann in a bear hug from behind while Nell kept Ann's head from banging against the wall. Mr. Grant, still blustering wordlessly, skittered out of the room like a round beetle, followed by Wells.

"Do you have any idea what might have triggered this?" asked Nella over Ann's shoulder. Johnson strained to see her. "Well, begging your pardon, but no one's been able to get her to really talk about what happened until you. I figured this must have been from digging up all those memories. But there's no help for it. *Someone* has to find out how all this happened."

"I apologize," said Nella, "next time I'll be more prepared. I assumed her lawyer or at least the original investigators had already gone over it with her."

Ann snapped her teeth and Nella instinctively flinched.

"No," said Johnson when Nella had recovered, "When the investigators found her, she was even worse than this. They couldn't get her to calm down enough to talk. And her lawyer-" Johnson scowled, "He's just waiting for you to declare her incompetent. In fact, I'm sure his ban on sedation was in hopes that something exactly like this would happen while you were here. He just wants to get the whole thing over with."

"He's never talked to her about what happened?" asked Nella, incredulous.

"The TEETH! THE TEETH MUST GNASH THROUGH THE BEAST ROOM DOORS!" screamed Ann and Nella moved her hand, but too late. Ann clamped her teeth down and twisted. Nella sucked in a sizzling breath, but managed not to yell. Ann immediately opened her mouth again and Nella quickly stepped back before Ann's jaw could snap shut again.

"Oh God!" said Johnson, watching the skin between Nella's thumb and finger split and swell with blood, "I forgot you didn't have gloves on. Wells! Wells get back here!" she shouted, struggling to hold Ann still. Nella saw tears streaming down Ann's cheek and she pushed Ann's tangled hair out of the prisoner's face with her good hand.

"It's okay Ann. It's okay, I know you didn't mean to."

The pain in Nella's hand coupled with the natural, humid heat of the blood on her skin made Nella nauseous. She tried not to imagine what it would have been like to be slowly torn apart by the teeth of several Infected. Her whole body ached in empathy even as she pushed the thought out and carefully held Ann's forehead away from the wall she was trying to smash it on. At last, Wells cam running back, a capped syringe and small glass bottle in his hand.

"Jesus, Doc, are you okay?" he asked.

Nella managed a small smile. "Sure. I just wasn't paying enough attention." Wells handed Nella the bottle and syringe and took Johnson's place holding onto Ann.

Nella looked at the vial for a moment. "Sorry," she said, "I don't think I can do this with one hand."

"Here," replied Johnson, "I'll do it, I was a combat medic." Johnson filled the syringe.

"Okay Ann, officer Johnson is just going to give you something to help you sleep for a while. Is that alright?" Johnson waited for Ann to reply.

"Stop the teeth," sighed Ann, "Stop the teeth

and the screaming beasts."

Johnson nodded. "Yes, Ann, we'll stop the teeth and let you rest."

Ann didn't even flinch as Johnson administered the sedative. She rocked back and forth, no longer thrashing but still frantic.

"Ann," said Nella, "Do you remember your mother and father?"

Ann stopped rocking. She looked up and to everyone's surprise, Ann's eyes caught on Nella's face.

"Did they tell you bedtime stories Ann? Can you tell me a bedtime story?"

Ann smiled. Wells and Johnson shared a shocked glance.

"Once upon a time there was a queen who wanted a little girl very badly . . ." Ann began. The queen hadn't even pricked her finger with her needle before Ann was slurring and drooping. Johnson helped her lie down.

"Come on, Doc," whispered Wells, "You need to get to the infirmary."

Nella hesitated for a moment. Johnson looked up from smoothing Ann's hair. "Don't worry, I'll be here and she's going to sleep like a log for a while. Thanks for standing up to Grant, Dr. Rider. He's been worse than useless this whole time."

Johnson grinned and Nella thought it made her look nicer. "No problem," Nella said grimly. A burst of pain splashed over her and she followed Wells out of the cell and down the hall, trying to hold her hand against the cloth of her skirt so she wouldn't drip on the floor.

"We'll be at the infirmary in a sec and the nurse will clean you up." He looked at her hand doubtfully. "I think you might need stitches," he said.

Nella gently covered the bite with her good hand. The wound sizzled and popped, a burning flare in her mind. She said a silent prayer that the infirmary was still stocked with increasingly rare and desirable modern pain killers.

The officers in the infirmary were kind, but Nella suspected she had more actual medical training than any of the nurses. Still, she thought her hand would heal without too big of a scar. The drug cabinet had been stocked, but its pain killers were limited. It seemed even the military could no longer procure medical grade narcotics. Nella was thankful she didn't need major surgery. She looked at the two slim, white tablets in her palm. Nella was no addict, but as the pills slid down her throat, she thought that the production of a simple aspirin tablet might be what would launch what remained of humanity back into a civilization.

The nurse patted her on the shoulder and gave her a compassionate smile. "Be careful," the nurse said, "I know it's just aspirin, but if you've had the same experience as the rest of us, it's been a while since you've taken one. It will probably hit you faster than you expect and make you dizzy."

Nella laughed. "You know, I used to pop these like breath mints when I was in college for headaches."

"Didn't we all?" asked the nurse, "and now you'd be hard pressed to find anyone under 20 who remembers even having seen one." They were both quiet for a moment. Then the nurse roused herself, "Ah, but I'm sure we'll be making them again soon, don't you think?"

Nella nodded. "If they were able to bring us hot showers within a year, I'm sure someone is working on aspirin tabs after eight."

Nella felt the buzzing numbness of the aspirin spread down her arm. She looked down at herself. The side of her skirt was stiff and purple where she had pressed her hand. She looked around for her suit jacket and winced as she saw the spatter on it. At least her shirt was unstained. "Do you have a sink I can use?" she asked the nurse, "I have another appointment and I can't go like this."

"You sure honey?" asked the nurse kindly, "I think they'd understand if you rescheduled."

"No, I need to keep this one and I'm already late. Besides-" Nella laughed, "I don't think I can drive while the aspirin is working. I must be becoming a lightweight."

Nella was still desperately scrubbing the hem of her skirt with a wet towel when Mr. Courtlen walked into the infirmary.

"I heard Dr. Rider has been injured-" he began speaking to the nurse.

Nella looked up and dropped the towel into the red laundry bin. "I'm okay," she said, more brightly than she felt, "I'm sorry I'm late, I was just trying to clean up." She waved her good hand across the remaining bits of blood.

"Of course, no need to apologize."

"I'll be right there. I've just got to get some books out of the car that Dr. Pazzo wanted."

"Let me do that for you."

Nella hesitated.

"You're injured," said Mr. Courtlen, "I won't search for any case notes or anything, I swear." Mr. Courtlen held up his right hand and grinned.

Nella fumbled for the keys. "Thank you," she said, "There is a box in the trunk.

"No problem." Frank closed his hand around the keys, brushing her palm with the tips of his fingers. He was so warm. Nella kept expecting his skin to be cold and damp like an Infected. She shook her head. She had to stop thinking of the Cured as they had been when they first woke up. It had been six years since the Infected had started being Cured. Did she really know no one else who had been Cured? She was startled to realize that she did not. She didn't even know what happened to them after they left the medical camps she had worked in. Oh, she knew that a great deal of them- something like thirty percent committed suicide and almost half of those remaining had lasting psychological problems like depression and addictions. It was constantly in Sevita's broadcasts. But Nella didn't know how or where they lived, if they kept to themselves or mingled with the Immune population. But then, Nella reasoned, she didn't even know her next door neighbors.

She was late to meet Dr. Pazzo. Nella put herself back together as best she could and headed back down the hallway to the common room.

WE'RE ALL VILLAINS

"Good morning, Dr. Rider. I had heard there was some unpleasantness with Miss Connelly this morning. Do you wish to reschedule?" Dr. Pazzo tried to look gentle and sympathetic, but his desiccated skull made him look sinister instead. Nella tried to sit at the plastic picnic table without thumping her wounded hand.

"No, thank you Dr. Pazzo, I'm fine."

"Good, good. I have all the time in the world of course, but the world- well, the world doesn't have all that much time left in it. So better to have this over quickly."

"You keep saying that Dr. Pazzo. Care to tell me why you think the world is in danger?" asked Nella.

"We'll get to that," said Dr. Pazzo and Nella swallowed a smirk at his deflection. "As I said, I hate to repeat myself, so we'll wait for Mr. Courtlen before we go into it. I want to show you both some of the video diaries I made during the onset of the Plague. I requested that they be made available for my defense after I was Cured and taken into custody."

"So you knew even at the beginning of the Plague that you would be arrested?"

"Come now, Dr. Rider. That's not really the question you wanted to ask. Drop the therapist facade and have some intestinal fortitude."

"Very well. Are you saying that you knew how devastating this Plague would be from the very beginning?"

Dr. Pazzo grinned, but it was a bitter, angry grin. His teeth glimmered like fresh boiled bone. "Yes," he said.

"Yet you warned no one? You just waited to be

caught?"

Dr. Pazzo sighed. "What could I have done? The bacteria had already been released. I had even taken Ann to the hospital during the incubation period because the symptoms didn't match what was expected. When I realized that it was, in fact, *our* bacteria that caused her aggression and irrationality, the best I could do is isolate us and hope that we hadn't been infectious to others yet. Of course, I didn't know Dr. Schneider would be able to break out. I had hoped someone would find my notes, but I never dreamed we'd survive to be *put* on trial."

"Would you have fled if you'd known you would end up here?"

Dr. Pazzo frowned and his face was filled with gothic angles, a breathing statue. "No. There was no fleeing from this. Besides, I hate it when the villains get away in the end."

"Do you think *you* are a villain Dr. Pazzo?"

"Is anyone who is now living *not* a villain? Did you really not kill *anyone* in the past eight years to survive? Or let someone else die so you could escape?"

Nella was silent, watching the guard behind Dr. Pazzo shift self consciously. The prisoner's voice rose and his face began to blanch. "Oh, but those were just 'zombies' you killed, right doctor? Just monsters without compassion, without souls. Wrong!"

Dr. Pazzo slammed his open hand down on the table and bright droplets of spit flew from his frowning mouth. Nella didn't flinch, but sat calmly, as if she were the calm heart of a storm.

"Those people were *ill* Dr. Rider. Not only did the Immunes kill sick people, they killed sick people who ultimately could have been *cured*. People that could have led normal lives again. People with spouses and parents and siblings. People with children. Tell me doctor, do you really think the

Immune survivors deserved to live any more than the Infected?"

"Of course not," answered Nella in a steady, clear voice, but her heart slammed angrily into her rib cage. *There wasn't supposed to be a cure,* she thought, *they TOLD us they were mindless, relentless. A victim of their own urges. Unnatural and utterly incurable. That's what the government said from the beginning. How were we supposed to know that was wrong?*

Mr. Courtlen walked into the room with the box of books. Nella looked at his open, friendly face, partly shattered with scars, and was stricken with guilt. She did not let it show.

"Don't mistake me doctor," continued the prisoner, "I'd have done the same in your place in order to survive. My point was simply that we are all guilty now. Murderers and looters, each of us."

Dr. Pazzo paused in time to observe Nella watching Mr. Courtlen. He squinted, making his shrunken eyes even smaller and more menacing. "Even Frank here. You wouldn't think it to see that gentle, honest face, but that's why he makes such a good criminal defense attorney. Do you know, Dr. Rider, how they found him when he was Cured?"

"Dr. Pazzo, this is neither the time nor the company to discuss my-" Mr. Courtlen began quickly, but the prisoner spoke over him.

"He was covered in infected bites and scratches from the child that originally brought the Plague into his bunker. He had a festering bullet hole through his hand and into his shoulder where his wife, an Immune, had shot him in a desperate attempt to survive and a jagged slice taken out of his face from the same battle. For months his body suffered infection, his flesh rotting around him untreated. For months his brain, that intelligent, articulate mind that he's always had, was reduced to indiscriminate rage, tormenting hunger and pain. Around him were the clean, gnawed bones of his wife and the child. He *ate her alive* Dr. Rider. You've had just a hint of that this morning. You can't imagine what a brutal death it must be. I hope he started with her throat so she didn't have to suffer long." Mr. Courtlen dropped the box of books on the table and walked out of the room without speaking. "And when he woke up, he was so traumatized he couldn't speak for months. Who was the villain? Maybe the question should be who are the good guys? Because they don't seem to be around any more."

Dr. Pazzo coolly picked through the books. Nella sat in silent shock for a moment.

"You think I'm naive," she said quietly, "But if you've done your research, you know I've worked with the Cured for six years now. The conditions they survived in no longer surprise or frighten me, they just make me sad. I realize you are feeling powerless and are frantic to change the dynamic by shocking me or withholding what you seem to think is vital information. And I know you are trying to feel more powerful by exposing Mr. Courtlen, but I'm warning you, it's going to backfire. It's in your best interest at this point to be civil with anyone who is trying to help you. The world isn't on your side. Mr. Courtlen is."

Dr. Pazzo stared at her. He turned toward one of the guards. "Would you please fetch my lawyer? I want to have this over with as soon as possible. Thank you." He smiled sweetly at the officer and Nella felt a stone growing cold and tight in her belly.

When Mr. Courtlen returned, Nella blushed in empathetic embarrassment. He sat next to her without looking at her. Dr. Pazzo sat alone on the far side of the table. Nella stood up abruptly. "You know," she said, "I think I *will* postpone this meeting.

After everything that's happened, I don't think I'm comfortable continuing today. Dr. Pazzo, I will see you tomorrow instead," she turned to Mr. Courtlen and held out her unbitten hand. "I'm so sorry for wasting your time Mr. Courtlen." She tried not to flinch as the rough scar tissue in his palm brushed against her. Dr. Pazzo sneered and pretended to ignore them, his face ugly with anger.

Nella was halfway down the hall when Mr. Courtlen caught up. "I would have told you, eventually. Everyone knows the story," he said, and she stopped and looked at him. "It's not even that original of a story, I'm sure hundreds of people have a story that's similar." He blushed as he met her eyes, "Still, I wish he hadn't told you that way. I'm sorry."

Nella was quiet for a long moment. "Are you hungry?" she said at last.

"What?" asked Mr. Courtlen, confused.

"It's been a pretty awful day. For both of us." Nella held up her bandaged hand. "I'm done for today. How about you?"

Frank smiled and the tension seemed to slide out of his limbs. "Yeah, I'm done feeling like a punching bag for today too."

"Come on," she said, and pulled out the extra dose of aspirin the nurse had given her. "I'll buy you lunch if you'll drive."

THE DINER

They ended up at a diner. Nella hadn't ever been inside before, and it was busy, catering mostly to the electric plant's workmen and laborers from the Farm. She was surprised and pleased to be surrounded by so many others. Frank worked his way through the crowd to the back and found them a table. Nella sat down, her head a little dizzy.

"Are you okay?" asked Frank, leaning over the table toward her.

Nella grinned in genuine comfort. "Yes, I just haven't heard this many voices talking at once in- I don't know, years? Do you eat here a lot?"

Frank shrugged, "Once in a while. They have good food and I know many of the regulars." He looked around with a smile. "Not the kind of place you'll be able to talk confidentially though," he said, raising his voice to be heard. They were late for the lunch rush and the diner soon emptied, but the comfortable bustle of the waitstaff and kitchen still filled it with life and warmth and Nella was happy they had come.

"How's your hand?" asked Frank. She opened and closed it gently.

"Sore, but not too bad. It should be okay in a few days."

"Look, I'm sorry for how Dr. Pazzo acted today. He's not usually like this."

Nella shook her head. "You're his lawyer, not his mother. You aren't responsible for what he says. Besides, he's just flexing his muscles, trying to make us both uncomfortable."

An older lady with an eyepatch and a clawmark wriggling down her arm gently laid a cup of grain coffee in front of them. Nella smiled at her and Frank thanked her. He turned back to Nella, absently stirring the cup although there was neither sugar nor milk on the table.

"Aren't you?" he asked.

"Am I what?"

"Uncomfortable."

"I worked in the Cure camps for two years. It was my job to listen to far worse stories than yours. Before that, I worked in a mental hospital where I heard stories beyond anything Dr. Pazzo has up his sleeve. He's going to have to try a lot harder to shock me." She leaned forward and put her hand near his on the table. "You shouldn't let him make you uncomfortable either. He's only trying to make himself feel more powerful."

Frank smiled, but it wasn't a happy smile. "Nothing he's said isn't true." He put down the spoon and slid back, his legs brushing by hers as they stretched out.

"Just because he aired your dirty laundry doesn't mean nobody else has any. Including him. And Mr. Grant." Nella frowned at the bad taste his name left in her mouth. She looked up and saw Frank watching her. She smiled gently. "And me," she said.

He was silent, but he continued to watch her. She blushed. The waitress brought their food.

"Why did you agree to do this trial?" he asked.

"The simplest answer is that I was asked to do it. You don't really say no to the Military Governor if he asks you for a favor. And he told me about Ann. I hope that I can help her. He told me it would be one of the most important trials in history we needed to be sure that it was fair." Nella sighed. "Although, from the attitudes of the people I've spoken with, that seems to be an incredibly optimistic view."

"Dr. Rider, I know I said that acquitting Dr.

Pazzo wasn't my goal-"

Nella shrugged. "You were just being realistic," she interrupted.

"I hope this world is still as decent as you seem to think it is. I hope that, whatever the outcome, the trial is fair. I just don't expect it."

They ate in a comfortable silence. The waitress brought their check. Nella sighed. "What's wrong? Is your hand hurting?" Frank asked.

Nella smiled. "No, I just don't want to leave yet. This was nice. Well, this part of the day anyway."

Frank laughed. "Really? I haven't just depressed you more?"

"It's nice to just be able to be me and not a psychiatrist for a while. Even if our conversation wasn't light. It's nice to be around normal people, doing normal things."

"We can come back."

Nella smiled and paid the bill.

The day had turned gray and dull as they returned to the prison. Yesterday's snow was slithering into the gutters in dirty silver slumps. Frank stopped the car next to hers. "Has the aspirin worn off enough? Will you be okay to get home?" he asked.

Nella slid out of the car. "I'm fine," she said, "and I'll go slow. It's not like there's much to run into any more."

"That's true. But if it snows-"

"It's okay, I'm just down the road. I'll see you tomorrow." She began to shut the door and changed her mind. She leaned down to see Frank's face. "Mr. Courtlen- maybe it's not my place to say- we don't know each other that well. But since no one else seems to have told you, I guess I will. You don't deserve to be treated the way Mr. Grant and Dr.

Pazzo did today. What you did when you were sick- none of us can say we were any better. Not the Cured or the Immunes." Nella blushed. "Okay, good night," she said and shut the door before he could respond.

She found he had parked in the same spot the next morning and half expected him to be sitting in his car in the same clothes as the day before. But he was inside already, laughing with Officer Kembrey and Terry, the nervous soldier was nowhere in sight.

"Good morning Dr. Rider," said Stan, "I heard you were injured. Are you feeling better today?"

"Yes," Nella lied. The pain had been flashy and sizzling all morning and the willow tea she'd had was a very poor substitute for the little aspirin pills she'd run out of.

"Good. You'll be glad to know that Ann has been doing fine today, thanks to your orders and we haven't heard a peep."

"That's great news. Maybe we'll start to make some progress now."

Stan exchanged a quick glance with Mr. Courtlen. Nella ignored it. "I guess you'll be wanting Frank then," he said.

Nella smiled. "If you're ready Mr. Courtlen."

"As I'll ever be," said Frank, "Have a good day Stan."

Officer Kembrey waved them off. "How long have you two known each other?"

"Stan? He was at the prison before I even got here. We play poker sometimes with a group. And I introduced him to his wife. She was in the same Cure camp as me. He's a good friend."

They had reached the dented metal door. "Last chance. You can go home and call in sick if you want," said Frank with a grin.

"No," sighed Nella, "let's get this over with."

Dr. Pazzo was already sitting at the plastic

picnic table as if he'd never left. Nella sat down across from him. Mr. Courtlen sat next to her rather than crossing to his client. She guessed that he hadn't forgiven him for yesterday yet.

"We're all ready then?" Dr. Pazzo asked brightly, as if nothing had happened, "Good, let's start the show."

A guard wheeled in an old black television set and Nella took advantage of Dr. Pazzo's distraction. She lightly squeezed Frank's arm and gave him a comforting smile when he looked over at her. She was relieved that he smiled back.

INFECTION

"This is video diary number thirty-five in the Recharge Project. I am Dr. Gerta Schneider. Assisting is Dr. Robert Pazzo and Anne Connelly."

Nella stared at the attractive blonde woman on the screen. She could swear she'd seen the woman somewhere, but she couldn't place the memory.

"As previous videos have stated, the goal of the Recharge Project is to develop a vector that can administer both a dopamine pre-cursor and amphetamine to the brain for a very specific amount of time. The goal being to provide those with high pressure occupations such as police officers, medical personnel or soldiers with a safe and effective alternative to pharmaceutical substitutes."

A very young Dr. Pazzo spoke up from the background. "We also want to address long term treatments for post traumatic stress. Don't forget to say that."

"Yes Robert, I was just going to get to that," said Dr. Schneider, but Nella thought she looked anything but gracious. Dr. Schneider turned back to the camera, her arms crossing her chest. "We have encountered numerous pitfalls while choosing a vector, trying to find a harmless bacteria that is resistant to most commonly prescribed antibiotics, so that it will be effective in a majority of cases without complications. We also needed to find a bacteria that could easily infect the central nervous system without causing inflammation which could cause side effects. At last, we have chosen a weak strain of antibiotic resistant streptococcus. It should not make the host ill, but can withstand courses of almost all antibiotics on the market today, ensuring that this will benefit almost everyone. This video diary is being made to document our first animal test."

The screen blinked for a minute and was suddenly focused on a window into a room filled with cages.

"Wait, can you pause this please?" asked Nella.

The guard paused the video and Dr. Pazzo looked at her expectantly. "Are you having trouble with the jargon Dr. Rider?" he asked.

"I don't think so," she said, "From what I understand you were trying to make a natural drug that caused euphoria, alertness and extra focus without causing side effects."

"That's correct."

"But you chose a virtually unstoppable bacterium as your delivery system, why?"

"Well, we chose to use bacteria in order to get a more natural bump in delivery as opposed to a huge spike than would come from injecting a drug. It was meant to be used to aid people, not for recreation."

"No," said Mr. Courtlen suddenly, "I don't think Dr. Rider was asking why you chose bacteria, I think her question was why you chose an *incurable* one."

Nella could see the scar on his cheek flashing red against his pale face. His voice was steady but she could see his anger rising.

"If we'd chosen something susceptible to antibiotics it would have been wiped out before it even had a chance to work. Anytime it was given to someone who had caught an STD or the flu and went to the doctor and was given a round of medicine, it would have killed a more vulnerable strain. Besides, it was supposed to be weak, so the host's body would naturally defeat it, but not until after the amphetamine and dopamine precursor were delivered. It was incurable because it was *supposed* to be harmless."

"So what happened?" Mr. Courtlen hissed.

Dr. Pazzo shifted nervously in his seat. "Watch and see," he said and indicated that the guard should start the video again. The screen again showed the window into the room with animal cages. Two figures in light blue biohazard suits came into view. One of them pressed a button near the window and spoke into the intercom.

"We are administering the first dose via injection. After today, this room's air will be filtered in a closed system where the streptococcus bacteria that the animals breathe out will be refreshed with more amphetamine and dopamine precursors. The goal is to monitor both short and long term effects of exposure." The speaker was Dr. Pazzo. The other figure was busy opening one cage door after another and administering the bacteria.

"For this series of tests we are using Macaque monkeys."

A young woman stepped in front of the camera smiling. "For all my animal rights friends, I just want you to know for the record, we've done our research, this should be completely harmless to the monkeys. They should feel happier and more alert. Also, they are only in the cages for the administration of the injections. You'll be happy to know that the room behind me opens into a communal living area for the Macaques once they have received their injection."

"Thank you Ann," said Dr. Pazzo.

Nella could actually hear the eye roll in his voice. She felt a pang of sadness as the pretty young woman walked out of frame. So that was Ann as she had once been. The video reeled on, silent now as the two doctors administered the injections.

"Was Ann your student?" she asked.

"No, she was Gerta's intern. She was in all ways the responsible party when it came to Ann's fate." Dr. Pazzo's mouth twisted, as if he'd tasted something rotten.

"Ann's fate?"

"Just watch," Dr. Pazzo spat.

Someone focused the camera more closely on the cages but the animals seemed calm and Nella was unsurprised when the screen went black a few moments later.

"I'm going to save you hundreds of hours of recording. Results were normal across the board. No aberrations, no warning signs for four weeks. In fact, I think the test was going exactly as planned until the video I'm about to show you." Dr. Pazzo paused and leaned toward them over the table. His expression was solemn. "I *think* this day was when the Plague actually began."

Nella felt a painful tide of tight goosebumps cascade down her arm and over her wounded hand.

The screen blinked and a haggard Dr. Pazzo appeared. His eyes had great dark pouches beneath them and his jaw was shadowed with a patchy brown beard. He scrubbed his face with one hand. Nella thought he looked overly stressed for someone with a flawless experiment and she began to grow suspicious.

"Um . . . Okay. This is video diary number . . . 69. There is nothing new to report, all quiet on the monkey front. Seriously Gerta, I don't know why we need to be doing round the clock observation when we're filming all this. And when are you going to show up for your shift? Ann and I are ragged." Young Dr. Pazzo shrugged. "You won't even look at this tape anyway. But I'll make the morning report regardless." Dr. Pazzo's face split into a bitter grin. He held up a clipboard. "Okay, the animals are consistent in their activity, logging three more hours on average of play movement. Their natural sleep cycles are still reduced to three point five hours . . ."

Dr. Pazzo kept talking but Nella completely forgot to listen. Behind the haggard figure of the scientist was the window into the animal room. The cages had been moved and Nella could see a climbing habitat with several monkeys actively interacting. In the center of the habitat, sitting on the floor, was Ann. She was asleep in the contaminated room in her street clothes. As Nella watched, Ann stirred and yawned.

"Oh my god."

"What is it?" asked Mr. Courtlen. He had obviously been listening to Dr. Pazzo's report. Nella got up and walked to the television. She skipped the video back a few seconds and pointed with a shaking finger to Ann. Nella stood mesmerized as the video reeled on. Ann got up and exited the animal room. Dr. Pazzo was continuing his report, completely oblivious to the fact that his intern was now carrying the special strep strain on her clothes, her breath, her sweat. Mr. Courtlen began to stand as he watched the figure of Ann walk up behind Dr. Pazzo, as if he could somehow physically stop what had happened. Ann reached an arm around the shoulder of Dr. Pazzo and she kissed his ear suggestively. Nella winced thinking of the thousands of bacterium that had just been introduced directly into Dr. Pazzo's system.

Dr. Pazzo turned toward Ann. "Hey," he hissed, "Not on camera."

"Oh relax," she said, smiling broadly, "No one is ever going to watch this disc and you know it."

Dr. Pazzo relented and turned toward Ann and kissed her on the mouth. Nella felt nauseous. She walked slowly back toward the table and sank unsteadily into her seat. Dr. Pazzo was looking down at his hands, not raising his eyes to see either their reaction or his younger self in love upon the screen.

"How did you get so much energy?" asked Dr. Pazzo, still oblivious. "I'm completely wiped out."

"I have my ways," Ann grinned mischievously, "No sign of Dr. Schneider?"

"No. I don't think she's showing up today. Listen, do you mind taking a turn for a while at the computers? I'm so tired of staring at screens. If I could just get an hour's nap I'll be okay."

"Sure," said Ann brightly, still hanging on his hip. The two walked out of frame and the camera was left watching monkeys swing and climb through the glass window.

Nella turned to look at the prisoner. "You think this was the first time Ann went into the animal room without a suit?"

Dr. Pazzo shook his head but didn't look up from his hands. "No, but it is the first evidence I can find of it. From her incubation period and the alteration of the monkeys' behavior, she must have been infected for two weeks before this video."

"How can that be?" asked Mr. Courtlen, "You said that you taped everything."

Now Dr. Pazzo looked up and Nella saw his thin face drawn even tighter with anger. "When Dr. Schneider was on shift, she took the camera into the lab so she could talk continuously to it and document her work. Any of those shifts Ann could have gone into the animal room. I know Dr. Schneider was the one that persuaded her to do it in the first place."

"Why? Why would Dr. Schneider risk Ann or even her experimental results by infecting a human?" Nella asked.

"Dr. Schneider was convinced the bacteria was rendered harmless, and all the results *seemed* to be showing that. But she was impatient. The tests would have had to continue for months, years maybe before human trials could begin. She wanted her results now, not later. So Dr. Schneider left us alone to do round the clock observations for longer and longer periods. And then, when we would go home for some sleep there would inevitably be some trivial 'emergency' just a few hours later and we'd be called back in. She was *hoping* one of us would crack from the exhaustion. We were both bordering on irrational at that point. If Ann hadn't been persuaded to take advantage of the 'free boost' of dopamine in the animal room, then I eventually would have made a mistake. With my suit or the door or a sample. Infection was pretty much inevitable. And Dr. Schneider made sure of that."

Mr. Courtlen shook his head. "I don't understand. You said the experiment was going smoothly. How did we go from happy, besotted, alert interns to- well, to enraged cannibal?"

Dr. Pazzo scratched his cheek as he thought about his answer. Nella wondered if he were getting ready to lie.

"Of course, I can't be sure because by the time I realized what was going on, I didn't have time to conduct a real laboratory examination, not the kind I would want to do. But my *guess* is that either one of the monkeys or Ann herself were carriers of a competing strain of strep bacteria. Either that, or the strain we had infected the monkeys with just mutated as it passed into a human. It caused swelling in the brain. That's why the first symptoms were shambling or uncoordinated movement. It was followed by aggression and eventually uncontrollable pica- cannibalism in this case."

"And it couldn't be cured because you used an antibiotic resistant strain," sighed Nella.

Dr. Pazzo raised his hands and held his head, pulling at the thin strands of hair that were left on his scarred skull. "That's not the worst of it," he mumbled. Nella was startled to find herself empathizing with the man's distress, even after his nastiness.

"What do you mean?" asked Mr. Courtlen.

"Normally when people get a strep infection they manifest symptoms within three days, like sore throats, colds, earaches, rashes. Things that would send people to their doctors. With a normal strep infection the medical community would have been alerted very quickly. With this strain, nothing happened for four to six *weeks*. Even I didn't see it until week five or six in Ann and I was trained to look for it." Dr. Pazzo stopped talking and took great shuddering breaths. Nella thought he must be crying.

"Jesus. Five weeks. How many international flights could have delivered the Plague in that amount of time?" Mr. Courtlen sat stunned.

Not just planes and boats and cars, Nella thought, *How many crowded movie theaters and shopping centers is that? How many hospital waiting rooms when symptoms did start being recognized?*

"The world had already died by the time I found out. It just didn't know it yet," Dr. Pazzo sobbed, and Nella felt a pang of sympathy for him, "What was I supposed to do? What good would warning people do? It was already too late."

"Maybe we should take a break," suggested Nella in a gentle voice. Dr. Pazzo was still audibly weeping and Mr. Courtlen looked shell shocked and was completely still. Nella stood up. She gently squeezed Frank's shoulder as she passed behind him. He shook himself.

"Yes I think that's a good idea. Robert, perhaps we should call it a day. I'm sure Dr. Rider can ask the nurse to give you something to help you sleep."

Dr. Pazzo laughed bitterly. "Why should I get to sleep peacefully Frank? When everyone else is troubled. I know how rare sedatives are these days. Since I am the author of all this," he raised his hands and spread his arms around him, "why should I be the one that sleeps? Besides, we can't stop now. There is no time."

And for the first time Nella felt a cool stone of nervous doubt at the base of her throat. Maybe he wasn't bluffing.

"At least let's take a break then. We'll come back in an hour okay?"

Dr. Pazzo nodded looking defeated. "Yes, that's acceptable," he said, "but we need to finish the diaries today. We can talk about what happens next tomorrow."

The stone in Nella's throat grew heavier and icy. "I thought you said we had enough time," said Nella.

"We do. All the time that's left in the world." Dr. Pazzo stood up from the table and shuffled down the hall toward his cell. Frank stared after him and then shook his head. He looked around and saw Nella still standing behind him. He smiled to break the tension.

"Come on," he said, "I'll buy you the worst lunch you've ever eaten."

Nella laughed and immediately felt better. "I don't know," she said, "I've seen some pretty rough times in the past eight years. It can't be as bad as the medical camp food."

"Want to bet?" he said and walked with her toward the cafeteria.

WE NEVER EVEN HAD A CHANCE

It really was one of the worst meals Nella had eaten in a long while. She didn't care. The cafeteria was bright and open after the windowless cell block. A few administrative personnel and infirmary staff were scattered over the area, but for the most part she and Mr. Courtlen were isolated from the quiet conversations of the others.

Nella looked at the shriveled pile of canned fruit on her plate. She sighed and then laughed.

"What is it?" asked Frank

"I was just thinking how much I miss bananas. A peanut butter and banana sandwich. I think I miss bananas more than I missed hot showers."

"Hmm, I don't know if I would go that far, but a banana would be pretty wonderful. I never would have imagined that I would go almost a decade without fresh tropical fruit. I wonder what parents feed their infants now?"

Nella poked the shrunken pear with her fork. "Not this I hope. Maybe after the trial I'll buy a boat and sail to New Guinea and start a banana farm."

"I can think of worse places to retire."

Nella was trying to keep both of their minds off of the disturbing task still before them. "What do you want to do after this is over?"

He leaned back in the plastic chair. "I hadn't really thought about it. Everything's moved so fast, I'm still not entirely sure how I got this far," he perked up, "Maybe I'll come with you. I'll start a pineapple plantation next door. It'll be our cover, we'll really be partners in a rum running operation. I'll cook the books, you cook the rum."

Nella laughed. "Deal. You take the east half of the island, I'll take the west side."

"Wow," he said, "that was easy." He raised his coffee to his lips and suddenly stopped. "Wait, why the west side?"

Nella shrugged. "I like to sleep on the left side of the bed."

Frank coughed on his coffee. He laughed deeply and it was like a warm wind rolled across the world. Nella could count on one hand the times she'd heard anyone laugh so freely in the past several years. For a moment she was bewildered by it. A guard walked up to their table and Nella felt a pang of real regret knowing their break was over. Even the guard looked hesitant to interrupt.

"Mr. Courtlen, Dr. Rider, the prisoner's ready to begin again."

Frank straightened up and began tidying up his tray. "Thank you, we'll be right there," he said.

The guard walked back toward the cell block. Frank looked at Nella. "Are you ready? Are you still in pain? We can stop at the infirmary if you like."

"No thank you, I'll be okay. Besides, the aspirin makes it hard to concentrate."

They both stood up from the table. "Listen," Nella touched his wrist to stall him, "Did you know all of this before you saw it on the video?"

Mr. Courtlen's brow tightened and he looked troubled. "The version he told me was- well, it was highly edited. I'm not a medical professional, so I still don't know if I quite grasp all of it. But I knew it was Ann who was first infected and I knew Dr. Schneider had coerced her into tampering with the experiment. But I didn't know they started with a resistant strain. And I didn't know that it had been kept secret for so long." He rubbed the scar on his cheek with two fingers. "Six weeks. We never even had a chance did we?"

Nella shook her head. "Maybe a few rural populations wouldn't have been reached by then, but the cities would have been heavily infected. And then as the outbreak began, infected people would have fled to those rural areas without even knowing they were carriers. But you're his lawyer. Why didn't he tell you all of this?"

"I don't know. He hasn't told anyone this much. The other doctors- he wasn't lying when he said you were the fifth one. He'd string them along with the same version I got until they started asking him personal questions and he'd try to get them to answer personal questions of their own. And when they wouldn't answer, he'd refuse to see them again."

"What kind of personal questions?"

"Well, he usually asked them what they did to survive the Plague or what they did to help the Cure."

"So why hasn't he asked me?"

Mr. Courtlen shrugged and picked up his tray. "I can only assume it's because your history with the Cure is already well known. It was clear to me that the judges were tired of trying to placate Dr. Pazzo and decided to hire you to work some kind of miracle on Miss Connelly rather than do much with Dr. Pazzo. They are expecting her to tell the whole story. But it looks like Dr. Pazzo decided to start telling it anyway."

"Mr. Courtlen," she said, and the icy boulder that had lodged in her throat reappeared, "I'm starting to think you were right about Dr. Pazzo."

"What do you mean?"

"I think he really has something important to tell us. I don't think it's a bluff anymore. And I don't think it is anything good."

Mr. Courtlen stared at her. "What do you think he's trying to tell us?"

She felt sweat spring out on her forehead and tears prickled in the corners of her eyes. She whispered so the scattered occupants of the cafeteria wouldn't overhear. "I don't think we've seen the last of the Plague."

HOW IT SPREAD

Dr. Pazzo had recovered his usual reserve, but Nella's chest was tight with anxiety. She'd seen no indication of madness in Dr. Pazzo yet, nor did she expect to. Beyond a fairly normal case of narcissism and an understandably high level of depression, he was remarkably healthy. His hints of withholding vital information were all the more frightening to Nella because of this. She could see, however, that Mr. Courtlen was becoming more suspicious of his client. Nella was increasingly convinced that Dr. Pazzo was telling the truth.

They resumed their seats. Nella heaved an inward sigh at the contrast between the bright and airy cafeteria and the grim, hunched narrowness of the cell block. She was glad she would get to walk out at the end of the day.

"Dr. Pazzo," she began, "You said it took you several weeks to notice Ann's symptoms. How did you finally find out that she was infected?"

"It was the day I took her to the hospital. She had accidentally cut herself on some broken glassware. If I had known what we were dealing with at that point, the cut would have been enough for me to suspect something."

"What do you mean?"

"Ann was never klutzy, but over a few days preceding this incident she was stumbling pretty often. I thought it was the exhaustion. She would slur her speech every so often as well and we had some really nasty fights in those last couple of days. What else should I have thought? It was a normal reaction to lack of sleep. But- well let me show you."

The video began again. The camera was still focused on the window into the animal room. The monkeys seemed sluggish, but Nella thought, perhaps it was the beginning or end of their sleep cycle. Somewhere off the screen came a loud, splintering crash as glassware was dropped.

"Oh Jesus, Ann. Oh God. Are you all right?" Dr. Pazzo's voice moved away and Nella heard Ann mumbling but couldn't hear what she said.

"Okay, just stay there. Don't. Move." Nella heard footsteps run past the camera which tilted as Dr. Pazzo ran past. Now it pointed partly into the lab. Nella could see computer screens and equipment as well as the animal room in the corner of the screen. She still couldn't see Ann but could hear her whimpering. Something black thudded across the screen. It was Dr. Pazzo.

"Here, we have to keep pressure on it. Look at me Ann, I need to call for help. Can you keep pressure on it?"

Nella didn't hear any response from Ann. She heard the quick skid of Dr. Pazzo's shoes as he ran back toward the camera followed by a stumbling, irregular trot that was Ann. They came on screen, Dr. Pazzo dragging Ann and pressing a towel onto her upper arm. He fumbled with a phone for a minute, trying to dial with one hand and hold Ann's arm with the other. "Hello?" his voice was shaky and loud, "I need an ambulance at-"

Nella tuned the rest out. She was watching Ann intently. Ann was not looking at anything in particular, her eyes wandering in the pattern Nella now recognized. She was rocking gently back and forth and seemed utterly calm. Nella could see the towel darkening on her arm. She watched the two run past the screen and heard a door open and slam and then everything was quiet. The video cut out and returned, refocused on the animal room.

Nella heard the door open and the heavy tread

of Dr. Pazzo. "Robert, is that you?" Dr. Schneider's voice sounded distant but Nella heard the sharp clicks of high heels head steadily toward the camera. "Where have you been? I come in and the lab is abandoned with broken glassware everywhere-"

"Ann cut herself. She had to be rushed to the hospital." Dr. Pazzo stooped into the frame fiddling with the camera.

"What? Where is she now? What kind of tests did they run at the hospital?" Dr. Schneider's voice was shrill and panicked.

Dr. Pazzo looked up from the camera, his tired face drawing into a scowl as he turned away towards Dr. Schneider. "She's at home sleeping. Jesus, do you even care that she was injured?" Dr. Pazzo shook his head in disgust and turned back to the camera. "Christ, this thing is a mess," he mumbled and picked up the camera, carrying it with him to a desk. A cloth swiped over the lens and the camera was lifted to shoulder level as Dr. Pazzo looked through the eyepiece. Nella felt slightly dizzy, but at last the view settled onto Dr. Schneider's angry face. "She needed stitches and the emergency tech said she seemed exhausted, which I agreed with. So they stitched her up and sent her home to sleep. Why would they need to run tests?"

Dr. Schneider hesitated, frowning at Dr. Pazzo. "Nothing. Never mind," she said.

The camera was abruptly set on the desktop. "No, what did you mean? What tests?"

Dr. Schneider was silent. Dr. Pazzo came into view, rapidly crossing the space between himself and Dr. Shneider.

"Gerta, what tests? What did you do?"

"She was exposed to the Recharge bacteria."

"She's infected? How did she become exposed?" Dr. Pazzo threw up his hands. "No, you know what, I don't even want to know. When was she exposed?"

"Calm down Robert. It's a harmless strain, you checked it yourself. Don't you see? This is good. This will push the trials forward-"

"Shut up. Where did you get your doctorate anyway? Mail order? It *was* a harmless strain. Every time it crosses species- every time it infects someone new, in fact, it has a chance to mutate. This whole experiment was supposed to be about control. The dopamine and amphetamine levels, yes, but also keeping a pure strain. We have no idea what mutations may have occurred at this point." Dr. Pazzo clutched his head. "Jesus, Gerta, she could be exposing others right now. How long ago was she exposed? Are we infected?"

"Relax! My guess is that it's been about four weeks. She's fine. We're fine. There's nothing to worry about."

It startled Nella to see Dr. Pazzo run out of view. A few seconds later, she heard a violent retching. "Really Robert, there's no need for all this melodrama. If it will make you feel better, I'll run some cultures when she comes in tomorrow and show you it's the same strain."

"No. I'm going to go get her now." He came back into view, clutching one of the pale blue biohazard suits. He walked up to Dr. Schneider and pointed a shaking finger at her. "And you're going to stay right here until I get back."

Dr. Schneider laughed. I don't think so. I have a fundraising dinner tonight."

"I don't give a damn about your fundraiser Gerta. We have to figure this out. You're going to take a sample of the bacteria in the animal room. Then, you're going to sit your ass down and do some actual lab work. You need to compare it to our original strain. I'm going to get Ann before she infects anyone else. Maybe it's not too late."

Dr. Pazzo began stepping into the biohazard suit. "Hey, I'm the lead scientist on this project," Dr. Shneider said shrilly, "I don't take orders from you."

Dr. Pazzo stopped with one arm in the suit. "I don't care about seniority Gerta. Don't you understand? We fucked up. We have to find a way to fix this."

"There is nothing to fix! Everything is fine." Dr. Shneider rolled her eyes. "This is ridiculous. I'm going home."

"Gerta, if you take one more step toward that door, I'll have to do something we'll both regret. We have to maintain quarantine."

"Quarantine?" she hissed, "Do you even hear yourself?" She shook her head and then started walking past Dr. Pazzo toward the door. Looking grim, he punched her in the jaw and then caught her as she fell.

Nella felt Mr. Courtlen tense in surprise. She watched in shock as the young Dr. Pazzo dragged the unconscious woman back to the desk chair near the camera. He slumped her onto the chair and then reached for a roll of medical tape sitting nearby. Nella could hear the loud squeal of ripping tape as he bound Dr. Schneider to the chair. He paused to rub a hand over his eyes and Nella could see he was crying. He rocked back and forth on his knees and held his head in his arms. He was so close to the camera that Nella could hear the crackling rustle of the suit. "Please let it be okay," he whispered, "Please let it be okay."

Dr. Shneider groaned and began to stir. Dr. Pazzo stood up, his eyes still streaming. "I'm sorry Gerta, but you've got to stay until I figure this out."

"Idiot," she spat.

"I'm going to get Ann now. I'll be back soon."

"If she is infected then you're already infected too," Gerta sneered, "I know all about you're little trysts. That suit isn't going to protect you."

Dr. Pazzo shook his head. "It's not to protect me from Ann," he said, "It's to protect everyone else from us." He pulled the plastic helmet over his face and walked away.

TURNING

The video cut out and Nella turned to Dr. Pazzo. He was shaking and held up one hand as if to forestall her questions. "I think," he said in a low voice, "I'm going to leave you both to watch the next pieces alone. I will answer any questions you have tomorrow, but I don't think I can live through the next part again. If you'll excuse me," he rose from his seat, "Mr. Courtlen, Dr. Rider goodnight. And thank you for the books." Dr. Pazzo shuffled down the hall followed by his guards.

Mr. Courtlen took a deep breath and puffed his cheeks blowing it slowly out again. "Do you know what is on the next tape?" asked Nella.

"I haven't watched it, but I can guess that it is at this point that Dr. Pazzo secluded himself and the others in the lab. Dr. Pazzo's notes say this is a key piece of evidence, but I'm not so sure- I think we've pretty much seen all the evidence that matters. Let's get to it though."

"I'm not really concerned with evidence. Did he tell you about his relationship with Ann? Or Dr. Schneider?"

Mr. Courtlen shook his head. "No, I didn't know he and Ann were sleeping together. I guess it's not really that important for the trial."

"It might explain some of his actions. Why didn't he contact the authorities?"

"I have a feeling Dr. Schneider was at least partially responsible for that part. And you saw how panicked he was. He probably thought he could get ahead of it. If anyone found out- about *any* of it; sloppy laboratory practices or sleeping with interns, he could lose his job and his reputation would be permanently scarred."

Nella picked up the remote and started the video again. The camera still showed Dr. Schneider taped to the chair on the side of the screen. She appeared to have fallen asleep. Two blue suited figures walked in, one supporting the other. Dr. Pazzo removed his helmet and guided Ann into a nearby chair, where he removed her helmet as well. She was awake, but to Nella appeared exhausted or drugged. Her eyes stared toward the camera but didn't seem to register anything around her. She seemed to have been chewing on her lip, there was a thin line of dark, crusted blood just below it and there were minor scratches on her face.

"Stay here Ann," said Dr. Pazzo and Nella saw Dr. Schneider start from her sleep.

"You're back then," said Dr. Schneider.

"Yes, we're here."

"Are you going to let me go?"

"Are you going to help me figure this out?"

"She looks fine Robert, just tired. Why don't we all go home and get some sleep and in the morning-"

Dr. Pazzo crossed the room with surprising speed. He shoved Dr. Schneider's chair and she rolled rapidly toward Ann. The two women were about a foot from each other, but Ann didn't even blink. Dr. Pazzo grabbed the back of Dr. Schneider's head and forced her to look at Ann.

"Look at her," he said, and his voice was low and threatening, "She can't walk straight. She's been scratching at her face." He pulled the glove off of one of Ann's hand. The tips of her fingers were pulsing with blood. "She's been eating her hands Gerta. Does that seem fucking fine to you?"

"Let me go," said Gerta, "Okay, I get it, let me go. We'll do the samples now."

"You aren't going to try to run?"

Gerta sighed. "No, if there is really something

wrong it's too late for me to go anywhere now."

Dr. Pazzo began removing the tape. Dr. Schneider silently moved off screen and returned with a first aid kit. "Get the lab ready," she said, "I'll work on her hands."

The camera cut out for a second. Dr. Pazzo appeared on screen talking into the camera.

"I'm not sure who I'm leaving this for, but I hope that someone will find it. I would send it out over the internet, but Ann- well, Ann had an episode. The modem is in pieces and Gerta has confiscated my cell. Some nonsense about damage control. As if there could be any control after this." He scrubbed his face with his hand. "I've put Ann in the animal holding area for now and locked the door, so that she can't destroy anything else. Gerta is going over and over the tests, but I'm afraid there is no doubt. The strain of strep has mutated." Nella saw tears starting up in Dr. Pazzo's eyes as he backed a few feet from the camera and sat heavily down into a desk chair.

"I guess that answers the question," said Mr. Courtlen. Nella nodded and turned back toward the screen.

"Ann's antibody levels are abnormally high, even in the presence of strep. The closest thing I can compare her behavior to is Autoimmune Neuropsychiatric Disorder, but I've never seen it in an adult before. She is unable to walk without lurching and stumbling. She won't stop chewing on her bottom lip and her hands. In fact, she seems not to even notice that she is doing it." Dr. Pazzo stopped and Nella watched a tear slide down his face. He cleared his throat. "She has become erratic and aggressive which are not normal traits for her at all. She smashed a good deal of equipment before I could sedate her and contain her in the animal room. I didn't want to do it, but there is only one other room with a lock on it, and that is the closet for cleaning supplies. I can't tell if Gerta and I are infected or not. So far our blood tests aren't showing anything, but it could just be a matter of time. Whether or not we will experience the same symptoms as Ann, I don't know. There is really no way to conclusively test for inflammation of nerves in the brain. I hope Ann is the exception. But to be safe we are going to have to quarantine the lab. Gerta doesn't accept this and I'm afraid I may have to force the issue if she doesn't come around. Until we have proof that this strain is not as dangerous as it has become for Ann or we are past the incubation period for ourselves, we can't risk exposing anyone else. Eight weeks should be sufficient to evaluate our symptoms and to see if our bodies will be capable of fighting the infection off naturally. If Ann *does* have a form of ANDAS, her body's defenses are unfortunately fighting her brain and not the bacteria. In our quest to develop a bacterial mule that would succeed in the greatest number of subjects, Gerta and I-" Dr. Pazzo shook his head, "No, not Gerta, *I* chose a bacteria that was resistant to all known antibiotics. There is no known cure. I cannot realistically hope that the infection has been isolated to the lab, but still I have to take precautions. All I can hope for is that the bacteria remains harmless to the rest of the population. If not, I hope this record and our data will help someone develop an effective antibiotic quickly. I am going to close up the lab now. I will leave a disinfected copy of this video in the-"

A banging sound came from behind Dr. Pazzo. He turned swiftly in his chair. "Jesus," he said. He stood and walked toward the animal room behind him. Standing at the window was Ann. She was slapping the glass with her hand. Nella couldn't see much of her face, she was too far from the camera.

"I'm hungry Robert," she yelled. She smacked the glass.

"You just ate Ann," said Dr. Pazzo trying to maintain a reasonable tone.

"I'm hungry," she smacked the glass a little harder, leaving a pink streak where the bandage on her hand had slipped. "I'm hungry, Robert, I'm HUNGRY!" She was yelling louder now. Dr. Pazzo ran a hand through his hair, distressed. "I'M HUNGRY, I'M HUNGRY! I'M HUNGRY," Ann was screaming louder and faster now, flinging her whole shoulder against the glass with deep, nauseating thuds. Suddenly she stumbled deeper into the room away from the glass. Nella heard the shrieking of dozens of monkeys, along with Ann continually screaming, "HUNGRY," over and over. This went on for several seconds and Dr. Pazzo began slapping the glass window. "Ann, Ann," he called. Something smacked the window with a wet crunch, as if several carrots were snapped at once. Nella jumped. Whatever it was smacked the window again, leaving a smear of blood and silver fur. Ann came up to the glass holding a limp monkey just in front of Dr. Pazzo. He backed up slowly from the window. "Hungry," Ann said and buried her face in the carcass. Dr. Pazzo sank down into a crouch, his head swallowed in his arms. "No, no, no," he cried and rocked back and forth. The video cut out.

QUARANTINE

When the screen shifted from blank black, it showed a small closet and Nella's ears were filled with the incessant buzz of an old florescent bulb and the muffled sobs of a woman somewhere outside the closet. Occasionally there was a sharp, rhythmic banging.

"Don't do this Robert!" Dr. Schneider's voice was pleading and raw even through the wall. "I'm not sick. You can see that I'm not sick."

"I'm sorry Gerta. I have to do this. I can't trust you to maintain quarantine voluntarily. Ann is locked in as well and I'll be locking myself in next."

"Someone's going to come looking for us," sobbed Dr. Schneider, "You won't get away with this."

"Someone might come along, but they'll have to ignore some pretty massive signs warning them. Then they'll have to break through several palettes I nailed across the door."

Nella paused the video. "Mr. Courtlen, I don't know if I should see this. Dr. Pazzo isn't charged with kidnapping but he could be."

He ran a hand over his head for a second. "I know you don't have to keep anything confidential, and I'm not asking you to. I don't think a kidnapping charge is anything Dr. Pazzo has to worry about. Not just because I don't expect him to win his case in this trial. Holding Ann and Schneider was necessary to protect the public. I don't think he will be charged even if it gets that far."

Nella was worried by his bleak outlook. She started the video without further comment.

The banging resumed for a few moments.

"What's your brilliant plan for getting us out of here once our quarantine is done?"

There was a lengthy silence. The electric hum of the lightbulb seemed overwhelming.

"Or are we just supposed to slowly starve to death in here?" Her voice wavered like a candle in a breeze. Nella winced, sensing Dr. Schneider had been on the verge of hysterics.

"We're not going to starve. There was an emergency supply of food and medicine in the basement for just this sort of incident. I've supplied each of us with enough for almost a year. If I'm overreacting, then someone will break the quarantine before then. If I'm not- well, I guess if you are still not sick by then, you'll have the strength to break through these few boards. If you are really prepared to live alone in a dead world."

"You're mad Robert! We're fine, we're not sick."

"Speak for yourself Gerta."

"It was just a bad reaction that Ann had. We'll fix it together. But I can't do it in an office kitchen." There was only silence. "Robert? Robert!"

There was a squeal of hinges as the closet's metal door opened. Dr. Pazzo stumbled through and grabbed the camera, his face filling the screen.

"I can't remember what video number this is. I'm sorry. I'm having trouble with the details now. I'm making this particular entry in case I've been wrong about this whole thing and I need to defend my actions." The camera spun around to show the closet's interior. "Of course, if I'm right about the extent of damage this disease can cause, our collection of video diaries may help survivors figure out how this happened and maybe, someday, a way to cure what we have done."

The closet had been cleared and all that remained was a low cot, a pile of books, and a mop sink. It still looked cramped.

"As you can see," Dr. Pazzo began, "I have provided us with the basics. For water and toilet necessaries, we all have a drainable sink- actually Ann has a basin that is automatically filled regularly as part of animal care. But both Dr. Schneider and I have sinks. I've loosened the spigot in both, so that there is a constant small stream of water. For when we can't remember to turn it on by ourselves."

The camera shook and Nella realized Dr. Pazzo was crying silently. She heard Mr. Courtlen utter a strangled sigh beside her.

"Anyway," continued Dr. Pazzo in an exhausted voice, "We don't have to worry about water or light, since the lab was converted to solar power during the university's green initiative last year. The gas generator should kick on if the snow covers the panels and we have enough for a long while." The camera spun around to show a small shelf cut into the wall. "This is a food dispensary of sorts. I've programmed the timer for the animal room to release ration packets once a day to all of us. With the reluctant help of Dr. Schneider and some spare vent hoses from the maintenance room we should be well supplied for about a year. You may be wondering why I felt this system was necessary." Dr. Pazzo walked out of the closet. Nella saw with some shock that the desks and lab tables were gone, nailed in large panels over the visible doors and windows. The lab was left a gray wasteland ruled by a silver web of exhaust hose draped from the ceiling. Even the loose cords and computers had been carefully bundled to the far side. For a moment she wondered why such care had been taken in what had surely been a very hasty preparation. Dr. Pazzo lurched forward and stumbled, almost dropping the camera. Nella guessed that he must already have been very ill at the time of the video.

"It has been almost two weeks since we discovered Ann was infected and her symptoms have become dramatically worse." The camera swept over toward the glass window of the animal room. Nella wanted to cover her eyes. She heard Mr. Courtlen draw in a sharp, shocked breath. The window was smeared, edge to edge, with blood and fur and greasy matter. It was almost opaque with gore, except where the light shone through the yellow fats like a greasy paper bag.

"I have been into the animal room twice since she killed the first monkey. Once to move a cot in for her and once to attempt to clean that. But Ann attacked me so violently that I would have had to harm her to stop her. So I left and have not tried again. Instead I have relied on the internal video feed to observe Ann's symptoms." Dr. Pazzo paused and when he continued, his voice cracked.

"Ann can no longer speak articulately. She will sometimes shriek or grunt, but no one has heard a word from her in a week. She also no longer seems to recognize us by sight or voice. Even the animals- Ann used to lobby for us to treat our lab animals with all the kindness we could. Without fail she would bring them toys or interact with them even through the plastic suit we had to wear . . .

She killed them all. All the monkeys, one after another. Within two days, fifteen in all. She gorged herself on them. The only thing I can think is that she is suffering from a strange compulsion. She is certainly not hungry. I don't know, however, how much is just the constant aggression and hostility she is displaying and how much is the need to eat. Anyhow, this is why I put the food distribution system in place. So each of us would get the calories we needed every day without killing ourselves by eating too much, too quickly."

Dr. Pazzo walked over to a bank of light switches. "It became clear that we would have to separate ourselves not only from the outside world, but also from each other after Ann's numerous episodes of violence. And since we do not know when or if we will all suffer from the same symptoms, we had to act as quickly as possible. This is why we are in isolated, secure cells. Ann's is locked from the outside. Gerta- Dr. Schneider's kitchen has no lock, so I boarded the door with a few slats. It won't be enough to hold her back for very long as long as she remains well and rational enough to use tools. But it will discourage anything as impaired as Ann has become. Whether that thing is trying to get out or trying to get in. God, how I hope I'm mad and this will all be over soon."

Dr. Pazzo began flicking light switches, consigning section after section of the lab to windowless dark. The animal room glowed pink and yellow, a smeared cathedral window into hell. A crack of gold outlined Dr. Schneider's kitchen and a thin path to the closet drew Dr. Pazzo down it toward his prison. Dr. Pazzo sobbed loudly when he reached the door. Nella felt something in her chest snap in sympathy for his loneliness.

"I don't know if I'll have the dexterity or intelligence to use the key once the disease truly takes hold," he said, and then rolled a shimmering key in his hand so that the camera picked up its light. "But I'm not going to take the chance." Dr. Pazzo placed the camera on the floor facing the doorway. For a long, long minute nothing happened. Nella could hear a low, drawn out moan as Dr. Pazzo wept. Then a shaking hand carefully placed the key in front of the camera. Nella felt pure, irrational panic reach up and choke her. The hand pushed the key, shooting it through the crack at the bottom of the door, off into the sea of darkness beyond.

Dr. Pazzo picked up the camera and spun it to face him. "That will do for this video I think. I will try to record more if I can, so that any future researchers will be able to track the symptoms of this disease." The screen went black.

Nella turned toward Mr. Courtlen. "How long were they like that?" she asked.

"Ironically, they were some of the first Infected to be Cured. But I think Dr. Pazzo said he and Ann were there about fourteen months. Their rescuers said both were very emaciated, to the point that a few days more might have meant they starved to death. Dr. Schneider escaped after only about two weeks after being confined and has never been seen again, that we know of."

"Funny," said Nella, "I could swear I've seen her face before, but I've wracked my brain and I can't place where or when."

"Maybe you knew her Before? I gather she was quite well known in scientific circles."

"Maybe," answered Nella doubtfully.

"If you *do* remember, the prosecutor would certainly like to speak with her."

"I'm sure most of the world would like a chance to speak with her. Maybe she just has one of those faces." Nella shook her head.

"It looks like there is only one video left. I know it's been a long day, but we should try to get through it." Mr. Courtlen looked for a moment and Nella's bandaged hand before continuing. "Should we stop for a minute and get you some more painkillers?"

Nella's brain screamed an emphatic yes. Her hand was a pulsing, creeping fire. But she knew how precious each pill was, so she clenched her teeth and then said, "No, I'm okay." Her smile was hardened plastic. "Besides, I wouldn't be able to drive home if I took anything."

Mr. Courtlen hesitated and then nodded and started the last video.

Dr. Pazzo was propped against the closet wall. His beard was full and thick, but Nella could see large patches of hair on his head were missing. She wondered if it were part of the disease or simply stress.

"Um. I can't remember which video this is. My watch says it's been about ten days since I locked us away."

He sounded slow, almost drunk, and he concentrated hard on every phrase. "My speech has been getting worse, though I didn't realize how much until now. My conversation to this point have been limited to a few words spoken through the wall to Dr. Schneider. She seems fine, but refuses to tell me if she is seeing symptoms in herself or not. I don't have much room in here to turn around, so testing the deterioration of my motor skills has been a little inconclusive. I do know they were deteriorating rather rapidly before I locked myself in here."

Dr. Pazzo paused for a minute and Nella could see him blushing. At last he said, "I'm having considerable difficulty concentrating on the words in my books." He turned the camera toward a pile of shredded paper. "As you can see, I became very frustrated yesterday. I don't even recall what finally set me off. I do, however, remember actually doing it. It was an exhilarating moment to just be ripping and tearing. I find that disturbing, but I'm not sure what I can do to stop it."

He turned the camera back to his face. "I think I'll give up reading for a while," he said with a rueful grin, "at least I'll have some toilet paper when I run out. If I'm still aware enough to want it. God knows

Ann wasn't." The grin turned into slow tears that Dr. Pazzo mopped at clumsily with one arm. He cleared his throat.

"Unfortunately, I feel physically fine. We've made the strain both too resistant to be cured and too weak to cause any real damage until it is already well entrenched in the brain. It's never going to kill the host by itself. Hosts may kill each other due to hostility resulting from the bacteria's effect, but it's probably not going to burn itself out like other epidemics. It's not even going to show up in doctor's offices or hospitals until it is far too late. It's so mild until the end, that no one will seek medical attention for this. I can only pray that we caught it in time, that we are the only three who are infected. And if that's not the case, I hope that someone has a new antibiotic waiting in the wings that will work on this superbug we have created-"

"Robert? Is that you?" The voice was muffled but Nella could understand what was said. Dr. Pazzo rolled his eyes without even looking at the camera.

"Yes, of course, who else would it be?" Nella was surprised by how snappish his response was.

"I have something I need to confess."

"Are you finally admitting that you are sick?"

"What does it matter if I am or if I'm immune? I'm going to die here either way."

Dr. Pazzo ran a hand through his thinning hair and closed his eyes. He gently knocked his head against the wall, thick tears leaking through his beard. He took a deep breath. "All right, what sordid thing did you do? I hope it's naughty," he said with a faint smile.

"No Robert, this time I'm serious."

The smile dropped from his face and he opened his eyes.

"Robert? Are you still listening?"

"Yeah, I'm here."

"Remember how we discussed developing a strain with NDM plasmids?"

Dr. Pazzo sat straight up, his eyes flying wide. Nella watched his adam's apple jump and throb like an erratic heartbeat. "Gerta," he called, his voice raised more now, "We said we weren't going to do that, that normal resistances were good enough. We said we weren't going to play with anything that dangerous."

"I know we said that."

Dr. Pazzo stood up, the camera in one hand. He leaned against the wall between him and Dr. Schneider, his ear resting on it. "Gerta, please don't tell me that you went ahead and tried it anyway."

"It was supposed to be harmless, Robert. You said it would be harmless. It was controlled, only the one plasmid changed."

"Jesus," Nella whispered.

Mr. Courtlen paused the video. "What is it? What are they talking about?"

"It's been a long time since medical school but I believe they were talking about creating a strain of bacteria that is completely immune to all antibiotics. Something for which there is no cure, there can be no cure, not even a miracle one like the one that saved us this time. And a different strain means even the Immunes wouldn't be safe this time."

Nella could feel the sweat gathering at her hairline, but she shuddered and hugged herself.

Mr. Courtlen stared at her in shock. His face was so pale that his scar was like a shadow at midnight. "They couldn't have. He would have told me. He would have warned someone."

"We have to know." She grabbed the remote and started the video again.

"Good God. Why? Why would you do this? You didn't even finish the testing with this strain."

"I thought we could test them at the same time, get both pushed through at once. I wanted to patent the stronger strain and have the weaker one as backup. It was supposed to be harmless, why would anyone need to cure it? If it could withstand everything, then everyone, even people with chronic illness could benefit from it."

Dr. Pazzo was shaking. He stroked the wall with his free hand. "Please Gerta, please tell me you only thought about it. Please tell me we aren't infected with an NDM strain."

"No, we are infected with your strain."

"Thank God."

"But I did create it. It's stored in a private laboratory. I didn't tell anyone about it. It's locked away, but I didn't expect this to happen. I don't know if it's safe, that's why I fought you on the quarantine."

Dr. Pazzo started laughing.

"This isn't funny Robert."

"What does it fucking matter? The disease we released needs a miracle cure. By the time anyone realizes it, all the labs, all the governments, they'll all have collapsed. There's no cure coming. The disease that lurks in your lab has no cure at all. What does it matter? The world is going to tear itself apart human by human."

"Stop talking like that Robert. You're crazy."

Dr. Pazzo stopped laughing. "*I'm* crazy? *I'm* crazy? You delusional *bitch.* This whole thing is *your* fault. You're greedy and impatient. You couldn't wait to follow protocol so you purposely exposed Ann. Then you let her walk out into the world. You *murdering bitch.* You've killed us all for the sake of a few dollars."

Dr. Pazzo pounded on the wall with every sentence. Nella could see his face twisting into a bitter rage.

"I have to leave Robert. I have to undo this and see if I can stop the NDM bacteria from being discovered and released."

"Don't you dare!" roared Dr. Pazzo, thumping the wall. "You will infect everyone you meet, you'll kill the world even faster."

"I *have* to Robert. I can't stay here any more." There was a splintering squeal of breaking wood.

"No! You can't leave! You can't do this!" Dr. Pazzo was banging and kicking the wall, forgetting the camera in his hand. There was another crash from beyond the wall and Dr. Pazzo roared, no longer forming words. The camera bashed again and again into the wall and the guttural roar was unending. At last the camera's image shattered into bright white pixels and the video stopped.

FRANK COURTLEN

Nella could hear her blood pounding in her head like a giant helicopter rotor. She didn't dare to look around at Mr. Courtlen until it had faded into the background. She started to get up, but she shook so much that she thought she might shatter. She sat back down.

"What do we do?" she asked in a quiet, lost voice. All her training, all of her desire to remain professional and collected was stripped away. She could remember hearing almost the same news spilling out of the television in her university's lounge. The same vivid panic reached out of the memory and squeezed her chest with unbearable weight. She turned to look for Mr. Courtlen.

He was as lost as she, still staring at the blank screen. His face was yellow and waxy with sweat. He was motionless but his bones still seemed to want to leap forward without his skin and he was all angle and sharp corner. His terror made him hideous. Nella had time to realize that she didn't care, she was glad he was sitting with her. At last he passed a shaky hand over his face and then looked at her.

"Look, I know you aren't bound to hold anything said here in confidence, but I think we can both agree that until we find out more, the less said to strangers the better. Don't you think?"

Nella was silent for a moment. "But someone's got to find this lab and destroy the bacteria-" Nella's voice was shaky and rushed. Mr. Courtlen put up one hand.

"I know, I know. Dr. Rider I'm not asking you to keep this secret indefinitely," He leaned toward her and spoke low into her ear though the guards had all left with Dr. Pazzo, "but we don't know who would try to use this to their advantage. Like the government. Or who would go off the deep end and try to save the world in an ill fated blaze of glory. I know the soldiers here, they are all brave, they all want to be heroes. Hell, I'm thinking about doing it myself. But until we know where Dr. Schneider's lab is, or even Dr. Schneider herself, we can only make things worse by spreading panic."

He held her arm gently so she would look at him. "Can we agree on that?" he asked quietly.

Nella nodded. Of course, he was right. What good could they do with an unverified piece of information? They'd have to wait until morning to find out more.

"Will Dr. Pazzo know where her lab is?"

"Possibly, but I'm going to call in a favor with a friend in the military police headquarters. They've been able to pull up old addresses and driver's licenses for a little while now. He won't ask questions and I don't want to wait until my client feels like telling us." His face was grim. He got up from the table, but turned back toward her. "Listen, don't leave all right? I mean, you're free to go where and when you like of course- I just, that is, I would appreciate it if you wait for me. I don't like the idea of walking out onto that dark parking lot alone just now." He pulled the disc from the television and placed it in his jacket pocket.

"Sure," she said, grateful that he felt the same way she did, "I'll check on Ann and meet you at the entrance."

She was done with Ann far sooner than she expected and waited nervously near the heavy glass entrance door. The combination of the aching pain in her bitten hand and impotent terror made Nella rock on her heels and fight not to cry. Mr. Courtlen came up behind her and she tried to pull herself together.

He looked out at the parking lot and sighed. "I don't know about you Dr. Rider, but I've never needed a drink more than I do right now." He smiled down at her.

"Thank God," she said, venturing a shaky grin, "I hate drinking alone."

He laughed and opened the door.

"Come on," she said, "I think I have a bottle or two stashed at my apartment. And if it's okay with you, I'd rather not be sneaking into bootleg clubs today."

"Sure, but we're taking my car."

Nella shook her head, confused. "Why? I'm not drunk yet."

"No," he said and reached into his pocket as they walked toward the cars. He pulled out a bottle of aspirin, "but you desperately need these and don't pretend you don't, I could see you wincing all afternoon."

Nella's eyes went wide. "Where did you?"

"Relax, I didn't steal them. The apartment I was given, it must have been a hypochondriac's house. They didn't clean anything out before they assigned it to me. She had literally hundreds of bottles of various drugs and cleaning products. I carry around one of the bottles because they are so useful for trading."

He shook out a dose into her hand. She stopped and looked at the smooth, gleaming aspirin in her hand, like tiny teeth. "I don't like to owe anyone," she said doubtfully.

"Well, I think a bottle of something stashed in your apartment should cover it," he laughed, "Don't worry about the car, I'll pick you up in the morning and drive you back. Besides, I want us both to be here as early as possible tomorrow. I don't like sitting on this secret. Not at all."

"No, I'm not comfortable with it either. Is your friend going to get back to you soon?"

"He said the old address should be in the university's record, so he expects to have something for us tomorrow." Mr. Courtlen opened the passenger side door for Nella. "No more about that today. Let's let the world take care of itself for one more day." Nella swallowed the tiny tablets and slid into the dark car. It was cool after the warm prison and it smelled as clean as Mr. Courtlen had. Nella closed her eyes for a moment as Mr. Courtlen got in and started the car.

"You okay?" he asked, then quickly added, "I mean besides the obvious."

She chuckled. "Sorry, I always do this for a second at the end of a long day."

He smiled and took his hands off the wheel. He sat back and closed his eyes, crossing his long arms over his chest. She smiled and leaned back on the headrest, her face turned toward him. He took a deep breath and let it out.

"You're right," he said, "That is much better." He leaned forward and shifted into gear. "Now let's go get snookered. Don't fall asleep! You have to tell me how to get there."

Nella laughed. She struggled to put the day out of her head and searched for something to distract them. "By the way," she said, grinning, "We can't make rum out of pineapples and bananas. The best we can hope for is weak wine."

"What? Not acceptable. One of us is going to have to switch our plans. We can't be wine runners after all."

"You're going to want to turn here. We could be wine runners I suppose, but I think people would pay more for rum." Her breath was light and easy again, and though she knew the aspirin couldn't have hit her that fast, her hand ached less.

Mr. Courtlen slowed to a crawl in front of a brightly lit mansion. "Woah, is that what I think it is?"

Nella was surprised. "You mean you've never been through here before? That's the house the government gave to Dr. Carton after he released the Cure."

"Have you seen him?"

"No, no one has seen him. He's very private, never comes out at all."

"I wonder what he does in there all day?"

Nella shook her head. "I don't know. It must be just as hard to be seen as the savior of humanity as it is to be seen as its destroyer."

Mr. Courtlen let the car pick up speed. "I wonder where either of them thought they would be by now."

"I thought I'd be doing research at a lovely, well funded facility by now."

"And I thought I would be representing divorcees with deep pockets. I barely finished law school though."

"I never quite finished med school. I still had a few months of residency left. But since there are so few doctors left, I guess no one thought it mattered so much."

They were silent a while, rolling down the empty streets.

"Is there a lot of demand for lawyers now? Do you do other cases?"

"I know there are some for looting or when someone gets out of hand in a fight. But mostly people seem to forgive small things. And no one seems interested in committing the big crimes anymore. Besides, those cases are all taken by more experienced lawyers than me."

"Did Dr. Pazzo ask for you to represent him?"

Mr. Courtlen shook his head. "No. I was the only one willing to represent him. I wasn't even practicing law when the preparations for the trial began."

"What were you doing?"

"Actually, I was assigned to repair power lines as the City expanded. The labor department thought I couldn't speak. I guess that it was a common thing with Cured, because they just threw me in the manual jobs pool without really worrying about it."

"More common than you'd think," Nella said grimly. "What made you decide to represent Dr. Pazzo?"

"I saw on the news that there was a long line of people vying for positions in the prosecution and that as of yet, Dr. Pazzo and Ann Connelly were not represented at all. I was very angry then, at what had happened. You have to remember that this trial has taken years to prepare for. I had just been Cured and I didn't think I could live much longer with what I had done. I was angry and I wanted to know why this had happened. I know enough about law to know that the prosecutor and the public were never going to know the whole truth. Never." Mr. Courtlen held up one long finger. "But, the defense would. As much as there was to be known, the defense lawyers would know. I thought if I knew why, then I could accept it. That it would make sense."

"Some things are too terrible to make sense," said Nella sadly, "Some things just are and have no reason or sense behind them."

"So I am slowly discovering," Mr. Courtlen sighed.

They were quiet until they arrived at Nella's apartment building. She led him up the narrow staircase past all the silent doors that she'd never even knocked on. She sighed with relief as they walked into her apartment. He stood a little self consciously just inside the doorway.

"Look," she said smiling and turning on a few lamps, "We're both exhausted. Don't stand on ceremony, just get comfortable, because I'm not going to wait on you."

He laughed and she immediately felt better. "Oh all right, I guess I'll make you dinner, but only because I'm hungry too." She pulled a bottle of amaretto and a half bottle of rum down onto the counter. "Well, you look like a scotch man, but unfortunately, beggars at the end of the world can't be choosers."

"It's better than anything I have," he said, already opening cupboards in search of glasses, "I'll just close my eyes and pretend I'm taste testing in New Guinea."

Nella pulled a box of produce from the refrigerator. The Farm had a good harvest week so she had plenty. She did pine for premade meals from time to time, and today was definitely one of those days.

Nella felt the stiff collar of her shirt scrape across her neck and realized how much the combination of pain and stress had made her sweat. "Uh- Mr. Courtlen, excuse me for a minute, I'll be back in a minute."

"All right," he said amiably, "but if we're going to be drinking buddies you might want to start calling me Frank."

She flashed him a startled smile. "Well, then you'd better call me Nella. Enough with the Dr. Rider crap."

"Well, especially since I now know you played hooky in med school."

She laughed and went to change. When she

returned, clean and refreshed, Frank was flipping pages in a cookbook. "How many of these do you have?" he asked.

Nella blushed. "It's kind of a hobby. I like to collect them."

He looked up at her. "Books or cookbooks?"

"Cookbooks. It's rare to find a recipe I have all the ingredients for these days, but I like to remember when I used to." She blushed more deeply. "I look through the recipes and imagine cooking a huge feast someday for my friends with exotic dishes."

"Like tropical fruit."

She smiled. "Like tropical fruit yes, but also things like chocolate and cake with finely milled flour instead of the stuff with pebbles in it like we have now."

"It's so odd to think that just a few thousand survivors have run out of those things so quickly isn't it?"

"Oh," she replied, "I think there is more out there, probably just a few miles away, but it is in the Infected zone and even the best scavenger teams aren't allowed past the military's cleared points."

He looked steadily at her. "You know it's going to get better right?" he asked, "The world's going to get better. The Infected zones are going to get smaller and the people that are left will pick up again and go forward."

She felt tears prick at the corners of her eyes. She laughed at herself. "Well, if all I have to worry about is a few luxuries, then things can't be that bad right?"

He closed the book in his hand. "That's not what I meant."

"I know," she said, "But I think you were right this morning. No one is going to come along and put the world back together the way it was," she picked up a glass and poured it half full with alcohol. "I think people expect this trial to do just that. They are expecting to find someone to blame, something to make sense of the whole thing. But I think the world is just too broken for that to work. Sometimes there's no real explanation, no justification for things that happen."

"Some things just are?"

She nodded.

"I still think people need some sort of attempt at an explanation."

"But we've just seen the closest thing to an entire explanation that there is. I don't feel any better, do you?" She really was crying now, and though she tried to stop, it just kept coming. Before she could wipe her eyes again to see, Frank had crossed the bright kitchen and folded his long arms around her in a hug. She didn't try to push him away.

"No," he said, "I feel worse. But it's a relief to know anyway. Don't you think?"

She felt a fast hitch start in his chest and realized he was trying not to cry as well. She reached her arms out to hug him back. They stood there like that for several minutes, two almost-strangers aching for the world that was lost in the gnashing jaws of disease and worrying for the world that was found on the other side of it. At last, when she felt his breath warm and calm again, she stepped back, wiped her eyes, and said, "Sorry, I didn't mean to make you feel worse."

He cleared his throat. "You didn't. I feel calmer than I have all day." He reached for her hand and pulled her toward the kitchen. "Come on, I'm starving. And I think I found a recipe we can actually make."

A SETBACK

The rum was gone. The amaretto was making angry bubbles in Nella's stomach, but she didn't care. Her hand didn't hurt and her heart didn't hurt and she wasn't alone in the silent apartment building. In the dark, empty world.

Frank sat across from her, unfolded like a carpenter's rule on the couch. He was looking at the bookshelf beside him, his fingers tracing the cracked spines. His face was softened in the lamplight and though the scar that shattered his cheek still glowed like an almost-dead ember, Nella thought he didn't look quite as ugly as she'd thought before.

"My wife had some of these books," he said, without looking at her, "I think she would have liked you."

"Really? What makes you think that?"

He thought for a minute. "The way you treat people. You seem ready to believe that people are better than they appear at first. That there's a reason they are the way they are. And the way you are kind to people like Ann, people so damaged they appear to be monsters to others. And that you defend them from people that want to treat them that way. She would have liked that. *I* like that."

"What was she like?"

He pulled a battered book from the shelf and played with the fray in the spine. "She was kind and funny and intelligent. She challenged me. She was a lawyer, like me. But she helped write cases for human rights violations at international tribunals, unlike me."

"Is that why you decided to participate in this case?"

"I think it was part of it," he glanced up at her

with a small smile and then back at the book. "I thought it would make her proud, even if she couldn't forgive me."

Nella leaned forward, "I don't understand Frank, you were ill, how could you think she wouldn't forgive you for something you had no control over?"

He sighed, and retreated into the couch. "It's not that- I mean, it is that, but it *was* my fault." He shook his head. "I don't want to talk about it with you."

"I'm sorry, I didn't mean to pry-"

"No, you don't understand. It's not that I mind you knowing. I just, I don't want to be one of your patients. I don't want you to see me that way."

Nella was startled. "I don't. I don't see you that way." She paused, still confused. "How do you want me to see you?"

Frank grinned and relaxed, leaning forward again. "Don't pay any attention to me," he said shaking his head, "It's been a long time since I had any alcohol. I think I can safely say that I'm very drunk."

Nella smiled. "I'll get you some blankets, we should get some sleep."

"Are you sure?" he asked, "I can walk, you can come pick me up tomorrow."

She laughed. "Of course you aren't walking. I'll be right back. The bathroom is free if you want it."

She tried to make the couch as comfortable as she could, but she knew it was about a foot too short for his frame. Frank returned from the bathroom still smelling impossibly clean after a long day in an old suit.

"Thank you," he said, "I swear I wasn't angling for an invite."

"I know. To be honest, I'm glad you're staying.

The world seems far too lonely after today. Sometimes I feel like a stray pebble rattling around in an empty shoe." She hugged herself, then shook her head and smiled at him. "Never mind my rambling. I'm a little drunk too. Goodnight Frank."

He grinned. "Goodnight Nella." He touched her arm. "Things will look better in the morning you know," he said.

Nella smiled, but her eyes filled with tears again. She nodded and then walked into her bedroom.

It was much later than she expected when she finally woke up. She swore under her breath and sat up, wincing at the immediate headache. She got dressed in a daze and wandered out into the living room. Frank was calmly ironing his over shirt on her counter. His right arm was covered with small, jagged moons of raised, angry skin and one rough starburst in his shoulder. An exact opposite of the sky. Nella tried to hide her shock when he looked up and smiled at her. He ignored her stare and said, "Good morning," instead of offering any explanation and made no move to put his dress shirt on. "I hope you don't mind I used the washer. I guess I'm still not used to normal procedures, like private property." He chuckled.

"No, of course not. Anything you like," she said almost absently. "I'm sorry, I know you wanted to get to the prison early and I've completely overslept."

"I don't think we're going to get an interview with Dr. Pazzo today," Frank said and his face was grim.

"What? But what about finding Dr. Schneider's lab?"

Frank sighed. "I called the prison this morning to see when he would be ready for us. The guard told me he was refusing to speak to either of us for the day. Yesterday exhausted him and he needs time to recover he said." He looked up from his shirt. "Do you think this is more stalling on his part? Because eventually my contact from the military police is going to call me back. Should I tell Dr. Pazzo that and see if it forces his hand?"

"No," said Nella and paused for a moment, thinking. "That will just make him angry. The minute he thinks he has lost control of us he'll turn to someone else that he thinks he can control. And we can't afford to let anyone else know about the bacteria."

"So you still think he's using this information as a way to gain the upper hand?"

"I was surprised that he actually had valuable information to back up his hints, but his attitude coupled with his complete enmity for Dr. Schneider tells me he is still using the information to get *something*. I don't think he's necessarily trying to escape trial and sentencing any longer. I think he is trying to make it urgent that we find Dr. Schneider so she won't escape. I don't think he's going to give us the information we need to find the bacteria until we find her. He'll give us the location of the lab, eventually, but it is only because he doesn't believe the bacteria is still there. He thinks we'll find her, or some trace of her there."

"What do we do then? For all we know the bacteria is already destroyed. Dr. Schneider presumably escaped the university lab in order to destroy it. We just need to find her and ask."

"Maybe I can find out from Ann."

"Nella, I know you're good at what you do, but Ann is permanently damaged. No one can even get a coherent version of events from her. What's the likelihood that she'll even remember Dr. Schneider's old address let alone be able to tell us in any logical way?"

"We have to try. I think there is more in her mind than we've seen so far. She's our best bet for now."

Frank turned off the iron and picked up his dress shirt. "Okay, if you really think you can get something from her, I'll try to persuade Dr. Pazzo to meet with us or at least tell us what he knows. I can try my contact again too."

THE MANSION

They were rolling past the silent mansion again on their way back to the prison when it hit Nella like shattering glass. She grabbed Frank's arm and the car slid across the empty lanes. "Stop the car," she said, "I remember where I saw her. Stop the car."

"Jesus, Nella! Okay, don't kill us."

She barely waited for him to pull off the side of the road. When she opened her door, the tires were still spitting gravel at her ankles.

"Just a second! Where are you going?" Frank yelled out the open door. Nella walked back toward the mansion, her hands shaking inside her jacket pocket as they fumbled for her phone. Frank ran up behind her. "What are you doing?"

"Do you know if there is cell service here?"

Frank stammered. "What? I've never been here- I guess so, I mean we're close enough to the prison that the tower there should cover it. I don't know which ones have been fixed out here."

Nella swore and started dialing. "Sevita, pick up the phone. Sevita, it's me, pick up the phone. I need to know when you recorded that footage of Dr. Carton's house. The one with the woman. It's extremely important. If you can meet me at the prison in half an hour I can almost guarantee it will be more than worth your while. I really need you to do this for me." She hung up the phone and turned toward Frank. "Remember I told you I knew I'd seen Dr. Schneider somewhere before?"

The early spring sun made a weak, cold halo around him. "Of course," he said, "You mean you saw her *here*?"

"I saw a film of her here. Sevita Das, the reporter who is covering the trial-" she paused.

"Yes, I know who she is," said Frank.

"She's been my friend for a long time. Since the Cure began. She's always wanted to find Dr. Carton. It's been her obsession since the first day we administered the Cure. I don't know if she wanted to thank him or curse him for putting this burden of guilt on everyone. But she's always wanted to know. She's tried everything to get him to agree to meet her, but she can't find anyone who knows anything about him and so far he hasn't answered the door. So in her spare time, she comes out here and films the house. She says that he has to get groceries from somewhere, he has to have contact with the outside world once in a while."

"And she found something?"

"She thought she did. I mean, there's always the postman and the deliveries from the Farm, but they never go inside. There's an interior door that's always closed when the outer door is open. That's how deliveries are made." She became embarrassed as he stared at her expectantly. "Sevita makes us watch hours of footage to make sure she doesn't miss anything. But this one time, about a month ago, she taped someone coming out. No one has ever come out before. At least that we saw. I'm almost positive it was Dr. Schneider."

Frank shook his head. "What would she be doing there?"

"I don't know, but I'm going to find out before we run out of time." Nella began walking toward the massive iron gate. Frank grabbed her arm.

"Wait," he hissed, "we don't know anything yet. If you go pounding on the door you could alarm her. We can't afford to lose what little bit of a lead we have. Besides, you said no one answers the door. It can only make things worse. Let's at least go to the prison and see if we can get some more information first. You said your friend spent hours videotaping this place. Maybe she can at least point out all the exits in case Dr. Schneider is in there. I hardly need to tell you that we can't get the military police involved."

"But what if she's in there right now? What if she's got the bacteria right there. What if today is the day it gets lost or released or stolen?"

"This isn't the place to argue about this."

Nella reluctantly began walking back to the car with him. He took a deep breath.

"Maybe this is the day, Nella. Maybe this is the very last day. But what is banging on the front door going to do about it? You think they're just going to hand over the bacteria because we say please? There's a reason Dr. Carton doesn't want the world to know who he is. There's also a reason that Dr. Schneider was in there when no one else has been allowed. I'm not saying those reasons are questionable or honest or anything else. I'm just saying they exist. And until we find out what those reasons are, we're going to have to tread carefully."

"I can't just wait around."

"We're not, we've got a plan. Let's follow it. Someone will tell us something, and then we'll have to decide what we're going to do."

Nella slid back into the car. She flexed her wounded hand after closing the door. It was stiff, and she had a heck of a hangover. She shut her eyes as Frank turned the car on.

"Have you thought about that?" he asked as he pulled the car back onto the tar.

"Have I thought about what?" she asked, her eyes still closed.

"What we're going to do once we know where Dr. Schneider is?"

"I guess that depends on where she is. You do

realize that the chances of her remaining unfound in a Cured sector are pretty remote don't you?" she opened her eyes to squint at him.

"I've thought about it, yes." He was quiet for a moment. "I'm not a soldier."

"I know. I understand if you don't want to go with me. I can do it alone."

"I just don't know if I could shoot someone. Not knowing they could be Cured. Not even to defend myself."

Nella smiled gently at him in the mirror. "Well," she said, "let's not borrow trouble. Let's just get through today."

The prison was a flat, dull blotch. Nella felt her chest fill with lead as soon as she stepped out of the car. They walked toward the door silently. Nella reached for the handle, but Frank put his hand over hers to stop her. "No one can know, not even your friend," he said.

"I know. She can be trusted, but she won't ask if I don't offer. I won't say anything."

"I'll see you soon," he said and let her go.

She hesitated for a second, not wanting to walk away into the madness of Ann's cell. She realized she was truly frightened. Nella became angry with herself and pushed herself forward through the heavy door. She forgot to say anything to Frank and she felt immediately guilty. But she didn't turn around. She had to be professional. She felt ridiculous instead.

WHAT ANN SAW

Ann was calm and Johnson looked well-rested, even cheerful. "Good morning Doc," she said.

"Good morning. Everything seems to be going well here. How is Ann?"

"Like a new woman. She let me brush her hair, and she hasn't tried to bite her hands at all today, I even took the straitjacket off."

"That's wonderful," said Nella.

"Yeah, and Wells got this idea to line the exercise room with old mattresses from the empty cells. We're going to see if she'll be okay out there for a change of pace. That is, if it's okay with you of course."

Nella smiled, "I think as long as she stays like this, that will be fine. I'm going to post a standing order for sedative if she becomes unmanageable or can't sleep. That means you and Wells and her night guard are in control, not Mr. Grant, got it?"

"Do you think we can keep her this way if we do?"

"I do. I think she was only as bad as she was because she didn't have medication for so long. I'm going to order some tests though, with the infirmary. I don't think anyone's done a serious evaluation of what kind of damage she is really suffering. I'll be able to tell you in a few weeks whether she'll be able to adjust to less constant supervision or not."

Wells came in, half out of breath. "Hey Doc, how's your hand?"

Nella smiled, "Much better, thanks."

"It's almost ready," Wells said to Johnson, "but I'm going to need a hand with the last few so we'll have to wait."

"Oh," interrupted Nella, "that's okay, I think I

can handle Ann for a few minutes, if you both want to go."

Johnson looked at her doubtfully. "Are you sure?"

"I think so," said Nella, "I was going to ask for a few moments alone with her anyway, I need to ask some confidential questions for the trial."

"Okay, but remember, if you need someone, press the green button and we'll all come running."

The guards began walking reluctantly away. Nella didn't want to waste any time, so she didn't wait to see them out the door.

Ann was sitting on the floor of the cell making echoes with her voice and looking pleased. Nella sat down next to her. "Good morning Ann."

Ann looked over at her in surprise, but it quickly faded out, and Ann lost her focus.

"How would you like to go out into the sunshine today?"

Ann closed her eyes and smiled. "The sun is coming back today? There hasn't been any warm sun since before the teeth. Before the beast room."

"Yes Ann, warm, quiet sun outside. We can go see it, but first I need to ask you a few questions. Is that okay?"

Ann looked wary and her bandaged hands tapped nervously, but she still did not look toward Nella.

"We won't talk about bad things today Ann. I just want to know where Dr. Schneider lives."

Ann wrinkled her brow. She shook her head.

"Did she ever have you send things from the lab? Or deliver things?"

"She wanted monkeys. But Robert said she hated the monkeys. She hurt them. So I didn't bring them."

Nella could see Ann becoming agitated. "Okay

Ann, we don't have to talk about the monkeys. I just need to know where Dr. Schneider's house was."

"She had a boyfriend. Robert didn't like him. He said Dr. Schneider's boyfriend would steal."

"Who was her boyfriend Ann?"

Ann looked at Nella as if she were an idiot not to know, meeting her eyes directly. "Dr. Carton was her boyfriend. Dr. Carton from Kingsfield. Robert says you shouldn't talk to him. He's a thief. But Robert didn't know-"

Ann trailed off and started her echo game again.

"What didn't Robert know Ann?"

Ann ignored her. "What didn't Robert know about Dr. Carton?" Nella sighed in frustration. Ann looked at her and smiled.

"I like you," she said, "You don't hurt the monkeys."

Nella smiled despite her worry. "No Ann, I won't hurt any monkeys."

Ann looked up at the ceiling. "Robert didn't know that Dr. Carton took the vial. In his pocket. It shouldn't be in his pocket. Dr. Schneider said. But he took it. And Robert didn't know. I couldn't tell." she clapped her hand over her mouth and shook her head at Nella.

"What was in the vial Ann?"

"I can't tell. Dr. Schneider will hurt the monkeys if I do. Burn us all up if I tell. She says Robert is slow, too slow. If he knows I smelled the vial he'll get mad. He'll get mad and maybe he'll hurt the monkeys too. Burn us all up to save the world. So I was quiet. Even when Dr. Carton stole the vial. But the monkeys died anyway. Maybe because the camera saw him take it. And Robert always saw what the camera sees. All the monkeys are gone." Ann started to cry.

Nella hugged her, careful not to relax in case Ann became to agitated. "It's okay Ann, it's okay. Let's go see if the sun is out." She helped Ann to her feet. Ann sniffled but shuffled obediently alongside of Nella. They walked out of the cell and through the nearby door. Wells and Johnson were stuffing the last mattress against the concrete wall. The small yard was soaked in bright light. Even Nella squinted in the spring sun. Ann stopped moving and lifted her face, closing her eyes. Warmth pulsed around them and the soldiers looked relaxed as they lounged in the daylight.

Something was scratching at the back part of Nella's brain. For a man who had spent his time meticulously documenting the lab procedures, Dr. Pazzo had certainly seemed to miss a lot. How could he not have known about the altered bacteria until Dr. Schneider told him? Nella was uneasy as she watched Ann bask in the golden day of early spring. Something crept up her neck and crawled behind her eyes with pricking insect legs. If she could only think of what exactly was bothering her . . . But a guard walked through the doorway. "Dr. Rider," he said abruptly, "You have a visitor. She's waiting for you at the entrance."

"Thank you." Nella turned to Johnson. "Are you and Wells going to stay with Ann?"

"Sure Doc," said Johnson, "I've never seen her so calm. We'll be fine."

"I'll make sure I write that order for sedative use. You remember what I said. You're in charge, not Mr. Grant. And I'm going to order those tests for the next few days. She will have to be transported to a facility that has the correct equipment."

"And that will tell us if she'll- if she'll stay like this?" asked Johnson.

"I hope so," said Nella. She watched Ann turn

in the sun one more time and then went to meet Sevita.

Sevita was pacing at the entrance. "What's going on?" she asked as soon as Nella came in view. Nella sighed. She wanted to just tell Sevita, but Frank would be upset. "I can only tell you part of it," she said apologetically, "I need to get into Dr. Carton's house."

Sevita snorted. "So do I, but that doesn't mean it's going to happen. How many hundreds of hours have we watched that housed? We've only ever seen one person go in or come out."

"Yeah, and I need to know where that person went."

"What? Why? I thought this was about Dr. Carton."

"I can't tell you Sevita, not yet."

"Well, what did you need me for?"

"I don't know all the entrances and exits like you. I need to make sure that the woman we saw on the tape, if she is inside, that she doesn't get out until I've talked with her."

Sevita sighed. "Can I at least come with you?"

"It might be dangerous, Sevita. Not just for you, but for Christine too."

"What are you talking about?"

Frank touched Nella's shoulder. She jumped and then blushed when she saw him.

"Sorry," he said, "didn't mean to startle you."

"Frank, this is Sevita Das from HCN. She's going to help us get into Dr. Carton's house."

Sevita gave Nella a strange look and then smiled as if she knew something that Nella did not. She shook Frank's hand. "Pleased to meet you," she said.

"Likewise. I've watched all of your documentaries," Frank said.

"Look," said Sevita, "I don't know what you're up to, but I'm coming along. I realize it's probably confidential because of the trial and I promise not to air anything until you tell me it's okay, but there is no way-" she held up her hand to stop interruptions, "Nella, there is no way I'm not going into that house with you after all this time. You want my help? Sure, of course I'll help you Nella, you're my friend. But I'm not going to pass up an opportunity either."

Nella glanced at Frank. He seemed slightly troubled. Sevita saw it too. She folded her arms and looked at Nella expectantly.

"Okay," Nella said, with an interior wince, "but I'm serious that this could be dangerous. If I tell you it's time to leave, then you leave and don't wait for me or for Frank. And Sevita, if I tell you we can't go home for a while, you have to trust me. For Christine's sake."

Sevita still had her arms crossed but she was biting the corner of her bottom lip and Nella knew she was nervous. "Yeah, okay Nella, I won't ask questions but I can see you're worried. I'll be a good girl scout and follow directions."

Nella glanced at Frank. He looked concerned but saw her look at him. He shrugged and smiled. "If you think this is best Nella, then we'll all go together. Why don't we go somewhere that isn't so public to discuss the details though, okay?"

Sevita nodded. "Nella's apartment is closest. But I brought the bike. I don't have car privileges like you important folks." Nella laughed. Sevita squinted at Frank and looked particularly sly. It made Nella's skin prickle apprehensively.

"Frank, can I catch a ride with you? I'll show you where Nella lives."

Frank looked startled and shot a glance at Nella. "Sure," he said quickly, but Nella blushed, knowing Sevita was not fooled. But Sevita showed mercy and didn't say anything, just walked toward the door. Frank turned toward Nella. "Dr. Pazzo won't tell me anything," he said quietly, "and my contact hasn't been able to find any labs connected to Dr. Schneider, all he has is her home address."

"I don't think it's actually Dr. Schneider's lab. I think it's Dr. Carton's. Ann said Dr. Carton lived in Kingsfield and that Dr. Schneider was in a relationship with him. That's all I could get from her."

"Kingsfield? That's still in the Infected zone."

"That's just where Carton used to live, maybe the bacteria is somewhere else. Wherever Dr. Schneider is. Maybe even in the mansion." She paused and looked at him. "I know you don't want to tell Sevita anything, but we can trust her. She's my friend and we've been through a lot together."

Frank nodded. "For her own peace of mind, though, perhaps the less we tell her, the better." He followed Sevita out to his car. Nella glanced back down the hallway. If only she could place what was bothering her. Just a few minutes and she knew she could figure it out. The worry was palpable, tasting acrid, like burnt sugar in her mouth. She shook herself. She didn't have time for this. Nella sighed and pushed through the glass door into the bright, sunny afternoon.

She worried what Sevita was telling Frank in the other car. The two women hadn't met until the Cure, but Nella, like most other Immunes, was not innocent of blood shed. She had felt a serious twist of guilt shoot through her when Dr. Pazzo had laid bare the fact that Immunes had killed people who were merely ill. People who were not in control of themselves. Nella knew that others had killed too, that people had defended themselves or even sought out people like Frank as if they were prey. But her feelings were of overwhelming *personal* guilt. As if she ought to have known better. And she didn't want Frank to know what she had done in the past. She worried that he would be disappointed somehow, that he would turn cold and unfriendly if he knew. It made her feel deeply alone.

Sevita was already drawing a diagram of the mansion on Nella's table when she came in. Frank was rummaging in the kitchen for lunch. Sevita looked up with a wicked smile as Nella walked through the door. Nella should have been exasperated, but she was not. She was relieved and comforted to see them both there, in her home, relaxed.

"So when did you want to do this?" Sevita asked.

Frank looked up from the cutting board. "As soon as possible," he said. Nella laid her keys on the counter and walked over to the table.

"Shouldn't we wait until dark if we are going to be sneaking in?"

Sevita shook her head. "It won't matter, that place is lit up like a pre-plague Times Square at all hours. If there is any actual security, they'll be less likely to expect someone during the day anyway." She pointed to the diagram. "As far as I know, the only entrances are the front door and the side door here. But I've recorded hundreds of hours of video and never seen anyone go in. So I either have really bad luck, or there's another entrance somewhere."

"Where?" asked Frank.

"Maybe underground," suggested Nella, "If he has a lab in there it'd be easier to control the climate if it were built underground."

"But that means the entrance could be anywhere. How are we going to monitor it if we don't know where it is?"

"I don't like it either, Frank, but I think we're going to have to take some chances. If we can sneak in somehow, then maybe we can locate the lab when we are inside without being caught. What we are looking for will be there anyhow."

Sevita gave Nella a sharp, worried look, but she didn't say anything.

"We should probably go through the side door then," said Frank, "but how are we going to get through the gate without being spotted?"

"That I can help with," Sevita said. "A while ago, I tried to get close enough to the house to peek in the windows." She blushed. "I just wanted to see if I could Nella, don't look at me like that. Anyway, in the back here, this is all hedge. He must not have a very industrious gardener because the deer ate a patch back there and left a gap. It was wide enough to slide through when I was there last time, but I don't know if it's grown in since then. The hedge is about neck high- er, maybe chest high to Frank. So we can come right up to it without being seen. It's only crossing the yard to the door that we might get caught. But like you said Nella, we're going to have to take a few chances to do this."

Nella walked toward her bedroom. "Where are you going?" Sevita asked.

"For supplies," she replied grimly. She could hear Frank and Sevita still talking quietly over the diagram as she moved the trunk that was sitting in her closet. Even Sevita didn't know that Nella had kept them. While not exactly illegal, Nella had a feeling that still having a gun in a Cured area would make her a person of intense interest to the military police. She also had a feeling that she wasn't the only one who had them. She looked at the long wooden case and felt guilt smashing down on her. How many people had she killed with these? At the time she hadn't thought of them as people. At the time she believed they were monsters. After the first few, there hadn't even been any hesitation. As if they were all just paper targets that could run. She hadn't hunted them, like some of the Immunes had. She only killed when she thought she had to. But Nella wasn't in denial any longer about what she'd done. She knew better now. She knew, and she felt the weight of each bullet that she'd shot. But she'd kept the guns. How could she have kept them? Why was she thinking about the need to use them again? This time, though, it wouldn't be to escape. And it wouldn't be against sick people. A doubt about whether she could handle using the guns again flitted through her mind for an instant and then was gone. She was sure. She pulled the box out of the closet. She walked out to the kitchen and set it silently on the table. Sevita looked at her and then opened the box.

"I can't Nella," Frank said quietly. She looked at him and was startled to see how sad his face became.

Sevita just looked at her. "It's okay," said Nella, "I can. If I have to. If you can't, then don't take one with you. It will just make things worse. I hope it's unnecessary. But we both know what's at stake. Sevita, you'll just have to trust me when I say it's better to be prepared."

Sevita picked up one of the guns without comment. She zipped it carefully into her camera bag and then added a small box of ammunition. Nella quietly did the same, putting both in the oversized pockets of her spring jacket. Then she closed the box and placed it carefully back in the closet. Frank went back to making lunch without any further observations, but Nella could see the sweat spring out on his head like tiny glass beads.

They finalized their plans as they ate, but Sevita tried her best to lighten the mood and Frank played along, though Nella could see they were both as nervous as she felt. In the end, it was almost dusk by the time they were ready to go. Sevita had decided she needed another camera and to see Christine. Frank said he would drive her so that he could grab some less conspicuous clothing. All Nella could do was wait. At first she tried to use the time to untangle whatever it was she had forgotten at the prison. She soon concluded that whatever it was, wasn't coming back just yet. She ended up trying to memorize Sevita's crude diagram of the house and pacing the apartment floor. Sevita and Christine startled her when they came in.

"Chris, what are you doing here? And where is Frank?"

Sevita and Christine shared a look. "Told you," Sevita said.

"I came so you don't have to walk," said Christine, "Or were you going to park out front? Besides, there's no way I'm letting Sevita go somewhere that requires a gun, Nella, without knowing where she is and having medical supplies nearby. And your friend thought it was a good idea."

Nella blushed. "You're right, I'm sorry. I'm glad someone else is thinking of these details."

Christine hugged her. "Nella, I don't know what you've got yourself into, but maybe you should wait and call the police. You don't have to do this, whatever *this* is."

The panic she'd been struggling with for the past two days threatened to burst out of her and infect the room in sharp, yellow shards. Nella fought it. "I wish that were true Chris, I really do. But I can't. The police will only make things worse."

Sevita smiled as she set her camera bag on the floor. "And Frank is on the way. We just beat him here is all. He seems very nice by the way."

Nella was confused. "Yes he's very pleasant," she replied at last.

"And I won't even ask why he didn't ask for directions here in the car."

"Oh! We just wanted a drink and I-"

"I said I wouldn't ask," Sevita winked. Nella felt her throat dry up in embarrassment.

Christine grabbed Nella's hand and scowled at Sevita. "What happened to your hand?"

She was still busily disinfecting Nella's wound when Frank knocked on the door.

Nella tried to calm down as they drove toward Dr. Carton's house. Sevita put a sympathetic hand on her arm as they sat together in the back seat. "I've never seen you this scared," she whispered, "It's going to be okay you know."

Nella shut her eyes to keep herself from crying. "You don't understand, Sevita, I'm not worried about getting caught."

"Obviously. I'm not naïve Nel. I've known you long enough to know you don't just commit felonies for the heck of it."

"I don't think there's such a thing as felonies anymore."

Sevita grinned. "You know what I mean. Look, you don't have to tell me or even confirm my suspicions, but I figure this has something to do with the trial, otherwise why would Frank Courtlen be involved? And if it has to do with the trial, it has to do with the Plague. And the only thing I can think that would make you this upset would be if you knew something very, very bad about it. Like maybe it's not over."

Nella rubbed her eyes dry. Sevita hugged her

awkwardly. "It's going to be okay Nella. The world's going to go on spinning, the trees will go on growing, and the rain will keep on falling."

"What if we're not here to see it?" whispered Nella.

Sevita sighed. "I'm not entirely sure that would be such a bad thing. Look how badly we screwed up. And we still treat each other like crap. Even with only a few of us left. Some days it feels like we'll never learn anything."

The car rolled to a stop. The gun was so heavy that Nella's hip felt bruised. Her chest ached as if she'd been holding her breath for too long. She opened the door and slid out into the chilly evening air. They were on a side street a little way past the mansion. The streetlamps were still off and the sun was just setting, giving the sky an illusion of warmth that Nella could not feel. She rounded the front of the car with her hands in her pockets, her good hand touching the warm metal of the gun. She stood near Frank as Sevita kissed Christine goodbye and grabbed the camera bag.

"What if she isn't in there?" Frank asked.

"At least someone may know where she's gone. Remember, as far as we know, she escaped in order to destroy the bacteria. She may already have done so. We just have to find out for sure."

He looked at her, his face serious. "Why bring the gun then?"

Nella was grim, but she didn't apologize. "There is a reason no one has seen Dr. Carton, even though he's humanity's savior. There is also a reason no one has seen Dr. Schneider since her escape. Maybe Dr. Carton is just shy and retiring. And maybe Dr. Schneider just wants to have a little love nest with the guy. Or maybe she is desperate to avoid prosecution for her role in the Plague. Or maybe they are still delusional, thinking they can perfect their bacteria so that it doesn't have these terrible side effects. Maybe they are already infected. The gun is for the maybes."

Sevita walked up to them. Christine was still wiping tears away and smiling encouragingly. "Ready?" Sevita asked in a low voice.

The three of them slipped into the empty overgrown lot across the street.

MEAT

The mansion sat in an empty section of the City. It, like almost every other existing building, was left over from Before. Nella seemed to remember it as a large bank in its former life. It was one of very few large buildings still maintained and in use. The military government was beginning to demolish empty buildings that were in danger of collapse, but for now, most of them sat slumped and shuddering in the wind. They smelled green and rotting and the pavement in front of most of them had been eaten away by rain. Wild silver grass grew long and tangled in the cracks. The clamor of birds coming home to roost in the crooked roofs and rusting cars made Nella feel even lonelier than normal. At least they would be unnoticed in this part of town. Sevita led the way and the three of them reached the hedge in a few short minutes. It shocked the eye, a wall of bright, almost supernatural green against the wild golds and silvers of the dead trees and grass around them. Something thriving in the winter land where everything else just survived until spring.

They were silent now, not knowing if someone patrolled inside the hedge. The sun had set and left a haze of pale blue in the evening sky. Sevita found the gap by feel and ducked into it, holding Nella's hand. Nella reached out for Frank and pulled him through the thick, scratching branches. They stood on the lawn in an odd twilight as the natural sun faded and the floodlights of the house tried in vain to take over. "Look," hissed Sevita, "There aren't any lights inside."

"Maybe the curtains are closed," whispered Frank. They didn't waste time arguing. Leaving the shadow of the hedge they sprinted across the small backyard to the side door. No one stopped them.

Sevita fumbled with a small pouch from her camera bag. It was a tiny toolbox. Frank shook his head and held up his hand. Sevita froze as Frank tried to slowly turn the doorknob. The latch clicked and the door opened a crack. The air hit them as if they had just opened a tomb. It was rancid and smelled like raw excrement. Frank quickly closed the door and held the other hand over his mouth, trying not to retch.

"Someone is dead in there Nella," whispered Sevita.

Frank shook his head. "No," he whispered, his face pale and shining with sweat, "that's not death. Someone's been eating meat."

"What?"

"That's someone that's been eating a lot of meat. You just aren't used to it because no one can afford it anymore. Trust me, I'd know that smell anywhere. I never wanted to smell it again." He had to stop again trying not to retch.

"Well," said Sevita, "I guess if anyone ought to be able to afford the last few tins of canned meat it ought to be him."

Nella shook her head. "He'd have to be eating a lot of meat to make the whole house smell like that. I don't think even he could afford that many cans."

"You think he's got a cow in there?" said Sevita.

"I don't know. I don't want to think about it," whispered Nella. She put her hand over Frank's on the knob. "I'll do it," she said. She took a deep breath of clean air, then pushed the door open halfway. The smell hit them again and Nella could taste rotted egg on the back of her throat. She took a few shallow breaths to try to get used to the smell and stepped quietly inside. It was dark, not lit by artificial light at all, only the leftover glow of the sky coming through the windows. At least the curtains were open. Nella waited for her eyes to adjust as Frank and Sevita came in beside her. They were in a small, uncarpeted hallway. The smell had made Nella think the house would be filthy and unkempt but the hallway was clear of any debris or furniture and the floor shone even in the weak light. Nella walked to the left down the hall and through a doorway at the back of the house. She found herself in a small, immaculate kitchen. A light in the oven hood was turned on casting a dull gold light over the countertops. As Nella passed through toward the opposite door, she noticed a slab of meat defrosting in the sink, white and red, but odorless.

"Nella," Frank whispered. She looked back and he pointed to the oven. It was set to preheat. "Someone is coming back."

Nella felt panic clutch at her arm muscles making her ache, but she just nodded firmly and passed out of the door into a darkened formal dining room. She needed to let her eyes adjust again but she didn't want to wait, so she kept creeping forward, hoping she wouldn't bang into on of the massive wooden chairs. Where was the damned lab entrance? Even the outer light was failing fast and Nella knew they were going to have to risk turning on artificial lights soon or be caught in complete darkness, something she was desperate to avoid. Between avoiding heavy furniture and worrying about the light, Nella didn't notice the towering grandfather clock until she was standing underneath it. Then the tick, tick, tick was like a hammer pounding nails into her heart. She let out a shaky breath and looked up to see the pale, stern face of the clock and relaxed, her flesh feeling like abruptly dumped water. The far end of the dining room opened into another hallway. Nella opened a side door to find a tiny bathroom and she quickly shut it again, before the rancid sulfur smell could overwhelm her.

"Sevita," she whispered realizing she could no longer see if Frank or Sevita were behind her.

"I'm here," the answer floated back toward her.

"Do you have a light on your camera?"

"Sure, but it's pretty bright."

Nella hesitated. Frank's voice was a low thrum behind her. "It's either that or we start flipping switches."

Sevita gingerly slid past Nella and turned the camera light on. It was almost blinding after the natural dark. "I don't think anyone else can see down here without lights either, so there is probably no one on this floor right now," she said.

"What about the oven?" Nella asked.

Sevita shrugged in the harsh light. "I didn't say the place was empty, just that there wasn't anyone on this floor at the moment. If we start seeing lights turn on I'll turn off the camera light."

They walked slowly toward the front of the house. Nella began to relax in the bright light of Sevita's camera. She began to notice that the house was extremely quiet. Except for the ticking of the clock she had almost run into, there was no other sound. No dripping faucets, no humming electricity, no natural creaks. And as they passed through the second of two large living rooms, Nella noticed there was nothing out of place either. No books lying open or chairs pushed invitingly out from desks. It wasn't just tidy, the house felt completely unlived in. The oven and meat in the kitchen had been the only sign that someone existed between the walls. At last they came to the large entry hall. It was cold and bare. Nella wasn't sure if it was just because of the rapidity with which they had moved or their limited scope of vision but she didn't recall seeing a single picture or mirror on any of the walls. She was tempted to run back to the small bathroom and check there, but recognized it as foolish impulse. Frank caught her hand and squeezed. She looked at him and realised she could partially see his face though Sevita was facing another direction. He pointed up the large staircase and Nella saw a light at the far end of a long hallway. Sevita turned around. "I think I found it," she whispered. They turned toward where she shone the light. A sleek silver elevator door waited just across from the completely unguarded front door. Nella was no longer relaxed.

"Where is everyone? Where are the guards? The owner? The cook?" Frank's hand was shaking slightly around hers. She squeezed it to calm him down.

"Should we go up or down?" whispered Sevita.

"I think the lab will be downstairs," said Nella, "and whoever is upstairs doesn't know we're here yet, so they won't run or alert anyone.

"But shouldn't we check first?" asked Frank, "We may be able to find Dr. Schneider and she'd be away-" he looked hesitantly at Sevita, "she'd be away from any sort of weapon."

Nella considered for a moment. But while they stood there, the silver door slid open with a smooth woosh of air. And the decision was made for them.

The man in the elevator was startled and immediately reached for the button, but Sevita sprang forward and held the door from sliding shut. "You're Dr. Carton aren't you?" she asked.

The man was in a wheelchair and his skin hung in loose folds and wrinkles as if it were slowly melting from him. This man couldn't be Dr. Carton. He had to be at least thirty years older than the pictures Nella had seen of him on the news.

"What do you want?" the man asked.

Frank stepped into the elevator next to him.

"We aren't going to hurt you. We just need to find Dr. Carton and Dr. Schneider as soon as possible."

The man sighed. "I knew this day was coming. I'm Dr. Carton. And I haven't seen Dr. Schneider in weeks."

The man oozed the raw sewage smell from every pore. Nella forced herself onto the elevator with him. Sevita stepped in too and trained the camera on Dr. Carton.

"We know there is a lab here Dr. Carton. And we know about the incurable strain of the Recharge bacteria." Nella said it calmly but it fell in the elevator like a steel bat across the old man's face.

He raised a shaky hand to his face. "Jesus," was all he said. Sevita stared at her as if she too, had been struck.

"Why don't we go down to the lab, Dr. Carton? Maybe you can tell us where Dr. Schneider has gone."

"Jesus, don't kill me. I don't know who told you about the Recharge bacteria but it isn't what you think. I beg you not to try to find it, it won't solve your problems. All it will do is make things worse."

"We know," said Nella grimly. Frank pressed the basement button on the elevator.

Nella wheeled Dr. Carton into a brightly lit room with lined with steel tables and unmarked silver doors that looked like refrigerators. Frank and Sevita hurried past her, moving swiftly and quietly down the lab.

"Why are you doing this?" Dr. Carton asked, "Don't you know it will destroy the world if you release it."

Nella was startled and looked down into the choppy sea of frightened flesh that was Dr. Carton's face. "We don't want to release it Dr. Carton. We want to destroy it. Dr. Schneider was the last person to know where it is. We just want to find her."

"What? Then why did you break in? How do you even know about it?"

"We were reviewing the evidence for the Plague Trial." Nella held out her hand, "I'm Dr. Rider. I'm the court appointed psychiatrist for the trial." Dr. Carton took her hand with some reluctance. She noticed his hand was still shaking and wondered if it was actually palsy and not terror.

"So Dr. Pazzo told you then."

"In a manner of speaking, yes."

"He didn't know the whole story," Dr. Carton hesitated and squinted at Nella. He slowly added, "Or if he does, he didn't tell it to *you*."

Frank and Sevita joined them. "She isn't here," Sevita said, "but there is an exit. Its overgrown with weeds, I don't think anyone has used it in weeks."

Nella looked at Dr. Carton. "Would you care to tell us what you think is the whole story?" she asked.

Dr. Carton sighed and wheeled his chair around so that he was facing all three of them.

DR. CARTON

"I don't know what Robert Pazzo has told you or how much you believe to be true. He probably told you that Dr. Schneider and I stole his version of the Recharge bacterium. I won't lie. Dr. Schneider and I did obtain a sample without permission. He also obviously told you that he and Dr. Schneider argued at length about how durable the strain ought to be. The idea was to make it resistant to most or all treatments administered to treat harmful diseases or used as prophylactics. Robert was afraid of making it too strong. He was afraid to lose control. But then, Robert Pazzo was always spineless and short sighted." Dr. Carton shifted uncomfortably in his chair, his drooping jaw growing dark red with anger and resentment. "He couldn't see how much more efficient it would be to test the most durable strain immediately."

"That's probably why some of us survived," interrupted Sevita.

Dr. Carton nodded and his smile was jovial as if she had told a good joke. "Ah, you would think that. But my company offered to not only fund his research for the duration of the trials, but also to loan him state of the art laboratory space for as long as he needed, provided he test our version first. In our facility there wouldn't have been a leak. Not only would the sniffers have caught any infection present in the lab and isolated it, but untrained personnel like Miss Connelly would never have been allowed into dangerous areas in the first place. If Dr. Pazzo had listened eight years ago, all this wretched misery might have been avoided. But he is stubborn."

Nella crossed her arms over her chest. "Ann told me it was Dr. Schneider who persuaded her to infect herself after depriving both Ann and Dr. Pazzo of sleep for days."

Dr. Carton sighed. "Gerta can be overly impatient and has foregone protocol in the past in order to prove a point. Again, my lab wouldn't have allowed her to sidestep the process or overwork her staff.

"Regardless of what might have been, it's over now. Yes. We stole a sample of the weaker strain in order to develop a bacterial delivery system that was usable even in patients that required high doses of antibiotics. Their small experiment was only a stepping stone in what was to be a revolution in medicine."

Frank smacked his open hand on a steel table hard enough to leave a ringing echo. "Enough with the damn posturing. Did you make an incurable bacteria or not?"

Dr. Carton shook as if the chill in Frank's voice cut to his bone. "Yes," said the old man quietly.

"Has it been destroyed?"

"No. The lab was set to begin trials on it when the outbreaks began. By the time Gerta escaped from her lab to warn us, the social fabric was already failing. Everything changed so fast. You have to remember that people were infected within days, hours maybe, by Ann, and those people infected others. For weeks the Plague was incubating without anybody knowing. When it hit-"

"We remember. There was a massive tide of mob violence and then- and then the world was different." Nella's stomach clenched. She had woken up to it as the Plague overtook her apartment building. At first, she had opened her door to see her two neighbors fighting. They clawed and bit and bashed without slowing. They didn't seem to register that they were injured. They weren't even swearing at each other, just roaring endlessly from the pit of the throat. Other neighbors came to their doors within seconds. One young man ran at the two brawlers with a yell. Nella thought he was going to try to stop them, to break up the fight. It shocked her to see him simply join in, making fresh wounds on each combatant with his teeth. More people ran from their doors and the apartments around Nella quickly emptied. They were a swirling, jerking mass of cracking bone and splashing blood, snapping teeth and crushing pistons made of limbs. Nella had simply stood, completely uncomprehending for a few long minutes. Then she realized she was the only one left to stop the brawl.

She yelled at the top of her voice trying to cut through the strange, creaking growl that they made at each other. "Hey! Cut it out! What the FUCK?"

The mob stopped and was ominously still for a second. Each member turned toward Nella, untangling the twisted knot into a crowd of people again. Their breathing was a ragged, uneven ocean of sound and the copper smell of blood. She had time to pick out details. Like 4A's girlfriend was missing an eye and didn't seem to notice at all. And 7B's arm hung the wrong way as he reached toward her. And everywhere faces were slick and shiny with dark blood but teeth shone through the crowd like a recurring nightmare of peppermint, maroon and white. They began to run toward Nella. She slammed the door and locked it even as it shivered in its frame. Within seconds the people had turned their attention back toward each other and continued to tear each other apart.

Nella had tried the police several times that day and in the week following but no one ever answered. The brawl had eventually either burnt itself out or moved to another floor leaving a wake of blood and dead flesh behind. Nella spent the week curled in a ball on the floor in front of the television. She didn't start crying until the news anchor turned feral on camera, his voice going from slurry but rational to a low, meaningless groan within seconds. She turned off the television before he could attack the cameraman. The power had gone out later that day. She still tried to call someone, anyone she knew over and over. She got only voice mail until her phone had died for good.

Within a few days, the building began to reek. The hallway buzzed with flies caught in the tacky, rotting mash on the rug. Nella knew that she would have to leave, have to see for herself what was left of the world.

"What? You've never heard of a phone before?" Sevita's voice broke through the haze of Nella's memory and she shook herself back to the present.

"By that time the lines were either jammed with panicked people or maybe Dr. Schneider's phone was dead. I know mine was," said Dr. Carton, his voice gone whiny and waspish.

Frank leaned into Nella. "Are you all right?" he whispered, and his breath was warm and alive in the well of her ear. Nella nodded.

"Look," Sevita was saying, "I don't even know why we're arguing about this. At some point Dr. Schneider found you right? And she told you how dangerous this bacteria was and you went back to the lab. That's what happened right?" Nella could hear a bitter edge of panic in Sevita's voice. Dr. Carton rubbed his temple as if agitated. Nella noticed his palsy was more pronounced. She leaned forward to look at him more closely.

"No," said Dr. Carton, "I mean- yes, she found me. But, I wasn't- I wasn't quite myself when she found me."

"What do you mean you 'weren't yourself?'"

"He means he was infected," said Nella, realizing what the shakes in his muscles and confinement to a wheelchair resulted from.

"You were infected? But how is that possible? You cured the Plague." Frank ran a hand over his smooth head in confusion and frustration.

Dr. Carton began to slowly wring his hands and his voice shifted from petulant to teary. "Actually, neither of those statements is correct."

Nella felt her throat tighten and lift and her chin ached with pressure. "Oh God," she managed and ran to the nearest sink. Dr. Carton frantically wheeled after her trailing a bewildered Frank and Sevita.

"Dr. Rider, please understand, I didn't know what caused the Plague until much later, not until Gerta told me. I didn't know how it worked on the Infected, I was only trying to sur-"

Nella retched so violently that the world went a hazy noiseless ash color and she missed the end of the word. She tilted her head sideways so that she could get a breath of air. Sevita was trying to keep Dr. Carton in her shot, still unsure what was happening but knowing it was important to catch on film. Nella reached up and turned the tap handle. She wiped her face with the cool water, but she could still feel her disgust as burning acid at the base of her throat. She turned back to Dr. Carton.

"You were a scientist. A doctor. How could you do-"

"I never killed anyone," Dr. Carton interrupted, speaking quickly, "Not then. I thought if I smelled like them, if I acted and looked like them, if even my sweat blended in, then I wouldn't be attacked. I only ever-" he paused and began again in a low voice as if he did not want the world to overhear, "I only ever ate the leftovers."

Nella retched again, but this time it caught in her gut, a spiky ball of horror stretching painfully against her innards.

"You mean you ate the dead?" Frank asked. He was pale as chalk. Nella could hear a sudden rattling of plastic as the camera shook in Sevita's hands. Frank tried to calm himself. "You mean you were infected," he said, "like everyone else. It's okay, it wasn't you, it was the disease-"

"No, Mr. Courtlen. I wasn't ill. At least not ill with the Plague. I felt no compulsion to eat humans. It was- it *is* abhorrent to me both in theory and fact. I couldn't keep it down the first few times. I didn't slur or stumble or have any tics like the Infected. I had to adopt those. I hid in the lab for about a week, watching what they did. I felt it was necessary for me to blend in as much as possible if I was to survive."

"But you must have seen them attack each other too," said Sevita.

"Only when they were hungry. I followed a group of them after I left the lab. As long as I was careful to stay in places with- with rich pickings and didn't move quickly, they ignored both me and each other. They only went into a frenzy when the pica returned. It worked, here I am, eight years later."

Frank held his own face in his hands and Nella thought he might be crying. Nella cleared her throat, her breath scraping against the raw spots where her stomach acid had lain. They were all silent for a moment, the dripping sink echoing with a metallic ping and the florescent bulbs buzzing like mad flies trying to escape.

Nella folded herself onto the cold floor. She brushed her sweaty hair off of her forehead and felt as if she were wearing away, eroding under the weight of the world. "So Dr. Schneider eventually found you in this- condition?" she asked wearily.

"Yes, Dr. Rider. It took almost a year. You can imagine I wasn't completely in my right mind by then. I was ill with something and despite my best efforts, I'd been attacked and bitten several times. I was close to starving when Gerta found me. We made it to what was left of military headquarters. Gerta didn't tell anyone what we'd done and as soon as I was well enough, we left and set up a lab in secret to work on the Cure. Gerta didn't want to waste time with testing procedures." Dr. Carton paused, rubbing his temple again. "She said she had to fix it, that it was all her fault and she had to fix it. It was my job to pull in Infected to test on. The first tests- they didn't go very well." Dr. Carton swiped at his eyes and sniffed, and his voice was wheedling and teary again. "Gerta told me to get rid of the bodies. She said we had to emerge from this thing with a clean image. And we couldn't do that with dead patients. So, I did what I knew how to do. And Gerta promised not to tell anyone, as long as I did what I was told, she wouldn't tell anyone what I was."

"You mean you continued to cannibalize the dead?" Sevita asked, her voice dry and papery.

"Yes. Once I was used to it, it was easy."

"If you did all of these terrible things to keep your secret, why are you telling us now?"

Dr. Carton closed his eyes and sighed. "Because you already know the worst secret and you know it's still out there, waiting to kill everything. Because I've become convinced that one more old villain like me will just fade into the woodwork in this beat up corpse of a world. Because I'm tired of pretending to be the savior of mankind. At best Dr. Schneider postponed our deaths with the Cure. I was nothing more than a lab assistant. But Gerta threatened to tell the world what I had become if I didn't claim the Cure for my own. She didn't want to be found. She still doesn't."

"But she knows where the incurable strain is?" asked Frank.

"She said she was going after it. She was going to return to the lab if she could and destroy it before anyone else could. That's what she said when she left a few weeks ago. She said it'd been weighing on her. I told her not to worry about it. It's still far into the Infected zones. It's not like the Infected will find it. And I highly doubt there are scavengers out that far. But she was insistent. She packed up a carload of all the survival gear I could still wrangle from the military and a stock of Cure darts and took off."

"We need to know where the laboratory is." Frank's voice was low and threatening and Nella felt her skin curdle at the violence in it.

"Didn't you hear me? I said it was overrun. There's no way you'll even get close. It was a suicide mission for her and it will be for anyone that follows her."

"You survived."

"I had to act like the Infected. And I was fleeing toward what was left of civilization."

"Someone is eventually going to reach that lab Dr. Carton. It may not be soon, but someday, somebody will. If we go now maybe we can stop the next plague before it begins."

Dr. Carton sighed and shook his head. "Very well. It's your neck you're risking, not mine. Come upstairs with me and I'll draw you a map and get you some Cure darts from the safe."

The thought of getting into the elevator with Dr. Carton again made Nella nauseated all over again. She pressed herself into the corner as far from his stench as she could and tried to think of anything except what she'd heard in the past hour.

They made a quick exit after that, especially when it became clear that he was about to prepare his dinner. None of them wanted to think about the slab of defrosting meat in the stainless steel kitchen sink. They slunk out of the side door again and through the hedge, not wanting any passers by to question them. Christine was waiting for them in the car, her face like an angel of sanity. In six years Nella had never seen Sevita cry, but she did when she got in the car and Chris kissed her.

"Let's get out of here Chris," she said, "I never want to see this house again."

Christine took the long way to Nella's apartment so they wouldn't have to pass by the mansion again. Christine didn't ask any questions and they were silent until they parked. They sat in the car for a long moment without moving.

"Chris, why don't you take the car tonight. You don't need to ride your bikes in the dark. I'll walk over Monday morning," Nella said at last.

"Are you sure?" Christine asked, "That's an early morning for you."

"I'll pick you up before court Nella, we can pick up your car after the session on Monday," Frank offered.

Nella smiled. "There, it's all set then." She slid out of the car. Frank followed her.

Sevita rolled down the window. "Nella," she called. Nella leaned down to talk to her. "What are you going to do?"

"I'm going to forget it tonight, maybe forget it until Monday. Then I'm going to go to court for the first day of trial, just like you. Just like Frank. Then I'll think about what I need to do. I'm the only one who only has to make occasional appearances in court."

"You can't go alone," said Sevita.

"Let's not talk about it today. Just say goodnight Sevita."

"Goodnight. See you on Monday."

Nella waved as the car pulled away. Frank was a solid shadow in the dark beside her. "Do you want me to say 'goodnight' too?" he asked.

She thought he might be smiling but she couldn't see. She hoped that he wasn't. "No," she said, and she wasn't smiling. She took his hand and led him through the dark parking lot and up the silent, lifeless stairs.

She felt a sigh of relief travel from her throat to the base of her foot as she stepped through her doorway. She immediately felt guilty. "I'm sorry Frank, you probably want to be home in your own space relaxing."

Frank grinned for the first time in what seemed like days. "Are you serious? Neither of us would be relaxing if I was at home. I'd be pacing the floor worrying about what you were planning. And you'd be- well, you'd be planning."

Nella laughed. "I'm too tired to plan."

Frank's grin faded. "You aren't going alone."

"Let's not worry about it just yet. I'm sick of being scared."

He gently grabbed her chin and turned her face toward him. "We don't have to talk about it right now Nella, but you aren't going alone. I may seem like an amiable pushover sometimes, but I mean it."

Nella dropped her eyes for a second and then looked steadily at him. "We don't need to argue about it now."

"Or ever," he said. She shook her head and smiled. She walked away from him toward the bathroom.

"Where are you going?" he asked.

"To brush my teeth. I can still taste that house in my throat."

"I'm going to get a change of clothes from the car then."

Nella turned around. "Do you want me to come with you?" she asked.

Frank looked confused. "No, I know right where my bag is. Are you okay?"

Nella smiled but it wavered like a false

reflection. "Yeah, just nervous I guess."

"I'll be right back, I promise."

"I know," she said and went to clean off the stench of Dr. Carton.

She was in the closet carefully packing away the guns when he came back. She jumped when he said in a low voice from behind her, "I'm glad we didn't have to use those."

"Me too," she said and shoved the trunk back against the closet wall. It hit with a bang she hadn't intended and she tensed again.

"Nella, you have to calm down. What is it you are scared of? That old man?" She could see a ripple of revulsion pass up Frank's frame. "He's sick, there's no doubt about that, but surely this isn't so far afield from things you've had patients dealing with during the Cure, is it?"

Nella waved a hand dismissively as she backed out of the closet and shut the door. "No," she said, "it's not Dr. Carton. I've just had this overwhelming feeling of dread since we left the prison today. I don't know why, but I keep thinking I'm overlooking something important. As if everything depends on me figuring it out and as if something or someone is going to stop me before I can."

Nella shrugged. "I don't know," she sighed, "it's probably nothing. I think the pressure is just making me jumpy."

Frank's face was tight and anxious. Nella laughed and patted his arm. "Don't worry. I'm not quite cracked yet. A little paranoia is healthy." He didn't relax. She looked at him for a moment. "I'm glad you're here," she said.

"Me too," he said with an immediate smile. Nella felt her interior gravity shift. It startled her and she walked into the kitchen before he could say or do anything else.

"Come on," she called back to him, "You must be starving. I am."

"Really? After hearing all that, you're still hungry?"

Nella paused for a moment. "Surprisingly, yes."

"All right. Let me change first. Besides I made lunch, it's your turn to cook," he said and disappeared into the bathroom.

Nella watched the steam curl out of the bottom of the bathroom door as she cooked. She had always been comfortable in her apartment. She didn't go looking for things to add to it, they just sort of found her. Gifts from friends or things she'd saved from empty, abandoned places. Like her cookbooks. Her life was like a net gathering bits of flotsam after the storm. She didn't go looking for people to add to her life either. She didn't push people away, at least, she didn't think she did. But sometimes people seemed to swirl around her and stick when she was least prepared for it. Less and less lately. She watched the warm, clean mist creeping out of the bathroom and wondered if Frank was one of those people. She realized she was lonely. Nella sighed. What was she thinking? She was a psychiatrist hired to be an impartial observer for the most important trial in history. Even having the defense counsel over for dinner was seriously questionable. And now they were both privy to something that could change not only the outcome of the trial but the fate of civilization as well. She tried to be rational. *I'm a logical person, not some weak-willed woman who runs after other people for affection or protection.* Nella immediately felt ashamed of the thought. Why was she feeling so judgmental? Was it what others would think? Or what she thought of herself? She rapped her wooden spoon on the side of the pot in an angry burst. Why did she even like him? She knew very little about him. He was pleasant, but she had met many pleasant men over the years and never thought twice about it. Perhaps it was simply the pressure of the trial. But she rejected that as well. She had survived far worse without turning to intimacy for comfort. He was not pretty. Even now, she could admit that. Too thin and and angular, dark scars twisting his face and arms, and still visibly fragile and pallid from long illness. No one would think that he was handsome. But it had been a while since Nella had found him ugly, despite all that. She was having a terrible time trying to convince herself that he wasn't attractive. Because, of course, he was. She didn't know if it was something physical, like the grace with which he moved his ridiculously long limbs when she expected him to constantly be tripping over himself, or if it was something deeper and less defined. Nella had noticed Frank's patience with people even when he was unfairly treated and she didn't ignore his kindness to everyone around him and most especially toward herself. Nella was modest, but she wasn't blind. Frank had been sending clear signals. She knew he was just waiting to find out if she felt the same way about him. She felt a pang of sympathy when she realized he had reasons to be less confident than she. She wondered if he'd been rejected many times since the Cure or if he'd ever been able to move past the death of his wife. Nella felt ridiculous and self conscious. She scolded herself into concentrating on what she was doing. The constant, quiet splash of the shower ended and Nella could feel panic set in. *That's enough,* she thought, *stop being silly Nella. I can't do anything until after the trial. Otherwise we'll both lose our jobs.* She thought she had convinced herself into rationality by the time Frank walked quietly out of the bathroom.

"That smells great," he said, coming into the kitchen. He rummaged around the cabinets looking for silverware. He was humming something without knowing it. Nella watched him as he set the table. *How the hell did I ever think he was ugly?* She wondered. He turned around and saw her watching him. He stopped humming and smiled self consciously. "What?" he asked.

Nella blushed and returned his smile. "Nothing. What were you humming?"

Frank thought for a second. "I have no idea. Sorry, does it bother you?"

"No, not at all. I was just curious." She turned back to the stove and filled their plates so she could blush in private. *We should have dinner and then I should send him home. Not should. Will send him home.*

But her resolve weakened as the evening wore itself away. He seemed comfortable with her, unwound even, as if he had been screwed together too tightly for far too long. When she met him, she had thought he was too introverted to be a lawyer. He had been friendly but it had seemed rehearsed, like something he often got wrong. But now she wondered if the world had made him that way after the Cure. He had been so subdued with both Dr. Pazzo and Mr. Grant. It was easy to believe Frank was so ashamed of what the infection had done to him that he became deferential to anyone who treated him poorly, that he really thought he deserved it. She was hesitant to shatter what comfort he had found with her by sending him away.

He looked at her intensely for a moment, but Nella's mind was so far away she barely noticed.

"Stop psychoanalyzing me," he said, "I told you I didn't want you to think about me that way."

"I wasn't-"

Frank laughed. "You're a terrible liar. But I guess that's good in a doctor."

"Well how do you want me to think about you then?"

Frank got up and picked up his plate. He leaned over her and paused as he picked hers up too. "Now you're changing the subject," he said gently and then walked to the sink. Nella's ribs felt too tight. She tried to ignore it.

"What makes you think I was psychoanalyzing you?"

Frank turned the water on and spoke over the splashing, but didn't turn his face toward her. "Because you were staring at me for a while. And I think you've gotten over your revulsion of my scars by now, so it wasn't that-"

"I was never revolted by you-" Nella tried to interrupt.

"You were," Frank laughed and it was dry and brittle like an old leaf hanging between them. "You tried very hard not to show it, I know. Maybe you even tried very hard not to feel it, but I could see you flinch every time I came near you-"

Nella sprang from her seat and across the kitchen. "I'm not revolted by you," she said when she reached him. He turned off the faucet and calmly began wiping the clean dishes. Frank looked at her.

"I know. Not any more, anyway. So I know you weren't watching me because you were frightened or disgusted." He handed her the dry plate and she stared dumbly at it because his fingers had touched hers as he passed it to her and the sizzling it left in her mind made her too dizzy to put the plate in the cabinet.

"But you weren't staring into space, Nella, you were staring at *me*." Frank smiled, "All I can think is that you were either analyzing me or you were trying to figure out a way to toss me out for the night without feeling guilty."

Nella blushed. "I wasn't psychoanalyzing you."

He handed her the other plate. "If you want me to go," he said quietly, "All you have to do is say so. Nothing will be different tomorrow. We'll still be friends."

"I don't want you to go," she said and then rushed to put the plates away so that she wouldn't see his face.

"Good," he said, "because I'd like to stay. Your couch is comfortable."

She laughed despite her anxiety and turned back toward him. "How did you know what I was thinking about?"

"Because I've thought about it too. I'm an adult, Nella, I know how the world works. I'm not supposed to like you. And you're supposed to be impartial and everyone is supposed to play by the rules. If anyone found out that we weren't strangers to each other, the world would riot. And that's just the trial."

"What do you mean, 'that's just the trial?' Is there something else?"

"You're an Immune. You're supposed to be registering with DHRS and marrying another Immune so you can have lots of little Immune children. And I'm an Infected-" he held up his hand to stop her protest, "whether I've been Cured or not, I'll always be an Infected. I don't have the genetic resistance to pass on to the next generation. I'm supposed to die out, wither out of the gene pool."

"I don't care about that-"

"You might not. Your friends might not even care. But the rest of the world will. People like Mr. Grant will. Maybe we'd lose our jobs or be shunned or cheated at the market. Maybe we would have to live in more dangerous places than this." Frank sighed. "I know you aren't naïve Nella. I realize you've thought about this already. That's what you were thinking about before I interrupted you. I just don't know what you decided."

"What did you decide?"

Frank leaned against the counter and crossed his arms as if he were preparing for a blow from her. "That I gave up caring what the world thought of me a long time ago. That I already took the bitter leavings the world tossed at me every day, why shouldn't I accept the beautiful things it put in my path too?" Frank reached out to touch her face, but stopped short and pulled back. He stopped looking at her and looked toward the door, expecting to be walking through it. "But I still care about what the world thinks about you and what it would do to you if I were involved with you. This life is hard enough as it is. We both know that. I don't want to make it any harder."

The sink plinked a sorry tune between them as Nella thought about what she wanted to tell him. "Frank," she said at last, "the world isn't just nasty people like Mr. Grant and his cronies. It's also people like Sevita and Wells and Johnson. The world has always had bigots in it. I think it always will. If the Plague proved anything, it proved that. Even when we're on the point of extinction we still waste energy on hating each other. Living according to the standards of the Mr. Grants of the world isn't going to make them go away. And it will only make you- *us* miserable." Nella reached up and touched the scar on Frank's cheek with the fingertips of her bandaged hand. "How could I ever be revolted by you? If I ever did, I'm sorry for it now. You've shown nothing but kindness and patience, even to people who treated you badly. Even to people that I couldn't bring myself to be patient with or kind to. How could you make my life anything but better? If the judge wants me to recuse myself I will. If the Mr. Grants of the world want me to stop practicing, I'll do that too. But I don't want you to go."

Nella was a little amazed to realize how much she really meant it. She smiled and looked up at Frank. But his face was grim and still. He hadn't moved, even when she'd touched him. Nella's smiled withered away. "What's wrong?" she asked before her throat could snap shut with panic.

"I'm not what you believe. I'm not patient and I can be cruel, Nella. I can't do this." He gently moved her aside and walked toward the door.

"Frank wait." The lamp sparkled on his face like frost. The rest of him in shadow, slipping away, his hand already turning the door knob.

"Wait," she said again, but she was calm, not pleading. He waited, turning toward her, but didn't move from the door. The light behind him made his face a dark room she couldn't see into.

"It's not for you to decide," she said, "You may think you're protecting me from some mistake by leaving, but it's my mistake to make," she smiled, but her eyes felt pinched and there was a rough stone in the base of her throat. "And it's already been made."

Frank's shoulders sagged. He shook his head. "You don't know me. You don't know what I've done."

She wanted to tell him she didn't care, that whatever it was, it couldn't be that bad. But in the world that remained after humans had slaughtered each other with their bare hands and sick people had been executed not only to insure safety, but also for sport even after the Cure, in *this* world, that wasn't true anymore. The little voice in the hollow still place of her chest said that, yes, it could be that bad. So she was calm, too rational to tell him what she really meant, when she said, "How will I know if you never tell me?" She took a step toward him. "You can stay the man you've made yourself into, and I'll never know what you were before. No one's going to betray you, no one's going to tell your secrets." Nella paused and crossed the remaining space between them so she could see his face in the dim light. "Or you can tell me what it is you think you've done. You can spill it out in the most wretched language you like and be free of it. And let me decide."

He was silent. She desperately wanted to watch his hand on the knob, as if it, alone, decided what happened next. Her hand ached to take his away from the door. She forced herself to focus on his face. He shifted his weight and she shut her eyes so she wouldn't see the door open. "It isn't a kindness, this way Frank. It isn't sparing me anything to just leave with things half said."

She felt his sigh like a slide of warm sand shifting against her side. She opened her eyes and he had let go of the doorknob.

"There was a kid, Nella. That's why we were Infected." he sat wearily on the couch.

YOU HAD A CHILD?

"You had a child?"

Frank shook his head. "No, this was after the Plague started. We had this bomb shelter. It'd come with the house when we bought it. I just kept it stocked because it seemed like a good idea and a safe place to store emergency supplies. You know, in case of a bad storm or something. But then, the Plague began spreading. It hadn't reached our area yet, in fact, I think we were one of the last places to become infected. But we heard on the news that the incubation period was very, very long. We didn't wait to see if we'd get sick. We closed ourselves in the bomb shelter and just tried to wait until it could burn itself out. It had it's own air filter, we had enough water and food for years. We were safe, my wife and I. All we had to do is stay sane and keep the door closed and we would've been fine. *We were safe.*"

Nella sank down onto the couch next to him but she didn't try to touch him.

"But then, a few weeks later, there was this pounding on the door. Sarah, my wife, begged me not to open the door. We had already discussed it, we'd agreed that no one, not family, not neighbors, nobody was going to come in. But I heard this little voice." He put one long hand on his head. "This small voice that was *so scared.* It just kept saying, 'Let me in, please let me in! They'll eat me! I'm not sick, let me in!' And on the other side was Sarah, pleading for me to come away from the door, for heaven's sake not to listen. She kept saying, 'It's a trick. They'll rob us or throw us out.' But I had to. I had to open the door. It was someone's baby. Someone's whole reason for being. And he was begging for anyone to help him. Nella, how could I not open the door?"

He looked at her as if she had some answer, but she was silent.

"I let him in. Sarah, bless her, never said another word about it, just acted as if it was the plan the whole time. As soon as the door opened she acted like she was the boy's own mother."

His chest hitched and he choked back a sob. His hands kept moving, sliding over his face, rubbing his knees, flying in front of him like startled birds.

"But he was sick?"

"Yes, he was sick. It took us a few weeks to realize it. He was slower and slower. He stopped talking. But we just kept pretending like it was okay. We kept telling him we were just going to wait a few days for him to feel better, and then we'd all go find his parents. We never had our own, we were so young. We didn't know what the hell we were doing, but we did the best we could for him. There were no doctors to call, no medicine we could give him or even anyone to ask advice from. There was only us in that tiny metal tube, watching the time run away from us so slowly. And then about a month after we let him in, he bit me. I yelled for him to stop, just to *calm down* and stop, but he wouldn't. He just kept clawing and screaming and there was blood everywhere. I kept trying to hold him back but he was so wild. I didn't want to hurt him. He was just a little boy, maybe eight. Maybe younger. And Sarah shot him." Frank stopped a small groan with his hand over his own mouth. "Sarah shot him because I couldn't do it. She wanted to shoot me too. I begged her not to. I told her we could be immune, we weren't sick. And the bites weren't how it spread. She listened. I should've let her shoot me then." He put his head in his hands and his whole body shook. "I should've let her shoot me."

Nella didn't know what to do. She'd seen

dozens of people cry in the past several years and she always knew what to do. But not now. Her skin ached to touch him, to glide her fingertips over his back in soothing strokes. But she sat motionless beside him instead.

"Was she Immune?" her voice was low and thick around the lump of sympathy in her throat.

"I'm not sure," he said, trying to wipe his eyes. Nella resisted the urge to hand him a tissue. "She said she felt very slow over the next few weeks but she never seemed to show symptoms other than that. But maybe that's why she waited too long. Maybe she was thinking so slowly she missed my symptoms."

"Maybe she thought you'd get better."

Frank nodded. "Yeah, she would have hoped that." He rubbed his shoulder. "Some days, I think she missed on purpose. But I didn't get better. And if she was sick, then she held on longer than I did. We were arguing about the boy again. We had wrapped him in a blanket and some old plastic sheeting I had stored in the bunker. I thought he ought to be buried. And I meant to do it. But every time I got close to the door, Sarah would panic. She'd beg me to wait just one more day, not to leave her alone with those things waiting for her outside the door. I tried to tell her that anything that was out there would've moved on, but she was convinced that if I opened the door again we'd both be dead. We were both sure we were Immune. But the infection was already inside. It was already too late. But I kept putting off burying the boy to appease her. We argued about it every day for weeks. In the back of my mind, I knew he was rotting, that we were breathing him in. I couldn't smell it- maybe because we never opened the door for fresh air, so it kind of just crept up gradually. We never smelled him, but in the back of my head it drove me crazy to think about him in there with us, slowly falling apart, liquefying. I used to lie awake thinking about it." Nella felt Frank's shudder pass through his body and into hers as he spoke.

"So this last day, I could barely get the words out. I was trying to climb up the ladder to the hatch and hold his body at the same time. He kept slipping inside the plastic and I could feel the bones shifting and wiggling in there. And I just wanted it done. My feet didn't work right, but only sometimes, so I would get a few steps up and the bag would slip, and I would yank it up again. Then I'd lift my foot up to take another step and instead, slide backwards. It took a long time and I was getting angry. I had started while Sarah was asleep, because I didn't want her to stop me again. This time I *had* to bury him, or I'd go mad. I knew it. I only had three steps left to reach the hatch when she woke up. I knew it would take me another fifteen minutes or so just to manage those steps, but I thought if I could just get the door open, she'd stop being upset about it and I could take my time with the rest. I was covered in sweat and so tired. The boy couldn't have been more than fifty pounds. Something I wouldn't normally struggle with. But that day- I don't think I've ever been that tired before or since. I felt like all the water and air had been squeezed out of me and I was just this paper thing, just a husk being thrown around in a strong wind. I managed another step and I could almost reach the door handle with one hand. Almost. If I hadn't been carrying the boy I could have reached it." Frank stretched his arm in front of him as if the hatch were before him now, always just farther than he could manage. Nella wondered how many nightmares had featured that hatch over the years in Frank's mind.

"But if I reached as far as I could have, the boy would have slipped out of my other arm and fallen.

Sarah was just stretching but she saw me pretty quickly up on the ladder and she sprang out of bed.

'Frank,' she said, and she was already crying, 'Don't go today. Please, just one more day I promise.'

I put my forehead on the ladder rung in front of me, trying to focus on the cool touch of the metal. I wanted to cry. I couldn't turn back. Not now. This small trip up a ladder, a trip that would have taken all of thirty seconds when I was well, had taken over an hour. I think some part of me knew I was really sick. I don't think I would've come back to the shelter if I'd left that day. Sarah would have been safe.

"The ladder wasn't that long, maybe twenty rungs in all. I could stand at the bottom and reach halfway up to the hatch. I didn't have the greatest grip on the boy by now, I just kept readjusting as he slipped, so part of him was dangling below me. It was low enough that Sarah could reach it if she stood up on her toes.

'Sarah,' I said, 'It has to be today.' and that was all I could manage to say without forgetting which word I wanted to say next. I just kept repeating, 'It has to be today' over and over. I lifted my foot to put it on the next rung.

Sarah was yelling at me, begging me not to do it, but all of my concentration was on that one foot. I just had to get that one foot onto the next rung without slipping. She didn't wait for that though. She started pulling on the plastic around the boy. She wasn't just gently tugging either. Sarah was desperate to stop me. She yanked as hard as she could. The boy slipped away from me and landed with a greasy pop next to her. But the sudden shift in weight threw what little balance I had completely off. I fell too, landing on my back on the cement floor. I think I blacked out for a second and the wind was knocked out of me. I could see Sarah leaning over me as I lay gasping there. She was crying and her hair brushed my face. The bunker light made a halo around her head, sparked and shone on her skin. And I had my last charitable thought then. I thought, she's just scared. She didn't mean to hurt me, she's just scared.

And then it was as if someone came along and blew the little candle that was my soul out and left an empty, cold place behind. All I could think of was how much pain I was in from the fall, from the disease, how hard I had worked to get the boy up the ladder and Sarah had smashed me back into the ground. That she was always holding me back from doing what I knew needed to be done. That I had to get rid of her, so I could be free. And while she was still leaning over me, trying to see if I was all right, trying to *help* me, I grabbed her hair and wrapped it around and around my hand, pulling her down toward me."

Frank looked at Nella and his face was like a cracked mirror that could only show grief. His voice wavered. "She must have been so scared. I'd never even raised my voice with her before that. She must have been terrified and heartbroken. Her whole face was almost blank with shock. And I knew, even then, that she was frightened. I knew and I was *glad*. It was a fierce, hot joy, as if I was filled with vengeance. But for what? She hadn't done anything. And I did the most painful thing I could think to do. I bit her behind the ear. I bit her so hard that her skin and scalp started to come away from her skull."

Nella felt her stomach boiling away even as she tried not to shudder. Her teeth ached in protest at the image.

"I bit her where I used to love kissing her the most. And I still felt nothing but visceral delight in doing it. I let her hair go though, when she screamed and she leapt back. It took me a few seconds to get up off the floor, because it really had given me a blow to land that hard. Sarah didn't waste those seconds. She found the gun and had it pointed at me. She was crying, begging me to stop. She said I was just sick, if I could calm down, she'd get me to a hospital and everything would be okay. I stood there, this hulk of a thing, my mouth dripping with her blood and I could feel the grin splitting my lips. She was trying to save me, and all I could think of was how good it had felt to bite her. Like it filled some part of me I'd never known was empty before. I could see the end of the gun shaking and I knew she wouldn't be able to do it before I reached her. And I didn't care that I was going to kill her and I didn't care that I was going to die too. All I wanted was that feeling back. There was nothing left in me but this growl, this grunt that grew and grew until I leapt at her and I couldn't even hear her screaming over the growl coming from my chest.

"If there had been any mercy at all left in me, I would have tried for her neck and ended it quickly. Instead I scratched and hit her face. She had lost control of the gun, I was far too close for her to raise it again. She reached behind her and found a glass bottle and smashed it across my face. That's how I got this." Frank rubbed the purple jag on his cheek. Nella's eyes were too blurry with crying to see his face very well. She wasn't sure she wanted to see it at that moment anyhow.

"The shock of it pushed me back about a foot and Sarah managed to raise the gun. She was still crying. She wasn't angry with me, she wasn't trying to hurt me. She was just crying. And she shot me in the shoulder as I sprang again for her. I wasn't glad anymore. I was angry. Hideously, blindly angry. I snapped her neck with my hands. And she was gone.

And I was alone with my rage and that never ending hunger. How could you possibly love somebody like that?"

Nella swept the tears from her face. Frank was looking grimly at her, but Nella didn't think he was really seeing her.

"Dr. Pazzo wasn't lying when he said they found me just a few months later surrounded by the bones of my wife and the boy. I didn't bury them. I didn't even leave them in peace in the silent bunker. I was surrounded by bottles of water and over a year's worth of food. But I ate the bodies as they rotted around me. After the Cure, when I could think rationally again, I realized what I'd done. I wished that they'd left me in the bunker to starve. I didn't want to live, but I believed it was a just punishment, that killing myself would be worse than everything that I'd done before. Every following breath was hell, until I met you. I could feel them inside me, I could remember their taste, the texture of their skin and organs. I could taste it all the time, no matter how many times I scoured my teeth. I could smell the rot on my skin no matter how much I scrubbed. How could you kiss someone like that?"

Frank sat motionless as Nella got up to stand in front of him. She warmed his scarred cheek with the palm of her hand. "I wish I could tell you that Sarah would forgive you. I think she would, but I didn't know her." Nella watched his eyes fill again. "I don't even know if there is anything to be forgiven. You were ill. The whole world was sick. It still is. Infected and Immune alike. I don't have to love the person that did those things. He's not real. He never was."

Nella threaded her fingers through one of his long hands. "I know these hands did those things. And I forgive them." She brought his hand to her lips.

She traced his mouth with one finger. "I know this mouth did those things. And I forgive it."

She watched his eyes for a long moment. "But your heart didn't do those things. I don't have to forgive it for anything."

She leaned down and kissed him. She felt Frank sob and he held her around the waist as if he was drowning. She bent her head and whispered, "Please stay." But she never knew if he heard her.

NEWS FROM THE LAB

Nella woke to the phone ringing. The couch had made her stiff and sore. She still hadn't showered and she felt grimy and scratchy. She sat up slowly. Frank was not next to her. The phone was still ringing, but she ignored it. She checked the bathroom, but it was dark and silent. "Frank?" she called, walking into the bedroom. But the bed was made just the way she'd left it. The phone stopped ringing and Nella panicked, thinking maybe it had been him. She stopped on the way to the kitchen when she saw a flutter of white wave to her from the door. Her heart sank. It was a note. She tore it from the door.

"Gone to the Farm. You needed groceries. Be back soon."

Nella relaxed. On her way to the shower the phone rang again. Everything itched to be cleaned, but she stopped to pick it up with a sigh.

"Where have you been?" said Sevita.

"Sorry, I just woke up. What's up?"

"I told Christine."

"Sevita, how could that have helped?"

"I know, I know. But how could I not tell her? Especially since she's ready to have a baby. The only thing that's keeping me from telling everyone is that you think it's important to keep it secret for now. I think they have a right to know."

"It's not that people don't have the right to know Sevita, it's that there's a dangerous weapon free for anyone to pick up lying out there in the wasteland. If we tell the wrong people-"

"Okay, okay, I understand. The thing is, one of her scav buddies did a preliminary sweep of that lab months ago. They were looking for medicine and equipment for the hospital and they couldn't wait for the military to clear that zone. Nella, the guy said the place was ransacked, but not in a Looter kind of way."

"What do you mean, 'not in a Looter kind of way'?"

"I mean there were top of the line drugs scattered over the floors, portable equipment and first aid kits were left behind, even narcotics were lying neatly in drawers. But in the upper labs, the ones even these guys refused to go into- you know, the kind you have to walk through an airlock to get in or out of? They were trashed Nella. Tables overturned, papers in messy piles like someone had gone through them one by one only to drop them, even some floor tiles were pulled up."

"Maybe the Infected went on a rampage before they abandoned the building."

"That's what the scavengers thought at first too. But the vault where they keep all the frozen samples- the door was standing open and the generator had failed. Of course the samples must all be dead by now, they said they thought the generator had been sabotaged years ago."

Nella was silent.

"Well, aren't you going to say anything?"

"I don't know *what* to say Sevita. I don't know if this is good because it means Dr. Schneider destroyed the bacteria long ago or if it's bad because it means someone knew it was there and got to it before she could."

"Who would have known it was there?"

"I think only Schneider, Carton, Ann Connelly and Dr. Pazzo. But I'm not entirely certain. It would make sense that they would be the only ones who knew exactly what it was, Dr. Carton said it wasn't due to be tested until the week after the world went to pot."

"But Dr. Carton was busy playing sick, if we believe his story. And I don't really think he has a motive to make up something like what he told us yesterday. There are less elaborate lies and more attractive ones too, don't you think?"

"Yes, I believe Dr. Carton was telling us the truth."

"And you watched Dr. Pazzo lock Ann, Dr. Schneider and himself in right?"

"Ye-es," Nella said slowly, but something in her brain sent up a little flare. She couldn't figure out why though.

"And Dr. Schneider later escaped, after telling Dr. Pazzo she was going after the incurable strain to destroy it. And Dr. Pazzo and Ann were found found almost a year later, still locked in. So the only person it could be was Dr. Schneider."

That little flare kept digging at Nella's brain. "Something isn't right," she said, "when did the scavengers reach the lab?"

"Christine said it was something like six months ago, while the hospital was overrun by flu."

"But Dr. Carton said that he had seen Dr. Schneider about a month and a half ago. And she said she was going back to the lab to destroy it. That they hadn't been able to reach the lab before then because of all the Infected in the way."

"Then who?" asked Sevita, "Looters wouldn't have bothered with a biohazard vault. Even stupid ones. And why would they leave highly valuable drugs and equipment lying around? It doesn't make any sense."

"No, it doesn't. I've got a bad feeling about this. I think I'm going to have to get to the lab as soon as possible to see for myself. I'll have to go after court on Monday- I'll give my findings on the mental state of the defendants and I'll leave immediately-"

"Woah, hang on Nella. I think we should talk about this. You can't go alone."

"We can't tell anyone else about this Sevita, and you and Frank have to be in court for every session, otherwise everyone will know something is wrong. I'm the only one that *can* go."

"What does Frank say about all this?"

"It doesn't matter, the facts are the same."

"Bullshit. Put him on the phone, I want to talk to him."

"He's not here."

"Oh Nella, you didn't blow it with him did you? I'll never forgive you if you did. He's a far more decent person than you've ever been with since I've known you."

"Sevita, be rational. How could a defense attorney be caught dating the supposedly neutral psychiatric counsel?"

"I don't think the world cares about that stuff anymore. In case you didn't notice, we've run out of lives as a species. If that's what's holding you back Nella- just don't be an idiot. Call me when he gets there."

Sevita hung up and Nella sighed and walked into the bathroom. She had just finished dressing and was sitting on the edge of the bed lost in thought when Frank returned. She was concentrating in the quiet, trying to puzzle out what was eating away the corners of her conscious thought. It was something to do with Dr. Pazzo, something about his videos.

She was so absorbed in the memory, she didn't hear Frank come in until he knocked on the open bedroom door. She started and then brightened to see him leaning against the frame.

"Are you okay?" he said.

"I'm sorry, I didn't hear you come in." She

blushed as if he'd somehow seen more of her than she had intended simply by catching her daydreaming. He hadn't touched her, hadn't even returned her kiss. Nella felt exposed and awkward and not exactly sure what he wanted from her.

"Do you need help with the groceries?" She asked so she'd have a reason to divert his attention from her. She stood to go into the kitchen, but he didn't move, his tall figure still blocking the doorway.

"No," he said, "It's all fine where it is."

Nella nodded and felt her face warm. She stood there, awkwardly, as he stared at her, unmoving. All of her adult life she had been still and waited for her patients to begin speaking. She never felt the need to interrupt or prod or fill the silence. Now it was unbearable. *He's changed his mind,* she thought, *He's decided I'm not what he wanted after all.* And her interior gravity shifted again, this time crushing her ribs inward. She focused on remaining calm, trying not to let her shrinking lungs make her breath ragged.

Frank was still just watching her. "I'm sorry about last night," he finally said in a calm voice, "I shouldn't have done that to you. It wasn't right."

Nella felt tears spill from her before she could stop them and her voice was stricken even to her own ears. "You didn't mean it then? You aren't staying?" she asked, convinced that he had decided she was a mistake.

Frank looked as if he'd been slapped. But it was only for a second. He moved so quickly that Nella flinched and threw up a hand to protect herself. Then his arm was threaded around her waist and he was brushing her cheek dry with his other hand. And he kissed her. He kissed her as if he were drawing his breath directly from her lungs. The scar on his shoulder pushed through his shirt and into Nella's hand, a warm, thick starburst. She wished it would burn itself into her hand, a jagged brand that she could hold even if he left. He lifted her feet from the floor and she felt the soft give of the bed behind her. She pushed him, just an inch, and tried to catch her breath.

"Don't cry. Don't cry. I meant it." Frank was whispering so quickly that she wondered if he'd already been saying it when they had kissed. He blew the words gently over her eyes, her brow, her cheek, evaporating her doubt with his warm, living breath.

Nella brushed her fingers over the back of his head, feeling the rapid heartbeat in his skin and the sudden goosebumps her fingers made, like ripples in a pond. The perfect, fragile bone of his skull pressed against the thin bandage on her palm.

"I meant it. I meant it," he whispered into her neck. She twisted the fabric of his shirt in her hand and gently turned his face toward her. She stopped his mouth with her own.

His hands that hadn't been lawyer's hands in a long time, warm and weathered like driftwood, scraped lightly on her skin as her shirt bunched underneath her and left a corner of her hip exposed. She gasped, startled as he slid his hand farther up onto her stomach and sent echoes of heat bouncing against all the places he hadn't touched yet.

The phone was as sharp as breaking glass and Nella stiffened with the first ring. She hissed a swear and tried to slide away from Frank. He laughed. "No way," he said, pulling her in. She realized she hadn't told him about Sevita's call. The ring came again.

"Frank, I have to-"

"Why?" he mumbled, his lips already brushing her neck, "It's not the judge, not on Saturday."

"No, it's Sevita," she sighed and gently tried to push him off. He pulled back and looked at her, his face still half laughing but a little hurt too.

"You don't have to answer it, you can call her back."

"No, I'm not going to answer it, but I have to tell you something."

He rolled onto his side next to her and propped his head on his arm. "This is like every dream I've had since I met you," he sighed, but the sting had gone from his smile. She half sat up and leaned over him.

"I promise it's important. And I promise I'll still be right here afterwards."

THE PLAN

Nella didn't get very far in explaining the break in at Dr. Carton's lab before Sevita knocked on her door.

"Thank God," she said, when Nella answered the door, "I was afraid you'd panicked and left without me. Have you told Frank yet?"

"I was just doing that," Nella replied, "But maybe you'd better finish, you can answer his questions better than I can."

Nella tuned most of what Sevita said out, having heard it before. Something about the whole mess seemed off, almost predictable, like a trap. What Nella couldn't decide was who the trap was for. To know that, she thought, she'd have to know who set it in the first place. She had to find Dr. Schneider and she had to do it without filling the trap.

There were people that would want Sevita silenced, that was easy to see. The reporter practically ran the news channel, and was given free rein to air the stories when and how she wanted. She was dangerous and powerful.

Frank was the only defender and voice of the man most people blamed for the Plague. Dr. Pazzo was the supreme architect behind the annihilation of the human race, according to popular opinion. And Frank was trying to keep him safe from the people's vengeance. Even the man representing the co-defendant had publicly humiliated him. Nella shivered, wondering how he managed to get home every night without being shot. Then she remembered that the trial hadn't even started yet and most of the population didn't know who he was. Yes, there were people that would like Frank out of the way.

That left herself. As far as she knew, she hadn't made any personal enemies- at least, not ones that would really want her gone. Most of the public didn't know who she was, wouldn't know who she was even after the trial. And the occasional person that did, wouldn't have cared. She was just the court appointed psychiatrist. No more partial or important than the bailiff or stenographer. She was just part of the machinery. And not even working machinery. She was a prop to make the court look as if it ran with some degree of fairness and impartiality. Just part of the fairy tale that the world told itself while sharpening its knives. No one would miss her if she was suddenly not a part of it anymore. So it had to be her that went. She had to spring the trap before Frank or Sevita could. She decided this while they were still talking, still trying to devise a plan.

"Look," she said, breaking in, "I'm the only one that can go. It's no use arguing, we all know that I have to be the one. If you can figure out how to cover that distance between one court session and the next without alerting anyone, you let me know. Until then, you're just going to have to accept that I'm the one that has to do this."

"No way," said Sevita, "the area is still crawling with Infected. And Looters. None of us should go alone."

"It's time to call the military government Nella. We can't do this by ourselves anymore," said Frank.

"No," said Nella, "we can't tell anyone until we're sure this thing has been destroyed. What if the military government wanted to keep it as a weapon? Or some hot shot who didn't know how to handle it correctly found out about it and went after it without informing his superiors? Or just some greedy Looter who wanted to cash in by holding the world hostage? The more people that know about this, the closer we are to the disease being released."

"We can't do anything until after court on Monday, regardless of what we decide. We all have to be there for the first session. We'll just have to think of an alternate plan before then." Sevita looked at Frank with some significance. Nella was too distracted to pay much attention. Frank smiled and squeezed Nella's knee.

"We said we weren't going to discuss it until then," he said, "I think that's a good plan."

"Okay," said Sevita, standing up from her seat, "I'm just glad you didn't take off without telling me Nella."

Nella didn't promise anything, though she knew that's what both Sevita and Frank wanted.

"It's not that I think you aren't capable or that I'll be any better at this. I just care about you Nella, and I think we should go together." Sevita smiled and Nella hugged her.

"I know. I just don't see a way around it."

"Just think about it until after court. I will too. We'll figure something out."

Frank was strangely silent and it made Nella nervous. What was he waiting to say?

"Well," said Sevita, "I guess I'd better go then. Before Chris thinks I ran off after you. I'll see you both on Monday morning."

After Sevita had gone, Nella expected Frank to continue trying to persuade her to get the military involved, but he didn't. He just started putting groceries away.

"Is this your way of fighting with me?" she asked after a moment. Frank laughed.

"Why would I fight with you? You're right, we have to find Dr. Schneider no matter what. And if we start a panic by letting the authorities know, or worse, as you've said, nothing good will happen. So it's up to us. Us, Nella, not you. You think you'll wear me down, but you won't. I said you weren't going to go by yourself and I meant it. Even more now. I just have to figure out how to go with you." Frank shrugged his shoulders, "So what's the use of fighting about it?"

"Am I the only one who thinks this whole thing is some kind of set up? How is it that the only people who know about the bacterium are conveniently locked up or otherwise distracted, not for a few days, but for years- think about it, *years* Frank. Yet when the scavenging teams finally reach that sector, only a few months ago, the only thing missing out of a very resource rich lab is that one strain? Not only that, but we happen to find out about the disease only weeks before the military is scheduled to start Cure sweeps of that area. How long has Dr. Pazzo sat on this information? Why did he only tell us now, right before his trial?"

"I'm sure he wanted to find people he could trust. What else could he possibly gain from waiting?"

"Maybe he was hoping to trade for leniency. Or maybe he just wants Dr. Schneider to get what he thinks she deserves. And now the trial will proceed without any prosecution of her, unless we find her, and fast. Or maybe, he's just making a desperate play for time and he thought saving it until the last minute would get you killed, causing a postponement until they could replace you." Nella saw something open up in Frank's face, like an idea flickering over his skin. She didn't like it. "It's a trap, Frank. I just don't know for sure who set it." She crossed her arms over her chest as if they were a shield.

"Maybe," he said, and curled his arms around her, "If it is, I'll have you to protect me."

"I was being serious."

"So was I. Even scavengers don't go into Infected areas alone, and they are trained for this. It would be foolish if either of us tried to."

They were quiet, standing in her tiny, sunny kitchen, wrapped in each other. She wished the day would stretch out, longer and longer, hold its breath. She wished they could freeze like a photograph because she couldn't see a brighter moment coming down the line. But Frank stepped back and let her go.

"I have to go get my opening statement notes," he said, "I need to make some changes before Monday."

"Are you coming back?" she asked, not certain what exactly she meant.

Frank looked surprised. "I'd like to, Nella, but I've a lot to finish by tomorrow. Maybe it's better if I just pick you up in the morning," he looked nervous as he picked up his bag, "will you be angry?"

Nella laughed and shook her head. He kissed her again in the doorway, the warm afternoon sliding down around them. "Next time I'm not sleeping on the couch," he said smiling. She closed the door slowly behind him, still floating like a dust mote in the golden sun.

COURT

Nella sat on the cold cement steps in her best suit. The gauze on her hand had been replaced by a single bandaid. She tried not to scratch it. She had spent the night rereading her notes on Robert Pazzo and Ann Connelly while trying not to worry about what would happen after court.

She had a nervous headache and the raucous calls of returning birds made it worse. After the human population of the City had plummeted, the bird population exploded. They filled the silent world almost the same way that television and radio had filled it before. Nella tried to block it out, but it occasionally poked through, drowning her thoughts in competing songs. She was too restless to wait for Frank inside and too nervous to contemplate being late.

She jumped up as his car rounded the corner and pulled up in front of the building. He got out, not realizing she was already waiting for him. His suit fit perfectly and Nella wondered for a moment how he managed to find it, as gaunt and tall as he was. But then he was next to her, his face cheerful and relaxed. How did she ever think he was ugly? Perhaps it wasn't his face, but the covering of guilt he threw over himself every time he was self conscious that did it. The thought flitted through her brain so quickly she only understood a part of it.

"Are you ready?" he asked.

"Yes, let's go," she picked up the heavy hiking pack next to her, trying not to wrinkle her jacket. She was surprised that he didn't say anything about it, but just opened the large trunk for her. Then she saw a similar pack already lying on one side.

"Frank," she said turning toward him, "You

can't-"

He pulled the pack gently from her shoulder and laid it in the trunk and looked at her. "It'll be alright," was all that he said and then closed the trunk and walked back toward the driver's seat.

"Are you nervous?" he asked in a bright tone.

"Aren't you?" She slid into the passenger side and smoothed her suit so that her fingers wouldn't tap and dance along her knee.

"Yes, but I'm ready for this whole thing to move forward."

They rode the few minutes to the courthouse in comfortable silence. Nella was relieved to see her car already in the lot next to Sevita's camera van. It meant both Christine and Sevita were already there. She brushed her skirt down as she stood next to Frank's car and straightened her cuffs.

"You look fine," Frank said without her asking. He curled one hand around hers and she looked up at him. "It's going to be alright Nella, just trust me." Then he let her go and they walked separately toward the courthouse steps as if they didn't know one another.

Nella drew a quick whistling breath through her teeth when she saw the number of people in the auditorium. They had expected many spectators, converting an old concert hall into a courtroom, but Nella wondered who was left outside, making what was left of the world run. Not only was every seat filled, but people were packed into the aisles as well. *If someone really wanted to*, she thought, *they could take out the rest of humanity right now. With, say, another bacteria.* She felt her heart thud as if it were being dropped down a flight of stairs. She scanned the hall as well as she could, not even knowing what she was looking for. Eventually the bailiff, a cranky looking older woman, came to find her.

"Are you Dr. Rider?" the bailiff asked.

"Yes, I'm sorry, were you looking for me?"

"I've got a seat set aside for you away from the mob up here. It will make it easier when you need to testify. Follow me."

Nella followed the willowy woman who knifed her way through the crowd. Nella struggled to squeeze through gently. She was pleased to see that she was close to Sevita and only a little way in front of Christine and the large black cameras. It made her less nervous to know that her friends were nearby. *If something is going to happen*, the bitter part of her brain added, *at least we'll all go together*. Nella tried to shut the thought out, looking for Frank at the defense table below her. She could see Mr. Grant looking sleek and wearing a self-satisfied smile. She wished Frank didn't have to sit next to him. Ann was already sitting next to Grant, obviously unsedated, but Wells and Johnson were both behind her and they kept her from harming herself and seemed to be consoling her. Dr. Pazzo was crouching in his seat, a grim gargoyle surveying everything around him. Nella felt the skin on her neck prickle again and she looked quickly away from him. Frank's seat was empty. He wasn't near the Judges' bench either. Nella looked over toward the prosecution. A few aides were sitting there, already taking notes on nothing. But Ms. Jacobsen, the lead prosecutor, was nowhere to be seen. Nella leaned over toward Sevita.

"Has the prosecutor arrived yet?" she whispered.

"Yes, everyone is here."

"Where are they?"

Sevita shrugged, "It looked like Frank and Ms. Jacobsen were taken to the judges' chambers before you sat down."

"Why not Mr. Grant?"

Sevita shook her head. "I've no idea. No one has made any announcements."

Frustrated and anxious Nella sat back in her seat. She started to scan the court again fretfully, but then she zeroed in on Pazzo. For some reason her gut told her he knew more about what had happened, what might happen, than anyone else in the court did. She paid attention to who he looked at, his expressions, even his reactions to Ann and Mr. Grant beside him. The crowd was a wave of warmth behind her. It was so foreign to hear so many voices at once that Nella had a hard time concentrating. She followed threads of talk until they disappeared into the tangle of noise again and then she'd refocus on Pazzo and the empty chair beside him.

At last there was a snowy pop as the microphones were switched on and the crowd sat down immediately. They leaned forward, craning and silent, a flock of starving birds hovering over the killing floor. Nella felt mildly sick. Judge Hawkins, the head justice, walked up to the central microphone. "I would like to request that Dr. Rider and Ms. Das come to the judges' chambers please," he said without sitting down. He held up his hands as the crowd rustled and sighed in a great wave. "Folks, we'll be starting as soon as possible." Judge Hawkins turned around and left the court room, his robe trailing rumour and panic behind him. Nella got up and shot Sevita a nervous glance. Sevita just shrugged. They followed the slim, cranky bailiff back into the hallway and down the stairs to the auditorium basement. She rapped briskly on a wooden door and then opened it for Nella and Sevita. Ms. Jacobsen was arguing loudly with one of the other justices as the door opened.

"-don't even know if it's true. This is just another ploy by Mr. Courtlen or his client to delay this trial-"

"Ms. Jacobsen," interrupted Judge Hawkins, "that's hardly fair. Mr. Courtlen has not asked for any postponements before now, unlike yourself and Mr. Grant," he held up his hand to stop Ms. Jacobsen's interruption, "Not that I'm ready to grant it. Ah, Dr. Rider, Ms. Das, I understand you may be able to help us verify Mr. Courtlen's story."

Sevita tried to catch Nella's eye, but Nella was too shocked to pay attention. "Your Honor," she stuttered, "I'm not sure what you mean."

"Dr. Rider," Judge Hawkins replied, "I understand you and Mr. Courtlen very recently uncovered the possible existence of a more powerful strain of the Plague, but are still trying to discover its whereabouts."

Nella stared at Frank, who didn't look toward her. She didn't dare deny it. "We agreed that in the interest of keeping all of us safe, that we would keep it secret. We can't risk it falling into the wrong hands if it hasn't already."

The other justices and Ms. Jacobsen gasped as Nella spoke. Judge Hawkins alone, did not seem shocked. "I know, Dr. Rider, and I agree with you. Which is why the people in this room are the only ones who will hear of it until the threat is contained. Is that understood?" He looked at each of the others.

"But surely the military should be notified," said Ms. Jacobsen.

"Believe me," Sevita said, "We've discussed that at length. I'd give my left arm to take that route rather than what Nel- Dr. Rider has planned. But if we notify the military it will have to go through several people before any action at all is taken, and every person it goes through is a potential leak to the outside world. Someone out there knows where this thing is. The only hope we have of stopping it is making sure whoever has it doesn't realize that we know about it."

Ms. Jacobsen crossed her arms. "So far, I've heard no evidence that this bacteria is anything more than a stalling attempt by Dr. Pazzo."

"Ah," said Frank, "I think Ms. Das and I can help with that." He pulled a video disc from his briefcase and Sevita rummaged around in her camera back and brought out another.

Frank tapped his disc on his open palm. "Your Honors," he said, "the disc in my hand contains evidence pertinent to the trial. In the interest of safety I am turning it over now, but I trust you will view it without prejudice and allow me to properly introduce and screen it in court when the time comes. The disc Sevita has contains an interview with Dr. Carton- one that you may find shocking that also pertains to Dr. Schneider's trial when and if she is ever found."

The justices turned to one another and talked in hushed voices. While they waited, Ms Jacobsen walked over to Nella and Sevita. "Look," she said in a low voice, "I like Frank, but if I were him I would do everything I could to delay the trial too. But you have no vested interest in either defendant, correct?"

Nella shook her head. "No, we were both appointed because we were meant to be neutral parties."

"Then if you tell me this super bacteria is out there, I'll withdraw my objection to postponement," she looked distraught, "look, I'm begging you to tell me this is just a ploy. I've got kids- everything is just getting put back together."

Nella placed a warm hand on the prosecutor's shoulder. "I'm sorry," she said, "I wish I could say it wasn't true, but everything seems to verify that this bacteria is not only real, but is also missing from where it's supposed to be. We have to find it. Or find Dr. Schneider. Or both."

Ms. Jacobsen nodded, visibly paling. She stepped back and cleared her throat. "Your honors," she said, interrupting their discussion, "I withdraw my objection. You don't need to rule on watching the videos, they can be shown in their proper place."

Judge Hawkins looked surprised. "Very well," he said, "all that's left is to decide what should be done and how long to keep the world in the dark about it."

"We have a plan for that," Frank said quickly, before Nella could speak up. "The best place to start is by looking for Dr. Schneider."

"We've been looking for her for years," Ms. Jacobsen said.

"I know, but Dr. Carton gave us new information. We think she is headed back to his old laboratory to destroy the sample. But someone else got there first and the sample is gone. Dr. Schneider is the only one who knows if someone else could have discovered what it was or wanted to use it. We have to find her to find the sample."

Nella watched one of the justices sink down into a chair as if he were suddenly twenty years older. The others looked just as grim.

"Since myself, Dr. Rider and Ms. Das were the only people to know about it, we had planned on going after her ourselves. But we can't be here and there at the same time."

"What about Dr. Carton?" Judge Hawkins asked, "You said he was the one who told you about Dr. Schneider. What if he warns her? Someone has to watch him while you are gone." He turned to Sevita. "Mr. Courtlen said it was your surveillance of his house that got you an interview. Could you do it again without being seen?"

"Sure," said Sevita, "but not by myself. While we were there we found an underground entrance that Dr. Schneider has been using to pass in and out of the house unnoticed."

"I've suddenly found myself with some free time," Ms. Jacobsen said dryly, "I can help you watch the other entrance."

"The only other people to know are the defendants, correct?" asked Judge Hawkins.

"As far as we know," Frank replied.

"Then the other judges and I are probably the best people to keep an eye on them. We'll make an extensive inspection of the prison in order to make sure they are being treated as they ought and we'll keep our ears open," Judge Hawkins sighed and shook his head, "If this were a decade ago I'd have to arrest all three of you for withholding evidence and then call in the CDC. But I guess things change. I don't like it. Especially sending two people alone into a heavily Infected zone. But I don't see any real alternative without causing a panic, does anyone else?"

The other justices shook their heads.

"Then I guess we are agreed. I'm going to allow a postponement. I want you to leave those videos with the bailiff to keep. If either of you is not back in ten days, I'm going to use them to find out where you've gone and I'll be sending in the military. Please get back here by then whether or not you've found anything. I'm going to tell the court that this recess is due to illness." He turned toward one of the older judges, "Richard, will you stay here and be our flu victim?" The older judge nodded and remained in his chair looking drained.

Judge Hawkins looked sternly around at each of them. "I hardly need to tell you all that this is secret. If anyone breathes a word of it before Mr. Courtlen and Dr. Rider get back- well, the panic you create will be worse than anything that I can do to you, but I *will* throw the book at you as hard as I can." He straightened his collar, "Okay then, let's go."

Nella and Sevita walked back to their seats, pressing themselves through the roar of the impatient mob. Frank and Ms. Jacobsen walked back to their seats. Ms. Jacobsen looked a little pale, but nothing else was visibly different. Frank didn't look at Dr. Pazzo and his face was impassive and quiet. Nella watched Dr. Pazzo almost exclusively. The crowd went silent and stood as two of the three judges walked to the bench. There was a traveling rustle as everyone sat again. Judge Hawkins tilted the microphone. "Ladies and gentlemen," he said, "This court is in recess for one week as Judge Crag has taken seriously ill. We will reconvene after he is well. Thank you." The judges got up and walked out of the courtroom as the crowd exhaled in a deep, expanding rumble. Nella saw the slow grin she had been waiting for unfold on Dr. Pazzo's face. Her throat clenched with sudden fear. Frank didn't look at his client or Mr. Grant. He just packed his case files and turned to glance up at her. Nella rose from her seat as his gaze hit her, and they both left the courtroom through opposite doors.

Nella found Christine on the edge of the sluggish clot of people in the auditorium lobby. She pulled her friend past Sevita, who was pretending to interrogate Frank for her camera and the crowd. Nella walked with her hand in the crook of Christine's elbow until they got to the relative quiet of her car.

"I know Sevita has told you," said Nella, and she pressed a key into Christine's hand, "You already have the car key and the apartment key. I want you to use them if you need them. If we don't come back, or if something else gets back before us, this is the key to the gun chest in the bedroom closet. Chris, if it starts again, don't hesitate. It's not going to get cured next time. They're not going to come back anymore."

Christine's hand closed around the key. "What about you?" she asked, "Won't you need them?"

Nella shook her head. "I've got Cure darts for getting there. I don't want to hurt someone who can be helped. I'll take a pistol, just in case, but if this thing is loose- well, I'd rather not see what happens if it's too late. If you hear *anything*, if Sevita starts talking about hearing rumors or the scavenging teams come back with weird stories- anything like that Chris, find somewhere airtight and hole up as best you can for as long as you can."

Christine hugged her tightly. "Good luck, Nella."

Nella gently patted Christine's stomach. "See you soon baby. Be safe Chris, and make Sevita be safe too," she said and walked over to Frank's car. He was already waiting for her. She wished she could say goodbye to Sevita, but the crowd was still thick around her and her camera crew.

"Ready?" asked Frank.

"Let's go," she said grimly and slid into the car.

THE ROAD TO THE INFECTED ZONE

Frank started the car and glanced at her as he pulled out of the auditorium lot. "Don't be angry. You said yourself that we didn't have time to wait until a break in the trial. And you couldn't have gone alone. Not just because of- of us. We have to find and destroy that bacteria. If you disappeared how would anyone have known if it were still loose out there somewhere? This was the only way."

"You could have been fired. Or jailed."

"We all could have, but what else could I do?"

Nella sighed. "I'm not upset. Just worried." She looked out the window as they turned onto the desolate highway. It was like the blank page at the end of a book. Empty, with nowhere left worth going. "We aren't going to be able to take the car past the Barrier," she said to break through the overwhelming feeling of loneliness.

"I know, but I don't want to leave it at the house. If I do, neighbors will start asking questions about why I'm always home."

"You're neighbors care whether you are home or not?"

Frank looked confused. "Well, I don't know if they necessarily *care*, I hope they do, in a good way. But they'd definitely gossip. Wouldn't yours?"

Nella shrugged. "I don't know," she said, "I've never even met mine. Anyway, what's your plan?"

"We're going to the wrecking yard where they dumped all the abandoned vehicles. I have a friend that works there pulling parts and siphoning gas. He'll watch it for me without asking why. It's only a few miles to the Barrier. But I don't know how we're going to get through without attracting attention."

"I have my old medical badge. I was planning on telling the gate guards that I was due to rendezvous with the last Cure team but got delayed. I wasn't expecting you to be with me though. I think we'll be okay if we talk and move fast. They're trying to keep Infected out after all, not keep anyone in."

Frank shook his head. "That might have been true a few days ago, but you and I have had our faces broadcast all over the news by now. Most of the population may have been in the auditorium, but I guarantee anyone who wasn't able to be there is watching it live. Even in the guardhouse. I'm not worried about being stopped, I'm worried about being noticed."

"There's the smuggler's entrance," Nella said hesitantly.

They turned off the highway and onto a pitted gray road. The tar looked like dirty ice pack slowly evaporating from the dust underneath. "What's the smuggler's entrance?" Frank asked.

"Its where the scavenger teams dump extra things that were special requests. You know, booze, contraceptives, that sort of thing."

"You mean anything the DHRS has deemed illegal. You're lucky I'm a public defender Nella."

"Hey, I didn't say I'd ever used them. I just know where the entrance is. Christine told me a while ago."

The car stumbled to a stop in front of a wide metal gate. Frank rolled the window down and pressed a buzzer. "How does Christine know where it is? No, nevermind. Why did she tell you where it was?" He gave her a wicked look.

Nella laughed. "It was nothing bad. I needed a sedative for a patient who was having very bad nightmares. I could have requisitioned some from the military stockpile, but those are becoming scarce and were more powerful than my patient needed. So I asked Christine to find out if there were any over the counter sleeping pills available from the scavenging teams. She said they'd been forbidden in case of suicide or accidental overdose. But she said if this man really needed some that I should go to the smuggler's entrance and talk to her friend. The time I went, it was completely unguarded. No one knows where it is except the people that are supposed to know, and things move out of there so quickly that they don't even bother trying to defend it. And even if someone is there this time, they aren't going to want to blab about seeing us."

A little man covered in sweat and grease walked up to the gate and started opening it. He grinned when he saw Frank.

The car rolled slowly through the blinding glitter of glass and chrome that lay snarled around them. The little man who had opened the gate jogged beside them. "Pull it around the shed Frank, I've got a tarp you can use."

Frank waved a slender hand at him to show he understood. They rolled past a rusting corrugated metal shack with dusty windows. The only part of the wrecking yard that wasn't littered with shattered glass or twisted strands of rubber was the green patch of grass behind the shack. Frank carefully parked the car on it and got out, followed by Nella.

The sun was unbearably bright, reflected like empty mirrors from the broken metal around them, but it was still cold and distant and the grass still crunched softly under Nella's feet from the frost. She pulled their packs from the trunk as Frank talked to his friend. She wished they'd had a chance to change at the courthouse. At least she could ditch her heels. She left them in the trunk and pulled on her heavy boots. She wanted to rummage around and find her warm clothes but she didn't want to draw more suspicion than they were already risking. They'd have to wait until they found somewhere that had been left empty. She patted the side pocket and felt the reassuring shape of the dart gun without opening the pocket.

Frank's friend was eyeing the large packs as Frank handed him the keys. "Where'd you say you were going Frank?" he asked.

"This is Dr. Rider. She's taking me out with her to the Cure team while the court is in recess. I wanted to get in contact with a witness on the team and she knew where they were. Unfortunately, as you know, no cars outside the Barrier. So we're walking."

The little man's face rippled into a gap-toothed smile. "Oh, well hey, it's kind of cold, you guys have jackets?"

"Sure do Jim, thanks for asking. Just watch after my car for me until we get back, will you? Don't strip it for parts or put sugar in the tank."

Jim laughed, "No problem Frank, it'll be here and in good order when you get back. I'll see you next week." Jim waved and walked back around the corner into the piles of wreckage. Frank picked up his pack.

"Sorry," he said, "I don't like to lie to a friend, but I thought it was the easiest way."

Nella nodded, heaving the pack onto her shoulders. They headed casually toward the metal gate which still stood open. The road split and stuttered into gravel as they walked toward the Barrier. The land around them had been scraped and flattened by the Barrier in great arcs as it pushed outward, farther and farther retaking the Infected zones. Left behind were artificial plains that were slowly clothing themselves in short grasses and brush. Unlike the City, where it was easy to find shelter and food among the few humans that remained, the birds here did not flock in great numbers. The early spring wind blew without stopping, chilling Nella's legs and pinching her eyes. She looked back toward the wrecking yard almost regretfully. The empty plain that already stretched between her and the big metal gate made the glittering junk yard seem like a far away reflection of water, a mirage, a memory of humanity in the great barren world. Nella sighed and turned back toward the road. Frank walked ahead of her, seeming to glide on his long legs above the dirt and wind. She struggled to keep up.

Frank turned to check on her and waited when he saw her lagging behind. "Are you all right?" he asked.

"Sure, just cold. Aren't you? Your head must be freezing." She pulled the pack down and searched through it, finding her wool hat. She handed it to him. He looked a little awkward in a suit and tie with an old winter hat, but she stopped shivering when she looked at him.

"Thanks," he said, "We're going to have to find somewhere to change into warmer clothes or we're going to freeze."

"When we turn north to get to the smuggler's entrance I'll be able to find some old shacks where the first camps were. I think the medical huts for the doctors were left behind. It shouldn't be much farther."

Frank matched her pace and walked beside her, blocking the gusts of wind that rolled across the road like massive waves. Nella was instantly warmer. She slipped a cool hand into his as they walked. It was only half an hour until they caught sight of the Barrier.

"It's gotten much farther out than I thought," said Nella, "we should turn here so we aren't seen by the guards. We can get closer to the Barrier after we turn north, away from the gate."

They left the road and cut across the rocky scrub. The world was gray, as if the wind had swallowed it up. The sky was colorless metal with a hole cut into it for the sun to poke through with a cold glow. The grass and brush were dead and silver, rustling and twisting and spitting themselves in pieces into Nella's face. The Barrier loomed like a black mountain on her right side and there was only bare pale dirt in its shadow. Nella was glad that the snow was gone. As it was, her eyes started to muddle the earth and sky after only a short time and she looked for anything that would provide a break in the horizon. She pulled them closer and closer to the Barrier, hoping it would provide some sort of windbreak, but it was facing the wrong direction. Even Frank was becoming tired, holding his arm across his face to protect himself from the wind and slowing his pace even below hers.

Nella felt a soft bang as something smacked into her shin. She leaned down and picked it up. It was a bandage wrapper. She looked up. Off in the distance was an uneven smudge of darkness holding still against the wind.

"Everything okay?" Frank asked.

"Yeah, I just found a piece of trash from the camp, we must be getting close. I think it's that black line over there," she pointed.

"Good," he said, "This is rough. I can't imagine how cold your legs must be."

"I should have changed in the car. I wasn't thinking, I was too startled at the change of plans."

"Sorry."

"Don't be, I'm not." She smiled at him and he grinned back. They trudged on toward the camp, too cold and uncomfortable to stand still and talk.

SCARS

The debris from the camp grew as they walked. Farthest out were just a few fluttering scraps of paper caught in the brush by the wind. As they approached the perimeter of where the tents had been, the trash became heavier. Plastic bottles gleamed and flashed as they rolled ceaselessly in the wind. Nella squinted against the added light. A few broken cot springs and lost gurney wheels were piled against the corner of the abandoned medical hut. Nella shoved them aside as she pulled on the flimsy plywood door.

It was dark and still inside except for an occasional stray gust that made it through the gaps in the door frame. Nella sighed with relief and pushed further in to make room for Frank. She pulled her pack down and felt around for the battery powered lantern. It had been an expensive trade but she'd never regretted it. The doctor in her occasionally tried to force herself to conquer the basic fear of the dark, but after what she'd seen during the Plague, she doubted if she would ever be able to walk into a dark place without a bristling pang of adrenaline rippling up her back.

The lantern lit up the small hut completely. It was empty except for a jumble of cots in the corner.

"Didn't anyone clean these sites up before they moved on?" Frank asked.

Nella struggled to pull a cot free of the tangled mess. She dropped her pack onto the cot and began hunting for warmer clothes. "This was one of the first camps I think. As soon as we knew the Cure worked, there was a mad frenzy to push outward and retake areas as quickly as possible. We were routinely given a day to pack after the patients had recovered. The Barrier was moved outward on that day, and then we hiked to the next site," she said as he dropped his pack beside hers. She shrugged. "I *did* always think someone came behind us to break everything down that was left. I guess I was wrong."

Frank took off his suit coat and began unbuttoning his shirt with one hand while the other searched his open pack. Nella turned toward her own pile of clothes with a blush. She pulled off her boots and jacket, trying to think of a way to change without him looking at her.

"Is it far from here to the smuggler's entrance?" he asked, startling her.

"No-" she said and turned around. She sucked in a shocked breath. He was half turned away from her and small shattered moons glowed dark against his skin. She had felt the edges of the rough craters in his skin before and had seen them briefly from across a room, but the livid twists of purple along his arm were different, more real this close.

"What?" he asked, turning his head to see why she had stopped. His face blanched, embarrassed as she reached out and touched one of the scars gently, as if it would burst open. "I know, it's not attractive. But you should have seen them when they were new," he turned to face her and rubbed one of the broken crescents stamped into his arm. "They were far, far worse. Trust me. It's taken years for them to fade this much."

She stepped in closer to him, tracing the edge of the teethmarks with a feather light finger. The arch was so small. She could see that the boy must have twisted his head at the last second, trying to take the flesh with him because the scar was pulled and stretched, elongated.

"I can't imagine how much that must have hurt," she said. She looked up at his face. "Sorry," she said suddenly, "I didn't mean to make you self conscious. I just didn't realize he'd bit you so many times and that hard."

She moved her hand from the curved punctures on his long arm to the shattered starburst on his shoulder. He was still, as if he didn't want to frighten her. But she felt a ripple start deep under his skin as her fingertips slid over his shoulder. She felt the pattern of his breath change, like wave racing in front of a storm.

He had been beautiful once, she could guess that. He carried himself differently when he was around her, as if he had forgotten his ugliness. As if it were a mask he could simply slip out of. As if he were falling back to an older self.

Nella had stopped thinking of him as ugly, but if she were honest, she knew he was not beautiful. It wasn't the scars, not really. It was the mark that severe *want* had left on him, in him. He was still so thin, even six years after surviving starvation. She could see the twisting cable of muscle in his arms too clearly. With no fat to soften them, it was as if his skin were peeled back and all the secret life within him exposed upon the air. Each bone in his chest was a cathedral arch pushing painfully through a thin canvas of flesh. Almost without realizing it, she kissed the jutting ridge of rib, half in sorrow, half in longing.

She felt his hands shake as they closed around her waist. Hunger wasn't the only want he'd held for too long. He baked under her hands, a frustrated flame consuming itself even in the chilled early spring air. The way he spoke- or didn't speak to people who abused him, as if he were no longer their equal because he was not one of them, because he had lost- something. Nella's eyes blurred as she thought of all the somethings, all the beautiful somethings, the world had lost, and she closed her eyes so he wouldn't see.

"Nella," he said, his voice thick and rough. He pulled her slowly into him. She could feel his heart under her palm. Every beat was thunderous with *yearning*. If she could just take away some of the *want*, fill it for a little while, maybe he would get some of himself back. She slid her hands around the back of his neck and felt a sigh travel from his chest to his throat and then warm in her ear as she pressed against him. She kissed the jagged scar on his cheek with soft lips.

The tight control he had maintained over himself for so long was gone. He turned his head and caught her mouth with his. For a second, he kissed her with so much force that she would have fallen backward if he had not been holding her so tightly.

But she sank into him, like water over dry earth, melted and curved around him and he quickly grew gentle again. He still held her with one arm. He tried to unbutton her blouse with the other hand, but he was shaking so badly that he only managed the top two before she took pity on them both and began to help.

Frank untucked the bottom of her shirt and slipped his large hand underneath the fabric, kissing the base of her throat as his fingers glided over the skin of her stomach and rested between her breasts. A ripple of joy started beneath his warm hand and spread like an echo bouncing over her skin. She became frantic to undo the last buttons as he pressed into her mouth again and his hand slid over her breast. She shrugged the shirt off at last and gasped as the cold air hit her back. She reached between them and unzipped her skirt. It fell onto the dirt floor with a soft puff of air.

He lifted her from the floor, both of his long arms wrapped around her. She locked her legs around his hips. Frank's breath was warm and wet through the thin silk of her bra and again on the overcharged skin of her stomach.

A small explosion bloomed in the center of her chest and spread outward. "Oh God," she whispered.

Frank stopped for a moment. He lifted his face to look at her. His breath was rapid and thin, as if he were drowning in her. He reached behind her with one hand and she tensed, waiting for the crash of the hiking packs being shoved from the cot. But it didn't happen. He pulled his arm back and began wrapping her shoulders in the warm fabric of her sweater.

"It's too cold Nella," he said softly. He relaxed his hold on her and gently let her stand on the ground. He traced her jaw line and her lips with his thumb and bent his head so that their foreheads touched. She could feel the pull of their breath between them, a whirlpool of warm air sucking her towards him more and more. His heart thudded against her hand, a rapid chant of "I want, I want, I want."

Frank let a ragged sigh wobble its way out of him before he lifted his head. He let his fingers trail down her neck and over her breast before dropping way from her. "I've never wanted anything so badly in all my life," he said quietly, "Not even Sarah. But not here, not in this place." She looked up and was surprised to see his eyes were red. He smiled nervously. "Besides," he said, "it's too cold, we'll freeze to death."

Nella warmed his wind-chapped face with her hands. "We have a long way to go, and not much time," she said, "I'm sorry, I shouldn't have- shouldn't have interrupted our preparations."

She let him go and pulled the sweater over her shoulders. Frank slowly buttoned the front, his fingers briefly traveling up her center like tiny solar flares as he pulled the fabric closed between them. He kissed the corner of her jaw and whispered into her ear, "If you knew how much I've wanted to touch you since I shook your hand the first time we met, you wouldn't apologize."

Then he drew away and turned back to finish dressing. Nella drew on her jeans and tried not to feel as if she'd trampled something.

BEYOND THE BARRIER

The shadow of the Barrier was creeping long and seeping into the plain when they reached the little break that made the smuggler's entrance. The Barrier had stopped there a few years before as the City's manpower reached its limits. There were simply no more people to guard the Barrier so it stopped expanding. Cure teams and scavenging missions still extended beyond the Barrier, but as fewer and fewer Infected were found and old resources grew ever more scarce, it looked as if the Barrier was now a permanent fixture instead of a mobile one. Someone had utilized a small gap between sections of the hollow cement wall that made up the Barrier and widened it into a tunnel with a rickety, squealing metal door at either end.

After checking the area to make sure that they weren't watched, Frank opened the door, wincing at the sound of metal scraping against concrete.

"Wait," said Nella, putting a hand on the door, "Have you been outside since the Cure?"

"Not since I walked to the City."

She put her pack down and knelt beside it, opening the side pockets. She pulled out a dart gun and the box of Cure darts Dr. Carton had given her. She silently loaded it. She hesitated for a moment and then drew out a pistol from the other side pocket. Frank crouched beside her.

"Nella, I don't think I can. No matter how bad it is out there."

"I know you think that, but until you see you aren't going to know what you're capable of."

She handed him the dart gun. "This has a long lasting sedative in it along with the Cure. But it won't be instantaneous. If an Infected person is chasing you- us, we will have to outrun it long enough for it to take effect. That's a long time Frank. The best thing to do is dart them from a hiding place." Nella passed him the box of darts. "You need to know that this isn't an easy out," she met his eyes and held them, "This is a slow release sedative. It takes the average person a few *days* to recover. When we did this before, we hooked people up to IVs to keep them hydrated and fed while the Cure worked. You and I don't have that. Administering the Cure on people that are malnourished or dehydrated may kill them before they wake up again. In addition, the sedative is dosed for a normal adult. Smaller people and children may die from the sedative if we dart them. Larger people may not be sedated enough and it will still take three days for their brain activity to return to normal as the antibiotic works. Not that I expect anyone is overweight anymore," Nella sighed, "That's not even mentioning the psychological danger of darting someone and leaving them behind without explanation if they do wake up. But time is a luxury we don't have. The best we can do is hope that we'll return the same way and get back to them before they wake up." She ran a hand through her hair and looked up at him. "Do you understand?"

Frank's hand closed over the box of darts. "I understand," he said, "and if it were me in their position again, I'd want to take the chance of dying from the Cure than spend another day as a monster."

Nella nodded. She began loading the pistol with bullets. "Why do we need *that* one?" Frank asked. She didn't look up.

"The Infected aren't the monsters out there Frank. The Immunes are." She strapped an empty holster around her waist and handed Frank a larger one for the dart gun. Shoving the pistol into its holder and closing her pack, she stood up.

"I'm not trying to scare you Frank," she said, her voice softening, "We'll probably not see a soul for miles. The military has done a good job of clearing out both the Infected and the Looters for a long way. If scavenger teams have already been to the lab, it must be safe pretty much for the whole way. I just want to be ready, in case." *And I don't want to be raped and killed in a Looter's camp while you watch or are shot for the fun of it,* she thought, but held her tongue. He looked nervous, the lines around his mouth drawing closer. She wanted to kiss them away, but she touched his hand instead. "It's going to be all right you know," she said and he smiled.

"Yeah, of course," he said. She wasn't so sure he wasn't thinking the same thing she had been. He opened the metal door again and they ducked inside the dimly lit tunnel. There was no one inside, though an electric bulb sat in the middle of the ten foot space. Each side of the tunnel had been made into storage for contraband inside the hollow Barrier wall. Frank was surprised that they had left it unguarded. But then, who was crazy enough to steal from scavengers or to come all the way out here? Nella pushed open the far door slowly, peeking out to make sure no one was around. A small shack nearby bustled with people and its lights were beginning to burn brightly in the dusk. The scavengers were having a party and everyone seemed too drunk to pay much attention to the tunnel. Nella waited a few seconds until a small knot of people on the porch headed into the warm building and then she and Frank slipped out and down the dirt road.

It was as if they had stepped into another world. Trees clustered close to the Barrier, cleared only far enough away that no one would be able to climb over. There were trees in the City, of course, even parks that had been allowed to turn wild, but those trees were smaller, still marked by their years growing under human rules. These were already large when the Plague hit and eight years had seen them grow still larger. Their dead had fallen and were half buried in bracken and dead leaves, undisturbed, erasing the road, rotting or burning as they would, unchecked. It had been a long time, even for Nella, since she had been outside the Barrier and she nervously wondered what had happened to the packs of feral dogs and cats that had wandered behind the Infected, scavenging. Nothing bunched here, not like in the City. What humans were crazy enough to live out here stayed separate and spread out for the most part, not cooperating or even meeting very often. The birds didn't congregate like they did near Nella's apartment because there were no easy pickings here. Even sound seemed spread out, thin and fragile. She suddenly felt small and alone. She looked back for Frank. He crept up next to her, soundless and quick as if he'd been doing this for years. He slipped his hand around her shoulder and squeezed it gently without saying anything. She felt better and they kept walking.

Though the wind had died down rather than battle its way through the thick trees, it was still too cold for them to risk sleeping outside and the dark was quickly swelling around them, welling up from the shadows of the trees, choking the light out of the dirt path. She kept hold of his hand. She told herself it was so they wouldn't lose each other, but she knew it was her fear of the dark. For a while she was in agony, both longing to light the lantern so that nothing could creep up on them and terrified to finally see what may be hiding in the dark. If they could just find the main road before night swallowed up her sight completely.

Frank stumbled over something beside her. "I

can't see anything. Do you know where we're going?" he asked, rubbing his ankle, a slim ghost of gray and black beside her.

"I'm trying to get back to the road. But if we use the lantern something- some*one,* I mean, might see us."

"At least we could see them coming if someone was trying to hurt us," he said, echoing her own thoughts, "I don't think we have a choice. If we get lost out here we'll die of exposure. We have to find some sort of shelter and I don't think we'll find it in these woods."

Nella pulled the lantern out of her bag, silently relieved that he had insisted on it. She stood up to light it, but an overhanging branch snagged the end of her hair. She jumped, dropping the lantern in her surprise. Frank caught it before it could smash onto the road. He turned it on and the pale light shot up, leaping over his face. It highlighted his thin, shell-like skin and the sharp edges of his eyesockets and nose. For an instant Nella saw only a spindly, hungering creature that was all claw and tooth, something wholly inhuman.

"What's wrong?" he asked, quickly standing. He was himself again, solid and kind and *with* her, even in the dark at the end of the world.

She laughed at herself. "Nothing, just nervous I think." She picked up her pack and felt its weight dragging at her. "I just want this day to be over," she said and struggled not to burst into tears.

"I know what you mean," said Frank. He held up the lantern and said, "Look, I think that's the road."

The moon was starting to rise by the time they reached the street, a still gray vein stretched tight across the silent world. Nella looked back toward the Barrier that was now miles behind them. A soft glow, like a lone coal buried in ash, rose from behind it, where all that was left of civilization waited to be saved. She turned back toward her destination. "No lights," she said softly, "No fires or headlights, street lamps or porch lights to call us home." She felt a hot tear slip past her and down her chilled skin.

Frank turned off the lantern and set it and his pack onto the cold tar. He turned her toward him and drew her into him. She closed her eyes and smelled the crisp fresh linen smell of him, let the heat of him sink through her stiff clothes and seep into her skin.

"Look," he whispered and stretched a long hand up toward the sky. She tilted her face up. "Look at all those lights. They'll never turn off or run down. They'll never stop calling us home."

She wiped her face, but felt great tears building behind her eyes again. She was exhausted. Frank let her go, sliding hesitantly away from her. He lifted his pack and turned on the lantern.

"Come on," he said with a small smile, "it's too cold to hang around here."

THE TIRE PIT

They passed by several dark houses without stopping, not wanting to be surprised by intruders while they slept in a strange place. Finally they settled on an empty gas station that fronted the road. Nella cautiously opened the glass door with a hand on her pistol. It was silent and nothing moved in the dull moonlight. She walked a few paces in and Frank followed, holding up the lantern. The store had been picked clean, even the empty shelves were all pushed against one wall. At least it wouldn't be a target for Looters.

"We're too exposed in front of this window. Anyone walking by would be able to see us and our equipment."

"There must be a stockroom," said Frank and moved toward the far wall. Nella turned back to the glass door. She flipped the small metal lock. It wouldn't really stop anyone, but at least they'd have to break a window to get in and Nella would have some warning.

The light disappeared for a moment and Nella turned around.

"Found it," Frank called.

She made her way over to him. The stock room was small, but empty. More important, it was windowless and relatively warm. She closed the door, shutting out the motionless, moonlit world. She dropped her pack with a sigh of relief. Frank grinned. He knelt on the floor and unrolled his sleeping bag and then hers. She sat down beside him and pried her boots off. The floor was hard but she didn't care. Frank lay back and stretched his long frame. Nella laughed as his fingers touched one wall of the small space and his toes the other.

"Not much room," she said. He folded his hands underneath his head and lay down looking at her.

"It is cozy. At least it will be warm."

Nella grabbed her pack and started searching its depths. After a few seconds she got fed up and dumped it into her lap.

"What are you doing?" Frank asked.

"Looking for the food. I'm starving, aren't you?" She dropped a wrapped package on his chest.

He sat up and opened it. "Yes, I forgot we hadn't eaten today. It seems to happen often. I just never feel as hungry as I did after waking up from the Cure."

Nella was stuffing a sweater in the door crack to keep in the heat. She heard him and stopped.

"Frank," she said, turning slowly around to face him, "do you mind if I ask you something very personal? I wouldn't- but I have this hunch that it's really important. Not about you- about something else."

"Sure," he said, picking pieces of sandwich off of the wrapper.

"On second thought," she said, "I'll wait until you're finished."

He set aside the food. "Sorry, I wasn't trying to be rude."

"No, it's not that, you weren't. It's just, not a great topic to discuss over dinner. Although it did make me think of it."

Frank looked at her, bemused. "Okay," he said, picking up the sandwich again. They ate in the bright lantern light, their limbs quickly thawing in the warmth of the small room. Nella was quiet, concentrating. Frank repacked her bag.

"All set?" he asked, "I'm going to turn off the light to save the battery if you are ready."

"Yes, okay," she said, noting that he was still dressed. She felt depressed thinking she had made him self conscious. He switched off the lamp and she heard the soft rustle of him sliding into the sleeping bag next to her. She slipped out of her dusty clothes. She curled herself into her own blankets, trying not to bump into Frank in the dark.

"What did you want to ask me?" his voice floated beside her in a half yawn.

"Please don't get upset. I'm not asking out of curiosity."

"It's okay, you can ask me whatever you want."

"When you were- when you were sick, you said there was plenty of food around you in the bunker."

"Yes, there was enough for about a year for my wife and I. So about a year and a half for one person by the time I became sick."

"But you didn't eat it. I know one of the symptoms is pica- strange cravings, this time for- for human. But, you said you were starving by the time the Cure team found you right?"

"Yes, I'd lost over a hundred pounds. I don't think I would have survived much longer."

"Did you not realize you were surrounded by food after- after you ran out of immediate stuff? Or did you choose not to eat it?"

"I don't remember being aware of it at all. In fact I probably would have died of dehydration if the toilet bowl hadn't kept filling, but there were gallons and gallons of water around me. Where is all this going Nella?"

"One more question, I'm sorry. If someone had somehow opened the package of food for you and given it to you would you have eaten it?"

Frank was silent for a moment. "I *think* so. It was like I was smelling things. And people- my wife, smelled good. And the food didn't smell like anything because it was wrapped up I think."

Nella raised herself on one hand toward his voice. "Remember the video Dr. Pazzo made of his preparations before locking himself in? He made a point of showing the food distribution thing he rigged up for each room."

"I remember."

"So, do you think that food and water was sent down loose like in a pig trough or neatly wrapped like a vending machine?"

"It would have to be wrapped, it wouldn't have slid all the way through the tubes otherwise. It would have caught and clogged-" Frank sat up and reached for her abruptly. She could feel the tension in his hand as it closed around her arm, like a wire suddenly cut loose or frayed free. "How did Robert and Ann survive for almost two years with nothing to eat or drink?"

Nella felt the hair on her arms rise as she heard him say it. "That's where this was going," she said.

"Someone must have been feeding them, but who? Dr. Schneider?"

"I don't know. We'll have to wait to ask her. But I doubt it. She was supposed to be with Dr. Carton for most of that time. How would she be able to travel repeatedly through the Infected zones to feed them and then return to Dr. Carton?"

"I don't like this." He let her arm go and fell back in the dark.

"Me either. Sorry, I didn't mean to worry you. I wasn't sure who else I could ask that kind of question though."

"I guess it won't do anyone any good to worry about it much until we find Dr. Schneider," he said, a yawn overtaking his last words, "I'll try to stay awake if you want to talk about it though."

"No," she said, "I'm exhausted. I only wanted to ask so I wouldn't forget to do it again." She was asleep almost as soon as she stopped speaking. She woke up a few hours later because Frank was shaking beside her. She turned on the lantern and saw he was shivering in his sleep. She didn't know how he could be cold, the stock room had become like a sauna. She could only assume it was a nightmare and felt guilty about asking about the Infection. She lay down, leaving the lantern on, her mind wandering to Dr. Pazzo and Ann. Ann could have survived for some of the time on the monkeys, Nella thought, but not long. Frank had only made it a few months and he had- she shuddered and tried not to gag. Shutting Dr. Pazzo and cannibalism out of her brain for a while, she turned toward Frank. He looked exhausted even asleep. She stroked his face, trying to wake him without startling him. He was warm, as usual, and his face became more drawn, sadder as she touched it.

"Frank," she whispered, "Frank, wake up, it's okay."

He gasped and opened his eyes. "You were having a bad dream, it's okay."

"Is it time to go?" he asked.

"I don't know. There's no window. I don't think so. Are you all right?"

"Yeah. Sure," he said, but his hands were still shaking.

"I'm leaving the lantern on. I have another battery." It wasn't an offer. She wanted it on too. The dark felt overwhelming. She closed her eyes. "I've made a mess of everything today," she said sleepily, "I'm sorry. I'll try to do better tomorrow."

The sound of the sleeping bag zipper was so loud it almost echoed in the small space. Nella's eyes popped open as Frank unzipped hers too.

"I'm not dr-" she started.

"I know. I don't care," he said quickly and slid in beside her. "You didn't do anything wrong." She felt the tension drain out of him, like air from an old balloon as he held her, already becoming heavy with exhaustion again. He traced a pattern on her hip and her bare back with one hand until she was asleep.

When she woke, the room was cold and the lantern was dark. She could see a length of daylight spilling over her pack because the stock room door was partially open. Frank was gone.

Nella scrambled for her clothes. "Frank?" she hissed but there was no answer. She grabbed the pistol and slowly pushed the door open farther, peering around the frame. The storefront was empty. The plate glass windows seemed to expand, to focus on her and lay her bare to the world. She crouched and crept beneath them heading for the door. She realized how bad this trip would have been to make alone. She choked down the thought that something had happened to Frank. She made it to the door and gently pressed it. It opened easily. Frank must have unlocked it. She felt a little better. She looked outside, but nothing moved. Nella opened the door and stood up slowly. She slid out of the gas station and slowly walked around to the back. Frank was sitting on the edge of a pit the station had used for old tires. The air still burned with the heavy smell of rubber.

"Frank, what's going on?" she asked. He looked up at her and she could see he was distraught.

"They were just left here," he said looking into the pit.

Nella sat down beside him to look. If they hadn't still had shreds of cloth around them, Nella would have thought they were just three small logs scattered among the tires. Even their thin fingers curled like twigs in the dust.

"I think this store was stripped clean a long time ago. And I don't think the Cure teams would have missed them. We were ordered out in grids, the areas we would have missed would be miniscule. People locked away, like you, would have been missed if not. I don't think anyone left them here Frank. Maybe they wandered in looking for food or water and couldn't get back out. It wouldn't take much, a broken leg or arm and they wouldn't be able to climb up again."

"Why would they come here?"

"I don't know, maybe they were attracted by the light of the City? Or the debris left by the scavengers and military teams." She put a hand on his knee. "I know you've heard stories about Immunes shooting the Infected for sport. I'm not going to lie and tell you it isn't true. And after the way you've been treated since the Cure, I don't blame you for being suspicious and sad. But I worked with the Cure teams, and they were *good* people, almost without exception. They wanted to find and help people. If anyone had known these three were here they would have brought them in for the Cure." She stopped for a moment and watched him. "It would make me feel better if we stopped to bury them," she said, "as best we can."

Frank nodded. "Me too," he said, "at least someone will remember they were human once."

They had no tools and there wasn't much to be had in the tire pit. The bodies had been there for a long while, not much more than dried corn husks dressed in rags. There was no smell and Nella was far less disturbed by it than she thought she would be. Less disturbed, but deeply sad. They were all broken, somehow. Slashed or bit or snapped as if they really were old wood. She tried not to think of how drawn out their last days must have been. In the end, they covered them with old tires, working silently, each wondering what kind of life the three had before the world got sick. At last, when the sun was already almost overhead, they were done.

"We should light it," Frank said bitterly, "let it burn forever so the City knows what happens out here. So they can't pretend the world is just going to go back to what it was. A permanent bad taste that lingers long after they've scrubbed all the blood from the corners of their mouths."

Nella was glad that there was no gas left at the station. She believed he meant to do it. She was quiet for a moment, watching his face harden like cooling wax. She squeezed his hand.

"It's time to go Frank. Let them lie in peace. God knows they're in need of it." She walked away from him without looking to see if he was coming and scrambled up the dirt side of the pit. She walked back to the stock room and began packing up, waiting for him to cry it out if he needed. She felt dusty and tired and the day wasn't half over yet. She badly wanted to wash her hands, but she didn't dare to use what little water they had. She'd have to wait until they found a stream or ditch. She lifted her pack and checked the map. Frank returned to the store. He lifted his pack.

"It's okay if you want to go back," she said, "I'll understand." But her mind panicked at the thought of continuing alone.

He shook his head. "No, of course not. I'm angry with the way the City has treated the Infected, but I don't want it to be destroyed. And definitely not the way this bacteria will destroy it."

He started heading for the door. "You *do* realize this is crazy though, don't you?" he said over his shoulder, "I'm a lawyer. You're a psychiatrist. We're supposed to be in dark, air conditioned offices charging exorbitant fees to rich clients. Not saving the world. Not chasing bad guys."

Nella shrugged. "If the world could predict who the villains and heroes were going to be, the crisis wouldn't exist in the first place."

They headed out the door and walked quickly, trying to cover the empty space between them and the lab as quickly as they could.

WHO FED THEM?

After a few miles, the road broke off in several directions. The Looters had mostly stopped using cars, preferring atvs when they could find the gas or bicycles when they could not. They no longer depended on the old roads. The military only maintained those it currently needed, so most roads had eroded into a mosaic of tar and gravel or had collapsed with their culverts into gaping ditches. Frank and Nella turned onto one that had almost completely been eaten away and swallowed by brush. There were times when the only indication that there had been a road once were the houses on either side that slumped themselves ever closer to the ground. The spring insects sprang up in misty gold clouds whenever Nella or Frank brushed by. The sun, which had been so distant the day before now glared and sank into their clothes and made them even wearier.

"I thought this lab was in a large town," said Frank.

"No, not from the map. Looks like they tried to hide it as much as possible. It looks like it's pretty far into farm country. Must be why it took so long for the scavenger teams to find it."

"Are we going to reach it in time?"

"We should get there tomorrow, but I don't know if we'll find Dr. Schneider there." Nella sighed and rubbed her forehead. "You're right. This whole thing is insane. We aren't even looking for the right thing. We're looking for someone who *maybe* can tell us where the bacteria is. And we don't even know if we'll find her." She slapped at a fly, disgusted.

"What else was there to do? She's the only one who knows for sure who had access to it and would know what it was."

"I'm becoming convinced that is not the case. Someone was feeding Dr. Pazzo and Ann. Someone knew they were there and had access to all their data and those videos."

"Maybe I was just different from others. Maybe I had a worse infection or something and my reasoning was even more impaired than others'. Maybe Dr. Pazzo and Ann figured out that food and water came out of that hose thing and I just didn't."

"We saw lots of people as malnourished as you Frank. Not all of them could have been completely out of food. I wouldn't have asked you last night if I thought you were the one stupid zombie in existence."

Frank laughed and pretended to be shocked at her language.

"Well, even if that is the case," he continued, "what would anyone stand to gain if they got there hands on this bacteria? Knowing what it could do, why would anyone not want to destroy it?"

"That's the question of the year. If we can answer that, we will know who has the bacteria."

"Why keep Dr. Pazzo and Ann alive if they were just going to destroy the world?"

Nella sat down on a stone porch in the shadow of a rotting house and rubbed her ankles. Frank pulled out a water bottle.

"Maybe they didn't have all the information that they thought they needed from Dr. Pazzo and Ann. Maybe they kept them alive hoping- or expecting- a Cure."

Frank squinted at her, "You think it was Dr. Carton? But he warned us away from using it, he seemed to want it destroyed."

"I don't know who it was, I don't know what to think. Maybe that's not even the reason. Maybe it was someone that just cared about Ann or Dr. Pazzo. Or someone who couldn't face committing murder on a personal level but has some vendetta against the world and didn't have as much of a problem wiping out humanity as a whole." Nella shrugged.

"But Nella, the governments are all gone. The churches are all gone. Poverty is a thing of the past. Pretty much. I mean, no one is living large, but no one is really starving any more either. The three biggest sources of conflict in the world are gone."

"Maybe it's someone who lost their family to this plague. Maybe it's someone who believes this is the God's vengeance and wants to finish the job. Just because most of us are gone, doesn't mean the rest of us won't find reasons to hate each other."

"Are you going to tell me it's some primal territorial drive in our brain, to fight each other? That this was the inevitable conclusion?"

Nella stood up and stretched. "I hope not. If it *is* a basic urge then as a whole, we've done a remarkable job thwarting it for centuries. I'm a psychiatrist, not an anthropologist. But I think we're basically social animals, we're meant to live together. But when you have eight billion people living together, a few of them are bound to be wired wrong. And maybe one or two are going to have the opportunity to act on that bad wiring once in a while."

They walked slowly back onto the grass lane where the road had once been.

"So we're looking for someone with a revenge fantasy against the whole world. It's been eight years. What is he- or she- waiting for?"

Nella stopped and stared at Frank's face, troubled. He stopped too. "I think whoever it is, is waiting to see what punishment the world thinks is justice. I think he is waiting for the end of this trial."

Nella felt filled with lead as she said it. She walked on, barely noticing as the suburbs changed into shrinking fields and spreading forest. Frank, too, seemed somber. Neither of them saw the first bleached cow skeletons erupting from the long grass like unfinished barrels. But they came more and more often, on each side of the road, tangled in the wire fencing, as if it were a trail into an Ogre's den. Nella finally tripped over a leg bone that had made it's way into the middle of the lane. She froze and looked around. There were clusters of bones almost everywhere she looked.

"Frank," she whispered, "Frank, stop." He turned around to look at her and finally saw the bones as well. He crouched, almost instinctively.

"Is it Looters?"

"I don't think so. They wouldn't have wasted any meat. They would have herded the cows into their camp before killing them."

"Infected then?"

"I think so, the skeletons are whole where they died."

"These are old though," Frank said, visibly relaxing, "They must have been eaten a while ago. Whatever ate this has got to be dead by now. Are they even finding Infected any more?"

"Not many," Nella said, "and those they do find report having eaten stray cats or dogs to survive."

"Could a person even kill a cow?"

"Not one person," said Nella, "but if several people cornered one, I guess they could do it eventually." She felt the hair on her arms prickle and her stomach slid lower inside her.

"But you're talking about Infected working together. Do they do that?"

"It was probably more like a feeding frenzy than cooperation. The initial wave of Infected must have wandered out of the City looking for food. Look, Frank, you're probably right. I don't see how people could survive for years on stray cows and dogs, and these bones look like they've been here for a while, but let's be careful."

It was another mile before the reek of decomposition hit Nella like a broken brick.

THE INFECTED

It floated over everything, like grease on water. Choking and sour and coppery. Nella could feel it sticking to her, coating her skin and throat, and Frank bent over the ditch on the side of the road and vomited. It couldn't have died that long ago, maybe in the winter, thawing in the warm spring sun as the snow pulled back and uncovered it, or in the early spring where it cooked in its own gas. Nella didn't want to look for it, but she knew she was going to anyway.

"Go back," she whispered to Frank, "I have to find it and see if there are Infected around. You go back and find some fresh air."

Frank was shaking and ashy. "No way," he hissed, "You aren't going closer alone." He spat and tried to wipe his mouth with a handkerchief. "Besides," he said, creeping toward her, "I think that was all of it. I feel a little better now."

They moved together, trying not to smell the terrible hot-slaughterhouse air and trying to find its source simultaneously. It was surprisingly far, hundreds of yards off the road near a dour, unpainted barn. Nella exhaled in relief to see that it was far too large to be a person. She tried not to taste it as she drew in another shallow breath.

"Horse or cow," she whispered to Frank, "It hasn't been dead very long."

"How do you know?" he asked, holding an arm over his face. Both of their eyes were watering. The thing on the ground was black and swollen, it's belly a cave slithering with maggots. For some reason the sight of it bothered Nella far more than the smell. Maybe because it wasn't slashed or torn open, the way a knife or even a claw would do. It was gnawed open, ragged rounded hunks taken away, a grotesque reverse puzzle.

"The plants around it are cropped. It was foraging here. Whatever was here before must have kept reseeding and growing after the Plague."

"I'll bet that's how most of the animals that survived made it."

"Yeah, until the Infected got them. Or some other wild thing."

"Do you think it was dogs?"

"I hope so. But you'd think the bones we found earlier would be scattered if it were dogs."

Nella carefully stood up to look around, but the field was silent and motionless. The long grass of several summers was matted and gray around them and she could see up to the tree line.

"Come on," Frank said softly, "there may be nothing here now, but I don't want to be around if something comes back. And the more distance we can put between us and this smell, the happier I'll be."

Nella looked back at the bubbling mass of maggots once more despite herself as she walked away, obsessively brushing her pant legs, paranoid of taking any of them with her. It was like carrying a tiny piece of death. Nella told herself to stop being a basketcase and think logically. As the smell diminished she became more successful at it.

The road was just more field at this point and Nella used the fenceposts and treeline to help her stay on it. It was cool and the shadows were shattered where the long, gold afternoon sun came through. The young frogs in the ditches spoke high and sweet to their neighbors and Nella became almost relaxed. They were less than five miles from where the lab ought to be. She wondered if they could make it that evening, but the way Frank's shoulders drooped and her own feet swelled inside her boots made her doubt it.

It was warm, and if they had to, they could sleep in a barn or outbuilding, it was even mild enough to stay outside if nothing presented itself- but even as she thought it, she heard a restless shuffling behind her, something dragging itself out of the ditch.

Nella turned around as Frank yelled at her to look out. She pulled the pistol out of its holster but the thing was on top of her and its momentum sent them both back into the ground. The pistol flew from her hand and lay glittering black and foreign in the grass.

The Infected's face was barely recognizable as one, more leather sack than head. It was streaked with dried blood and rotting meat. Gray pus oozed out of the myriad wounds around its eyes and scalp and it was bald in patches where scars boiled up in great tarry snakes. Its smell was even more powerful than the horse had been, but only Frank noticed. Nella's world had plunged down to focus on the matted, filthy beard and its yellow, broken teeth. Its tongue was black and swollen and it made wheezing whistles in its throat as its face lunged closer and closer.

All Nella could hear was Ann in her head, screaming: "THE TEETH MUST GNASH!"

Please don't let it hurt too badly, she thought, even as she realized it was going to be an excruciating death.

Her hand fluttered and flexed, looking for the gun somewhere beside her. The Infected's black and yellow talons, they could be called nails no longer, pierced the side of her shirt and left a scarlet, sizzling runner along Nella's side.

She yelled and heard it echoed from over the Infected's back. Frank was trying to pry it off of her, but the Infected had desperate hunger on its side and Frank still saw it as a sick human. He didn't want to hurt it if he didn't have to.

Nella kicked up with her tired legs, and the Infected's weight shifted so she could roll away while Frank pulled. But it was too late. The Infected's teeth snapped closed around her shoulder. It ground and pulled with it's jagged, sharded teeth and Nella screamed and kicked again.

Frank let go of the Infected's back and slid down next to her in the grass. The world shrunk and became too bright. Nella fought it, knowing if she lost consciousness, she was dead. She sucked in a deep breath as the Infected still scrabbled and chewed. Her eyes watered, but she focused on the thing's shattered leg. She aimed and gave it one last great kick in the seeping black wound on its shin. It released her with a half wheeze, half howl.

Nella forced herself to roll away before she fainted. She saw Frank raise a gun and the thought slid by in a blur, *I hope he's using the pistol or we're both dead.*

The sound of the shot shattered the veil that was dropping in great folds over her. Her eyes rolled back to center and She saw Frank's hand steady his shaking hand with the other as he shot again.

Frank bent over her and she could see he was crying. She wasn't sure whether it was because she was hurt or because he'd killed someone. The world fell away in little puzzle pieces of light and sound before she could find out.

It flared back with a sizzle as Frank pressed her bitten shoulder with his shirt. The sound came back with a great thudding, like a slow fan.

"Nella, wake up. Wake up, we have to go. Please wake up."

Frank's eyes darted from her to the woods nearby and back, then to the field behind them.

"Are there more of them?" She tried to sit up

but her vision blurred again and he pressed her back.

"Yes," he said, "but they haven't noticed us yet. They heard me- the gun, and are looking for us."

"Are there any buildings nearby? Can you see anything?"

"There's a farmhouse across the field but it's pretty far."

"We'll make it. Help me up."

"Can you walk?"

"If I get up slowly I'll be able to run as fast as you. I just have to stay conscious."

He lifted her onto her feet. It felt as if the ground were sand sinking away from her every second. She fought the dizzyness. The pack's wide strap dug hard into her chewed shoulder and the pain was a dark blanket over everything, even her fear.

"Where is the farmhouse?" she asked, trying not to panic as she watched the half dozen Infected slowly closing in on their location.

"Are you ready?" asked Frank. Nella nodded. He held her around the waist and they began to run. Frank's fingers pressed on the slice in her side and each step jarred her shoulder. The farmhouse looked very far. Nella stopped looking at it, looking instead at the long grass in front of her and trying to resist the urge to look behind her at the people who were undoubtedly chasing them now. They would have seen the movement as Frank and Nella began running. She hoped they had enough of a head start. Frank began to outpace her and she struggled to match him, stumbling forward.

The thud of bare feet began to grow behind them. Nella felt a jolt of adrenaline burst into her legs. They were almost there, but Nella's chest still cramped in terror as she looked up to see where the farmhouse was.

She could hear an Infected behind her,

wheezing and growling, like a tired dog. She tried to brace herself for the taloned grab she knew was coming.

But then Frank was pulling her up the rotted steps and across the porch. The screen opened with a screech and the wooden door with a bang. They were inside, in the dark and Frank was slamming the door and turning the lock. Nella collapsed onto the nearby staircase, a puff of dust pluming into the air as she sat down.

"I need to check if there's another door," said Frank and darted away. Nella eased off the pack and closed her eyes as the Infected slammed themselves against the front door. Frank was back after only a few seconds.

"We need to dart them before they break the window," Nella said, "Can you help me upstairs, I can do it from one of the upper windows."

"You're hurt, you need to stop moving. We have to stop the bleeding. I'll take care of the Infected."

"Are you sure, Frank?"

He brushed her face with his hand. "For you, I can," he said, his face grim. He slipped past her up the stairs. She heard the window slide open with a shuddering squeal. The dart gun was designed to be noiseless.

She pressed the thin fabric of Frank's shirt against her shoulder, hissing with pain. She had to clean it with something or it was going to be severely infected. She would probably need to stitch it too. She wondered if the house had been picked clean or if it had been missed by the scavenge teams. The presence of the Infected gave her some hope that the house was untouched. Maybe she could find medicine or alcohol to clean it out.

Frank glided back down the stairs. He peeked

out of the curtain, watching the Infected as they slowly stopped banging. "How did they survive this long?" he asked.

"It must have been the cattle. How many were left?"

"Including the one that bit you- seven so far."

"They probably wandered out of the City and began eating the herds of cows, one by one. I doubt there are any more. The one that got me was filled with gangrene. He was dying."

Frank peered out of the curtain. "None of the rest seem to be in very good shape either. They are all cut up and bitten. They must have fought each other between cows- or whatever."

Nella heard a thud. Then something slowly slid down the front door.

"That's two asleep," said Frank, "Come on, we don't need to watch the rest of them pass out. We need to fix your arm before it gets worse."

"Can you check the bathroom for, well, for anything really, but peroxide mostly. I'll see if I can pull out the first aid kit."

"Are you sure? I can carry you upstairs so you can lie down."

"Have you ever stitched a wound?"

Frank looked pale. "No, but I can do it."

"I know you can, you'll have to, but I need to show you how first, so it doesn't get infected."

"Okay, I'll be right back, I think there are two bathrooms." He went into the hallway.

"Frank," she called, "Check under the sink too."

She heard two more thumps from the porch and closed her own eyes, waiting for Frank.

GET IT OUT

The bathrooms had been better than expected. Nella was not surprised given the remote location and continued presence of the Infected. The team that had scouted Dr. Carton's lab wouldn't have bothered with a smaller target like this if there were a big safety risk. They would wait until the Cure team got around to the area and then clean out the smaller houses.

Frank had found some prescription ibuprofen along with the peroxide and bandages. Nella wondered if it was still potent. She would have traded it for a tab of penicillin in a heartbeat, but they weren't that lucky. Her arm was soaked by the time he had returned and she felt a light buzzing begin behind her nasal cavity.

"I have to lie down somewhere, or I'm not going to be much help," she said, noticeably slurring.

He picked her up and carried her up the dusty stairs. She hoped the bedrooms were cleaner. She yanked the blankets down with her good hand as Frank put her down on the clean sheet. Dust swirled at the foot of the bed and Nella lost herself a moment in watching it.

"We're going to need water," Frank said, "Can you hold on a minute? I saw a duck pond behind the house. I have purification tabs."

"I'm okay for now," she said.

"I wouldn't go if I didn't have to. I'll be right back," he said, as if she had argued with him.

"Be careful," she said, "Just because we only saw those doesn't mean there aren't more."

"I'll take the dart gun," he said and squeezed her good hand gently. Nella tilted her head back against the flattened pillow as he left. The room was bright, the thin curtain sunbleached in the window. She tried to concentrate on what was around her so that the pain only crunched at the corners of her mind rather than devouring it whole. She wondered where the people were. They weren't the Infected that had chased them- the house had been left in perfect shape. The bed had been made and she could see the clothes folded neatly in the closet. There was no disorder, no signs of scuffle or panic. Maybe they had come in to the City before things got bad. Maybe they had weathered it out in a shelter like Frank.

Nella heard footsteps on the stairs and her chest cramped in fear. But it was Frank, carrying an armload of supplies. He dropped them beside the bed and began fumbling with the envelope of water purification tablets. Nella could see him swearing under his breath at his shaking fingers.

"You have to calm down," she said, "It's okay. We're okay."

He got the envelope open and swished the tabs into the bucket of water. Nella hoped nothing dead had been lying in the pond.

"It's supposed to take half an hour, but I don't know if we have that much time. What should we do?"

"We have to clean the wounds. We can't wait, we'll just have to hope the tabs continue working while we do it."

Nella was still holding his shirt against her shoulder. It was sopping and warm. She was trying not to look at it, but the wet heat was spreading across her own shirt and over her chest. The adrenaline had worn off for both of them. Nella was exhausted. Frank gently unbuttoned her blouse and she felt nauseous when his fingertips came away red and dripping.

"Do you have any towels? I think I saw a linen

closet at the top of the stairs."

He looked doubtfully at the neat pile near his feet.

"I think I have enough," he said. She inched her way out of the shirt and clamped her hand back over her shoulder.

"Soak two of them in the water and hand one of them to me."

The towel he handed to her was frigid and heavy. It smelled like algae. Nella dropped Frank's soaked shirt beside her on the bed. She yelped as she squeezed the towel into a chilled bandage around her shoulder. She took a deep breath and calmed herself down.

He stroked her hair as he pressed still harder on the towel. "Can I give you the painkiller?"

Nella smiled. "I wish you could but not until we're done. I have a bad scratch on my side, I think it's already infected. Can you start there?"

She could see Frank tearing up, but he just nodded and began wiping away the blood from her chest and stomach. She flinched when he hit the groove the Infected's nails had made.

Frank sucked in a hissing breath in sympathy. "Sorry," he said.

"No, don't be. You can't be gentle. It has to be clean or it's going to get very bad, very quickly."

He took a deep breath, which she unconsciously mirrored. "Okay, are you ready?"

Nella clenched her teeth and shut her eyes as he scrubbed the long trench in her side. He sat up and she let her breath drain out of her in relief.

"Peroxide now?"

"Is there any dirt or sand left?"

"No, but it's very puffy and I'd say it's definitely infected. Was this from that guy's filthy nails? God knows what he had growing under there."

"Peroxide won't kill the infection. Did you find any antibiotic or burn cream?"

Frank held up a tiny tube of ointment. "Sorry, this is all I could find."

Nella was having trouble concentrating. "That's not going to be enough. I need you to find the kitchen. See if you can find any honey anywhere."

She closed her eyes as she listened to metal pots ringing as they fell. She tried to squeeze her shoulder tighter but she was becoming progressively more numb and exhausted. Frank came back, looking dejected. He held up a small jug.

"It's mostly crystallized," he said.

"That's okay, just try to mix the crystals in with whatever liquid honey is left and spread it on the scratch. We'll save the ointment for my shoulder." She felt the world swirling around her head. "Frank, we need to go fast now." Her voice sounded thick and furry in her ears.

He was a little rough in his panic and the tiny shards of sugar crystals pricked her back into clarity before they melted in the heat of her skin. He pressed bandages along the scratch and then gently took her hand from her shoulder. She tried not to look at the wound as he washed it. Every swipe seared and crunched, no matter how gentle he was. Nella couldn't help the small sounds of misery that leaked from her chest and she was slippery with cold sweat within seconds.

"I'm so sorry," Frank said, wincing.

She shrieked as he hit something jagged and he stumbled backward in surprise.

"There's something in there. Something is in me," she gasped.

Frank squeezed the wet towel over her shoulder, dousing in in cool water. He cautiously lifted a flap of torn skin. He was grim as he reached for the first aid kit.

"What is it? Can you see it?" she asked.

"I see it," he said, "I'll try to be gentle, but this is really going to hurt. You have to hold still. Can you?"

"What is it?"

"I'm not sure yet. I have to take it out first." But Nella could see from his face that he had an idea.

"Get it out." Her voice was panicked and shrill.

"You have to hold still."

Nella clenched her uninjured hand. "I'll hold still. Just get it out."

Frank wiped the tweezers with alcohol. He gingerly lifted the loose slab of skin on her shoulder. The tweezers bit the sore, ragged skin twice without finding the object. They burned on her exposed nerves like an electric shock but she didn't flinch. The third time they caught it and Frank pulled the object out. The relief was immediate, as if he had pried a large splinter out. He tried to hide it in the towel quickly, but Nella saw it anyway, gleaming white and wicked in the afternoon light. A shard of tooth had broken off inside her shoulder. She leaned over the far side of the bed and vomited. Frank stroked her head and waited until she was done and calm again. He gave her a bottle of clean water from their pack and washed her face.

"I think that was the worst of it," he said.

Nella nodded. "Okay, this time you'll have to use the hydrogen peroxide. Try not to use too much or it will make it harder to close the wound. You'll have to- to lift the loose skin again," she said gagging.

Her arm fizzed and bubbled as the dirt and grass particles streamed out of it. Frank pulled out a pill bottle. Nella shook her head, "Not yet."

"Nella, this is going to be long and painful. If these knock you out, then why not skip this part?"

"Because I need to tell you what to do."

"I know what I have to do. I need to sew the big chew mark closed. Then I need to put antibiotic on all the smaller wounds and bandage you up."

"But-"

Frank put his hand up. "You have to trust me. I'm not going to let you die and I know how to sterilize a needle and sew. It's not going to be pretty whether you are awake to watch me or not. Besides, these probably aren't powerful enough to knock you out for several minutes. But if you flinch with every stitch, it's going to hurt worse and take longer."

Nella held out her hand for the pills. By the time he was three stitches in, her head felt full of sand and she shut her eyes. He hadn't even finished the fourth stitch and she was fast asleep.

THE FARMHOUSE

The metal screech of the front door invaded Nella's dreams and she swam unwillingly back into consciousness. For a few seconds she just lay in the dark, feeling the hot throb of her shoulder like the breath of a panting dog, coming and going, but never gone. She squinted, trying to see Frank in the strange, darkened room, but she couldn't see him. The front door snapped shut below her, reminding her of what had woken her up. She sat up too quickly, fearing the Infected had entered the house. The world fell like shifting sand around her. Nella quickly bent over, wanting to vomit. After a breath or two, she lifted her head again. She swung her feet over the edge of the bed as a pair of thuds rose up from the stairway. She stood up and winced at the touch of the cold wood on her bare feet. Frank had taken off her shoes and bloody clothes and cleaned up the room. She shivered in just her underwear and tottered toward the bedroom door, which hung open like a broken jaw. A board betrayed her with a snapping creak, and Nella's heart froze solid in her chest as footsteps came bounding up the stairs. She fell the rest of the way into the hallway and pulled herself up on the doorknob. She scrambled backward, slamming the door as a figure darker than the night around it, reached the top of the stairs.

"Nella? Nella are you okay?" Frank's voice seeped through the wooden door like sunshine, like warm water. Nella slid down it in relief.

"I thought the Infected got in," she called. She crawled away from the door and he opened it. "Why don't you have a flashlight?" she asked.

"I was- it's cold and starting to rain. I couldn't leave them out there like that. I brought the people on the porch inside. They are still asleep and I couldn't carry them and the light at the same time. I should have grabbed one when I heard you, but I was worried you would fall- which you did. Sorry."

"I'm okay. Are they all inside now?"

"Yes, I just pulled the last one into the living room. There's a fireplace there and the woodbox is full."

"Have you slept at all?"

"It's early still. The sun only went down about an hour ago." He groped in the dark and found her, lifting her to her feet. "Do you think you can get down the stairs if I help? You need to eat and you must be freezing. A fire will make you feel better."

"You need to sleep too Frank."

"I will, when you are taken care of."

She slid her good arm around his back and tried not to wince as his fingers curled around her waist, brushing the streaking comet that ran down her side. "It's not your fault," she said as they moved slowly toward the stairs, "If he hadn't jumped me, it would have been you."

"But if I was ready, like you are, I could have acted faster. Maybe you wouldn't be hurt. Maybe I wouldn't have had to kill him."

Nella's knees felt shaky as they walked down the dark stairway. The rain made a harsh hiss on the porch in front of them. "I wasn't ready Frank, or I could have thrown him off easily. He was clumsy and weak, if I'd been ready neither of us would have been hurt. It isn't your fault."

Nella felt with her foot for the edge of the stair, and at last realized they had reached the bottom. Frank held a hand in front of him, looking for the hallway. The light from Frank's lantern hit her as she found the living room doorway. The Infected lay in a long row across the floor. Frank had covered them with blankets.

"I should probably try to clean them up," he said, noticing her watching the sleeping figures.

"They are going to need food and water more than a bath," she said. "I'll help you in the morning. We can leave them supplies and a letter so they know what has happened."

He lowered Nella gently onto the couch. "They will already know what happened," he said grimly, wrapping her in a quilt, "but at least we can tell them where to go next."

He slid the grate from the front of the fireplace. In a few moments they were sitting in front of a blazing orange fire. "The curtains!" said Nella suddenly.

Frank held up a hand, "It's okay, I already thought of that." He grabbed his pack and sat next to her, sighing with relief. He closed his eyes for a second in the pulsing gold heat. She thought he looked ten years older than he had that morning and realized with a pang how tired he must be.

She brushed the side of his face lightly with one hand, surprised to feel the bristle of stubble. He smiled and laid a hand over hers without opening his eyes. "You need to sleep," she said.

"Soon," he said, "but we both need food. You especially. And I want to check your cuts. We have to keep them clean." He opened the pack.

"Let's eat first," she said, "I don't want to look at the raw hamburger my shoulder's become and then try to eat after that."

Nella felt odd and criminal eating even a simple meal in the midst of the sleeping skeletons that surrounded them, and promised herself that they would either find ample supplies in the house or leave their own for the Cured before they woke up. Her wounds were clean and the puffiness had subsided from the scratch on her side. The fire made her drowsy, but something felt distinctly creepy about falling asleep in the living room, something that just wasn't the same as falling asleep in a Cure tent surrounded by lights and soldiers along with the Infected. She felt exposed, unprotected, as if the sleeping man beside the couch would suddenly reach up out of the dark and claw at her throat.

"Frank," she said, gently shaking him from a comfortable doze.

"Hmm?"

"I'm really sorry, but I can't- I won't be able to sleep here. Can you help me get back upstairs?"

He sat up rubbing his eyes. "Oh sure, of course. Just let me add a few more pieces of wood so everyone will stay warm."

They took the lantern with them up to the dark bedroom. Nella was exhausted and shaky by the time they made it back. Frank closed the bedroom door tightly and shoved the dresser in front of it without comment. He placed the lantern on top and collapsed like a wooden doll into the chair next to the bed.

"I thought you were going to sleep Frank," she said gently, stretching flat on the bed.

"I a-" his yawn cut off the rest of the word.

"Come to bed."

"I don't want to hit your cuts and hurt you."

She gently pulled on his arm. "It's okay, you won't hurt me. You need to sleep." He tugged his shoes off and began to get undressed. "We'll never get anywhere tomorrow if you are exhausted," she continued and he stopped, startled.

"Tomorrow? We can't go tomorrow, the lab is still four or five miles. You can't travel that far, you lost a lot of blood today."

"We have to. We don't have that much time."

"Then I'll go. You stay and rest." He yawned

again and crawled into the bed next to her.

"No way," she said, "what if something happens? I can't let you go alone."

He scrubbed his stubbly cheeks with both hands. "Nella, what are you going to be able to do if something does happen? I don't think you are going to be able to run. Or shoot the gun without causing more damage to your shoulder."

"I could if I had to," she knew it was a weak argument. "Besides," she continued, finding his sore point, "what if something happens while you are gone?"

"What's going to happen? This place is remote and safe from Looters. It's well stocked with food and water and medicine. All you need to do is rest until I come back."

"What if the Infected wake up before they are Cured? What if I get a fever and can't take care of myself?"

Frank groaned and rubbed his hand over his smooth skull. He rolled onto his side and looked at her. "I don't want to fight now. Let's fight in the morning when I can think."

She laughed gently. "Okay, we'll fight in the morning."

He leaned over and kissed her. They fell asleep as the rain made the swelling joints of the house creak around them.

It was still raining, cold and misty when she woke in the morning. Nella had slept only lightly, afraid Frank was stubborn enough to slip away in the middle of the night. Still, she felt much stronger than she had the evening before.

Still clothed only in her underwear, she looked around for her pack before remembering it was sitting at the bottom of the stairs where she had dropped it. But the dresser was wedged against the door and too heavy for her to move with one arm. Nella stifled a frustrated sigh.

She stood shivering in front of the dusty dresser. She hesitated, feeling slightly cannibalistic, as if she meant to wear someone else's skin instead of their clothes, but the chill won out. She wiggled the swollen drawers open, ready to leap backward if a rat scuttered out. But the clothes were undisturbed. They were neatly folded as if they had just come down from the clothesline yesterday. They were men's clothes, far too large, but perfect for her wounded arm and side. She pulled out a sweater that still breathed a faint trace of the wood fire it had dried over. She eased it over the bandages on her arm, holding her breath expecting pain as the thick cloth brushed over the aching flesh of her shoulder. She got it on without too much wincing and then rolled up the cuffs of an old pair of jeans. They were patched and faded and all the stiffness already worn out of them. She got an eerie feeling again, as the fabric bunched and pooled around her waist, as if she had stepped into someone else's memories. A half-formed hope bloomed in her chest that these people were alive somewhere, not Infected. She grabbed a thick belt from the top of the dresser and threaded it with difficulty through the large pants. Her mind wandered to the Infected sleeping below.

Nella raked her hand over her snarled hair in frustration. She would be able to find supplies, the house seemed well stocked, and even if it wasn't, she and Frank had more than enough to spare for the people downstairs.

But they couldn't wait for the Infected to wake up. There wasn't enough time left before Judge Hawkins sent the military after them. How would the people downstairs react with no one to counsel them when they woke up? A note was no substitute, no matter how eloquent. Nella knew the prospects even for those who underwent years of therapy through Cure programs wasn't very good. The current suicide statistics were something like thirty percent for the Cured, and not very much less for the Immunes.

They would remember the Plague, everything that had happened and what they had done after their infection. But they would only understand the events of the past eight years as they had happened for themselves. Without someone to explain, they could have no real idea what had happened to the rest of the world. Nella had seen it before, even after the Cured had been shown news footage, had seen communities of survivors, even after they had found some remaining family members- some of them refused to believe it. They would blame themselves, convince themselves that they were inherently evil somehow, instead of just ill. Nella picked up the pistol that Frank had laid on top of the dresser. *They will probably all be suicides,* she thought, *isn't it kinder to spare them the agony of realizing what they've done?* She looked at Frank,his skin outlined in silver rain-light. He kept going. Some of them did. *Some of* ***us*** *do,* she thought. She put the pistol down and walked slowly to the window. The City was invisible in the fog. All she could see was the pale young grass pushing up through the old silver corpse of last year's field and the dark, still pond and the rotting carcass of the Infected's latest kill, a cow maybe or a horse. Nella sighed. *The bullet or the Cure. Either way it's murder.* She placed her forehead against the cold pane and closed her eyes. Frank stirred behind her and she turned around.

He stretched and scratched at the stubble that was thickening on his cheeks. He sat up and smiled at her.

"Feeling better?" he asked.

"Much better," she lied.

"Sorry about your clothes, I didn't want anything dirty getting into your cuts."

She sat down next to him on the bed. "Liar. You were just trying to get into my pants."

He laughed.

"Come on," she said, "we need to get moving. I want to leave these people with plenty of supplies in case they wake up before we get back, and we still have a few miles to go."

She expected him to argue with her, but he just shook his head and pushed the dresser away from the door. He was right, though he never said so. Nella was almost useless, she couldn't even carry her own pack without opening the wound on her shoulder again. So Frank rearranged their gear and gathered supplies for the sleeping Infected while Nella struggled to write a note that could explain the world they were about to wake up in.

It took less time than either of them expected. By midmorning, the sleeping people were warmly covered and a pile of provisions sat in front of the fireplace. Nella attached her letter to the mantle.

"I wish I could be here to tell you this instead of

leaving a letter," it began. Nella stopped herself from rereading it. She tried not to flinch as Frank tightened the sling he had made for her. She didn't want him to change his mind and insist that she stay behind.

It was still gray and cool when they left the old farmhouse at noon. The fields were heavy with old, wet grass and Nella tried to lead them back to the road. It was broken and patchy, but the land around them was weedy and quickly filling with thorn bushes and small trees. The road at least, was still mostly flat and at least halfway clear of bracken. At first, when her energy was still high, Nella felt guilty that Frank was carrying everything. But she soon became winded and drained and she was grateful when he requested frequent rests. She suspected some stops he was adding for her benefit rather than his, but each time they sat on the cold, damp ground she sighed with relief. The trip to Dr. Carton's lab should only have taken a few hours. Instead it lasted for the rest of the day. The dull pearl of the sun sank behind its clouds as they reached the lab.

THE LAB

The building was larger than Nella had expected and seemed a giant cube of black glass planted in a large clearing. It was surrounded by old forest that seemed to be spreading its fingers toward the building. Even the gravel parking lot was almost invisible, covered by early grass and unopened dandelion heads. Nella had been outside of the City many times with the Cure team, and she had seen the roads and buildings begin to decay, to be drawn back into the ground, swallowed by grass and trees. But this place felt almost surreal. It looked so untouched. No windows were broken that she could see. The roof looked whole and wasn't sagging. There was no paint to peel, because it was all glass and she couldn't see if there were any disorder within because the windows were reflective. It was intimidating, this thing that stood impervious to the devastation that had spread around it, from it even, if Dr. Pazzo was to be believed.

"What if she isn't here?" asked Frank as they reached the dark, smooth rotating door.

"She left Dr. Carton's lab seven weeks ago now. Unless she's living here I doubt that she *will* be here."

"Then why are we here?"

"I want to make sure the vial isn't in the vault. And maybe Dr. Schneider left some clue where she went. She wouldn't have been very careful, she had no idea she'd be followed."

Frank began to push on the door and Nella stopped him. "Be careful," she said softly, "we can't see inside. We have no idea if anyone else is in there."

He pulled the pistol out of the pack and gripped it tight. They turned the door together, entering the building at a slow, careful crawl. It was still inside and completely spotless. As if it were all waiting for the light switches to be turned on and it would all start up again.

"The scavenge scouts were right. No one's touched this place in all these years," Nella said.

"I doubt anyone even knew this place existed, except for the people who worked here."

"And we know what happened to them. But why is the lobby so immaculate?"

"I'm sure Carton sent them home at the first signs of Infection. He was better equipped to recognize them than others," Frank said, his voice a dry, bitter rind between them.

"But he said he watched them from the lab for a week before fleeing."

"I imagine there were great crowds of people both sick and well moving on the road past here. Some of them were bound to wander by here. Some probably knocked on this door for help. And he just watched them get killed." Frank's mouth had tightened and she could see the edge of his jaw pulse as he ground his teeth. "Come on, Nella, let's get this over with, this place gives me the creeps."

He stepped behind the reception desk and finding an empty shelf, stowed the pack. He kept the pistol and handed the lantern to Nella.

"Is it okay if you carry that?" he asked.

"Yes, I'm fine." She held up the pale light and it made a pitifully small circle in the large lobby. "Frank, maybe we should find someplace to sleep and go over the whole place in the morning. We could miss something in the dark. And I didn't see anywhere else since we left the farmhouse."

Frank frowned. "I know it's not ideal," she said, "and I don't want to stay overnight anymore than you do, but I don't really see any alternative.

And I'm exhausted."

"Okay," he agreed, "but first we take precautions." He picked up a lobby chair and wedged it in the rotating door so that it couldn't move at all. "Let's see if we can find a first aid station and change your bandages. Maybe we'll even find antibiotics."

They made their way across the dark lobby and down a glassed in hallway. Nella tried nervously to block the lantern on one side with her body until she remembered that the glass was one way. Still, when they reached the first floor offices she felt somewhat more secure. The silence made Nella want to hold her breath. They tried each door along the hall, finding only desk after empty desk.

"There may not be a first aid station on this level," Nella whispered, "They may be on the lab floors."

"In a place this big you'd think there would be something on each level- surely a security office or something. They wouldn't have left something like this unguarded. Even my tiny law firm had a security office."

They had almost reached the end of the corridor, where it branched off to the right and Nella caught a flicker of blue out of the corner of her eye. She froze and switched the lantern off with one finger.

"Nella, what-" started Frank. She shook her head and he was quiet. There was another flicker, like the flashing reflection of water. Nella looked down the side hallway. It was a slim tube of night, blank, unmoving, dead. Every door was closed except the last. Blue and gray light burst and receded across that corner of the hallway. There was no sound, just the moving flashes. Frank gently pushed past her, one long arm pulling her protectively behind his slim frame, the other holding the pistol. They were slow, as if it were a dream, a nightmare of endless swimming. Nella held the lantern in her aching right arm and let the fingers of her left hand brush one wall so she wouldn't fall if she tripped on something unseen.

The flashes made the darkness worse. Her eyes couldn't adjust. She felt sweat pool in the inside of her elbow and at her neck.

There was a loud screech and Nella's knees locked, cramping almost instantly. She saw Frank straighten and freeze for a few seconds. *It's an office chair*, she realized, *someone stretching in an old swivel office chair.*

Frank started forward again and she tried not to stumble as she took an extra few steps to catch up with him. They were only halfway down the hall.

She had time to wonder what he was going to do if it was someone dangerous. Was he really ready to fire the gun? He hadn't been last time. She felt a twisting thread of pain spiral down her arm, as if it were being bitten all over again. She wished it were she carrying the weapon. But a wave of shame burnt away the oily fear that clung to her. He was trying to protect her. He had protected her yesterday, even if it was a little late.

They neared the door and Frank pressed her gently against the wall and out of sight. He swung the door open and stood in the frame. Nella shut her eyes, bracing herself for the gunshot. At the same time she made a fervent wish that he wouldn't be forced to use it.

"Dr. Schneider?" he asked, his voice panicked and unbelieving.

"Who are you? How do you know me? Are you here from the government?" The woman's voice sounded tired and there was another screech as she stood up from the office chair.

"No- well, yes, but we're not here for the reason you think," said Frank, lowering the gun.

"We?"

Nella stepped into the fluttering blue light. "Dr. Schneider, you have no idea how relieved we are to find you here."

Gerta Schneider

Gerta Schneider was far more worn and disheveled than the image Nella remembered from Dr. Pazzo's video. The light from the television screen only added extra shadows to her eye sockets and cheeks. She was surprised Frank had recognized the woman at all. Nella wasn't sure she would have.

"If you're here to bring me in for the trial, you'll have to wait. I'm doing something far more important. I promise I won't try to flee, and I'll come without giving you trouble if you just let me have a little more time." Dr. Schneider glanced first at Nella and then Frank. Her shoulders hunched like a cornered animal ready to spring away.

Nella and Frank exchanged a look and Nella took a step forward. "We know why you're here Dr. Schneider. Dr. Carton told us you came back to find the more powerful strain of the Recharge bacteria. We just want to make sure it was destroyed."

Dr. Schneider sank back into the squealing office chair. "So the world knows then. Are you military? No- no you're Robert's attorney aren't you?"

"Frank Courtlen, yes I'm Robert Pazzo's lawyer. But besides the three of us, very few people know about the bacteria. We came to make sure it's destroyed before it can be released or cause a panic. We don't have much time before the military shows up though."

"And who are you?" she said, turning toward Nella.

"Nella Rider, the court psychiatrist."

"How did you get caught up in all this?"

"Dr. Pazzo gave us some recordings from your lab."

Dr. Schneider smiled grimly. "I ought to have

guessed. Well, Dr. Rider, Mr. Courtlen, it would seem we are all far too late. Someone, or several someones have already been through here. Whoever it was broke into the lab vault. The *only* thing they took was the Recharge vial." She waved her hand toward the security monitors, "I've been looking for a clue in the security camera footage. Unfortunately, some time ago the solar panels for the generator were obstructed by leaves and dirt from storms, so the coverage is intermittent at best. I cleaned them off over a month ago, but if you are thinking of turning on the lights, I'd reconsider. There is still at least one herd of Infected wandering nearby, not to mention the Looters."

"We know," Nella said grimly.

"How far have you watched?" asked Frank.

"I've gone back four years now. So far only a scavenging team and a few herds of Infected have even shown up on the screen. Only the scavenging team entered, it might have been them, but they left with medical supplies over six months ago. If they had the bacteria, why hasn't it hit yet? Besides, the other samples in the vault are beginning to denature. Some of it would have died within months, but the freeze dried samples should be good for years. I think the vault has been open for a very long time."

"Was the Recharge bacteria freeze dried? Could it still be infectious?" Nella almost choked on the question.

"The samples we were working with were frozen but we had two backup vials freeze dried. They are all missing. The freeze dried vials could be good for a decade or more." Dr. Schneider rubbed her eyes with the heel of one hand. "What's worse is that the vials are small and require no special equipment. They could be anywhere, with anyone. Except here, where they are supposed to be." She sighed.

"We'll help you," said Nella, "we'll figure out who has them, we have to. But I'm badly hurt and need rest. Frank does too, and you look like you haven't slept in months. Is there an infirmary here or a first aid station? Can we sleep tonight and go over everything in the morning?"

Dr. Schneider shrugged. "Why not? It's been eight years, what's one more day? I can't look at this anymore today any way. Come on, I made one of the executive offices pretty comfortable when I came back. We can at least turn on the lights up there."

Dr. Schneider flipped off the monitor and the room was clotted darkness.

"Nella, the lamp," Frank's voice was low but anger writhed beneath it. Nella turned the lantern back on. Frank had raised the pistol toward Dr. Schneider again. Nella was startled but Dr. Schneider just looked exhausted, worn through like an old shoe.

"Let me make something clear Dr. Schneider," Frank's words were bitten off and Nella was frightened to see that his hands no longer shook around the gun grip.

"We know you were the one who persuaded Ann Connelly to infect herself and then let her wander out into the public carrying the germ. We know you stole a sample from your own partner in order to develop a bacteria completely impervious to any antibiotic, before you even finished testing the weaker version and against the strenuous objection of Robert Pazzo. You may not be *solely* responsible for what happened, but you bear the lion's share.

"We are not your friends. You *are* going to be returned to the City for trial in a few days, whether or not we find the stolen sample. Nothing good has ever come from you. Your entire existence has caused nothing but misery and death. Even the Cure did more harm than good in most cases. I don't believe anything good *can* come from you. But this is a chance to prevent more devastation from clinging to you."

Dr. Schneider's exhausted expression didn't change. "I'm not going to try escaping Mr. Courtlen. I know Robert probably painted me as a villain, but none of what I did before the Plague, or since, was ever motivated by any evil intent."

"Just greed," Frank sneered.

"Please," interrupted Nella gently, "can we find somewhere to rest instead of arguing?" She wasn't really as exhausted as she let on, but she thought it was the best way to defuse the situation before someone got shot.

It had the desired effect, Frank immediately lowered the gun and came to her aid. Dr. Schneider moved toward the hallway. "This way," she said, "Try not to hold the lantern too high. The windows may be tinted but even the smallest light shining through will look like a lighthouse beacon these days."

Nella leaned on Frank to prevent him from becoming agitated again and they started down the hallway. "What made you come here now, Dr. Schneider?" she asked, "After all these years, why now?"

Dr. Schneider's voice floated coolly over her. "I thought the bacteria was safe here. Dr. Carton used his position to keep tabs on where the scavenging teams were going and this place was untouched. I always meant to get back here to destroy it, but something always prevented me. After a few years I just let it go and didn't think about it very often. No one was going to dig up this place or any like it. It's just an office building to anyone who didn't know what it was. Not exactly a high value looting target. And if they did come here, why would they take anything from the vault? The warning signs alone would scare the pants off the average Looter. But then I got a report that the scavenging scouts had been here and that the vault was lying open when they arrived.

"Only someone that wanted to destroy what was left of humanity would let the most dangerous diseases in the world thaw out of deep freeze to infect the next unlucky person to walk by. Thankfully, the frozen ones denatured long ago, before anyone could be infected. And the freeze dried ones are in a stable state, they won't infect anyone without being properly prepared. But I came anyway, to see if the Recharge Bacteria was safe, to destroy all the remaining viable samples of anything left in the vault. And when I found the Recharge samples missing, I decided to stay and try to figure out who took them."

Dr. Schneider pressed an elevator button. Nella had a strange sense of disorientation when the doors slid smoothly open to a brightly lit interior. They took the elevator to the executive floor.

"You said freeze dried samples need to be properly prepared- what would a person need to do that?" Frank was calm, but Nella could feel goosebumps rise on his arms and he tensed as he asked the question.

Dr. Schneider looked suspiciously at them for a few seconds. The elevator doors slid open with an alarming chime. The next hallway was just as dark. "Whoever has the bacteria would have to know what they are doing. Ideally, you'd open a freeze dried vial in a sterile environment and then basically drop the sample into a nutrient rich broth and let it incubate for a few hours or days. But it wouldn't really take that much to recreate those conditions. Someone with access to bleach, alcohol or even vinegar can sterilize both the vial and an area to work. A good beef broth and some plain gelatin would do the rest. As long as the sample wasn't exposed to the elements, it would be viable even in a cool area within a few days. We aren't talking major surgery here."

Dr. Schneider opened a smooth wooden door and flicked on a light switch. Nella and Frank hurried in and shut the door. The windows in the large room were all covered with black garbage bags and a giant executive's desk was shoved against one wall. The rest of the room was relatively bare.

"There's an executive bathroom attached. I brought up all the first aid kits I could find, just in case. You are welcome to use them. Do you mind if I take a look?" Dr. Schneider approached Nella and lifted the edge of her shirt without waiting for an answer.

"Uh- sure," said Nella, beginning to ease her way out of the sling and her sweater with Frank's help. She didn't want to look at the wound, afraid it would be worse than what she imagined, but she couldn't ignore Dr. Schneider's sharp intake of breath when the bandages were removed. Nella looked at Frank instead of Dr. Schneider. Instead of smiling reassuringly at her, he had gone very pale and tightened his arm around her waist.

"Let's put her down on the sleeping bags," Dr. Schneider said, "I've got some tetracycline from the labs. It should work if she has a staph infection, which is the most probable. It was a bite wasn't it?"

"Yes," said Frank as he eased Nella down onto the pile of sleeping bags in the center of the room, "But the guy was- well he was basically rotting from the inside out."

Frank followed Dr. Schneider toward the bathroom. "Did you sterilize the needle?" Dr. Schneider was asking as they walked out of earshot. Nella pictured Frank rolling his eyes and smiled in spite of her worry. At least they were working together. She sank back into the blankets, wishing for dose of aspirin. *Who knew it would take more than the end of the world to turn me into a drug addict*, she thought with a wry smile, *or that aspirin would be my drug of choice? Just as the bite on my hand gets better . . .* She tried to turn her thoughts away from her wounds as she waited for Frank and Dr. Schneider to return.

Dr. Schneider seemed to think it would be easy to revive the bacteria, but Nella realized very few people would still have access to beef. Bleach or vinegar, maybe, alcohol was practically it's own currency these days. Who would have access to cows though? The military still raised and butchered them, the Farm raised a few, mostly for milk products though. When a bull was killed it was like a festival in the City though. Everyone got some, but it was barely a scrap. But Dr. Schneider had said just broth. And gelatin. Gelatin was from the bones wasn't it? Those would be less in demand, but someone would still have to wait around for the cow to be killed. And then know the right person to ask. Nella didn't know very many people that were able to keep cows. She'd seen a lot of chicken coops in the City, but those were easy. In fact Chris and Sevita had a few and Nella contributed her table scraps to keep them going. A cow required a lot more land. Those that lived on the outskirts maybe? Nella shook her head. This was the wrong way to go about it. She'd never expected to have to think like a detective and she kept starting at the wrong spots.

The real key would finding out who *knew* about the Recharge bacteria. Who knew about it and who would want to use it? Or did anyone want to use it? Maybe someone knew about it and wanted it destroyed. Why wouldn't they have simply stepped forward and said so? Well, Nella admitted, they hadn't exactly been shouting from the rooftops about the Recharge bacteria. Maybe whoever it was didn't know anyone had found out. Maybe they were involved with creating it. Nella sighed. It all came back to who knew about the bacteria in the first place. Until she answered that, nothing else was certain.

Frank came back from the bathroom and Nella saw Dr. Schneider setting several supplies on the large desk.

"What are you going to do to me?" she asked Frank with a nervous laugh. He didn't return her smile but looked grim.

"Do you think you can manage a shower if I help?" he asked.

"Of course. There's a shower here?"

Frank helped her up. "Executive bathroom with all the bells and whistles."

"I would have killed for an office like this back in the day," Nella said. Frank finally grinned.

"Back in the day when you were still a lowly student intern?" he said. Nella laughed. They walked to the bathroom.

"I can probably do this myself," she said softly so that Dr. Schneider wouldn't overhear. Frank hesitated. "Don't be disappointed," she laughed, "this is not going to be attractive."

Frank blushed and smiled. "It's not that," he said, his tone turned serious, "Dr. Schneider thinks you have a fever and with the blood you've already lost, you might faint if you get in the hot water."

"There's hot water?" Nella said, distracted from her embarrassment for a moment.

"Yeah, the solar cells were meant for the whole building to run on. One tank of hot water isn't going to touch it." Frank shut the door. "I can sit with my back to the shower if you want."

Nella shook her head. "No, that's okay. I'm not entirely sure how well I can clean it out by myself anyway." She forced herself to look at her shoulder. It had formed a soft, dark scab, but the skin around the wound glowed and baked. It wasn't as horrific as she'd been expecting. She looked in the mirror, gingerly touching the deep red gouge that ran from the bottom of her breast to her hip. She was relieved that it was only slightly sore and not crawling with heat like her shoulder.

"You'll forget it's there after a while," Frank said from behind her, "and at least it's not on your face so casual observers won't remind you constantly."

A pang of shame struck Nella. "I wasn't thinking of the scar. I'm just glad that scrape is clean."

He lifted the hair from her shoulder and away from her wound. He kissed the base of her neck just outside the hot puffy ring of her wound. "Nella, I'm so sorry. I should have-"

She turned around to face him and held his bristly chin in her hands. "There wasn't anything you could do. We both knew what might happen. I got off pretty lightly considering. You didn't do this to me."

"I should have made you stay at the farm. You were so weak. And now I've made you even sicker."

"I'll be okay. You got everything out," she shuddered, "and if we clean it now, I should start to get better." She let him go and he stepped slightly back. He laid the gun beside her on the counter. He turned and locked the door. She watched him in the mirror as he stopped and stared at the doorknob.

"What is it?"

He shook his head but kept staring at the knob.

"What's wrong Frank?"

He looked at her, his face stricken with shock. "I can't tell you."

"What? Why?"

"I just can't. I'm sorry. Ask me later, when-when everything is over. Ask me anything then Nella, but I can't tell you now."

Frank collapsed onto the toilet lid, limbs folding like a marionette that had been cast away. He squeezed his head in his hands. "This is insane. What are we doing here?" He looked up at her as if she had some kind of answer for him.

"Trying to save what's left of the world."

"Right. A psychiatrist and a lawyer. The stuff of legends."

"Hey," she said crossing the room toward him, "We made it this far, didn't we?" She stopped in front of him and touched his shoulder. He pressed a hand on her stomach, touching the edge of the scratch gently.

"Yes. We got here. But I ruined you. And what did we come all this way for after all anyway?" Frank stared past her at the door again. Nella laughed to cover her confusion.

"I'm not ruined." She turned his face away from the door and back toward her, "And you didn't cause any of this."

What had he noticed? She glanced at the doorknob but didn't dare to stare. She scraped the backs of her nails against his stubble. "This must be itchy," she smiled trying to refocus him. His smile was automatic and it never reached wherever his eyes had gone. Nella sighed and stepped back. She turned on the shower. The hiss of the water snapped him free of his thoughts. Nella fumbled with her bra for an achy, frustrating moment and then felt his long fingers brushing her hair from her neck and unsnapping the clasps.

"You never will ask for help, will you?"

She didn't answer, but stepped out of the large jeans and then her underwear without looking behind her. She stood quietly so that she could hear he thud of his heavy shoes, first one and then another hitting the floor. His belt clicked and jangled and then the soft ripple of clothes falling away. She looked at the shower and tried not to feel the ache in her shoulder.

"Well?" he said, "Are you going to get in?"

Nella took a deep breath. "This is really going to hurt."

"Dr. Schneider said she had a little bit of morphine if you needed-"

Nella whirled around in alarm. "Frank, promise you won't let her inject me with *anything*. I don't know her. I don't trust her."

"That's what I thought you would say."

"I can't believe you are leaving her out there unguarded after that speech downstairs."

Frank's smile vanished. "Where is she going to go? It's pitch black and there are Infected and Looters in every direction. Besides, I don't really much care whether she really goes back for trial or not."

"You don't? Why not?"

"No, I don't. The way I see it, she's never going to live happily ever after. Even if she escaped, she would be living out here, in constant fear and danger, without allies, without a safe haven. A lifetime of that is enough punishment even for my worst enemy."

"Then why tell her we are taking her back?"

"Because the world needs her to go on trial. They need some sort of justice for the people involved in this."

Nella frowned. "You mean the world needs vengeance. Not justice."

"If you like that word better. I guess, yeah, the world needs some kind of revenge for what it has lost. Because there isn't justice enough for what's been done to us. By us. It always seems to go that way, after bad times."

"But this was an accident at worst, not a planned attempt to wipe out the world. Why her and not Dr. Pazzo? Why her and not Ann? After all Ann was a willing patient zero. Who gets to decide?"

He put a hand on her hip. "Nella, I'm no

longer sure that it *was* an accident. I'm not so sure that whatever happens next wasn't planned before either of us got involved."

"What are you talking about?"

"Never mind, get in before the water turns cold, you're covered in goosebumps."

Nella realized she was looking at him without meaning to. She blushed and stepped into the shower. The water was too heavy, like thousands of flaming hail stones smashing into her bruised skin. The pain was so intense for a moment that she thought she would vomit, but then Frank was standing in front of her, holding her against his still-cool skin. "It's okay," he kept saying in a voice she felt, rather than heard, rattle in his chest. She didn't know why he kept saying it until the wave of nausea passed and she heard her own voice sobbing and felt her legs shaking underneath her. Her skin gradually stopped screaming as if she'd been peeled down to the raw nerves and the water started to feel softer and more natural.

"I'm sorry," she said at last, "You must think I'm such a coward. I can't handle even one bite and you had a dozen. I can't imagine dying this way, devoured alive." She shut her eyes and shuddered.

"I don't think you're a coward. It was excruciating and I was only bitten by a small boy. You had a piece torn off by a full grown man." She felt him catch a sob and hold it back, but his voice was thick, clotted, when he began again. "I try not to think about what it must be like to die that way either. I can't forget how sad and frightened Sarah looked as I leapt at her. I think of it every day."

She pulled back from him and looked up at him. "Frank, I'm so sorry. I should have thought before I opened my mouth."

Frank shook his head and pushed a strand of

wet hair off of her face. "Don't be sorry. I'm glad you can forget that detail about me, even if it's only for a moment. It's more than I deserve and I'm grateful there is someone in the world who doesn't immediately and perpetually think of me as a monster." He reached past her for the soap, quietly clearing his throat. "Real soap. Are you ready?"

It wasn't as bad as she had expected, now that the initial shock of the water had worn off. She was sore, but clean, feeling hollowed out and left to dry in the sun. The heat of the water soon made her dizzy and another wave of nausea passed over her, forcing them out of the warm bathroom. The cool, dry air of the exterior office was a relief, though Frank still had to help her sit beside the large desk. Dr. Schneider looked grim, but she was relatively gentle.

"You know," she said as she inspected the stitches in Nella's shoulder, "The Recharge bacteria was never meant to harm anyone. I don't know if Dr. Pazzo ever told you that. It was meant to help. It was supposed to change everything for the better."

"But you didn't follow normal procedures. Ones that were set up to avoid disaster like this," Nella said gently.

"It wasn't stubbornness or greed that made me speed up testing," Dr. Schneider snapped. "All the primary tests were exactly, *exactly* as predicted. Robert assured me there was nothing abnormal at all. This method was supposed to help people. It was supposed to help police and medical aid workers and firemen make it safely through crises. No more injuries due to fatigue or slow thinking. No more lives lost because of careless mistakes due to overworked specialists. It was supposed to help lift depression and alleviate all the ills stemming from exhaustion, stress and trauma. All without drugs. No risk of abuse or addiction. Very low cost, much lower than other treatments. Can you imagine the changes in society when everyone, down to the poorest could be treated for mental illness? Can you imagine the happier, healthier, perhaps even less violent place it could have been? This was something we needed *immediately.* The world was tearing itself apart and this bacteria faced years, decades even, of further testing and verification. It would have been lunacy *not* to test a more powerful strain at the same time."

Nella drew in a hissing breath as Dr. Schneider became more vigorous in applying antibiotic cream onto her shoulder. Frank grabbed Dr. Schneider's wrist to stop her and the doctor looked up. "Sorry," she said, "surely you can see why I'd want to move the testing along? People needed this technology as soon as we could produce it. Not ten years later. You must understand how beneficial it was supposed to be. It was going to change medicine forever."

"It did, Dr. Schneider. Here we all are, almost a decade later, and I'm in danger of dying from an infection which would have meant a simple trip to the pharmacy before. Medicine *has* changed. It's been set back by a century. Maybe forever."

"Not just medicine," Frank broke in, "Civilization, in fact. Our grandparents had easier lives than our children will. Than our grandchildren will."

Dr. Schneider unrolled a gauze bandage around Nella's arm. "I hardly think that's a fair judgment," she said quietly, "I *did* do my best to fix it."

Nella sighed. "It's not us you have to convince, though I can't say you are even doing that. Help us find the lost samples and maybe the world will find you more persuasive."

Frank's color rose and he glanced toward the bathroom door again. It was so quick that Nella barely saw it. Dr. Schneider taped the end of the bandage down and cleared away the first aid kit, walking away from them. Frank leaned against the large desk and watched Dr. Schneider. Nella watched him.

"You know where it is." Nella was shocked to realize it.

Frank looked shaken and she could see small points of sweat glittering on his head. "No!" he said loudly and then lowered his voice to a whisper, bending toward her. "I swear Nella, if I did then I'd tell you. I'd tell everyone, consequences be damned."

"Then you guess."

"Not even that." He glanced at Dr. Schneider to be sure she wasn't watching them. "I promise, the moment I know something, *anything* for sure, then I *will* tell you. My hunches though, would only do harm."

He leaned back as Dr. Schneider returned. She handed Nella a pill bottle. "These will help with the pain. No more than two at a time."

"That's my cue," said Frank grabbing the lantern, "I'll be right back with the pack."

Dr. Schneider looked nervous as Frank left the room. Nella was too exhausted to wonder why. She dry swallowed a pill and winced at the bitter powder it left on her tongue. She thought about slipping the sling back over her neck so that she wouldn't move her shoulder in her sleep. But then her elbow creaked and cramped in protest and she decided against it. Dr. Schneider had already slipped into her sleeping bag and was facing the empty wall. Assured that no one would interrupt her thoughts for a moment, Nella looked back at the bathroom door. What was so important about it? It was just a door. It wasn't special in any way, and she racked her brain trying to think if they had seen an identical one any where. No memories were triggered. It was just a *door*. But that wasn't right. He hadn't been looking at the door. He had been staring at the doorknob. Nella stood up. She took a few steps toward the bathroom when she heard the elevator chime down the quiet hall. Her limbs tensed as a painful jolt of adrenaline shot through her. *It's only Frank, of course*, she thought, but she retreated to the seat by the desk again, still puzzled.

"Fresh clothes," Frank said with a grin as he walked through the door.

"Bed," Nella said with a smile. Her limbs felt like giant kelp floating in a current and there was a buzzing tingle behind her eyes. She wasn't sure if it was fatigue or the drugs. She let Frank help her dress in something clean and then crawled under the sleeping bag. She managed to wait until he was lying beside her, his hand curled around hers, before she fell down the smooth grey well in her mind.

THE VAULT

The windows were blocked, so Nella had no idea whether it was day or night when she woke, but she sat up with only one idea in her head. It wasn't the door Frank had been fascinated with. It wasn't the doorknob either. *It was the lock.* But why? Nella looked around her. Both Frank and Dr. Schneider were still asleep. She thought about taking another painkiller to stop the gnawing grind in her shoulder, but the idea that Frank was bothered by the lock had grown enormous in her mind. Something important hovered just beyond her groggy thoughts. If she could concentrate, she knew she could find out what it was. She had the overwhelming feeling it was something she *ought* to know.

Nella fumbled in the dark for the lantern. She switched it on, blocking the light with her body and slipped out of the quiet office. The hall and the world outside were pale gray with early morning light. She switched off the lantern and left it just outside the door. For a moment she was at a loss. What was she doing? She decided to go to the vault. If anything in this place had to do with a lock, it must be there. She was no detective, but she had an undeniable urge to see it for herself, to see if there were any clues about who had been there before her. She walked down the hallway toward the elevator. When she got to the smooth little panel with the call button, she began to feel distinctly creepy. What if she called the elevator and it arrived with someone already inside? She told herself not to be ridiculous, but once she had imagined it, there was no shaking the idea. She became more and more certain that if she called it, there would *definitely* be someone inside. Would it be a decomposing corpse simply jumbled like an abandoned marionette against the back wall? Or a Looter armed to the teeth and ready to grab whatever, whomever he wanted? Or just an Infected, mad and starving, stretched hide over the empty drum of its ribs, all jaw and talon? Nella backed away from the elevator doors almost without realizing it. She decided to look for the stairs instead.

The stairs were almost worse. With a slim window every other floor, the weak morning light was barely a glow against the concrete floor. Every step Nella took was echoed three times in the small stairwell so that it sounded like there were a crowd running after her. She forced herself to keep climbing, more from shame at letting the idea of the elevator defeat her, than in any real desire to get to the vault alone. Nella was grateful that it was only one floor. She had to rest a the top, sitting on the last step in front of the stairwell door. Her shoulder pounded and her breath was harsh and loud in the stairwell. She worried briefly at her body's weakness, wondering if the infection in her arm might truly kill her. She'd been exaggerating the night before, trying to drive a point home with Dr. Schneider, but now it hit her as true. The drugs to help her were simple. Simple enough that they were still being reproduced in a rudimentary way, but not for public consumption. Not for an affordable price, anyway. Nella sighed, startling herself with the echoes. Her body was just going to have to shake off the infection by itself. And climbing stairs when it was unnecessary wasn't going to help her do that. She stood up and opened the staircase door.

She felt tiny ants of unease creep over her skin as she faced a rounded silver door surrounded by contamination instructions and biohazard warnings in bright yellow and black, like hornets descending upon her. The door, which was supposed to be failsafe, airtight, unbreachable, was propped open with what looked like an old shoe. Nella felt a dryness creep from a patch in the back of her throat until it filled her chest with desert sand. *Don't be stupid*, she told herself, *those doors haven't been necessary for years. Dr. Schneider, the scavenger scouts and whoever took the sample have all been inside and they are fine.* Still, she couldn't argue the instinctual dread she had of entering. It was so palpable that Nella could imagine the smell of infection, could almost convince herself that she smelled a slight sourness, like fruit turning or like the clinging scent where roadkill once died, years before. She knew infection didn't have a smell, but she almost smelled it anyway. She thought if she moved her head just right, she'd catch a whiff in the breeze her movement made. She reminded herself again not to be ridiculous and walked through the airlock door.

She was in a dark, tiny passageway. She found the light switch and powerful overheads clicked on. The small room was lined with benches and white plastic suits. At the far end was a sink and another airlock door, again held open with a shoe. The first one's mate. Nella wondered why there were no alarms. Wasn't there supposed to be an alarm when the airlocks weren't working correctly? She passed through the door and turned on the next light. The overheads competed with a small star of purple light sitting in the center of the room. She tried not to look at it, afraid it would somehow harm her and passed through the next open door, this one held open by a silver instrument cart. The drains in this room hinted that it was for decontamination showers, but nothing happened as Nella passed through, and she again wondered why none of the decontamination systems were working as intended. Was it because the samples were all dead? Or had they been disabled? And if they were disabled, who had enough knowledge of lab procedure to know how to do that? The airlock at the end of the shower room gaped open into a dark void. She held her breath without even realizing it and stepped inside, fumbling for the light switch, but it did nothing when flipped. She waited until her eyes adjusted to the dim, milky light seeping in through the high, dirty windows.

Nella immediately realized why no alarms were activated with the airlocks forced open. Whoever had opened the vault had attempted to incinerate it. She wondered how the rest of the floor, the rest of the building, actually, had avoided catching fire. All of the surfaces were covered with soot. The scavenger team and Dr. Schneider had left footprints in the thin layer of ash on the floor. Beakers had melted into coin sized puddles of glass, now dark medallions fused with the lab tables. Along the edges of the room were round vats, all hanging open like hell's buried treasure chests dug up. Nothing else was recognizable. Nella walked carefully over to one of the vats. They had no soot inside and the glass vials seemed intact, which meant they must have been opened after the fire rather than before. Except one. She could see it in the gray light, its lid cracked and blackened. She walked over to it. She could only see into the top part of the cylinder, but it was enough. The vials had melted in place, their rack holders surrounding a thin stem of collapsed glass. Three empty slots were all that was left of the Recharge bacteria.

"I found it like this, except the other storage containers were closed."

Nella whirled around, startled by Dr. Schneider's voice. She was relieved to see Frank standing by the door behind the doctor.

"I tried to find out if it had been misclassified,

or if the vials had been moved to another container." Dr. Schneider peered into the closest container. "I went through the records and surviving vials for all ten thousand samples. One by one. But the Recharge bacteria was gone. That's when I started on the security tapes," she looked up at Nella, "which I recommend we get back to. We only have a few days."

"Wait, Dr. Schneider. You never said anything about a fire. Aren't these labs designed to initiate a burn when there is a containment leak?"

"It's not automatic. You wouldn't want someone burned alive in here. There is a panel outside the next door and one in the security office downstairs in case of an accident. The burn can be initiated from either place."

"But the power would have to be on, right?"

"Well, yes. But the lab also has a back up generator. Besides, the entire building also has emergency power from the solar cells."

Nella walked toward the lab door. She noticed Frank looked nervous and shot him a confused glance. "How long was the backup generator designed to run?"

"Seventy two hours. But right now it's on the solar energy."

"But those panels were not functioning when you got here, right?"

"Yes, they were luckily unbroken, but they were covered with leaves and sticks that had blown over them through the years. Where is this all going?"

"When the main power went off, how long would it take to switch to the solar panels?"

"Dr. Carton said the solar panels were already working when he left the lab after the outbreak. In fact, he said he had planned to stay here, but the solar panels couldn't handle the whole building's power and he was worried about lack of heat and running out of food. That's why he left."

Frank stared intently at Nella. At last he said, "I think we should watch the first security recordings. Not work our way backwards."

"What?" asked Dr. Schneider, "Why?"

Nella turned to look at Dr. Schneider. "When I was in medical school, we were required to learn biosafety procedures, regardless of our final professions. Level four labs, which, I assume this is, are required to have the capability for a controlled burn of several hours in case of an accident. That means a steady stream of fuel. Which also means a steady source of power to control it. The solar panels just aren't reliable enough. Dr. Carton would already have drained the battery significantly after the main lines went out. It had to be when the backup generators were triggered."

"Well, that wouldn't have been until the solar panels weren't creating enough power to sustain this lab."

"Right," said Frank, "the outbreak was in December, remember? That's why it was so bad, because travel and public interaction was so much heavier than normal."

"I remember quite clearly, Mr. Courtlen. As I said, Dr. Carton was worried about the heat-"

"Exactly," interrupted Frank, "And how much less would the solar panels have produced when they were covered with snow? The backup generators must have kicked on within weeks, maybe days. Certainly within the first year."

"Whoever did this covered their tracks with the fire. And knew the control procedures were still in place and available for use." Nella said it slowly, thinking it aloud rather than announcing it. Frank looked downright ashen and seemed to sway like a tall tree in wind as she said it. Dr. Schneider turned and ran from the lab. Frank sprang after her. Nella felt exhausted, the pain from her shoulder leaking into her side as well. She thought about the stairs she'd have to take if she avoided the elevator again.

She stumbled out to the changing room and sat on the bench. She disliked waiting for help, but she knew that Frank would be back soon, disappointed that the crucial footage was missing. Nella already knew that a person didn't break into a level four lab, set a fire to cover their tracks and then smile at the camera.

She gently rubbed her sore shoulder, looking at the dead electrical panel near the airlock. Whoever did this had to have both the entry code and know how to activate the emergency purge. A lab employee? Or maybe someone that was able to get into the security office? It wouldn't have been hard with the building abandoned in the panic. Nella closed her eyes, half dozing as she tried to think through who would have known about and wanted access to the Recharge bacteria.

Dr. Carton and Dr. Schneider were both obvious choices. They both knew the building procedures for the lab. They both knew about the bacteria, and they, more than anyone else except Dr. Pazzo, perhaps, would want to keep it secret. Without the samples and documentation, no one would ever be able to prove that they had caused the epidemic. That, in essence, was what Dr. Schneider was doing here now. But someone else had beaten both Schneider and Carton to it. And that person hadn't destroyed the samples, just taken them away. What were they planning on doing with them? Why do nothing for almost a decade?

The only other people that knew about the existence of the resistant strain were Dr. Pazzo and

Ann Connelly, at least, as far as Nella knew. If the samples had been taken in order to blackmail one of the scientists, then the thief would have had to ensure that Ann and Dr. Pazzo survived in order to be witnesses. Nella opened her eyes. Whoever had taken care of Dr. Pazzo and Ann also stole the Recharge samples. She shook her head. What were they waiting for? The trial had already started without Dr. Carton and without Dr. Schneider. The time to come forward or to get what they wanted had already come. Maybe it wasn't blackmail.

Revenge? That seemed more likely to Nella. She had met many, many people who wanted revenge for what had happened. For what each person had faced, for what they had to do, even now, to survive. She had even met people so miserable and full of anger that they'd take the rest of the world with them by releasing the bacteria if it meant vengeance. She sighed as she realized that maybe even Frank had been that angry once. That maybe even *she* had been that angry once.

But then why keep Ann and Dr. Pazzo alive? They were readily available scapegoats. Nella looked back toward the seared lab. This had happened quickly. Too quickly after the outbreak for some elaborate plot of revenge. It was too fast. Who would have known that these particular people were responsible? It took the military years to figure it out. No one could know that fast. Unless Dr. Carton were lying about where he was after the outbreak. Or someone else was.

Nella was too tired to keep wearing out the circular path in her brain. She felt a buzzing behind her eyes and the heat from her shoulder was overwhelming. She closed her eyes.

SICK

Nella woke with a gasp as cool water hit her face. "Wake up Nella, please wake up." Frank was hovering over her.

"Is it the Infected? I don't think I can get to the farm house." It sounded wrong in her ears. As if she'd already said it.

"No Infected, we're safe. In the lab, remember?"

Nella tried to turn her head to see but she became dizzy and she shut her eyes again. The cool water splashed her again. She shivered.

"You have to do something!" She heard Frank yelling at someone. He was so angry.

"There's nothing I can do. She's got a massive dose of antibiotics already." The woman's voice was nasty and cold.

Nella opened her eyes again. "What do you want me to do, Frank?" Her voice was dry and her throat felt as if it held the sun. He bent over her again. "You don't need to do anything. Just rest." He passed a wet cloth over her face. She felt her shirt being unbuttoned and he pressed the cold cloth against her chest. She shivered again.

"It's too cold," the woman's voice floated over them again. Nella tried to remember whose it was but she couldn't. "If you make her shiver her temperature will only go up more. You need to put her in a warm bath."

"Is there a bath here somewhere?"

"Down on the clinical floors. There are a few patient rooms. I don't know if the water runs anymore."

The world tilted as Frank lifted her. "Let's go." Nella looked up at his face. It was pinched and menacing.

"Don't be mad, Frank," she said.

He looked down at her and brushed the sweaty hair from her forehead. "I'm not mad at you Nella." The world lurched as he walked toward the elevator. Nella tried not to vomit. She heard the elevator chime.

"Not there," she whispered, "not there, the dead people will get you." She drifted off again into a thick drowze.

Water crawled under her legs and Nella woke up again in a dusty tub.

"We have to turn the lights off," hissed the woman's voice. Nella forced herself to focus. Dr. Schneider looked even more wild and angry than yesterday. "The Infected or the Looters will see."

"Shut up. If you're that worried go find some blankets to cover the windows. Otherwise stay out of my way. You already told me there's nothing else you can do." Nella tilted her head back and saw Frank kneeling by her shoulder. Dr. Schneider slammed the door on her way out. Frank looked down and saw she was awake. He smiled and held up a white cup. "Can you drink something for me?" He tilted the cup toward her before she could answer. It was cool and soft on her throat. The bath water was warm and pooling around her lower back. She vomited up the mouthful of water he'd just given her.

"Sorry," she said.

He wiped her mouth with the cool cloth. "It's okay. We'll try again in a minute."

"Why are we here?"

Frank stroked her hair and she let her cheek cool on the dusty porcelain. "I have to cool you down. Your shoulder is infected very badly and you have a bad fever."

"Is there a tooth in there?" she asked and

immediately knew that was wrong.

She saw a tear roll down Frank's long cheek. "No, the tooth is gone. I took it out, remember?"

"Don't cry. I'll try to drink again."

He held the cup for her. She swallowed a little and it stayed. Frank shut the water off. He splashed her stomach and chest with the warm water.

She closed her eyes for what seemed like a moment. When she opened them, she was back on the sleeping bag and Frank was pacing the room. She didn't see Dr. Schneider. She was half lucid and sweating through the fabric underneath her.

"Did you find it?" she said, still not understanding why Frank was so worried.

He sat down beside her and pressed the damp cloth to her neck. "Find what?" he said.

"The lock. No the key. Dr. Pazzo's key. Or was it Dr. Schneider's? No. She broke out."

Frank went pale. "Nella, are you really awake?"

"Yes, I think so. I'm still confused."

He held up a cup and she swallowed some water. "Tell me what to do. I'm not a doctor and Schneider won't help. What do I do?"

Nella tried to think. She was so hot. "About the fever?" she guessed.

"Yes, what do I do? You have antibiotics already. We gave you another dose."

She tried to sit up but couldn't force herself up. Her shoulder blazed with pain. Frank caught her and held her up. She took the cup from him and swallowed another mouthful. Everything hurt, even her teeth. She looked at his worried face. "Nothing to do Frank. It's old medicine, no good any more."

Frank shook his head. "She said it should still work."

Nella shrugged and then winced in pain.

"Maybe it's not the right medicine. The fever means my body is working. It has to get the teeth out." Nella shook her head. "No, that's not right. Take me to the shower. It's too hot. I have to cool down."

He looked doubtful but he lifted her up. "Not the elevator. There's Infected in the elevator," she said, fading.

She woke up in the shower. He was holding her and the water was cool on her skin. "Don't die Nella," he was saying.

"Everything dies Frank." Her eyelids felt heavy and sore but she was truly aware this time. "It's okay. The world will keep going."

"Mine won't."

She lifted her face with an immense effort. "I love you," she said.

She felt a soft rumble in his chest as he laughed. "Tell me again when you're better and I'll believe you."

She heard the water turn off and he wrapped her in a towel. He carried her to the sleeping bag and she fell into a deep sleep where nothing chased her.

She woke up in the electric light of the office. Frank was sleeping beside her. She shifted to see if Dr. Schneider was there and Frank woke up. "How are you feeling?" he asked.

"How many days has it been?"

"Only two. Don't worry. We have time. I should have made you stay at the farm house. You need to rest."

She reached an aching, heavy arm to touch his face. "So do you. Go back to sleep."

He turned and kissed her palm. "No," he said, shaking his head, "Schneider said you need to eat if we're going to move you in the next few days. Do you think you can?"

"I think so. Will you go to sleep if I do?"

He sat up and rummaged through the pack. "Only if you'll sleep some more too." He found a can of beans. Nella made a face. "You need the protein," he said.

She smiled at him. "Thank you for taking care of me," she said.

Frank blushed and cranked the can opener.

THE MEDICAL REVOLUTION

It was almost laughably predictable. Nella watched Frank and Dr. Schneider comb through the first tapes for the third time without comment. She had tried to tell them that whoever set the fire in the vault must have had the security codes and it was unlikely that they'd left video footage of themselves behind. But Dr. Schneider was convinced that whoever it was would have missed *something*. There were so many power outages, that they couldn't tell when the cameras had been deliberately stopped and when the solar cells had been depleted.

Nella tried to use the time more wisely, attempting to engage Dr. Schneider in conversation, but the videos engrossed the doctor's attention. Nella had to wait until late afternoon, when they were all exhausted, to get Dr. Schneider to concentrate.

Dr. Schneider sat slumped in her chair not bothering to watch the video feed that never changed, where only the light moved. Frank had left, going back to the executive office to pack their gear in frustration. Nella sat, quite forgotten by both, and she watched Dr. Schneider.

"Who knew about the Recharge bacteria?"

"Huh?" Dr. Schneider looked wearily around at Nella.

"I know you and Dr. Carton knew, as well as Ann and Dr. Pazzo, but who else knew?"

Dr. Schneider pinched the bridge of her nose as she thought. "Well, if you mean the original version, the university administration had a vague overview of the project. Our funding partners had a few more details, but the in depth lab work was solely up to Dr.

Pazzo, Ann and myself. I brought Dr. Carton in later. If you mean who knew about the more powerful strain, then it was only the four of us. Dr. Carton and myself didn't want any extra attention until the trials were done. We were due to brief a team here on lab testing, but the outbreak happened first."

Nella watched her intently, allowing the reason for her secrecy to pass by unspoken. "Do you think Dr. Carton was telling the truth about where he's been since the outbreak?"

Dr. Schneider looked up with a sudden twitch of her head. Her eyes narrowed and her lips twisted into a nasty, secretive grin. "What has Michael told you about where he's been and what he's done? Not the real truth, surely?"

The question prowled between them. Nella began to revise her opinion of Dr. Schneider almost without realizing it. "He told me that he was in such fear for his life that he resorted to aping the Infected. He told me he wandered for months that way until you found him and brought him back to the City." She watched Dr. Schneider's grin sour slightly. "He also told me that you made him- eliminate the evidence of your experimentation with the Cure until you got it right." Nella felt her gorge rise, a painful stone scraping along her throat.

The nasty grin was back. Dr. Schneider leaned back in her seat. "Well, Dr. Rider, food was scarce. Waste not, want not, am I right?"

Nella kept her face neutral with some effort. "I thought you cared for Dr. Carton," she said in a casual tone.

"What does my relationship with Dr. Carton have to do with anything?"

"I think your relationships with all of your business associates are at the root of why we're here now. After all, it was your suggestion that Ann expose herself during your testing phase was it not? And your persuasion that convinced Dr. Carton to bypass procedure and steal a sample of the Recharge bacteria in order to work on a more powerful strain- against the express opinion of Dr. Pazzo. And your extended absences from the lab was a brilliant use of passive-aggression. After all, the sleep deprivation of both Ann and Dr. Pazzo caused them to miss not only symptoms they might have caught earlier, but also your activities with Dr. Carton's lab."

"I thought you were supposed to be impartial. I see Dr. Pazzo has persuaded you that I am the villain here. Let me remind you that he and Ann were free to leave at any point, they weren't my slaves or captives. I've explained to you that Dr. Pazzo assured me that the strain was *safe*, that all the experimental results were normal. What does it matter if I persuaded Ann to progress the experiment at a slightly accelerated level? What happened would have happened anyway."

"That argument may work in court with lay people, Dr. Schneider, but you and I both know that isn't true. If the testing went as it ought to have gone, the human testers would have been isolated and observed. The chances of an epidemic resulting from a controlled experiment would have been miniscule."

Dr. Schneider waved her hand dismissively. "Why are we even arguing? You've already decided that I'm guilty. Let me remind you that I was the one that cured the disease. What did Dr. Pazzo do? Nothing. He and Ann sat drooling in their monkey cages for months while I worked. Dr. Carton was demented, little more than a garbage disposal system. It was *me. I* cured all those people, without me, what's left of civilization wouldn't be here. We'd all be dead or bestial. It's because of *me* that society continues."

Nella laughed bitterly, her professional mask

flaking off in the heat of her anger. "Without you? Without you the world would be just as it was a decade ago. Without you, billions of people that are now dead would be living out their lives with their families. No one would be haunted by what they had to do to survive or what they'd done when they weren't themselves. You may have stopped the disease but you can't ever clean up the harm that you've done."

Dr. Schneider stood up, her dark eyes were empty holes in the pallor of her face. "Does this conversation have a point? You aren't my judge, I'm not here to justify myself to you."

"I was inclined to feel sorry for you before I met you. I was convinced that you were simply a victim of circumstance. I see now that I was wrong. You created the circumstance for yourself. I still might be sympathetic, except you, alone of all the people I've met Immune or Infected, you show no remorse at all. The point of this conversation was to find out if Dr. Carton was telling the truth about where he'd been. You've confirmed it rather callously, so I'll waste no more time on it. What we're looking for isn't here and I don't think you know any more about it than you've already said. The sooner we get back to the City and turn you over to the authorities, the better."

Nella began to get up and saw Frank watching them from the doorway. "I couldn't agree more," he said grimly. "Unfortunately, the sun is going down. I don't want to risk walking at night in the open. And Nella needs more sleep. We'll have to stay one more night."

Dr. Schneider sneered at Frank. "You *walked* here? The court must not want me that badly after all. We can take my car and get this over with. I don't want to be around you people any longer than necessary."

Nella looked surprised and Dr. Schneider whirled around toward her. "You underestimate me. You may be able to dismiss the Cure, but I assure you, most of the world will not. I've already retained the best attorney. When I find the stolen samples, and I *will*, I'll be heralded as a savior."

Frank's voice was quiet but menacing. "No one is ever going to believe you're a savior. I'll make sure of that."

"You're both officers of the court. You can't testify against me. It's a breach of confidence for Dr. Rider and a conflict of interest for you."

"Dr. Carton can testify," said Nella quietly. She stood up, ignoring Dr. Schneider's contempt for that suggestion. She and Frank headed back to the executive office, leaving Dr. Schneider to fume by herself.

"Sorry," Nella said into the silent elevator.

Frank smiled at her for the first time in what felt like days. "What for?"

"I didn't want to create more tension, but I needed to find out if she or Dr. Carton were lying about where the samples are."

"They aren't here. I don't think Dr. Schneider has any clue where they are."

The elevator doors opened and they walked slowly into the artificial dark of the boarded up office. Frank flipped the light switch as the door closed behind them. The smile had faded from his face and he looked as if he had swallowed something bitter. "This was such a waste of a trip." He turned toward her and gently untied the sling on her wounded arm. She sighed with relief as her arm relaxed.

"At least Dr. Schneider is going to be brought to trial," Nella said as he checked her bandages. He scowled.

"Her karma would have gotten her in the end.

It still will. She isn't worth you getting injured like this."

"What do we do now?"

Frank shook his head. "I don't know. What I don't get is why whoever has it has waited so long. What are they waiting for? Maybe the samples were destroyed after all."

"Frank, you don't know who has them do you?"

He sat down on the carpeted floor, hugging his long legs and staring off into space. "I don't. I realize you think I'm hiding something from you, and- well, I guess I am. But I don't think it is very important and I don't think it has to do with the samples. I've just got a hunch that something is off. I'm not even sure what it is exactly."

"Then I guess we're back to figuring out what to do next."

"We need to tell Judge Hawkins that we haven't found anything. I'm afraid that whoever has it has been waiting for this trial, or the verdict. If that's the case we need to prepare everyone somehow." He glanced up at her, "And you need to get some medical attention. That's going to cause questions as it is."

"But if we warn people, then whoever has it may forget their plan and release the bacteria immediately."

"What choice do we have?"

Nella sat down in front of him. "Give me a few more days. I know I've almost got it figured out. I can feel it, just beyond the edge of my thoughts. We can turn Dr. Schneider in to the prison and delay our conversation with Judge Hawkins until Sunday. That will give me tomorrow and the next day to work on it."

"If that's what you think would be best, that's what we'll do."

They heard the elevator bell and exchanged a glance but stopped talking. Frank helped her into the sleeping bag and they went to bed without saying anything further to each other or Dr. Schneider.

THE WARDEN

The sun was shining as if it were midsummer when they left Dr. Carton's lab. It made Nella feel more cheerful in spite of what she knew was to come. When the car emerged from the dark underground parking lot and onto the gravel, the exhaustion dropped away from her and she felt a skip in her breath, as if she were skimming over the world rather than in it. Frank was driving and Dr. Schneider had taken the passenger seat, so Nella couldn't catch his eye. She wished she could. In that minute, just for that minute, she felt as if everything was going to be all right. She didn't know where the Recharge bacteria samples were, or if they would be released, but for that minute, it didn't matter so much. The world would keep on going, the sun would be as bright and the spring would be as green with or without the last tiny anthills of remaining humans. Things would go on without her, too, and that was something that gave her great comfort.

Frank felt little need for secrecy on the return trip, and the only trouble they ran into was losing the road in the high grass a few times. He drove carefully and they were able to return to the military maintained road by late afternoon. Nella was fascinated in looking behind the car. She expected it to leave a heavy trail of tracks, but the grass was so thick from years of growth, that it mostly sprang up behind them, as if they had never passed there.

They stopped at the farmhouse around midmorning, wanting to see if the people they had cured remained. Frank got out of the car without saying anything, though Dr. Schneider kept asking why they had stopped. Nella waited in the car, afraid of what he would find. She heard him calling, "Hello!"

several times in the still warm air. He walked quickly back to the car and leaned down to her open window with a grin. "All gone," he said, "the supplies too. No- no casualties."

Nella leaned back, relieved. They made it back to the junkyard in a matter of a few hours. They abandoned the extra car to the cheerful junkyard manager over the strenuous objections of Dr. Schneider. Nella had little sympathy for her, and Frank predicted that she would need it no longer. The afternoon cast long cool shadows across the road as they drove to the prison in silence. The car, like Frank, smelled like clean linen and Nella relaxed as she felt sleep pulling at her, a thrumming tide that echoed the tires. Returned to familiar surroundings and the welcome sight of people walking in the warm evening, she slipped into a healing doze.

The slam of the door rocked the car and she woke, startled to find she had been sleeping so deeply. Frank was leading Dr. Schneider into the low gray lump of the prison. Nella straightened up, her arm stiff and painful in the sling. She tried to smooth the tangles out of her filthy hair with one hand and got out. She was mildly embarrassed to appear so disheveled, simply because she had striven to be professional since the beginning of the process. But if Frank could do it, so could she. She caught up to them just outside the heavy glass door. Frank held it open for her. His face was grim, but she knew it wasn't because of her. Dr. Schneider was almost scowling. Frank spoke briefly to a guard and then sat in an angular plastic chair as if at ease. Nella slipped into a chair next to him.

"We need to wait for the Warden Dr. Schneider," Frank said with a cold smile, "this may take a while, you may want to take a seat." Dr. Schneider just glared at him and continued standing.

It was a good half hour before the Warden arrived from his office, with several guards in tow. Nella wondered if it were for show or part of procedure. Some things just clung on like that, even after all that had happened.

She thought the Warden looked more like an elderly priest than a hardened prison guard. "Mr. Courtlen, Dr. Rider, to what do I owe the pleasure?" he smiled jovially and shook each of their hands in turn, the florescent light bouncing of his glasses like a secret chuckle.

"We're here to turn Gerta Schneider over to your custody. She is wanted in connection with the December Plague case. She has been cooperative and accompanied us willingly. If there is any reason to note that, please do so."

The Warden looked startled. "Mr. Courtlen, this is highly unusual. There are procedures that must be followed, even these days-"

Dr. Schneider spoke up in a calm, smooth voice. "I trust you to make the arrangements then, Warden. If it makes the paperwork easier you can claim I turned myself in. I want my day in court. The world will see I'm not the villain I've been painted as," She glared at Nella, "So have your guards read me my rights or whatever you've got to do, and let's get this over with."

The Warden shrugged and told the guards to take Dr. Schneider to his office. He turned back to Frank and Nella. "You look like you've been drug down a gravel road on a dry day. Where have you been?"

Frank shook his head, "Sorry Warden, if I was allowed to say, then I would."

The Warden threw up his pudgy brown hands. "Okay, not trying to poke my nose where it isn't wanted. But I see Dr. Rider is injured. Perhaps we can have the infirmary look at that while I pick her brain about our new inmate."

Frank thanked the Warden so effusively and looked so relieved at the prospect of proper medical care for her, that Nella felt another wave of panic about her shoulder slam into her. After letting the Warden know that she didn't believe Dr. Schneider needed a suicide watch, she was handed over to the uniformed medical staff. She felt grungy next to them in their clean rooms with the bright lights and cold beds. Frank disappeared with the Warden, but she was too worried about what the doctor would find to notice. But the doctor's eyes crinkled behind his mask and he told her not to worry. She didn't even protest as the nurse injected her with a powerful sedative.

THE CURED

She woke up in the passenger seat of Frank's car, with no memory of how she got there. They were rolling slowly through the long spring dusk toward Frank's house. Nella hadn't seen the other side of town since she was a poor graduate student. Since things like poor and wealthy had mattered. Now, she guessed, it was immunity that separated people. She had felt slightly depressed when she had been forced to choose a row house during school. All those people around her, she always felt so claustrophobic and unable to concentrate. Nella had felt like one tiny insect among many then and it had irritated her. Now, as row house after row house unrolled before the car, like an unending snake skin long shed, Nella was overwhelmed with loneliness. She kept expecting to see a mother on each porch yelling to their kids to come in for dinner. Or a couple of old men leaning on the metal fencing around their yards impassively watching the car pass by. But no one appeared. The houses were dark and the paint on the brick and doors were chipping, but it was the lawns that gave Nella an odd feeling of panic. People had been proud of their yards here, small as they were. Saturday mowing had been a ritual more likely to be kept than Sunday worship. It had been miles of smooth green squares without variation. But now the weeds had overrun the concrete sidewalks, pushed and tumbled the front stairs of homes, become long whorls matted by frost. Nella saw the faded pink plastic of a small child's tricycle reaching out of a silver tangle of old grass as if it were gasping for breath before being swallowed forever. She turned away from the window, tired of the emptiness outside.

Frank glanced over at her and and smiled.

"Are you awake?"

"Sort of. How long have I been out?"

"Just long enough to look at your shoulder and put in a few more stitches. The doctor said you should be fine, the infection is passing."

Nella sighed. "That's a relief. Where are we going?"

"I needed to pick up some of the case files to work on. We can stay at my house or go back to your apartment if you like."

"Do you live near here?" she asked, mostly so she wouldn't have to think of the house windows like opening eyes as their curtains rotted into dust.

"Just one more street up," Frank said, "they opened this part of the City after the rest filled up. Maybe I wouldn't have chosen the house for myself before, but it's reassuring that there are enough people left to fill up the rest of the City. And my neighbors are nice."

"You know your neighbors?"

Frank laughed and glanced at her surprised. "You don't know yours?"

Nella shook her head. "I honestly wouldn't even know I had any except for the occasional thump on the wall or the ceiling."

Frank shook his head. "Don't you miss people? I mean, I know you talk with people every day for work, but don't you just miss having normal conversations about things that don't matter? Things like the weather and people's jobs and what their kids have done lately?"

"More than you know," she replied, "But no one talks about those things anymore. Unless it's to worry about them. And if you get friendly with your neighbors, they might want something that you can't afford to give them."

"Ah, I see now. You're still in the bunker."

"What?"

"Your side of town are mostly Immunes, right? You, the people around you, had to survive through their neighbors becoming monsters, the government breaking down and looters taking what few supplies were left."

"So did you."

Frank slowed to a stop in front of a well kept block of houses. "Not exactly. I mean, I was technically one of the last people infected, so yes, I was aware that things were bad, but I was already in my shelter when things started to fall apart. Most of these people," he said, waving his hand around toward the houses, "never saw that. Once the infection took over, a person didn't think about how dangerous things were or how scarce things had become. They would have walked right by a fully stocked grocery store without even looking at it. They didn't notice that the government had failed everyone or that the streets were dangerous. The worst thing that could happen had already happened. The Infected didn't have the brain processes it takes to worry while they were sick. Now that we are the Cured, nothing can be worse than what we've been and what we've done, so there is really nothing worth worrying about anymore."

He turned toward her. "We're all the same here. There's no reason to fear each other, because we know, in some sense and with a little variation, what each person living here has done. People that were Immune- they had to do all sorts of things to get by. Things maybe they aren't proud of, because those things are as bad as anything the Infected did, except the Immunes don't have a brain altering disease that will explain what they've done."

Frank slipped a hand around hers before she could interrupt. "I love you, Nella. I don't care what you did to survive this long. I'll never ask and you don't ever need to say. Whatever it was, I don't think it could be as bad as what I've done, what the Infected did. But not everyone could say the same. The people around you avoid each other, not only because they may be ashamed of what they have done in the past or frightened of what they will find out their neighbors have done in the past, but also because they are still afraid of what they may have to do in the future. They're still in the bunker. Like Mr. Grant. They think somebody is going to come along and fix the world any day now, and they can forget this nasty spell and move on. No one is coming. We're the ones who have to fix the world. You know that right?"

"Of course. What else have we been trying to do all this time?" she asked.

Frank smiled and touched her cheek. "We can't always be running after rogue diseases and conducting trials. I know it feels like those things will take forever, but soon this trial will be over and we'll find the bacterium and the world will be safe. But it won't be fixed. Sometimes you have to do really brave things, like make friends with your neighbors. That's how the world gets fixed. Little bit by little bit." Frank sighed. "Listen to me, going on and on. Must be the lawyer part of my brain gearing up. Sorry about that." He let go of her hand and opened his door. Nella took a few seconds to look at the house they had stopped in front of before getting out of the car. The bricks had been whitewashed, like the others on that block, and recently. The fence had been uprooted, not just around his house, but around all of them on the block. Frank's yard was a little weedy, speckled with the old brown husks of naked dandelions, but most of the other lawns had been tilled, their dark innards thawing in the warm spring night, waiting.

"People are growing gardens out here?"

"Yes, the block has decided to grow herbs and aromatics for medicine or soaps, luxuries. The Farm just doesn't have enough space for things like that, but the old stuff is almost completely gone, even the furthest ranging scavengers are having trouble finding some things."

"Are you going to grow them too?"

Frank sighed. "I wish I could, I've just been so busy with the trial. I haven't even cared for the grass that was already here. But Mrs. Nichols- she's one of the neighbors, asked if she could try a pair of fruit trees in my yard. It's still too cold, but in a month we'll plant some apple seedlings we traded the Farm for. That way we won't have to go all the way there for fresh fruit." Frank laughed. "She wanted to find a citrus tree, she's afraid we're all going to die of scurvy. I told her it was too cold, we'll have to take our chances with other produce."

Nella smiled faintly. "We'll send her crates of oranges when we move to New Guinea."

A metal door clanged shut a few doors down and a teenage boy ran across the street and started knocking on another door. The pretty girl who came out to talk with him was on crutches because she was missing a leg.

"Gangrene," Frank said seeing that Nella had noticed. "Bites from other humans are unsanitary and they festered, sometimes for months on the Infected before they received medical care after the Cure. Sometimes amputation was the only option. You'll see it a lot here."

"I know. I was part of the medical team that first administered the Cure, remember?"

"Of course," Frank shook his head, "sorry, I'm just used to people staring."

"I guess that I *was* staring, but that wasn't why. I'm just not used to seeing anyone between six and twenty anymore."

Frank nodded. "There aren't many of them are there? It must be really tough."

"They would have been, what? Eight or so when the Plague hit?" Nella shuddered, thinking of how frightened they must have been before they were infected and how vulnerable even afterward. She looked at Frank for a long minute.

"You must really believe he didn't mean to do this," she said, "I don't know how you could do it otherwise."

Frank's brow wrinkled and he was grim for a moment. "I know that he developed something that escaped everyone's control. We've both seen the evidence of that. But he followed protocol until the end and tried to keep the Plague contained after he found out that Ann had been infected. I think Dr. Pazzo was as much an innocent bystander as the rest of us. If anyone can be said to be at fault, it has to be Dr. Schneider and even Ann. Don't you think?"

Nella hesitated. "Yes," she said at last in a low voice, "but I don't know if the same will be true if the incurable strain isn't destroyed." She didn't add that she thought Dr. Pazzo was still hiding something. If it helped him get through the day, who was she to disturb Frank's peace of mind with something she only suspected?

Frank walked slowly up the steps to his door. He stopped with his hand on the latch. "It's not like your apartment, Nella. They didn't clear out the old owner's things before they assigned it to me. I've done some cleaning but-"

"I'm sure it's fine," Nella smiled. Frank opened the door and stepped inside, his hand automatically finding the light switch. The smell of a long departed cat and old newspapers flung itself at Nella. She half smiled to herself, remembering her old rental. It had smelled the same, though she'd never had a pet. She thought all old houses must be steeped in the vaguely yellow smell. The hall was very dark and the house seemed smaller than she expected, but it was hard for her to tell because the thick curtains were all drawn. Frank glided around her in the dark reaching for lights.

"I've got to grab my notes from the upstairs office. Just make yourself at home. I'll be right back, okay?"

Nella nodded and looked around her as the steady creak of his feet on the stairs faded. She was standing in a living room that looked decades older than Frank. The wallpaper must once have been a vibrant maroon or red and white stripe, but now it was a pale blend of peach and gold, like a peppermint sucked too long and then put back in the package for years. The furniture was heavy and covered with lace cloth. She wondered if Frank had ever even sat in one of the chairs. The lamps and overhead were weak and missing bulbs, so that they just glowed with yellow light, not even illuminating themselves fully. But everything was immaculately clean. There was no dust anywhere, no papers or books set down where they didn't belong, not even a mug ring on the coffee table. Nella ached to see his office. She wondered if the house was like this throughout or if the office was where he really lived. Nella walked over to a nearby lamp and pulled the shade off for some more light. A familiar bag near the door caught her eye. It was the duffel bag that the Cured were given when they left the Cure camps. It usually had a scavenged set of clothes and some basic toiletries. It also had all the personal effects that the person had been found with. Most of the Cured hadn't wanted to take the bag.

They hadn't wanted the charity or the memories. And Nella couldn't blame them. She wondered what was in Frank's. She didn't look but she did notice it was still zipped and tagged with his name and the camp's label. He'd never even opened it.

Nella wandered into the kitchen and groped around for the light switch. She was oddly relieved when the bright lamp flooded over the sink and she saw a coffee cup sitting in it catching a drip. She didn't know if she felt better seeing the cup out of its place in the cabinet or hearing the drip of the imperfectly sealed tap. Either way, it was a sign that the house wasn't completely empty. She emptied the overflowing cup and placed it back under the tap, resisting the urge to tighten the handle and stop the drip. She was searching for another cup in the cabinets when Frank came down the stairs with a series of creaks as the arthritic boards rubbed together.

"I'm afraid I don't have much here right now- it was time for me to make a trip to the Farm too."

"That's okay, I was just going to get a glass of water."

Frank looked alarmed. "Oh! You didn't drink any yet did you?"

"No, why?"

"I forgot to tell you, we aren't on the same reservoir as the rest of the City. We have to use purification tabs or boil it first. Here, I have some in the refrigerator I think." He pulled open the fridge as Nella stared, confused at him.

"You mean there was a spill or something?"

"No, we just don't have access to the sealed reservoir. This part of the City drew water from somewhere else- the river maybe? I don't know, I was never interested in that stuff before. But when they moved us here, they told us we would have to purify our water until the pollutants were all gone or they could find a way to get us access to the reservoir. But there aren't many experts left and even their apprentices are busy with irrigation at the Farm and managing the reservoir the rest of the City relies on."

"Frank, did they force you to move here?"

He looked confused. "Do you mean this house? We were assigned space as it became cleared of Infected and all the dead were removed. It's not such a bad place."

"No, I know that, I was assigned my apartment too when I reached the populated zone. I mean, could you have stayed in your own home if you wanted to? Since the Cure had reached it?"

Frank hesitated and bent down to pick up the filtered water. He closed the refrigerator and brushed past her to grab a cup. He started to pour the water for her before he answered. "Yes, I could have stayed. They weren't ready to clear the dead, but I buried my wife and the boy after I was Cured anyway. I could have stayed or taken more of my things if I wanted. Most people had wandered pretty far from their homes since becoming sick and their homes were still in Infected areas, so they didn't really have the option. But I did. I didn't want to go back. I knew I couldn't live with what I'd done if I tried to live in the middle of Sarah's things. I was assigned this house, but when I left the camp, I went back once, to bury them. When I was done, I went back into the house to get some clean clothes because it was muddy and I was filthy and sad and tired. I thought I was also going to pick up our wedding pictures and some small things that I really wanted to keep." Frank handed her the cup without looking at her and sat shakily down at the scarred wooden table. He rubbed one long finger along the splintered grooves and looked down at the wood as he spoke.

"But when I walked in the door, everything smelled like her, like she had just walked by. And her last case file was spread over the dining room table as if she just got up to make herself a cup of coffee. I didn't want to see that, and I didn't want to clean it up either. I just wanted it to stay there, just that way, but not where I could see it. I didn't even stay to get my clothes. I just walked out and headed here. It took a week in muddy clothes, but I didn't care." He looked around the small kitchen.

"This place is far enough that I won't be tempted to go back again. If I'm lucky, it's burnt down or blown over by a storm or there are complete strangers living in it and all the memories of us are gone." He looked up at her, his hand pausing in it's endless track on the table. The scar on his cheek stuttered and shone in the bright kitchen light as he spoke and his face was so drawn and tired that Nella worried that she'd somehow made him ill.

"I'm sorry," he said, "I shouldn't be talking about this with you."

Although there was a chair next to him, she sat in the one across from him instead. "Because you don't want me to analyze you? Or because you wanted to make a clean break and don't want anyone to know who you were before?"

"No, nothing like that. I don't want you to think I've idolized or worship my wife. Or that I'm still in mourning. I've had six years to learn to let her go. I don't want you to think I'm not ready or that I want to somehow replace her. It's not that I haven't come to terms with her death. I haven't come to terms with myself for causing it."

She wanted to reach across the wooden table and curl her hand inside of his, but she drank a mouthful of cold water instead.

"Frank, how much did they tell you about me

before I met you at the prison?"

The worry on his forehead deepened and creased. "Not much. Just that you had been working on a team during the first days of the Cure. And that you had a good track record helping people who were recovering from long term Infection. That you were able to repair what seemed like permanent brain damage to other doctors. Why?"

Nella leaned back in the hard kitchen chair. "So no one told you why I left the Cure team?"

Frank shook his head.

"I know telling you that you were ill and that killing your wife was more of an animal instinct than anything you had control over won't make you feel better. And you live among people who have similar stories, so you know your experience is not unique or even rare. But you seem to carry around this idea that you're somehow not worth as much as other people. That you deserve to be treated badly. I can't fix the water or make people stop staring or being nasty. But you don't need to think that way about me. I'm not any different than you or anyone here. I'm not a pure, fragile doll who's been locked safely away since before the Plague." Frank started to interrupt her, but she shook her head and put her cup down with a hollow ringing.

"You think the only terrible things I've done were in the name of survival but that's not true." Nella took a deep breath and Frank leaned forward in his chair.

IN THE CURE CAMPS

"I assume you've seen Sevita's footage of the first people who were rounded up and Cured- everybody has. It was awful, all those people waking up to the world around them, to what had happened to their families and their friends- to what they remembered doing themselves. Everyone remembers Isaac Green's suicide because his was the first one and it was broadcast on television with the first reports. What most people don't realize is that he was just the first of many. *Hundreds* Frank, hundreds every day. We took all the precautions that we could, administering the Cure in smaller batches so we could watch them, eliminating weapons in the Cure tents once the Infected were sedated, even keeping people in the camp longer than they really needed to be there so we could make sure they were stable. It didn't matter. They found ways or they waited weeks until they left the camp and then did it on the road. They used the camp bedsheets to hang themselves or broke into the medical waste bins and injected themselves with needles full of air. Some of them drank cleaning supplies. A few even waited for hours underneath military vehicles for the one soldier who wasn't paying attention to run them over. Every day, over and over and over. My overseer, Dr. Taylor, kept telling us that it wasn't our fault, that the normal human mind wasn't equipped to function correctly after trauma like these people had seen. But I started to think maybe we shouldn't Cure them. Maybe it was better if they just stayed Infected, because at least they weren't destroying themselves with grief then. I told Dr. Taylor we should consider lifelong institutionalization instead. He told me I wasn't being realistic, that there weren't enough healthy humans left to sustain our own survival, let alone police, care for and feed thousands of Infected." Nella rubbed a few tears off her cheek with a rough hand and continued.

"But at last, Dr. Taylor couldn't take any more either. We had just administered the Cure to a new batch of people and they were sleeping off the sedative while the antibiotic did its job. I woke up and it was still dark, but someone was shooting a gun. The soldiers had orders to only dart any Infected that got too close to the camp, so that they would get the Cure. It was a big switch for many of them, they were used to thinking of the Infected as something to be eliminated, not as human beings with minds that could recover and lives that could be useful and normal. Sometimes a soldier disobeyed, but he was usually stopped by a superior before he could actually kill anyone. Not this time though.

"I got out of bed, confused, because the sound was coming from the patient tent, not the perimeter. Which was probably why no soldiers stopped him. I ran to the tent and before I even lifted the flap I could smell the gunpowder hanging in the air. And I knew they must all be dead. I lifted the flap and there was Dr. Taylor, moving from bed to bed on the last row of over one hundred people. He aimed his gun at the sleeping patient's head and pulled the trigger. I yelled for him to stop, and I ran toward him, pushing carts and beds out of the way. I tripped once and heard the gun go off again. He only stopped to reload and that's when I reached him and tried to grab the gun. He just coolly pointed it at me instead. 'Nella,' he said, 'you're a good person and a damn fine doctor in a world that desperately needs you. I don't want to kill you, but I will if you stop me.'

"He said it as if he were listing the symptoms of a disease to a group of interns. As if it were something he had said every day of his life. 'Why are you doing this?' I asked him. Dr. Taylor turned and shot the next patient before he answered me. 'We can't institutionalize them. We can't let them roam around the way they are and expect any sort of security in our lives.' He shot another. There was only one left and by this time I was sobbing, but he kept pointing the gun back toward me between patients, so I wouldn't come closer. 'The Cure makes them remember everything and I can't keep them from killing themselves. The last one couldn't be bothered to find anything to do it properly. So he sat in the sun in front of my tent for three days and refused water and food. He tore out every intravenous line we put in. He just died. I'm tired Nella. The only people that seem to survive are the people that would have been murderous pricks without the Infection.' Dr. Taylor shot the last patient, a child. He turned back. 'I might as well do the good ones a favor and put them out of their misery. And the world a favor by eliminating the ones that would just be criminal anyway.'

'That's not true!' I kept saying, but he wasn't listening. He cleared his throat and raised the gun to his own head. He shrugged.

'Don't feel bad Nella. I would have been a murderous prick either way.' And he shot himself."

Frank swore under his breath. "It wasn't your fault," he said.

Nella shook her head and wiped her face with her hands. "No," she said, "it wasn't. But it stayed with me. It crept up on me every time I was talking with a survivor or waiting for a Cure to work or receiving news about another suicide. We routinely interviewed our patients every day from the time they woke up to the time they left the camp. But it was very disorganized, especially after Dr. Taylor died. So you could be assigned five or ten patients one day and see a completely new set the other day, depending on who had left the camp or died the night before. One morning, I was making my rounds and I met someone that I recognized. It was nothing I expected, we were miles from anywhere I'd lived or worked. We were overworked and exhausted. I'd been with the medical team for almost two years at that point and we didn't have breaks or days off or even full night's rests most of the time. I must have helped to treat thousands of people by then and after a while, their faces and their stories just seemed to blur together. Like one long streak of bad luck wrapped around each day. I stopped looking at faces. I stopped listening to stories. Because they were all the same. I just started reading charts and the notes the other doctors left instead. That day, I had been specifically assigned to one particular case because I seemed to do better with people that weren't responding to the Cure the way they ought to.

"Sometimes, they had just been infected for so long that their brains had suffered permanent damage from the swelling. I think that's what happened to Ann. We didn't see too many, because most Infected killed each other, suffered accidental deaths or succumbed to secondary infections and starvation. But there were a few that survived that long. Most of these were kept at the camp until a family member could come and care for them or until the military developed an institution for their care.

Sometimes, they had a bad reaction to the antibiotic. Those were the easiest to treat. It was the same as other allergic reactions and we knew how to deal with it.

This particular case though, fell into the unknown pile. And that's why I was assigned. I had worked in a hospital during school as part of my training. Most of the time I saw a patient for a day, maybe two before they were released. A few though, barely made it out for a week before returning. One of them, a man named Martin, had a severe case of paranoid schizophrenia. He couldn't afford his medication, so every week the local beat cop would write him up on a minor infraction so that he could bring Martin in to the hospital for treatment. We'd give him his medication along with the few days' supply that we could get away with and then release him again for another week. It wasn't ideal and the entire staff knew it wasn't going to work forever, because he was getting worse even when we managed to keep him medicated. One day, maybe only a month or two before the Plague was at its worst, something finally snapped for good inside Martin. He found a crow bar somewhere and beat the cop that came to pick him up with it. The officer was so badly beaten that he was in intensive care- I guess until he was infected or died, I'm not sure. But Martin was taken to a permanent facility immediately. Everything happened so fast after that, I had never really considered what happened to him or to the officer. I'm still not entirely sure whether Martin escaped the facility somehow or whether an orderly decided to let the inmates out when things got bad.

However it happened, Martin was free, and he was Infected. He must have wandered for miles during the year and a half until he was Cured. I didn't realize it was him until I got to the side of his cot. He was sleeping when I got there. He was so filthy I didn't recognize him for a while. That's how the other doctors knew something was off. The first thing that most of the Cured wanted to do, once the initial shock wore off, was scrub themselves clean. In fact, we had to have nurses watch many of them so that they didn't physically rub their skin off or damage their teeth in order to believe themselves completely clean. I'm sure you understand what that urge was like."

Frank nodded. "The first thing I did was brush my teeth. Someone stopped me after a tube of toothpaste and twenty minutes were gone. But I could still- I could still *taste them* on my tongue. I would have kept going if I could."

"But this guy, he didn't care. He didn't want to shower or brush his teeth or have his haircut- nothing. He had blood and matter clotting in his beard and around his lips, he had sores from bites that were festering and stank like rotting meat. His nails were long and sharp, like brown, brittle claws and he didn't care. And when the nurses tried to wash him anyway, thinking maybe he was catatonic with shock, he attacked them, accusing them of trying to kill him. He was so vicious with his teeth smashing together and his long, sharp nails raking everything he could reach, that they thought the Cure had failed. The only way they were able to be certain that it hadn't was that they heard him speak.

When he did speak though, he claimed that we were trying to trick him. He said that the world was finally clear to him, that he could only survive and grow stronger by killing and eating his enemies. He was convinced we had drugged him and we were trying to lull him with false security. He swore he'd kill all of us so that he could be strongest. Of course, we kept him in restraints. And they passed him on to me. It was a very hot day in the middle of summer when I finally met him again. I sat by his cot although he stank more and more with the heat. He had been sedated, so even after he woke up he wasn't really sure what was happening. He recognized me before I recognized him. He was convinced I was a hallucination.

'I know you,' he said, 'but you aren't really here. You're back at the old hospital. Back before the world showed its true self. That was a nice dream.'

'Do you know what happened after you left the hospital?' I asked him, 'What happened when the world showed it's true self?'

He leaned in closer to me, but was pulled up short by the restraints. Still, his breath was so foul with old gore, that I thought I might pass out between it and the heat.

'Everyone took off their masks,' he whispered, 'and the last supper finally began. I won though, I ate them all. I'm the strongest. I was filled with righteous wrath. I ate so many I became God.'"

Frank shuddered with his whole body and Nella paused. The soft drip of tap water into the ceramic mug filled the room. She twisted her own cup back and forth on the wooden table.

"I didn't even try to convince him that he was delusional. I listened to him for a while as he went on about how the other doctors were trying to weaken him or hurt him. But he went on for hours, becoming more and more angry as the sedative wore off. And I eventually tuned him out, even though I stayed seated near his cot. I was thinking about how hard it was going to be to find medication for him in this dead, broken, stand-still world. About how little it had helped him before. And I wondered if he were ever really Infected at all, or if he just became absorbed in the way the world had become. I thought about how many people he must already have killed and how many he would continue on to kill if he were ever to be released or escape military custody. Dr. Taylor's words kept coming back to me over and over.

Eventually, Martin burnt himself out, like a small child after a tantrum. When he was asleep, I got up. I very clearly remember filling the syringe with too much sedative. It was so still in the plunger, no bubbles at all, no droplets left on the needle. I went back to Martin and didn't even hesitate, not even to clean the site of the injection. I just pushed through the layer of grime on his arm. It was so smooth that he didn't even feel it. I sat next to his cot for twenty minutes or so, until he stopped breathing. I was calm and rational and entirely without remorse. And then I got up and reported myself to the captain in charge of my medical unit.

I was never arrested, never tried, for Martin or anyone else that I'd killed during the Plague. They just rotated me out of the Cure unit and I never bothered to go back. The military found excuses for me, sending me hard to treat patients at my own clinic, one at a time and then, eventually assigning me to this trial.

It wasn't Martin's fault. I could have found him a bed somewhere they could have kept an eye on him. Eventually someone will start making the right medications again. I didn't dislike him. I'm not even sure that I really felt sympathy for him. I've asked myself for years whether I did it for his sake or the world's sake or just my own. I still don't know the answer for sure.

Don't let the world convince you that you are somehow inferior to the people that were immune, Frank. The things you did were out of your conscious control, like breathing. The people that never got infected- we can't say that. Every life we took was because we chose to take it. Sure, we can say it was for survival, and I think that's mostly true. But it wasn't involuntary, and we'll have to wake up realizing that every day forever. That's the price of free will I guess." Nella was finally quiet, drawing in a slow breath as if she were reversing a sigh. Frank was silent leaning forward in his chair, but his face was drawn and tight, a hundred angles of worried. Nella smiled at him but her mouth tasted bitter and dry, as if she'd swallowed all the ocean.

"Ah. You thought I was someone else, someone different. I did too. Once. But all around this little shard of the world people are having the same revelations. We can barely stand to interact with each other. It's no wonder there has to be a government agency on human reproduction."

Frank looked up at her, his face breaking into living curves again. "No," he said, "I think you did what you thought was right. Whatever your doubts now, I can't believe that you weren't convinced then. And that's what I would expect, that you do what you believe is right. That's who I think you are." He stood up and gently pulled her out of the chair. "You *are* different. You're the one thing that didn't get broken after all that mess." He kissed the bitter taste out of her mouth.

FRANK'S HOUSE

They decided to stay at Frank's house. Nella didn't yet know how to tell Sevita that the bacterial samples were still lost, and it depressed her to think about facing her failure. She scolded herself for being a coward, but it didn't make her feel differently. She was hesitant to leave Frank as well, and she wasn't sure he'd go with her to her apartment. He had been absorbed in case notes since he'd brought her up to the office.

He apologized, but Nella could see he was itching to look back at something in the case. She was more convinced than ever that he knew more than he was telling her. That frightened her. It meant that he would either try to find the samples himself because he thought it was too dangerous for her, or that it had something to do with his client. Both ideas were equally opaque and unsettling to Nella. She had let him read his notes in peace, claiming to have medical reports on Ann to go over. She did have the reports, they had been delivered to her at the prison, but she only made a show of reading them, watching Frank's body language instead.

Whatever he was looking for, he hadn't found it even after an hour of frantic reading had passed. Nella could tell by the way his hand smoothed against the back of his head over and over, and the way his legs waited to leap from the chair when he found it. The evening slid on and Nella grew impatient. At last, she couldn't take the way cold panic was crawling over her with a million sharp legs and filling the shadowy space between them with visions of plague and death and loss. "Why don't you ask me about what you are looking for?" she asked, "Maybe I can remember. I have a good memory."

Frank turned and smiled at her, as if realizing she were there for the first time. "I'm sorry, you must be exhausted. You still need lots of rest. Why don't you get some sleep, I'll be done in a bit."

Nella laughed at the obvious dodge. "Okay, you don't have to tell me, I just want to help."

"I know you do. I wish you could, but I'm not even sure I remember it correctly. I need the tapes of the lab."

"Did you give the only copy to the Judge?"

"No, but I don't keep evidence here. It's at the prison, in the Warden's vault, for safekeeping."

Nella looked confused. "Is that normal?"

Frank shook his head. "This case was so large that no one wants to be accused of tampering. The Warden agreed to keep the defense's documents and the Military Governor is keeping the prosecution's items in his office." Frank sighed. "Well, I don't think worrying about it is going to help tonight." He stood up and stretched, his palms almost grazing the ceiling. Nella put down the unread report on Ann Connelly. He led her into the cool, dark bedroom. Before he even flipped the light on she knew the bed would be perfectly made, the floor would be bare and there would be little to no extra furniture in the room. She felt particularly gritty and sweaty after their trip. She knew she wouldn't be able to sleep there. When the light snapped on, Nella laughed in surprise.

"What is it?" Frank asked.

"I just wasn't expecting this. It doesn't look like the rest of the house."

Frank shrugged and blushed. "This is where I spend most of my time. Do you like it?"

A massive bookshelf stood on the far wall. It was filled with books on shipbuilding, with a giant atlas and novels of exploration and shipwreck and discovery. The ceiling glowed blue with nautical maps that covered every inch of it. There was a desk with a half finished model sailboat sitting on it. She looked back at Frank. "You weren't kidding when you said you wanted to sail to a tropical island when this was over, were you?"

Frank's face relaxed and dropped a decade, even with the thick beard shadowing the bottom half. For a moment Nella thought she saw him as he was before, wholly beautiful, happy, in love. It shocked her for a moment to realize she was the one that he was in love with this time.

"Can you imagine how wonderful it would be? To rediscover a place?" he waved a hand toward the map, "these places are all lost, as if they never were found in the first place. There's been no communication with them for almost a decade. Chances are, most of them haven't found a cure. Chances are, few, if any people have survived. The people that have, well they must have their own ways of doing things by now. New laws, new rituals, new ideas. We could visit them, you and me. We could be the next explorers."

"Aren't you afraid? Other people could have turned to piracy or slave holders or people who worship dead computers. We don't know what's out there."

"That's exactly the point. It's exciting, not frightening. Well, of course we'd be careful, but aren't you dying to know what's out there? Aren't you tired of the same old gated City, the same sad people day after day?"

"Well, yes," she admitted, though she felt a serious gash in her heart when she thought of leaving Sevita and Christine behind. But his excitement swept the thought away like a stray leaf in a gale. He pointed to the map directly over the head of the bed.

"There's New Guinea. I've been thinking it would take us about three months if we sailed straight, but of course we would want to stop everywhere on the way . . ." Frank talked cheerfully about routes and boat building and supplies until Nella was dizzy. She didn't stop him, the conversation was as bright as their earlier ones had been dark. She wondered if that particular map had ended up where it was after their lunch at the prison. She suspected that it had, and hoped it had been a source of several bright dreams for him. At last, he wound down and sat on the end of the bed, patting the spot next to him. She recoiled and immediately regretted it when she saw the nervous hurt return to his face, wrinkling away the ease that she had just seen.

"Oh Nella, I'm sorry, I didn't mean- I have a spare bedroom I can sleep in-"

"No, no," she said quickly, "it isn't that. It's just that-" her voice dropped to an embarrassed whisper as if the neighbors might hear, "I'm *filthy*. I can't mess up your nice clean sheets."

Frank laughed and the worry scattered. He scratched his thickening beard. "Yeah," he said, "I don't think I could stand this thing for one more minute either. I can practically feel it crawling." He pointed to a dark wooden door. "The bathroom is adjoining, I'll get some towels for you."

She blushed and hesitated for a moment. Discomfort won out over pride. "Frank, I can't- would you help me wash my hair? I can do everything else, but," she half raised her wounded arm.

"Of course," he said, before she could finish.

He opened the door to a small bathroom and then left her to find towels. The room was badly lit and the mirror was spotty with age. But it smelled sweet and strong, like warm soap and shaving cream.

She felt less grimy just walking into it. "You can get in, if you want," said Frank from behind her, "I just want to shave first. I'll be quick. Look what I've found." He handed Nella a slim bottle of real shampoo and rubbed his own head with a grin. "I won't be needing it."

Nella smiled, but she sat on the edge of the tub and made no move to get undressed. She watched him mix shaving cream and draw out a slim razor, like a shining bone and set it on the lip of the sink. He scrubbed his face with water and then realized she was watching him as he straightened up.

"What?" he asked, dabbing foam on the stiff hairs.

She shrugged. "It's just that you're one of very few men whom I've met that still shaves every day."

"Ah. That's because shaving cream is hard to come by these days. And I can't imagine trying to shave without it. I had to carry buckets of water for the barber's wife, Mrs. Avoncetti, every day for a month before the water was turned on in this sector. After that he finally agreed to teach me how to make my own." Frank stopped talking as he picked up the flashing rib of a blade. She watched the scarred side of his face emerge as if the razor were erasing shadow and care with each long, slow stroke. It was impossible for her to watch the smooth, graceful flick of his hand on the razor and not think of him touching her.

She shouldn't be here. He'd already rejected her once, hadn't he? Why torture herself? But he had said that he loved her. He'd shown her only kindness and care. More than that, he'd *wanted* her. She had felt it. But he seemed to want nothing to happen until after the trial. And though she felt stronger than she had during her fever, she knew she ought to take it easy for a while.

She was jarred out of her thoughts when Frank groaned lightly and she realized she'd still been staring at him.

"Nella, please don't tell me you *like* the mountain man look. I don't think I could stand it."

She laughed. "No, I like seeing your whole face."

He squinted at her as if trying to decide if she were teasing him. He bent over to wash his face again. He sighed with relief as he ran a hand over his smooth chin. Nella looked at her feet and tried not to feel the gentle ache on the surface of her lips, longing to kiss the line of his jaw. She tried to bully herself into being rational, but it was too difficult, surrounded, steeped in the clean smell of him, sitting so near to him, in his own space.

"Well? Did I miss a spot?" he asked, leaning over her to turn on the shower. Nella smiled and reached up to stroke his smooth cheek. He caught her hand and kissed her palm. His lips were so much softer than she remembered, though she had kissed them just a few hours before. Tiny echoes skipped across her skin, as if he had kissed a hundred places at once.

"It's perfect," she said at last, remembering he had asked her a question. She stood up, feeling the steam creep up her back in warm puffs. He untied her sling and she straightened her arm cautiously.

"I think we're going to have to burn these clothes," he said as he peeled off his shirt, "They're never going to be the same after this week."

Nella had started to unbutton her shirt. She clutched it closed. "Frank, I just realized I have no extra clothes here. We left them with the other pack."

He grinned wickedly at her. "Oh no," he said, gently moving her hand and continuing to unbutton her shirt, "whatever shall we do?"

She laughed and blushed. "I'm serious!"

"Relax, I'll go to your apartment tomorrow and pick up some things." He drew the fabric gently from her wounded arm.

"Until then?"

He shrugged and unzipped her pants, tugging them over her hips. "I'll turn up the heat."

"I thought you wanted to wait- until after the trial."

His brows drew together in confusion and he stepped back from her, "What gave you that idea? I mean, I'm okay with waiting if that's what you want-"

Nella shook her head but couldn't speak past the boulder in her throat.

"Is this about what happened at the Cure camp?" The space between them evaporated and his fingertips grazed the side of her face. They were like tiny rocks in a pool, the feeling rippling and bouncing over her in larger and larger rings. "That place was filled with misery. The very air was tainted." He leaned forward and whispered into her ear, "You're sacred Nella, a bright dream at the end of the world. I don't want to remember you in that dark place. I don't want to think about that sad time any more."

She closed her eyes but they leaked anyway. "But I was in a place like that. For a long time. It's part of my life. It's part of your life." Her voice creaked at the end, though she tried to control it.

His arms slid around her, his skin warm and damp from the shower steam. "I know. I know it was. But it doesn't have to part of *our* life. Not any more." He let her go and cleared his throat. His eyes were red, but he smiled at her and continued undressing.

"Come on," he said cheerfully as he picked up the bottle of shampoo, "the water heater in this place isn't that big. I'll be washing your hair in the dead cold before long."

Nella stepped carefully into the warm cavern of the shower after him. The shower didn't hurt her shoulder as badly as it had done before and she took that as a good sign. She stepped into the stream of water, turning her back to him so the water soaked through her filthy hair. She closed her eyes. Her breath caught as one of his hands wrapped around her stomach and his fingers grazed the bottom of her breast. The other hand tangled itself in her wet hair. She could feel the strands of grass from the fight with the Infected hit her shin as they washed away, and the clots of blood that had caught in the ends from her wound dissolved as he carefully slid his fingers through the tangles. Her head felt heavy from the extra weight of the water, but the rest of her felt lighter, younger as the week's dirt sloughed away. His hands slipped away from her and she smelled the sharp sweetness of chemical citrus as he opened the shampoo bottle. She smiled to herself. It had been years since she'd even seen real shampoo, but she recognized the smell immediately. She felt the weight of her hair disappear from her neck as he gathered it up and the rough pressure of his hands on her scalp. He tilted her head gently to one side and kissed the base of her neck with his soft lips. The lobe of her ear vibrated with his breath. "You didn't think that I didn't want you, did you?" his voice was heavy in her ear as the feathery foam of the shampoo slid down the small of her back, tracing slow rivers into her skin. She shivered. The soft weight of her hair slipped back onto her neck as both of Frank's long arms wrapped around her waist and good arm. He kissed the top of her good shoulder and she felt the hard bone of his cheek brush her ear. She leaned back into him and he tightened his arms. The last of the shampoo dissolved and streaked away and she felt as if she could follow it. "You can go to your grave sixty years from now knowing that a day didn't pass since we met that I did not want you."

She turned to face him, his arms loosening to let her. The thin stream of water began to grow cool between them. She leaned through it and tilted her face up toward his. She kissed him as the water wicked the heat and soap out of her hair and down over his arms and her legs in a last warm gush. The water turned frigid and he let her go to turn it off. She stepped out on shaky legs. She began to wrap a towel around her, but he stopped her, tossing it aside and pulling her into him. His skin was sun-baked stone, a tumbledown ruin left to the wind, all the jagged edges smoothed away. He kissed her too roughly, almost biting and his hand clamped shut just below her wound and she yelped as a jolt of pain sizzled up her arm and into her neck and breast. He dropped away from her as if she'd shoved him. "Oh, God, Nella, I'm sorry. I'm so sorry." He gently lifted away the soaked bandages with fingers light as leaves. The wound was unbroken, but he was shaken and reluctant to touch her. She turned his face away from the red scar that laced her skin until their eyes met. She smiled and felt his frame immediately loosen. The shower plinked like a metronome in the quiet. She stretched as tall as she could. Her lips brushed the ragged scar on his cheek.

"It's too cold in here," she whispered. Her hand slid gently down his arm and her fingers tangled in his. She led him out into the bedroom. She kissed him, her cool hand making a slow current down his chest as she gently backed him to the edge of the bed. He sat down, his hands spread over her hips in long streaks of warmth. She eased him back and hovered over him, her thighs touching the outside of his, her wet hair like cool grasses passing over his baking skin. He closed his eyes. Nella paused to look at his face. She traced the gentle ridge on his temple, feeling the fragile bone beneath, the frail globe that held everything she cared about. She leaned in closer, her breasts grazing his chest. She closed her eyes. Her breastbone ached as if it were too small to hold everything in. Her cheek rested lightly against his.

"I love you Frank," she said softly and with one small movement, enveloped him, like a still lake closing over a stone. He cried out and his eyes flew open to meet hers. She kissed him, her hips were like the currents in the maps above them, moving endlessly over the same hidden rocks and trenches, without pause. He twisted one arm around her back, needing her ever closer, as if he could dissolve into her. His other hand smoothed her hair from her face as she kissed him. He arced up toward her, a stone bridge that shattered and then collapsed into something new. He pulled her down with him and turned sideways so that she lay beside him, their faces level with each other. She watched the great breaths pulsing in his chest. He pulled her chin up gently with one hand. She glanced at his face and burst into tears. She pressed a sob into the back of her hand.

Frank pushed himself up one arm. "Nella, what is it? Are you hurt? Is it your shoulder?"

She shook her head and slipped a hand into his. "I can't help thinking about the missing samples. Even now. It hangs over everything. Maybe this is the last day. Maybe this is the last time I get to touch you. For a while I could pretend we were going to find them. That everything would turn out all right. But now, when it matters most of all," she brought his hand to her cheek, warming her face, "now I doubt. Now it seems impossible and everything seems closer to an end."

He curled himself over her, his too thin chest, his patchwork of scars suddenly beautiful to her. His thumbs smoothed the tears from her face. "Nella, we *are* going to find them. *I* will find them. This isn't an end." A broad smile spilled across his face, "Trust me, we're going to be making love hundreds of times. Thousands."

She laughed in spite of herself. He touched her forehead with his own. "The whole world had to die before I found you. I've been through hell. I even became the devil himself for a while. I can't lose you now. The universe can't be that unjust."

He made love to her again, slow and powerful, until she forgot the samples, forgot the trial and the loneliness of the empty world. Until she was lost in the sharp, clean smell of him, the rough, sandy feel of his hands on her skin. Until every touch was a splash, a little ripple growing inward and colliding with each other, colliding and merging and smoothing again into stillness.

NELLA KNOWS

Nella woke up in the early morning hours and slipped quietly out of the bed. She padded to the bathroom to relieve herself and soak in the shower. She pressed the small tab in the center of the knob without even glancing at it. More second nature than modesty, she didn't even think about it. Twenty minutes later, she changed the bandage on her wound gingerly and then turned the doorknob. The automatic click of the lock releasing was minuscule, but in her brain it was as loud as a gunshot. She looked down at the knob half turned in her hand. She realized that Frank was already days ahead of her and she cursed her slow thought process. How could she have missed it? It must have been on the video-how had she not seen it? Even if not, common sense should have told her. Even her fevered unconscious had made the connection. *Closets don't lock with a key from the inside. They lock with a button or a knob. The key only opens it from the outside.*

Nella flung the door open and paced naked from the bathroom to the bed and back, wondering if she should wake Frank. Threads of questions shuttled by her so quickly she couldn't grasp any of them for long. *Was it an odd lock? Had she seen it? Would he have had the mental capacity to open the door if it didn't need the key? Yes.* She could answer that one with certainty. The Infected could turn doorhandles, could probably even remember to turn the lock knob. Nothing more complicated. In fact, the revolving door at Dr. Carton's lab would probably, had probably, defeated them unless they stopped pushing at the right spot by mere chance. Keys were definitely out. The thought of Dr. Carton brought the next thought crashing down on her like ice water on her shoulders. *Had Dr. Pazzo even been sick at all? Was there a person keeping him and Anne alive or had it just been him the entire time?*

Nella sat on the foot of the bed and bit her nails without realizing it. She jumped up and shook Frank awake, rather more roughly than she intended. He sat up, but he rubbed his eyes and looked ready to slump back. "What's going on?" he asked.

"The lock wasn't a key lock was it?"

"Huh?"

"The lock on Dr. Pazzo's side of the closet. It was a push button wasn't it?"

Frank's eyes snapped open and he stared at her. "You know? Did I-"

"No, you didn't talk in your sleep or anything. I realized it just now, in the bathroom."

Frank sagged with relief. "I wanted to tell you, but I have to protect my client-"

"Never mind that," interrupted Nella, "I know why you didn't tell me. It's not important now. What *is* important is whether or not that door lock was weird and locked from the inside with a key. That's what you were looking for in your notes wasn't it?"

"Yes, but I need the video. It's not in the notes, I never thought it was important. I'm still not entirely sure that it is. He was ill when he finally found out about the resistant strain. We saw the infection take over. There's no way he could have gone to steal the samples at that point. Besides, they found him and Ann locked in the lab still."

Nella raked a hand through her hair. She was shaking and her lungs threatened to close in the thick panic of the room. "Frank, he wasn't sick."

"What are you talking about? We *saw* it happen."

"No Frank," her voice was razor thin and insistent, "*he wasn't sick.* He was pretending. Just like Dr. Carton. Except he didn't need to go as far."

"Nella, calm down. You can't possibly know that." He pulled her onto the bed and wrapped the warm blanket around her shoulders.

"Remember the food system of his? We agreed that an Infected wouldn't think to open packaged food, even if they were starving. And it couldn't slide through the ramshackle tubes he made without clogging somewhere else- *you* said that."

"I remember."

"So either someone was feeding him and Ann, or he was. He wasn't sick."

Frank rubbed his forehead and Nella knew he was convinced despite himself. "Why would he do all that though? Why the elaborate set up, the tube system, the key sliding underneath the door? Why the complete breakdown *on camera*? Why lock Dr. Schneider up? What could he possibly have hoped would happen?"

Nella was silent for a moment, torn between panic and confusion. She felt stupid and slow, as if she were in a bad dream where she could never reach her destination no matter how long she walked.

"He knew. He knew before they locked themselves in. He knew about the samples, he knew about the severity and communicability of the original, he knew that millions were going to be infected. We just assumed he didn't know until the day Dr. Schneider broke out because that's what he showed us. But Ann said he watched all the tapes. He had to have seen Dr. Carton. He had to know. We just took it for granted that he found out at the end. Just the way we assumed he was safely sealed away because he made a point of showing us the key to the door and how he put it beyond his reach. He distracted us just enough."

"Why film it in the first place?"

"For exactly this sort of situation. What is it they used to call it? Plausible deniability."

"There's no way he could have known what would happen. Assuming he knew about the incurable strain and the severity of the original Plague, the way that you say, he would have believed the world would be destroyed completely. That there would be no one left who cared how it started or no one left with the technical know how to discover how it started. He's just not that smart. No one is."

"Yes, he is, Frank. Maybe he didn't know he'd be facing a world tribunal, but he had to know that in the end, someone's head was going to roll, and he was going to make damn sure it wasn't his. He might not have believed that anyone would survive after seeing the violence and lack of self care that Ann showed and that probably came through the news reports in the lab, but he probably would have *hoped* that someone would stop it, that something would be left. I would have, if it were me. I believe him, still, when he says that he never meant the original strain to harm anyone. I believe that it really was an accident. But he knew he had to get Dr. Schneider to admit she was responsible and to tell him the location of the resistant strain. So he locked her up and recorded her. It was all a setup." She rubbed her sore shoulder gently and her face twisted as if she had tasted something sour and sad. "He knew the samples were missing, because he was the one that took them. He let us see the video because he knew we would run after Dr. Schneider. We played right into his hands. This whole thing was about holding her responsible."

Frank's face relaxed and he even looked cheerful. "Then maybe he's already destroyed the samples. Maybe they aren't even a threat."

"No," Nella said, as grim as before, "He

wouldn't have destroyed them. He needed them as evidence. And as leverage against Dr. Schneider. In fact, he'd probably want them as close by as possible. In *his* control."

"How would he have gotten them in? Prisoners are searched when they are booked. Everything is taken from them."

"Everything?"

"As far as I know."

"Maybe he got someone else to bring it to him. Or send it to him."

"He doesn't have anyone, Nella. No matter what else he may have lied about, I believe him when he says *we* are the closest things to friends that he has. Besides, all packages- *anything* delivered to prisoners would be checked."

"Checked how? We're only talking about small vials here."

"I'm not sure." Frank ran his hands slowly over his head in frustration. He looked up at her suddenly. "But I bet Stan Kembrey would be able to tell us. I need to get the video from the Warden's office anyway, and I want to talk to Dr. Pazzo about all this-"

"No! No Frank, he can't know that we've found him out." She gripped his arm so hard that he winced.

"Ow. Why not? We've done what he wanted, we brought Dr. Schneider back for trial. Why would he bother trying to hide it now?"

"If he doesn't want to hide it, he'll turn over the samples when you tell him we didn't find them. It will help his defense. You don't have to tell him you know that he has them."

"I *don't* know that he has them. This is all guesswork. And you still haven't answered my question, why is it important to act as if I don't think it's him? I'm angry that he used me. Especially that he used you. You've been hurt because of him. He needs to answer for that."

She put a gentle hand on either side of his face. "Because I'm not entirely certain that's all that he wanted. What if there is something else? Something we are both missing? If he intends to *use* the samples, then telling him we know he has them would force his hand, he'd release them immediately. I need time to find them before he finds out we know, and before whatever deadline he's set has passed. If he turns them over of his own free will, then wonderful, we can all relax. But if you go to your next meeting with him and he says nothing when you tell him the samples have been stolen, then we'll know he's not done with them yet."

"Nella, this is assuming way more than I'm comfortable with."

"This is how I work. This is what I get paid for, what I do every day. You need evidence because of what you do every day. I'm not asking you to do anything, except to go on acting the same way, treating him the same way as you have all this time. I can do the rest, probably with less suspicion than you can. Please trust me. Let me do my job."

He closed a warm hand around hers. "I *do* trust you. Just tell me what you need me to do. If I can do it without compromising the case, I will."

"Judge Hawkins is holding a copy of the video right? We need to tell him the result of our search. We also need to ask him to keep it quiet for a little while longer. You can pick up that copy and we can check it without anyone knowing we accessed the evidence cache at the prison. When is your next meeting with Dr. Pazzo?"

"Normally, it would be any time between now and court on Monday."

"Would it be odd or out of the ordinary to

schedule a meeting with him this afternoon?"

"A meeting with you too?"

"No, just the two of you, to discuss court strategy."

"Then it wouldn't seem odd, that would be pretty normal."

"Did you tell him where we were going before we left?"

"No, but given Dr. Schneider's presence in the prison last night, he's going to know."

"Good. When he asks, tell him everything about the trip. Give him a chance to turn over the samples or give him enough rope to hang himself. Either way, we'll know."

"Nella, you are ignoring the possibility that someone else took them."

"Because the possibility is so small. Look, Frank, I've thought about this nonstop for days. There were only four people who knew about the resistant strain. I'm convinced we've eliminated three of them either through motive or capacity. Dr. Pazzo is the only one that's left."

Frank sighed. "What are you going to be doing?"

"I need to find out if anything was delivered or returned to Dr. Pazzo. I guess I'll start with Officer Kembrey. Do you think he can keep his mouth shut?"

"Stan? I'd trust him with my life."

"Okay then. I need some clothes."

Frank grinned for the first time that day. Nella laughed. Frank swung his legs out of bed to begin the day.

"Frank, one more thing." Frank turned toward her.

"What's that?"

"He can't know about this- about us. Don't give him any more power than he already has."

NO GOOD NEWS

Nella let the cold flickering light of the screen strobe over her without registering what she was seeing. It had taken Frank almost an hour to convince Judge Hawkins to give them more time before publishing a warning to the City about the missing Recharge samples. They had agreed that she wouldn't meet the Judge, so that the sight of her injury wouldn't cause an immediate and irreversible call to the military governor. She didn't know what he had said to finally persuade Judge Hawkins to give them more time, but she didn't envy Frank. He'd had to walk a fine line in the narrow space between the truth and implicating his client. His nature was too open to enjoy any aspect of it. Nella shook her head. How had he become a lawyer in the first place?

They sat in her living room combing through the images on Dr. Pazzo's videos, looking for a shot of the closet door. Frank kept on, frame by frame, pausing and playing, rewinding and pausing. Nella had stopped paying attention. She didn't need any more proof. She'd been convinced as soon as she heard the lock click in Frank's bathroom. Her thoughts instead, stuttered and sparked and prickled. She bounced between wondering what Dr. Pazzo was waiting for and how he planned to release the bacteria. It never occurred to her to wonder *whether* he would release it.

"I can't believe it," Frank said, shattering the vague haze that surrounded Nella's thoughts. He was leaning forward, almost tilting himself off the chair in his excitement.

A still image of the closet door sat on the screen in brooding green. A single frame as Dr. Pazzo smashed the camera against the wall in his staged frenzy. He had been so careful, showing only the walls or his face, even the panel of the door at times, but never the knob. But he'd lost track of it. He wanted to be convincing in his fury, to appear truly infected, that he'd forgotten to hide the lock. It was a push button, just as Nella had thought. She watched Frank sink back into the cushions beside her, almost felt his certainty and confidence drain away.

"I'm sorry," she said.

"What do I do?"

"Stick with the plan. Maybe he'll admit to having the samples when you tell him we didn't find them. But if he doesn't- we've only got one shot to find them. Once he knows that we suspect him, he'll push up any plans he might have for the bacteria. You have to play dumb, Frank. Let him think he's got the power."

"You were right all along. You told me he was trying to establish himself as the dominant one, but I didn't believe you. How did I fall for his story?"

"It was a good story. He said it himself. We hate it when the bad guy gets away. I think he's mostly telling the truth actually. His version of events seems to be verified by the others. I *don't* think he was involved in releasing the original disease. I think he *did* argue against using a more resistant strain. The question is, why did he fake his infection? Why did he wait to recover the resistant samples? And what's he planning on using them for? Why hold onto them for all these years?"

Frank stood up. "I guess we'll find out. I've got a meeting scheduled with him in twenty minutes. Are you going to come too?"

"I'll come to the prison with you, but the meeting should just be between you two. He's more likely to make a mistake with you. I seem to put him on edge. I want to talk to Officer Kembrey. Dr. Pazzo had to get the samples into the prison somehow in order to keep them safe or start to revive them. I could ask the Warden, but I have a feeling that Kembrey knows everything that goes in and out of that place."

"Stan will keep his mouth shut too. Isn't it going to look weird if you just go to talk to him though?"

Nella waved Ann Connelly's medical record. "I can use Ann's test results as an excuse."

Frank looked grim. "Is there anything you can do? Is she going to get better?"

She sighed and shook her head. "No. In some cases, there is just residual swelling in the brain and we can treat that. Even with medieval methods. But Ann's brain- the bacteria was active for too long. People that were infected early and treated late have holes in their brain, where the bacteria has actually eaten away at it over time. I can't put back what's not there any more. She won't get worse and we might be able to build different pathways in her brain for some things, but she'll never be even close to what she once was."

"There just doesn't seem to be any good news these days, does there?"

Nella stood up and slid the medical record into her briefcase. She looked up with a small smile. "There's us," she said.

Frank immediately brightened up. He pulled her into a quick hug.

"Come on," she said gently, "we're going to be late."

STAN KEMBREY

They were both too nervous to talk on the drive to the prison. The tension seemed to wind tighter around Nella with every turn of the tires, though she strove to keep herself calm, more for Frank's sake than hers. They got out of the parked car without speaking and entered the prison. Both of them wore calm, polite masks. Nella walked behind Frank to the metal detector. She was momentarily shocked at the ease of Frank's greeting with Stan Kembrey. His smile was the same as the day he'd met her. At first it unnerved Nella that he could be so casual. She realized if she couldn't tell how anxious he was, then Dr. Pazzo certainly wouldn't, and Nella breathed easier.

"Hey Stan, I've got a few minutes before my meeting, how about a cup of coffee with me and Dr. Rider. She hasn't had a real cup of coffee in years and I told her you had the last can in the City."

Officer Kembrey simultaneously laughed and scowled. "That's supposed to be a secret Frank. But now that you've spilled the beans, I guess Terry can take over for a while."

Frank groaned at the obvious pun while Terry, still looking as nervous as on Nella's first visit, cleared them. Nella followed Frank and Officer Kembrey into a small office hardly bigger than a closet and crammed with various lockers. Officer Kembrey sat behind his desk, just freeing enough space for Frank and Nella to stand side by side. Frank closed the door without comment and the smile fell off his face.

"All right Frank, what's this really about?"

"Look, I don't have time to explain all of it, and I honestly think you'll sleep better at night if you never find out. But Nell- Dr. Rider can tell you if you insist. She really does need some information and I know you can keep your mouth shut if you need to. I wouldn't ask if it wasn't important Stan."

"This is a good, steady job Frank. After the trial I've been guaranteed a similar post if this one is no longer needed. I don't want to jeopardize that, even for you."

"It isn't information that's illegal or even questionable," Nella broke in quickly, "it's just that we can't afford for anyone else to know that we're asking."

Officer Kembrey leaned forward, "I don't understand."

Nella glanced at Frank. "You better tell him," he said, "I have to go or Dr. Pazzo will get suspicious." Frank opened the door and slid his thin frame out of it before closing it again.

Officer Kembrey turned to Nella. "You better sit down," he said indicating a stool jammed into the corner, "I can tell this is going to take a while."

"How much do you want to know?" asked Nella, trying to arrange herself without knocking her injured arm against the wall.

"I suppose you'd better tell me it all, otherwise I'll be up all night imagining the worst."

Nella blew out a sigh.

"That bad, huh?" Officer Kembrey asked.

"I'm sorry to be blunt, but I don't think we have a lot of time. Dr. Schneider and Dr. Carton developed a very dangerous bacteria before the outbreak of the Plague. When Mr. Courtlen and I interviewed Dr. Pazzo, it turned out that he knew about it. Frank and I went to destroy the existing samples at Dr. Carton's old lab based on Dr. Pazzo's information. Instead of finding the samples, we found Dr. Schneider. The samples had been stolen some time ago. I think by

Dr. Pazzo himself."

"How dangerous is this dangerous bacteria?"

"It's the incurable version of the Plague and those that were immune the first time probably won't be as lucky this time."

"Incurable?" Officer Kembrey shook his head, "And you think Dr. Pazzo has it?"

"That's what I want to ask you about. But if he *does* have it and finds out we're asking, whatever his plans are, could change."

Officer Kembrey rocked back in his seat and scratched the back of his head. "He was brought in with what was on him when he was Cured. But he didn't get to keep much of it."

"What did he come in with?"

Officer Kembrey opened a desk drawer with a rusty squeal. He rummaged around for a second and then pulled out a thin, plain folder. He opened it on the desk and then fumbled around the cluttered desk for reading glasses. At last he said, "It looks like a set of clothing provided by the Cure personnel, a wallet, a dead cell phone and three fountain pens. Uh, it looks like the wallet had thirteen dollars, a state ID and a university ID in it and . . . Nothing else. That's weird."

"What's weird?" Nella asked, leaning quickly forward.

"Well, I've been an intake officer for years, since before the Plague even. Nobody walks into prison with just an ID. It just doesn't happen. Okay, I've seen people without credit cards or identification. I've even seen people come in without keys to their car or house. That happens. But I've never seen anyone, even a homeless person, come in without some of the normal stuff in their wallets. This guy had no bank card, no grocery card, no video club card, not even a library card- and he was a university professor. No metro ticket, no pictures, not even an old condom wrapper. Nothing. It would be written here if he had. Combined with the fact that he didn't have any keys at all, not even to the lab he was found in. . . It's like all he wanted us to know about him was his name. Like he *knew* what we'd be looking for-"

Nella stood up and banged her wounded shoulder on an overhanging locker. Officer Kembrey winced in sympathy but Nella hardly noticed. "Like he knew what you'd be looking for so you wouldn't look any farther. So you wouldn't look at any of the other things he came in with, because they'd be normal, easy, nothing to remark at, nothing to remember. What else did you say he came in with?"

Officer Kembrey glanced at the paper. "His clothes, a dead cell phone and three fountain pens."

"What would he have been allowed to keep?"

He shook his head. "Well, none of it. At least at first. He would have been given his wallet back without the cash. There's a note from the Warden saying he requested the fountain pens back and some paper after a few days. It looks like he was given those. Nothing else, not that there was much anyway."

Nella was confused. What good were fountain pens and an empty wallet? "Has he received any mail? Or had any visitors who could give him anything?"

He flipped through the few pages in the folder. "He's had a few letters from Frank of course. And the books that you brought in for him just a little bit ago, but no, he hasn't had any deliveries. As for visitors . . . Just Frank, you and- oh yeah, I remember this guy. Ned Glist. He was a jeweler that Dr. Pazzo commissioned. He wanted to get something nice for the defense attorneys. The Warden approved it, as long as Mr. Glist didn't bring any tools with him. The guy came in empty handed, we checked him thoroughly."

"Do you know what type of jewelry he was supposed to make?"

"No, we didn't ask. It would have to be checked back through here anyway when it was done and sent to the Warden's office for safekeeping."

Nella felt panic claw it's way up her throat. "Did the guy leave with anything?"

"Sorry Dr. Rider, we don't really check what people leave with, just what they come in with. You and Frank could talk to him though."

"Not without him talking to Dr. Pazzo."

"I bet you could if you were clever. You and Frank go talk to this guy, tell him that Dr. Pazzo recommended him, because jewelers are scarce now. In fact I think he's actually a wire wrapper down at the electric plant these days. I have no idea how Dr. Pazzo found him or what he's intending to pay him with. Anyway, tell him you two are shopping for a ring and hint at Dr. Pazzo's order and see if he'll gab. Tell him he has to keep the ring a secret though, because there'd be trouble at court if anyone found out you two were seeing each other."

Nella blushed and looked confused. Officer Kembrey smiled. "Yeah, I didn't think that was too far off the mark. But no one'll hear it from me. Anyway, what exactly am I looking for, in case these samples haven't got here yet?"

Nella collected herself and sat carefully back onto the stool. "The samples were in small glass test tubes. As long as they are still sealed in those vials they are okay. Once they are exposed to the air though, the bacteria will either die or start spreading."

"How long do they have to be open before the bacteria spreads?"

Nella shrugged. "Depending on the ease of transmission, a few hours to a few days? This is a more potent version of the Plague, so I'd bet on sooner rather than later."

He ran a shaky hand through his spiky, graying hair. "Well," he said brightly, "I guess that's good news in a way. We're either already sick or it hasn't happened yet, because nothing like that has come through in the past few days. Or ever."

"I doubt anyone would bring the test tubes in openly. And glass won't set off the metal detector."

"The only people who have been through here since you two took off were staff. Even Mr. Green hasn't been by. And if Dr. Pazzo has staff working for him, well, we might as well give up now."

"What could they be hidden in?"

Officer Kembrey stood up. "Listen, Dr. Rider, let me work on that. It's my job to find contraband, and to find it quietly. You can help by visiting that jeweler and by acting normal. We're going to find those samples. The fewer people that know about it, the less panic we'll cause and the less likely Dr. Pazzo- or *whoever* has them, is going to jump the gun. Are you sure he would keep them here?"

Nella stood up too. "Yes. Dr. Pazzo needs to be in control. Having them nearby would ensure that he could use them when and how he wanted without relying on outside help. It would also give him a sense of power even in here. Trust me, that stuff is *my* job."

"Okay then. Let's both get to work. I'll find a reason to get into his cell and soon. If I find anything, if I even guess anything, you and Frank will be the first to know. If the jeweler tells you anything, you let *me* know."

Nella shook his hand with her good one. "Thank you Officer Kembrey, it's such a relief to have help."

He put one hand on her good shoulder. "We'll find them Dr. Rider. It's going to be all right."

She smiled at him through her worry.

FOREVER IN A PLACE LIKE THIS

Nella passed the cafeteria on the way to the infirmary to discuss Ann's medical results. The clatter of warming pans reminded her of something Dr. Schneider had said. The bacteria would have to be revived in some sort of broth and was it jello? No, gelatin. Nella wondered if it would matter if it were jello. She wheeled around and headed into the cafeteria. A few shiny faced ladies were joking good naturedly as they lowered steaming pans into the cafeteria bar.

"Excuse me," Nella said, smiling.

The nearest lady looked up. "Hi honey, we're running a little late today, we'll be open in just a few minutes."

"Oh! You're fine, I'm not trying to hurry you," said Nella, "I actually came by to see if you had a record of what the prisoners have been ordering for their meals."

The lady eyed her suspiciously. "You aren't press are you?" she asked, "That's not really information we give out."

Nella stuck out her good hand. "I'm sorry, I haven't even introduced myself. I'm Dr. Rider, I was sent by the court to make sure the prisoners are healthy enough for trial."

The lady shook her hand, "Ah, well that's different. You want to make sure they are eating, right?"

"Yes, that's right. Do you keep track of what they order and how much they send back?"

"Sure, but we're about to get awfully busy. The staff lunch is about to start."

"I can come back, say, an hour from now?"

"All right then, Doc. We'll have the list for you. How far back do you want?"

Nella thought for a moment. It had taken a little over a month for the first Plague's symptoms to begin. "Is six weeks ok? For Robert Pazzo and Ann Connelly and of course, Gerta Schneider from now on." She thanked the lady and continued on to the infirmary. She tried not to wonder how Frank was doing, but in the hundred yards from the cafeteria to the infirmary she worried about him at least a half dozen times. She was distracted enough that she had forgotten why she had headed to the infirmary in the first place and spent several seconds trying to remember before anyone noticed her.

"Dr. Rider," said a nurse pleasantly, his cool, crisp uniform almost an aura of order around him, "did you want me to check your dressing?"

Nella shook herself, "Oh, no thank you. I'm here to talk to the physician about Ann Connelly's test results. Is he busy?"

The nurse's polite smile stuttered. "I'll grab him for you. But Mr. Green let us know in no uncertain terms that he wanted to be present whenever Miss Connelly was discussed- especially if it was at your request."

Nella sucked in a bitter breath. "Ah, I see. Well, I don't want to make trouble, would you mind contacting both him and the physician? I will talk to them together at their convenience. In the mean time, I'm going to see my patient."

"I'm sorry, Dr. Rider."

Nella shook her head and smiled. "Don't be, it isn't your fault. It's perfectly all right." She turned and walked down the hallway back toward the cell block. It *wasn't* all right. *You'd think after the world fell to pieces that the jurisdictional bullshit would go away too. I guess if we only have one small city left to fight over, we're going to fight over every inch.* Nella lightly rubbed her sore shoulder. *It would be one thing if Mr. Green wanted to be present to protect his client. All he wants to know is how soon I'll pronounce her incompetent and he can get back to the golf course. Or whatever it is post-apocalyptic lawyers do in their spare time these days.* Nella stifled a perverse laugh as soon as she thought it. She approached the heavy metal door into the cell block and peeked through the mesh filled window while the door opened, hoping to see Frank at the conference table. It was empty. She couldn't decide if that was good or bad. Where would they be meeting if not in the block? Was he already finished? Did he know where the samples were? She took a deep breath and headed for Ann's cell. Frank was right. She did over-analyze everything.

Officer Wells met her at the cell door. "Hi Doc. Geez, what happened?"

Nella half panicked, not having prepared a story for her injury. No one else had cared enough to be curious, not even the infirmary staff. "Oh," she said, far more calmly than she felt, "it was a stupid accident. I was trying to fix the tiller I borrowed from a neighbor. I got a rock stuck in the blade and I sliced my shoulder pulling it out." She was shocked at the evenness of her own voice. Her brain remembered the actual injury in excruciating detail and sweat popped out on her forehead, but she kept her face cheerful. Wells winced. "Ouch Doc. You sure are accident prone. You have to be more careful."

Nella chuckled although she didn't feel like laughing it off. "You're telling me. Pain killers are hard to come by these days. Anyway, how's our Ann?"

"She seems much better now that we've taken her outside a few times. She had to be heavily sedated when she was sent for those tests, but she's been pretty calm since then."

"Good. The more consistent we can be, the better she'll do I think."

Wells squinted and Nella was alarmed to see that he was on the verge of tears. "She's not going to get better is she Doc?"

Nella set down the briefcase and patted his arm. "I'm sorry Wells, she has some pretty bad permanent damage. I'm afraid the best we can hope for is more good days than bad. The more you let her walk around outside or talk with her, even about little things, the better she'll do though. Pieces of her brain are missing, but it can rewire itself. I took her off the antibiotics the physician had her on. He thought they were helping, but they were actually making things worse. From now on, she should get better at things like walking and responding to people, even her speech should get better."

Wells swiped at his eyes with a sleeve. "But she's never going to get out of here is she? Or another place like here, even if the trial goes well."

"She's going to need to be in constant care for the rest of her life. She's always going to have tics, like biting, and scratching. And when she gets emotional she'll probably always try to do herself some kind of harm. Those things just aren't in her control. She's never going to be able to cook a meal or drive a car- or even remember much about what happened after the onset of the Plague."

"That's what Johnson thought. We've been talking. We're both supposed to rotate out of here after the trial, that's actually why we both agreed to this post. It meant we could do something else after. But I think- *we* think, it might be best if we stay with Ann wherever she ends up. She's used to us and we understand her, most of the time. I mean, I know we'll have to get medical training-"

"Actually, I think you and Johnson have as much training as anyone else these days. I'm afraid medical training consists mostly of first aid and cpr now. And I'm sure you already know that much. I think it's an excellent idea. Ann couldn't ask for a better set of caregivers. Of course, I can't say for sure what the Judges' ruling will be, but I'm fairly confident that Ann will not pass her competency hearing. The Judges will decide where she should go, but I'll be able to make a recommendation. I'll certainly suggest that you two stick with her, if you're sure that's what you want."

Wells nodded. "We're sure. Thanks Doc."

Nella placed her briefcase beside the door with a smile. She began to pull the cell door open and turned back to Wells. "Brace yourself," she said, "Mr. Green is on his way with the physician to discuss Ann's condition and treatment."

Wells groaned and Nella walked into the cell.

A FUNERAL THAT HASN'T HAPPENED YET

Nella had a small migraine by the time she headed back to the cafeteria. She suppressed a sigh as she was handed the small novel that made up the meal record for Dr. Pazzo and Ann. She walked back toward the prison's reception area, giving Stan Kembrey a furtive glance on her way. Frank was not waiting for her, though more than two hours had passed since they'd split up. She couldn't decide if it was a good sign or a bad sign. Not seeing him and Dr. Pazzo on the cell block had caused a dull drumbeat of worry to start in her head and it had only grown since then. She sat in the chair closest to the door and began flipping through the list of prisoner meals. She tried to concentrate on what she read, but between her headache and growing anxiety, she couldn't decide what could be important and what was not.

At last she heard the quick, light clip of Frank's shoes on the hallway floor. She heard him call a goodbye to Officer Kembrey. She snapped open her briefcase and slid the meal record in for later. She closed it and looked up as he collapsed into the hard seat next to her. He set his own case on the floor and leaned forward, his hands scrubbing his face. The reception area was empty except for the two of them and the florescent lights hummed cold and dismal above them like an echo of the aching space in Nella's head. She put a soft hand on his bony knee.

"I'm sorry," she said.

He straightened up and put a warm hand over hers, squeezing gently. He tilted the back of his head against the wall and turned to look at her. He smiled. "Let's go home."

He stood up, pulling her up with him and they pushed through the heavy glass door, out of the gray, changeless world of the prison into the mild sun of early spring. The world smelled green, even the steaming parking lot. The sound of birds was almost overwhelming. Nella winced in anticipation of a spike of pain. But her headache seemed to evaporate instead. For an instant Frank was a dark shadow against the bright sky. A thin, elongated icon, a cave painting. Just a memory of what men had been. Nella felt a strange sense of displacement, again realizing that the world would go on, *was* going on, almost without change. Even without humanity directing it. This time, though, the thought brought no comfort. Her eyes adjusted and Frank was solid flesh again, but her mind lingered in the same deep, panic worn rut.

The car was silent and hot, a breathless tomb that had lost the crisp linen smell of him. Instead the air was limp and stale and Nella felt herself drowning in the stillness. She rubbed away a few weak tears before Frank could see them. He slid into the car and rolled the windows down. The car idled with a muted thrum as he stared blankly at the low gray prison. At last he shifted the car into drive. His voice was gutteral and rough. "For the first time in my life," he said, "I sincerely hope that Hell is real."

The car lurched out of its spot and tore away from the prison lot. "It'll be a much shorter eternity if I know *he's* burning alongside me."

Nella felt her eyes spark and pinch again. "Don't say that," she said quietly.

"Sorry."

Nella watched the road turn rosy in the last light of the sun. She could hear the frogs singing loudly through the open window and the breeze was soft and smelled like crushed grass. She watched a sprinkling of lights turning on, like a string with too many burnt out bulbs. The car swerved and she looked back at Frank in alarm. He was wiping his eyes with one hand and trying to steer with the other. The car swerved into the soft, muddy shoulder and stopped. Nella reached over and put the car into park before turning it off. She unbuckled as Frank doubled over, his head in his hands. He tried so hard to hold back that he shook and his chest was a collapsed, breathless cave. Nella wrapped her arms around him as well as she could without speaking. They stayed that way a long time. The fresh, clean breeze swirled through the car and the frog song an unearthly choir around them. She felt as if she were at a funeral that hadn't happened yet. She stroked the back of his neck with her warm fingers, but he was like a closed shell, a stone without cracks. She felt tears cooling on her own face, but she couldn't have said whether it was because of his grief or hers. She pressed her forehead gently against his cheek and at last he turned toward her. She pulled him further into her arms and he took a deep, ragged breath. She could feel the sobs shaking in his throat, but he kept them there after a struggle.

"What happened?" she whispered and held his face in her hands.

"I really didn't believe he had them. I thought he might, you know, when I realized that he hadn't really locked himself in, but I didn't really *believe* it. And then, when you said it out loud, I started to think I was wrong, but I still thought he wasn't really going to use them, I'd just talk to him and he'd hand them over. If he wanted to destroy the world, he would have done it long before I met him, wouldn't he?" His voice broke and his breath was a sharp, hot wind over her arms. "All I had to do was reason with him and he'd turn the samples over. Then everything would be all right. The world would be safe," he laughed a little and looked at her, though his eyes still streamed, "*You'd* be safe. I'd be a hero."

Instead of answering, she pulled his mouth to hers. She could feel the tiny explosions of breath against her lips as he tried to suppress his grief. She kissed him until his breath smoothed out.

"I promised you that I would find them. I promised you that everything would be all right, that this was just the beginning. But when I told him about Dr. Carton and about his lab and finding Dr. Schneider but not the samples- I would have known then, even if we hadn't figured it out before. He was so smug. He was like a snake closing in, tightening around all the time left in the world. And I knew before I even finished that he wasn't going to turn them over. I wanted to hit him," He shook his head, "No, that's not true. I wanted to kill him. Right there. With my own hands. I haven't felt that way since- in a long time."

He touched her shoulder gently, feeling the ragged scar through her shirt and bandage. "Everything is repeating. The world is still dying. I still can't protect what I love. And I'm still a monster. Nothing has gotten any better."

"You aren't a monster."

"Normal people don't think about killing other people unless it's to survive."

Nella laughed. "Yes they do Frank. Especially these days. The sane ones just don't go through with it." She drew her fingertips down the hollow of his cheek. "You don't need to protect me. We *are* going to find the samples, and the world will go on and the sun will rise and the summer will come just as it has always done. But Frank, if we don't- if the worst happens, you don't need to protect me. Whatever comes, you don't have to shield me. This is lonely enough without that."

His breath hitched and heaved again and he closed his eyes, trying to calm himself. She pulled away from him slowly and got out of the car. She walked carefully over to his side, her shoes sinking in the soft spring mud, the gnats making a halo of fluttering gold around her. She opened his door. He unfolded himself and she was again reminded of a cave painting, a purple shadow of what had been rather than what was. He reached for her and they stood leaning against the warm car on the edge of the empty road as the last of the sun retreated and the City edged the horizon with a thin vein of light.

MIDNIGHT MOB

The packet of meal records slid from Nella's limp hand as she dozed in Frank's office. It slumped white on the dark carpet and the slight breeze on her legs woke her up. She leaned over and scooped up the papers. She started to straighten them into a neat pile and then gave up, tossing them haphazardly into her open briefcase beside her. She'd finished with them anyway. Nothing pure enough to revive the samples had been served in the past six weeks. All she had to show for her trouble was the return of a thumping headache. Nella switched off the light and walked carefully into the bedroom, trying not to bump anything in the unfamiliar dark. Frank's back was a dark mountain range gently eroded by the blankets into softer lines. She undressed and stretched her wounded shoulder carefully. She was relieved to be free of the sling and decided not to wear it again. It just caused more questions than she wanted to answer. The sheets were cold as she slid onto them, but she didn't want to wake him, so she left the space between them open. Her eyes slowly adjusted and she could make out the tired lines on Frank's face. He remained sad and exhausted, even asleep.

She resisted the urge to smooth the worry from his face with her hand. Surely, he had to have defended people he knew had committed a crime before. He may not like to lie, but she'd seen him do it without too much trouble before. Admittedly, there had probably never been this much at stake before. Nella closed her eyes. She ought to be worried about whether she would blow it herself, rather than whether he would. Her thoughts fluttered like gray moths. Sadness for Frank, the strange visit of the jeweler, Wells's worried face. One by one they made their circuits and floated away.

A thunk and a chiming crash woke her with a start. She froze and sucked in a panicked breath. Frank's was already sitting up on one elbow. He brushed his fingers across her back, looking for glass. "Are you all right? Did it hit you?" he asked.

Nella was still disoriented. "What? I don't think so. What is it?"

"Fucking zombie!" floated up from the street, "Don't even have the decency to shoot the bastard when you're with him." The voice was oily and uneven.

"Drunk. Great, it's starting early." Frank stood up looking for his clothing in the dark. Nella sat up. "No," he whispered, "stay there. There's probably glass on your side. And this guy might have a gun or friends or something."

Nella grabbed his wrist. "Don't go," she hissed, "Just let them go away."

"I have to. I have to at least see who it is."

"No, why? They're all the same. What if there's more than one?"

"What if they want to burn the house down?"

"No Frank, don't-"

He leaned over and hugged her. "I have to. I'll be careful. Stay here, don't let them see you." He pulled his wrist gently out of her hand and padded into the hallway in only his shorts. Nella scrambled to find her clothes. She crept down the stairs after him as he closed the front door behind him. The pack from their trip was still sitting beside overstuffed chair in the living room. She felt around in the pockets and found one of the guns. She thought it was the pistol but couldn't be sure even by touch. She pulled the thick curtain an inch or two from the window and peered out into the dark street. The man was still yelling and the lights in the neighborhood were beginning to turn on, casting light onto the street in long, thick teeth of pallid gold. She could see the man half tilted over and holding a bottle by its neck. She couldn't see his face. Frank must have sensed she was there, because he moved in front of the window, blocking the man from her sight.

"Terry? Go home. I won't tell anyone you were here. Just go home and sleep it off." She heard Frank's voice as if it were far away, through water. *Terry? Wasn't that the new guard's name at the prison?* She tried to peer around Frank's back, pulling the curtain a little farther from the window.

"You're a piece of work you know 'at? Your neighbors know what you done?" Terry stumbled in a half circle, facing the growing pool of window lights. His arm flailed upward with the almost empty bottle. Nella watched as Frank walked calmly toward him.

"'Ese your friends? Nah. Zombies ain't got no friends. You eats each other 'stead."

Nella paced to the door and opened it just a crack so that she could hear as Frank told him firmly and quietly to get lost.

"HE ATE HIS WIFE. AND A KID. A KID," Terry yelled. A baby down the street began to squall and Nella watched as a few men emerged from their front doors. Most were half dressed, their scars twisting like vines on their faces and legs and arms. Some were missing limbs. A few were carrying weapons. Bats, hockey sticks, golf clubs, tire irons, all shining like teeth in the light from the windows. She watched Terry recoil, their presence reaching through the thick haze of drunk and hate. "I see," he said, nodding conspiratorially, "You're all zombies." He stumbled and Frank caught him before his face could hit the pavement. Terry shoved him off. "Ge' off monser. James Grant tole me whatchu done. I know whatchu are. 'ID YOU KNOW HE'S THE LAWYER

FOR PATS- PAAAAZ- FOR THE GUY WHAT DID THIS TO YOU? 'ID YOU KNOW HE'S GOING TO HELP THE GUY GO FREE. ALL OUR LIVES IS RUINT BUT THOSE THAT DID IT, THEY GETS TO GO FREE. AN' THIS ZOMBIE PROLLY GETS A SHITLOAD OF MONEY FOR IT. YOU BELIE' THAT?"

The neighbors began descending from their stoops. Almost at the same time. Some hobbling, some smoothly sauntering, but all closing in on Frank and Terry. Nella held her breath and she checked the gun in the light filtering through the crack in the door. Ten or a dozen men formed a half circle around the two. Nella could see Frank's posture change. He grew bigger, lengthening as his muscles tensed and straightened and his long hands clenched.

"Oh shit," said Terry.

One very large man in the group of neighbors growled, "You're awfully lost Immune. This is our home. You aren't welcome here."

"Can go where I want," said Terry, puffing his chest out in false bravado.

Another man slapped a tire iron on his open palm as he closed the distance between the crowd and Terry. "Yeah? You know what we do to Immunes here?"

Terry shook his head. A reedy man circled around behind Terry while the one with the tire iron kept talking. Nella felt like shrinking away from the door to hide, but she remained still. "Well," said the man with the tire iron, "When we get tired of taking chunks out of each other and an Immune wanders in . . ."

"We eats 'em!" said the reedy man in a falsetto shriek and snapped his teeth together with a sharp click that even Nella could hear. Terry screeched and scrambled away from the group. He dropped the bottle as he ran back toward the City's center, not even bothering to stop and pick it up. Nella heard the men erupt in low chuckles and the lights in the windows slowly began winking out. But Frank still looked ready for a fight and she couldn't bring herself to quite relax. He turned toward the collapsing circle of neighbors and she could see the stress lines on his brow even in the half light. His scar pulsed and jittered as if he were grinding his teeth. She half opened the door, but the large man said easily, "You okay Frank?" and the reedy man clapped him on the shoulder.

"Yeah," said Frank and she watched him relax and uncoil. She decided not to move and stayed in the shadow of the open door. "I'm sorry. I didn't mean to bring trouble to anyone but myself. I don't even know why I chose to do this anymore."

"No one could think ill of you if you decided to drop the case Frank," said the man with the tire iron, "God knows you've as much or more cause to hate Pazzo as the rest of us."

Frank glanced uneasily back at her. *Me?* She thought, *he's worried that I'll be upset if he drops the case?* "Even people we hate deserve to have their say. We've all done things we aren't happy about. Wouldn't we all want the same?" Frank asked, as if someone had argued with him. Nella suspected this had been a long and frequent discussion in the neighborhood.

"We know why you're doing it Frank," said the large man, "No one here's going to harass you about it."

"Thanks." She could hear the relief in his tone of voice.

"C'mon guys, it's late," yawned a neighbor. The others split gently, each shaking Frank's hand or slapping his back and calling "goodnight" over their shoulders.

"Go on," said the reedy man, pushing Frank back towards the house, "Your girl must be out-of-her-mind worried. And tell her I didn't mean any harm." He clicked his teeth together again, grinning.

"You shouldn't keep her cooped up like that Frank," said the big man, "It's not polite you know. My wife said she was a good Doc. Helped her a lot in the Cure camp."

Frank laughed, embarrassed, and Nella blushed behind the door. "Okay, we'll have a block party or something. We'll be more social I promise."

He padded easily back to the door and flipped on the light. "See, I told you they gossiped," he said, without commenting on the gun in her hand. She replaced it in the pack without apologizing for it.

"Are you okay?" she asked as he caught her around the waist.

"I'm okay. Are you?"

She nodded and blew out a shaky breath in relief.

"It won't be the last time you know," he brushed a loose length of hair from her forehead. "It won't be Terry, I think I can safely guarantee that. But it'll be someone. Maybe not drunk next time. Maybe mean and sober."

"I know."

"Maybe I should take you home. You'll be safer there until the trial is over."

"Don't you dare. You want me to lie awake every night worrying that you got killed? I'll just drive down here and sleep in the car every night." She pulled him up the stairs so he wouldn't think of it any longer. They carefully cleaned the glass up together and Frank pushed the desk over to cover the broken pane.

Nella was exhausted. She had barely fallen

asleep when Terry had thrown the rock through the window, and it had already been very late. She pressed her cheek against his chest. Her breath fell on him in a warm, curling mist. "Frank," she said, already more than half asleep, "I won't be upset if you want to give up the trial. I'll understand if you can't do it, knowing what you know now."

"I can do it. It's just going to be harder." Frank's voice was bitter and slow.

"We could find a boat. We could just disappear."

He stroked her hair with his fingertips. "Nella, would you really disappear with me? We might never come back."

Nella yawned. "I know."

"After the trial."

"Stan said we should go see the jeweler tomorrow. Say we're finding a ring. I think he knows I love you Frank . . ." She murmured, trailing off into sleep.

"What jeweler?" asked Frank, but she didn't hear him.

THE JEWELER

"I don't like this plan," Sevita grumbled. Nella sighed and strained to see into the power plant's dark interior.

"You couldn't think of a better one," she said, giving up and turning back toward her friend. "Besides, what could happen? This guy is just a jeweler. Pazzo wouldn't have any co-conspirators. He's too controlling for that."

"Why couldn't I have gone instead of Christine?"

Nella laughed. "You're too well known. It would have been career suicide. If anyone, it should have been me and Christine that went."

"You're no good at lying. He would have seen right through you."

"I know, I know. This way no one gets caught."

"That's so boring," Sevita grumbled.

Nella laughed. Sevita tapped her fingers along her knee and Nella rolled the window down for some fresh air. "You're sure that's all he brought in with him?" Sevita asked.

"Hmm? Oh, Dr. Pazzo, yeah, three pens, an almost empty wallet and a dead cell phone."

"Well did anyone check the lab where he was found?"

"Yeah, I asked Frank that too. He says they took everything apart inch by inch for the investigation."

"What about weird places, like inside the vending machines or those tubes he pretended were feeding them?"

"You aren't going to rest until you see it for yourself, are you?"

"Frank must have access to it, as part of the

defense team."

"Ask him."

"Can't you ask him for me? He's more likely to say yes to you. He'll say yes to anything *you* ask," Sevita smiled slyly at her.

"I doubt anyone will need much persuading. Go to Judge Hawkins and ask. They want you to document the case right? That's part of it I would assume."

"No, I asked already," Sevita pouted, "He said it would influence people's opinions unfairly. Too much gore, it would inflame emotions or something."

"Then don't get Frank in trouble!"

"I'm not! I just think we should check to make sure Pazzo didn't hide it there."

"He would've expected the place to be searched. Besides, I know he wants to keep those samples near him. He can't risk anyone finding them. But if you swear to me that nothing will get accidentally aired, I'll ask Frank if we can look around."

Sevita was satisfied and let Nella return to her worrying in peace. They didn't have very long to wait. Christine was blushing on her way back to the car and wouldn't meet their eyes. Nella was amused, thinking Frank must have kissed her to convince the guy. Frank was only a few steps behind and got into the car without saying anything. He looked nervous. Sevita leaned forward and picked up Christine's hand.

"Chris, you dope, you had my ring on the whole time. How's the guy going to believe you now?"

Christine glanced at Frank and he shook his head slightly. Nella just caught it. "We told him we wanted to upgrade," said Christine still blushing.

"Well? What happened?" asked Sevita impatiently.

Nella leaned forward, forgetting Christine's

confusion and Frank's warning. Frank started the car. "Dr. Pazzo was very specific about what he wanted. He ordered gold plated fountain pens for the defense attorneys. Even Dr. Schneider's, although we hadn't found her yet," he said grimly.

Sevita glanced at her. Nella collapsed back into her seat, all the feeling draining into her feet. Sevita kept her voice low so Christine couldn't hear. "That's it, isn't it?"

Nella nodded.

"Then why don't we just go get the pens from his cell? That must be where he's keeping them."

"What if they aren't there? Then he'll know we're looking for them. He might release it right there and then."

"Can anyone get into his cell without him knowing?"

"Not until he's in court. And then we've all got to be there."

"You don't, as long as you've already testified."

Nella leaned forward, speaking over the whipping breeze that filled the car. "Frank, when is he supposed to deliver them? And where?"

"He said he was supposed to deliver them to court on verdict day. Those were Dr. Pazzo's express instructions." He paused and the despairing look he gave her in the rearview mirror made her heart ache. "That gives us about two weeks."

"That short?" asked Sevita.

"I can try to stall, but I can't do very much. The prosecution elected to skip survivor testimonies at the beginning of the process. The government thought it would be bad for morale to rehash what people had gone through, especially since we've all been through it. It isn't like other tribunals where the world needs to be educated about what happened. We all know too well. I thought I was doing the right thing by agreeing to skip that part. And then there is Ann's attorney, but I have a feeling Ann's case will be dismissed in short order, right Nella?"

"I filed a finding that she was incompetent and I haven't heard any protest from the prosecution's side, so it will be fast."

"That leaves Dr. Schneider's attorney. I don't know her, we've never met before. But I assume it's in her best interest to gloss over most of the evidence and concentrate on the work Dr. Schneider did on the Cure. So barring a sparring match between the two of us or between the prosecutor and Dr. Schneider's attorney, it will probably be pretty fast."

"I don't think Dr. Schneider is going to have it all her own way," Sevita said, "Ms Jacobsen and I had a long talk with Dr. Carton."

"Jesus," swore Frank, "You're lucky I'm not representing Dr. Schneider. I'm going back to manual labor after this. There's no way I can do this job with you around."

They pulled up in front of Christine's apartment. Nella got out and Christine hugged her, pressing Nella's keys into her hand.

"I'm glad I didn't need to use these. Frank's a wonderful person," she blurted out and turned away, quickly climbing her stairs and disappearing inside.

"That was weird," said Sevita. "Don't worry, I'll ferret it out of her before long."

"Nella, would you mind driving?" Frank asked suddenly.

"Sure," she said, stretching her bad arm to test it. She walked around to the driver's side and got in. She glanced over, but Frank had walked away from the car and was talking earnestly to Sevita in front of the building. Sevita glanced nervously at her and looked away quickly. Nella was confused. Frank returned to the car.

"What was all that about?" Nella asked.

"Hmm?" he asked with a cheerful smile, "Oh that? I was just telling Sevita to remember that this was all a secret and to be careful who she told what."

Nella didn't believe him, but she held her tongue. He leaned back into the seat and brushed wind whipped hair off her face. "Let's not think about it any more today. We can't do anything else yet can we?"

Nella shook her head. "Then let's pretend none of this is happening. Just for today. Let's just be us."

"Okay," she said and flashed him a watery smile before turning the car off and getting out.

"What are you doing?" he asked.

"We're going to be us today. I thought we could walk to the Farm. Maybe see a guy about a boat."

He stuck his hands into his pockets and kicked a stone into the road. "You know a guy with a boat?" he asked.

"Mmhmm."

"And you settled for a guy like me?"

She laughed. "You have thicker, more luxuriant hair."

Frank rubbed the soft skin of his head. "Yeah," he sighed, "I've always been lucky that way."

He kissed her in the warm spring sun and they headed down the crazy cracked pavement toward the transformed park that now fed the last city in the world.

OPENING STATEMENTS

The crowd pressed in around Nella and Sevita, even more people packed into the large auditorium than there had been last time. Sevita reveled in it, but Nella could only think of how easy it would be to infect everyone at once with every steaming breath that rolled against her back and stuck to the windows. Someone sneezed off to the right and Nella recoiled.

"Sorry," said an elderly man with an early tan. He held up a bright handkerchief. "Hay fever," he confided to Nella. She smiled to show him she wasn't worried about it.

Frank was sitting with Dr. Pazzo, trying to make calm and cheerful conversation. She could tell by the way he gripped the side of the table that he was uncomfortable and nervous. Dr. Pazzo, on the other hand, seemed completely at ease, leaning back in his chair and talking casually to Wells as Johnson kept a gentle hand on Ann's shoulder. Ann was mildly sedated again, but the crowd was overwhelming anyway. She rocked slightly and chewed the bandages on her hands whenever Johnson was distracted. Mr. Green completely ignored her. He was laughing with Dr. Schneider's attorney, an attractive blonde who looked far too young to ever have finished law school. Nella knew better though. She had been a big name even when Nella had been in school. She wondered what Dr. Schneider had to trade to get her. Or maybe this lawyer did it just for the fame of defending the maker of the Cure. Nella looked over toward the prosecution. Ms Jacobsen looked exhausted and cranky. *Good* thought Nella *Maybe she'll contest the finding on Ann's competency and buy me some time.* But Nella suspected it had more to do with the last minute addition of Dr. Carton to the witness list and Dr. Schneider to the defendant list.

The microphones turned on with a loud crack and the bailiff called for everyone to rise. The three judges walked out on to the dais and everyone returned to their seats with a rustle and then silence. The judges straightened their files and the bailiff talked with them in a low voice. There was a loud hacking cough somewhere in the crowd. Nella saw Frank look straight toward her as her own heart jumped out of its setting. He quickly looked back at his papers, but she saw his hand curl even tighter on the outer table edge. She couldn't tell if Dr. Pazzo had noticed.

"Good morning ladies and gentlemen," said Judge Hawkins, "Ms Jacobsen, would you read the indictments please?"

Ms Jacobsen stood up and smoothed her jacket. She spoke clearly and loudly and was assisted by two sign language interpreters on either side of the room. The mass of people were utterly silent.

"Ann Connelly, Dr. Robert Pazzo and Dr. Gerta Schneider stand accused of violating the Geneva Biological Weapons Convention, the Nuremberg Code and the United States Common Rule of research.

Each of the defendants participated in the development of the Recharge bacteria and after discovering its rapid rate of contagion and the dangerous effects the bacteria had on the human brain, failed both to contain it or to alert the proper authorities to its presence and symptoms. The citizens of the world were the unwitting and unfortunate de facto test subjects of the Recharge bacteria. Each defendant directly contributed to the death of millions of human beings through reckless disregard of proper handling, testing procedure and containment practices. Dr. Robert Pazzo also stands accused of the wrongful restraint of Dr. Gerta Schneider and neglecting to seek proper medical care for Ann Connelly. In addition, Dr. Gerta Schneider stands accused of theft, transportation of dangerous materials without precaution, and the kidnapping and enslavement of Dr. Michael Carton."

The crowd erupted and even the two subsidiary judges looked shocked. Judge Hawkins called for calm. "Would the defendants please enter their plea?" he asked.

Dr. Schneider and Dr. Pazzo entered not guilty pleas in order. Mr. Grant stood up for Ann. "My client was directed to undergo a competency evaluation. I believe your Honors and Ms Jacobsen have the results in front of you."

There was a quiet rustle as the prosecution and the panel found the paperwork. "Does the prosecution have any objection to the findings?"

Please say yes thought Nella.

Ms Jacobsen glanced up toward her with a worried expression, as if she were trying to disarm a bomb and wanted a hint. "No," she said.

The judges turned off their microphones and discussed for a few moments between themselves. Nella glanced nervously back toward Frank and noticed Dr. Pazzo staring intently at the judges. He was leaning forward as if it would help him hear. She sat up straighter and watched him.

The microphones were turned back on. Judge Hawkins spoke for the panel. "It is the finding of this tribunal that Ann Connelly is incompetent to stand trial at this time. She is remanded to the state for ninety days so that she may be returned to competency. We can revisit this finding at that point if necessary."

Ms Jacobsen broke in. "Your Honor, the

military government has studied Dr. Rider's recommendations. We feel it is best for all involved that this matter not be revisited on the strength of Dr. Rider's findings that Miss Connelly will never regain the mental capacity for competence at trial."

"Very well. Then Ann Connelly will be remanded to the state for the remainder of her life. I'm ordering her to be housed at Harbor Home when they can find space based on Dr. Rider's recommendation. In the meantime, I understand she is getting excellent care where she is. And I thank you for your fine service." He nodded gravely at Wells who grinned and at Johnson who blushed.

"I object!" Dr. Pazzo was on his feet, his gargoyle face a pallid yellow with burning spots of red on his cheek and chin. His eyes glittered.

Judge Hawkins looked confused and Frank was trying to make Dr. Pazzo sit again, one hand over the microphone, the other pulling gently on the other man's arm. "On what grounds?" Judge Hawkins asked.

"On the grounds that I should have a say in who cares for Ann," shouted Dr. Pazzo. His voice was distant without the microphone but perfectly clear.

The other judges murmured behind Hawkins and he leaned back to talk with them. "Are you related in some way?" he asked at last.

Dr. Pazzo was breathing rapidly as if he'd just run a race. Frank gave up reasoning with him and sat down. Nella half rose from her own seat. "I'm the closest thing she has to a spouse or living relative," Dr. Pazzo said, a little calmer now that the judge was speaking with him.

"I'm sorry Dr. Pazzo, but even if you were actually her spouse, this is not that type of competency hearing-" He broke off as Dr. Pazzo began screaming incoherently over him. The bailiffs came over to help Frank calm him down and Nella was already working her way down to the floor. Judge Hawkins banged the gavel as the crowd began it's own dull roar. Nella followed the bailiffs out the door with the still shrieking Dr. Pazzo. She dimly heard Hawkins ordering a recess and Frank joined her in the holding cell with Dr. Pazzo. He waited until the bailiffs released his client and Pazzo dropped onto the hard bench without comment.

"What the hell was that about?" yelled Frank. He was angrier than she had ever seen him. Angrier than the situation seemed to warrant. "If you don't calm down Judge Hawkins is going to have you removed from court. Not to mention charge you with contempt. I hardly need to tell you, you aren't winning any friends out there and we haven't even got to opening statements." Frank ran a hand over his smooth head and Nella was close enough to see the sweat at his temple.

Dr. Pazzo ignored him and turned to Nella. "Is it true?" he asked, his face almost gentle, almost the young man she'd seen on the videos, "She won't ever get better?" Nella felt Frank looking at her in confusion but she didn't dare to break eye contact with Dr. Pazzo.

"You really care about her?" she asked, "This whole time you acted as if she were just a fling. And now you care?"

Dr. Pazzo gripped at his thinning hair and Nella was shocked to see his eyes turning red and filling with tears. "I always cared. I always cared. But you never told me anything. Either of you." He glared at them in turn. "You were supposed to be the best." He spat it bitterly at Nella. "I refused to speak to four other perfectly capable doctors because I wanted *you* to see Ann. It took years. *Years* Dr. Rider." He stood up and moved toward her. Frank instinctively stepped between them before Nella could stop him. Dr. Pazzo sneered at him as if they shared a nasty joke and Nella saw Frank's long hand closing into a hard fist.

"What on earth are you talking about?" she asked, mostly so Frank wouldn't hit him.

"You were supposed to bring her back. You were supposed to fix it. Fix it all. Why did she get damaged and I'm not?" Dr. Pazzo sobbed mournfully.

Nella paused and Frank shook his head in warning. She pushed forward anyway. "I don't know Dr. Pazzo, why *did* she become so much more damaged than you?" She pulled the photos from the CAT scan from her brief case and threw them at him. They slid glossy and bright and damning over the floor. "I'm not the one who created this thing. I can only fix what I understand. Why don't you tell me?"

He slumped back onto the bench. Nella knelt down on one knee so that Dr. Pazzo could see her face. She picked up a photo. "This is what I understand, Robert," she said holding it up to him. "See this dark empty void here? That's where Ann lived. That's where her memories of you were, all the memories of who she was meant to be. And see these small spots here? That one was where she was happy. And that one let her string together her thoughts so that I could understand what is happening in her brain, why she screams about teeth, why she can't stop hurting herself."

Dr. Pazzo took the photo and cradled it in one hand. "Can't you fix it? You were supposed to fix it. You fixed others, worse off. I know. I read about it. I've been watching you for a very long time Dr. Rider." He swiped at his eyes, so he didn't see Nella pull Frank's already swinging fist back with a sudden jerk. Frank paced to the other side of the cell and tried to breathe.

"I can't fix what's not there. Your bacteria ate away at her brain. She's gone, just like everyone else who'd been exposed as long as her. The people I helped- they were still in early stages. The swelling in their brains was the problem. Not missing pieces. Not even if I had access to the best medicine and technology. Which I don't, because the Plague took those too. Nobody this far gone can fully recover. Except you." She waited for him to respond and Frank watched them, waiting for her to finish playing her hand. Dr. Pazzo was silent, the photo's bright finish still flashing off of his hooded eyes. "Anything you want to tell me Robert?" Nella asked at last.

He straightened up and took a deep breath. He handed the photo back to her and she watched his face close into its severe lines again. "No," he said. He looked at Frank, "Let's get this over with. I'm looking forward to watching Gerta hang."

Nella stood up. She didn't dare to look at Frank so she busily repacked her briefcase as he and Dr. Pazzo filed back into the courtroom. She collapsed onto the bench as soon as the courtroom door closed behind them.

What have I done? She asked herself.

The day dragged on, mostly occupied by the prosecution's opening statements and then motions by Dr. Schneider's lawyers to suppress evidence from Dr. Carton. Nella was nervous and itchy, she wanted to fly back to the prison and search Dr. Pazzo's cell. She was terrified by his reaction to her questioning. But it would be suspicious if she left court after Dr. Pazzo's outburst. She'd have to wait. She tried to pretend she was taking notes. She didn't know if Frank was angry with the delays or with something his client was goading him with or even with her, but his scar jumped and flared on his hollow cheek and his knuckles were as white as teeth as he gripped the side of the defense table. He didn't look toward her for the rest of the day and Nella berated herself for acting rashly, for pushing Dr. Pazzo farther. But there were no more outbursts from Dr. Pazzo. He seemed calm and spoke to no one but Frank.

When the judge finally closed the day's session, she found herself in the back of the massive crowd and it took her almost twenty minutes to make it into the parking lot. Sevita grabbed her arm and pulled her toward her towering cameras. "Sorry," she hissed into Nella's ear, "I have to. It would look odd after all that not to do an interview."

Nella sighed but stood still.

"Dr. Rider, you're the court appointed psychiatrist for the December Plague trial, is that correct?"

"Why yes, Ms. Das it is," she said with an overly sweet smile. Nella scanned the parking lot both for Frank and the prison transport as Sevita asked her questions.

"Court was quite exciting today. You prepared the recommendation for Ann Connelly's competency trial is that right?"

Nella just nodded absently.

"And you found her incompetent to stand trial. The judge and the prosecution agreed with you. But upon hearing this decision, Dr. Pazzo had what I can only call an extreme outburst. Yet you found him competent to be tried. Do you intend to change your position?"

Nella looked at Sevita confused. "What? I mean, no. There is a difference between a temporary outburst and Ann's condition. Ann can't understand what is going on around her and she is in no condition to aid in her own defense. In this case, there is no way she would get a fair trial. Dr. Pazzo simply had an emotional response to some disappointing news."

Dr. Schneider's lawyer walked up to Sevita's cameras and flashed a brilliant smile. "Uh thank you Dr. Rider," said Sevita quickly.

Nella slipped away as Sevita turned to the attractive blonde beside her. The white prison transport passed her, glowing in the early dusk. She hurried to Frank's car. He was leaning against it, his back to her, the rest of the lot empty even of gawkers.

She curled her fingers around his hand and leaned into his side. "Sorry," she said.

He smiled. "You? What are *you* sorry about?"

"I shouldn't have pushed him so hard. I thought I could make him change his mind, get some kind of confession or something."

"Don't be sorry. It was a good gamble. I would have done it too, if I'd known how he felt about Ann earlier. It just didn't work this time."

Nella looked around to make sure they were still alone. "I need to get into his cell. I need to find those samples."

"I know. I already called Stan. He'll be ready to help during court on Wednesday. After today's episode it would look odd if you weren't in court tomorrow. Give it one more day and things will calm down."

"You think no one will notice if I'm not there on Wednesday?"

Frank glanced at her quickly and then away. "Well- I did something that might be bad. I'm sorry, it was the only thing I could think of and I don't think it will cause any permanent harm. At least, that's what Johnson said."

"What did you do?"

"I asked Johnson to call you that morning before court. She and Wells are going to make it look like Ann is having an- an episode. Dr. Pazzo can't see into the cell and it's fairly well soundproofed, so he'll never know that she isn't having one."

"Did Johnson ask you why?"

"No. She said if it were you asking, there had to be a good reason. Anyway, it should give you plenty of time to search the prison at least. If you don't find it there- well I'm running out of ideas."

"I'll find it," she said.

WAITING

Tuesday dragged by in a dull gray blur filled with the voice of Dr. Schneider's lawyer. Nella and Frank tiptoed carefully around each other, not talking about Dr. Pazzo's outburst or the plan for Wednesday. It was a growing bubble of disease between them. Nella went to bed exhausted and sad, but couldn't relax. The wind threading in the broken window and around the desk was strong and cold. A book was lying open on it and Nella could hear the fluttering with every gust. It was driving her mad. She tried to concentrate on her breathing, or on Frank's, so that she could sleep, but she could sense him, stiff and moveless beside her and she knew he wasn't sleeping either.

She sighed. "What time is it?"

Frank fumbled with the bedside clock. "Early. Too early."

"Have you slept at all?"

"No."

She rolled on to her side to look at him. "Is it because of tomorrow?"

"Tomorrow and today and yesterday and all the yesterdays before that. I'm sorry I took a swing at Dr. Pazzo. Thank you for stopping me. That could have been bad." He rubbed his temple and then turned his head to face her. "The thought of him watching you all this time, planning this- it was too much. I've had clients I didn't like before. I've even had clients that I thought were guilty. I know Dr. Pazzo isn't guilty- at least, not of what he's accused of. But I hate him. I've always felt used after I met with him, even from the beginning. Even before you told me he was just trying to exert power over me. But it was okay before. It wasn't so different from what I had already been through. I thought that maybe I deserved it." He shifted onto his side and ran his fingers over her cheek. "But I can't watch him treat you that way, especially knowing what he's planning on doing."

She slid closer to him, folding into his chest. "Frank, I know you don't want to hear this, that you want to stay angry with him, but he did all this because he loved Ann. Because he wanted her to have her own happy life back. And because he wanted to hurt the person he thought had hurt her. He used me to help her. He used us, and presumably the samples of the resistant bacteria, to catch Dr. Schneider. If you had to do the same for- for Sarah, wouldn't you have done it?"

"If that's true, then why hold on to the samples still? He got what he wanted. Why didn't he just tell us where they were yesterday? You gave him a chance and he refused."

"Because I can't fix it. I can't bring her back. Nobody can. His only drive now is to see that the people responsible for her illness are punished. That means Schneider and Carton, that means himself too. And maybe the rest of the world. Because why should anyone else be happy or healthy when she can never be either?"

"The whole world? Nella, I would do anything to keep you safe. Anything. But I wouldn't destroy the world if I failed."

"That's because you aren't a sociopath who becomes enraged when someone breaks his toy. I told you Frank, you don't need to feel inferior to anyone. It wasn't the Infected that were the monsters."

The whistle of the wind through the broken glass filled the room for a moment. Frank's warm palm pressed against her hip and he pushed her gently onto her back, propping himself up on his elbow over her. "You'll be careful won't you? Take precautions I mean?"

"Yes, of course."

The chilled breeze puffed over her bare skin and vibrated between them in little waves. The pads of his fingers were four molten stars dragging slowly down her throat and over her breast. She held her breath.

"I have a good poker face Nella. I've made a career out of knowing when to tell the truth and when to shut up." His fingers were featherlight on her thigh and his hand shook, as if it were afraid to touch her. "But he knows. I can't hide it. He knows that I love you. He taunts me with it every day because he can see how badly I want you every minute we're apart."

She cooled his face with a stroke of her hand. "Is that why you've been so angry?"

His hand tightened slowly around her thigh, his thumb sinking gently into the soft skin. A ripple of want shook her. "He said- it doesn't matter what he says."

Nella raised her face to his and kissed him. "No," she said as they parted, "it doesn't matter what he says. Because I'm here. You've got me, I'm yours."

Frank smiled, but it faded quickly and he closed his eyes. "He knows though. He knows how it would hurt me if anything happened. He makes a game of it-"

She shook her head. "Nothing will happen. I'll be careful, I promise. He doesn't know I'm going to search his cell, he doesn't even know that we are still looking for the samples. He's convinced he has us outsmarted. He's relaxed and smug now, waiting for the world to fall into his trap. It'll be okay."

His hand relaxed around her thigh and she felt somehow abandoned. He drew back from her a little. "Nella, do you really love me? You aren't here out of pity or until someone better comes along?"

"There's no one better in all the world, Frank. And if there-were, I wouldn't want him." She pulled him down toward her and gently guided his hands where she wanted to be touched.

He kissed her neck and she could feel his lips smiling. "Not even the old man with the boat?" he asked.

She laughed. "Well, it is a *nice* boat."

Frank's hands moved smoothly now, confident and powerful. "Yeah, but can he do this?" Frank asked with a wicked grin.

"Oh God," Nella gasped and arced into him.

THE SEARCH

"I don't like leaving you without your car. What if you need to go to the hospital?"

She swallowed the lump in her throat. "I won't need to go to the hospital."

"But if you find it and the vial is broken-"

"Then I won't be going to the hospital. Sevita needed the car. It didn't make sense to have it parked here all day."

"Then drive me to the courthouse and take this one."

The parking lot was cold and breezy, old leaves raking themselves across it and catching in the cracks like little flags. She straightened Frank's tie even though it was already perfect. "It would look odd if I'm supposed to be treating Ann and I'm at the courthouse."

"You're so stubborn," Frank sighed, "be careful."

Nella squinted up at him, the bright morning sun splintering and bouncing from the waving spring leaves and sudden tears, blocking her sight with bright sparkles. "I will be. As much as I can."

He leaned in and kissed her. "I'll be back after court."

"Okay. Good luck."

"You too." He got into the car and watched her walk across the lot to the prison. He was gone before she had opened the heavy glass door.

Yesterday had been torture. It had worn away grain by grain as she sat in the hot courtroom and listened to Dr. Schneider's lawyer drone on in her opening statements. Frank had been testy and anxious all night too. He had been frantic, almost desperate and panicky when he touched her. Neither of them had slept well and Nella felt like it had been weeks since she'd had a quiet, full night's rest. It was almost a relief not to be waiting any more. She tried to pretend that she wasn't on edge, but everything seemed grating and sharp. The florescent bulbs buzzed like a colony of dying flies and the smell of bleach and floor cleaner was dizzying. She brushed it off as she walked to the metal detector. Terry was slumped on a stool beside it. Shocked, Nella almost asked what he was doing there before she remembered that he hadn't seen her at Frank's house. He waved her through without concern. She hurried to Stan Kembrey's closet sized office. He was tapping a pen too quickly on the side of his knee and staring at the biohazard suits he'd hung from an upper locker.

"I don't like this," he said without greeting her, "I think we should let the military handle it."

"I understand. You go ahead and make a call to the Governor. I'll get started and he can catch up."

"It's not my fault it's gone on this long. You and Frank have been mighty close with all this."

Nella perched on the stool across from Stan. "I'm sorry. I didn't mean to snap. I'm as nervous as you. But we don't have time to wait for the military. You didn't see that courthouse. It's packed to the gills. If the samples somehow end up there-"

Stan stood up and patted her shoulder. He grabbed one of the biosuits and handed it to her.

"I'll go alone if you like. I'll understand if you don't want to go in there," she said.

He pulled the other suit off the hook. "No way. Frank would have my head. Besides, I know all the good hiding places."

The suit was sticky and hot and the mask itched and scraped. Nella tried to adjust to it as they walked toward the cell block. "Did you clear the block?" she asked as loudly as she could. She had to strain to hear Stan's muffled response.

"Yeah, we moved Miss Connelly to the infirmary for now. The only staff in the block are lab techs to help, you know, if we find it. They are wearing suits too. Could it be in any other spot than his cell?"

"It's possible, but very unlikely."

Stan glanced around bending to peer down the hall. "As far as anyone knows, this is a routine drill. Let's try to keep it that way."

Nella nodded to show that she understood. Stan opened the dented metal door to the block. He started barking orders as they entered. "You and you, search the common area. You and you get Ann Connelly's cell. You two on Dr. Schneider's." Stan grabbed her arm. "You're with me." He called after the scattering teams. "Remember, treat this as a real biohazard event, not a drill. If you find the goods, don't handle them. Call me. Is that understood?"

A chorus of affirmatives echoed back at him. He looked at Nella and she could see the sweat rolling down his forehead. "God I hope you're right," he said.

"Me too."

They walked into the small cell and closed the door behind them. There was barely room to pass by each other and Nella was grateful that she wasn't claustrophobic. "You said they'd be in vials. Where should we start looking?"

"I think they are in the pens. The jeweler is making fountain pens for the defense lawyers and you said he came in with some. Maybe he's replaced the cartridges with the vials."

Stan nodded. "All right, you try on the table there and I'll check the bookshelves here. As you go, make a neat pile of things you have checked to one side so we don't repeat. Remember to check the spine of books and open them all, a lot of prisoners will hide things in the spine or cut small holes into the pages. We'll empty out the whole place if we have to."

Nella reached for the small cup of pens and pencils on the desk. She tried to keep her hands from shaking. Two of the three fountain pens were sitting in the cup. She gently picked up the first one. She slowly unscrewed the handle and pulled the cartridge out. Just ink. She clicked her suit's small flash light on and checked the hollow where the cartridge had been and then the empty space in the handle. Both empty. She put the pen back together and placed it beside her on the window sill. She reached for the next one. The handle unscrewed easily but the cartridge was stuck. Nella clicked the flashlight on. She couldn't see what it was stuck on. It looked like a normal cartridge. The suit was clinging in several places because she was sweating so profusely, but she felt a chill growl up her spine and bite the back of her skull. There was no help for it. She had to get it out. "Do you have tweezers Stan?" she asked.

"On the lab cart. One second." He left the cell and Nella stood there praying that she wouldn't break the cartridge. He hurried back, handing her the tweezers. "Did you find it?"

"I don't think so. But I have to make sure. Maybe you should- step out for a minute."

Stan tapped his mask. "That's what these are for. I'm not leaving you alone in here, not for anything."

Nella nodded. The seal over the nose piece slid and her eyepieces fogged. With a shaky hand she pressed the seal down on her sweaty nose and waited for the lenses to clear. She poked the tweezers into the pen and grasped the cartridge, trying not to squeeze too tightly. She tried to wiggle the cartridge but it didn't come loose. She hesitated for a moment and then yanked. *Please don't break, please don't break, please don't break.* The cartridge came free. Just ink. Nella realized she'd been holding her breath and let it out in a rush. She saw Stan watching her and shook her head. She reassembled the pen and put it next to the other one. One by one she checked each of the ball points, just in case, and then the cup. She moved on to the small pile of books as Stan quickly and thoroughly emptied the shelf. By the time she had finished what was on the table, he was already removing the mattress to search it. They found the last fountain pen under the bed, but it was filled with ink as well. Discouraged, they continued on, checking hollows in the little bit of furniture, the air vents, the plumbing. It took them almost two hours to search and put the room back together. The other teams were already finished. Stan sat wearily on the bunk and looked up at her. "You're sure the jeweler didn't take any cartridges or vials with him?"

"Frank got him to show him the pens without any problem. He wouldn't have been that open about it if he had. Frank said they were hollow, ready for cartridges but not filled." Nella sat on the other end of the bunk. "Maybe Dr. Pazzo keeps them on him all the time."

Stan shook his head. "I don't see how. They are searched pretty thoroughly when they leave the prison and again at the courthouse and then again when they come back."

Nella sat silent in disappointment.

"What I don't get," said Stan suddenly, "is why he would go to all this trouble."

"What do you mean?"

Stan got up and checked the door, making sure the other teams weren't listening. "Well, you said this bacteria is even worse than the first one, right? And that every last one of us was probably going to get it,

Immunes and all."

"That's right, as far as Dr. Carton explained it."

Stan scratched his head through the suit's plastic cover. "Well, it's not like Dr. Pazzo is going to escape it then right?"

"Not unless he finds a bunker somewhere. I don't think he wants to escape it anyway. He'd want a front row seat to watch the world fall apart. It's revenge for him."

"Why bother with trying to secretly transport vials in pens or body cavities or whatever then?"

"I don't follow."

"Why set an elaborate trap when he could be the trap himself? Why not infect himself and then just walk into court and talk to as many folks as possible, shake as many hands as possible, heck, even testify and cough a bit? You said the courthouse was packed. How often do that many people get together any more?"

Nella felt the bottom of the world fall away. "Oh God."

Stan stood up when he saw her reach for the table for support. He helped her up. "Don't panic Dr. Rider. It's weeks to the verdict, he won't have done it yet. We just have to find the vials. It's not like he can just pop 'em open and swallow 'em right?"

She regained her balance. "No, he needs some special ingredients to revive the bacteria. But I don't think he'll wait very long." She pushed past him into the common room where the other teams were waiting. "Is there a lab tech here? Someone that knows how to do a culture? Anyone who knows how to grow specific bacteria?"

"Sure," came a muffled voice, "Kevin was studying microbiology before the Plague."

"Where is he?" asked Stan.

"Right here, sir." One of the biohazard suits stepped forward. Nella walked up to him. He squinted at her through a crack in his thick glasses. "Sir, is she-"

"She's cleared to be here, you can answer her questions," said Stan.

"Kevin, if you know the answer, I'll spend every last ration I have to get you a pair of glasses without a crack. Did you ever revive frozen samples in school? Or have to speed up cultures without contaminating them with other strains?"

"Sure. We don't have many incubators anymore and power's at a premium anyway. We find ways to speed up cultures all the time in the infirmary."

"What do you need to do that?"

Kevin squinted at her. "What do *I* need or what could a prisoner use to do it?" The others closed in, suddenly interested. Nella glanced at Stan. He looked worried, but she decided to risk it.

"What could a prisoner use?"

"Well, it'd have to be sterile, so nothing could contaminate the sample. But if he could get his hands on bleach or alcohol or even vinegar he could do it if he was careful. And then he'd need a growth medium. We usually use agar, but he wouldn't have access to that. Gelatin would work or even beef broth but you need meat for that and that's mighty scarce these days. The cafeteria still serve the old kid's stuff?"

One of the others chuckled. Stan shook his head. "Haven't seen any in years. All got used up in soldiers' mess kits for quick protein fixes."

Kevin tried to push his glasses up with one hand and hit the lenses of his mask instead. He shrugged. "A potato would do it pretty well I think."

Stan was already talking to the cafeteria on the intercom. "How fast would it grow?" Nella asked.

"Enough to do what?"

"To infect someone with that strain."

Kevin glanced at the others. She could see them shifting uncomfortably as if they were ready to run out the door. "Well, it depends on the bacteria, but it could be a day, maybe two."

She saw Stan casually pull out the service gun he wore on the belt outside the biohazard suit. He was standing behind the group so that they couldn't see him. She smiled brightly at Kevin, willing them all not to panic. "Okay, Kevin, last question pays for all. If this theoretical prisoner's bacteria was primed and ready, how long from being infected would a person be contagious, say, through casual contact or breathing on others?"

Kevin shrugged and tried to sound casual, but his voice cracked in the middle. "Depends on the bacteria. Worst case scenario? A few hours to a day."

Nella heard running footsteps outside the door. Her companions turned toward it. "Sir?" asked one of them.

Stan held the gun at his side, pointed toward the ground but clearly visible to everyone. "This isn't a drill, is it?" asked Kevin.

"I'm afraid not. I'm sorry boys. I ought to have told you, but I really didn't think there was anything to it. But we've all trained for this and we've got our suits, so everyone just sit tight and I'm sure we'll be decontaminated and released quickly."

A few of the soldiers relaxed and sat down at the picnic tables scattered over the common area. Stan put the weapon away when he saw that no one was going to bolt. He spoke through the intercom again. Nella walked up to him and Kevin trailed behind her. Stan turned toward her. "Sorry Doc, that means you too."

"How long ago did he break the vials?"

"The Warden said Dr. Pazzo requested permission to start a small vegetable patch in the yard sometime last week. He got seed potatoes from the cafeteria. And Sunday night he reported that he was sick and requested cleaning materials for his cell but refused the guards' offer of help and also turned down a visit to the infirmary."

"Bleach?" asked Kevin.

Stan sighed and nodded.

Kevin tried to push his glasses up again, hitting the eyepieces of his mask. "Sunday. Where are the potatoes? And where are the vials?"

"Who knows? Flushed maybe? They weren't important after he'd infected himself. And they might have led to his getting caught."

Nella grabbed Stan's arm, her glove slipping on the smooth plastic of his suit. "Stan, that means he could be contagious right now! All those people at court- Frank-" She started for the door but Stan held her back.

"You can't go out there Dr. Rider."

"Someone has to stop him and warn them. What if he's not contagious yet? He wouldn't have done it until the night before last, after he found out about Ann's condition. What if there's still time? More than half the City is in that courthouse right now Stan-"

"I know. I already notified the Warden. He's calling the Governor right now. I'm sure the courthouse will be cleared in a matter of minutes."

"But he needs to be isolated-"

Stan firmly pushed her onto a bench. "Everything that can be done is already happening. There's nothing we can do without risking even more people."

Nella's eyepieces were misting up and she couldn't tell if she were crying or sweating or both. Stan sat down beside her. "He's going to be okay. Frank's harder than he seems. I've known him a long time Nella," he patted her knee and the plastic crinkled, "He's going to be mad with worry about *you*, but he's going to be okay."

"We can't just sit here Stan-"

"We didn't just sit here. We caught him. If you and Frank hadn't figured this out when you did," Stan sucked in a whistling breath through the mask, "Well, now we still have a chance. A *good* chance that we got ahead of Pazzo. And, please don't take this the wrong way Dr. Rider, now it's time to let people who know better what we're dealing with take over and do their jobs. We've done our part and then some. Just try to relax and I'm sure we'll be playing cards with Frank in light quarantine by the end of the day."

"Um, sorry to interrupt sir . . ." Kevin was still standing near them and he shifted his weight to one foot nervously.

"That's okay, Kevin. What's on your mind?"

"It's just that- well, if we're going to get sick, we were sort of wondering what we might be infected with. Some of us are Cured sir, and we just want to know what to expect this time."

Stan patted Nella's knee again. "I'll handle this," he stood up, "You just stay quiet."

"But some of them may-" Nella began.

Stan shook his head. "They won't. And if they look like they're going to, well, you can jump in then." He walked over to the soldiers. "Listen up boys," he yelled.

Nella didn't know how long it was before they were sent through the decontamination shower, but it felt like years. The plastic suit was scratchy and slimy with sweat and her hair was sticking to her skin. Even her breath felt sluggish and thick, like she was in a sauna and she had to fight the urge to rip the face mask off more than once. She could tell the others were having trouble too. But at last another group of soldiers in biohazard suits, a different color, led them out of the cell block and into the parking lot where the chemical shower and a large bus were waiting. As soon as they were through the shower, the suits were allowed to come off and Nella heard audible sighs of relief around her as her group removed the hot plastic. The cool afternoon breeze made her feel like a hollow reed. They piled onto the bus and were driven to the City's unused hospital. Her heart raced in her chest as the bus pulled up to the defunct ambulance entrance. There were a number of other buses sitting in the street. The exterior lights had been turned on and large barriers in orange and red made a ring around the building, as if it were a pustule about to burst and flood the City with illness. Soldiers in plastic suits scurried in and out or stood at the barrier with conspicuous guns.

A masked soldier shouted a muffled order at them. Stan led them into the hospital. The floor they were taken to was empty and Nella's heart sank. She'd hoped to find Frank or Christine and Sevita at least. The masked soldier stood on the counter at the nurses' station. "Folks," he shouted, "Thank you for your patience. I understand you've all been briefed on the situation-"

One of the group shouted, "We were the ones

that discovered the situation!"

The masked soldier continued, "Yes. Then you know how grave it really is. At the moment we're hopeful that none of you have been exposed. You are free to roam this floor as long as you stay on it. The general populace has been informed of the situation through the news network, but I understand some of you may wish to contact loved ones. The phones in the patient rooms have been turned on. However, there are several hundred people on the other levels of the hospital who came from the courthouse and as you know, our phone system is limited at best. Please have some patience when you're trying to get through to your family. I understand you folks haven't had chow since breakfast. Someone will be around with dinner shortly. Later on several doctors will be coming around to assess the chance of your exposure. Please cooperate with them. We don't want you to have to be here any longer than necessary."

"How long is that exactly?" asked Stan.

"Best case scenario, a week." The men around Nella groaned and she felt her own chest tighten with panic. The soldier raised an arm for quiet. "I know it's not ideal. But the last thing any of us wants is to carry this out into the City, back to the people we care about. We all know how serious this is. From what I understand, there's no hope for a Cure this time. Our only recourse is to contain it. I know I don't need to tell you, of all people, the extremes we will take to keep it contained if we have to. Please cooperate and we'll all get through this together."

The soldier hopped down and headed to the elevator. The small knot of soldiers broke apart, some headed for bed, others for the television set. Nella felt lost, unmoored, bored and terrified at once. She wandered into a patient room. They'd been hastily set up with an army cot and a folding chair, the old furniture scavenged long ago. She sat on the cot and stared out the broad window into the bright spring sparkle of the City. The trees were waving in the breeze but the windows were sealed shut. She snapped on the air conditioner. A phone rang distantly down the hallway.

"Dr. Rider?" someone shouted, "Nella Rider?"

Nella walked out into the hall. "Yes? Here I am."

A man down the hall waved a phone receiver at her. "What room number are you in? Someone's looking for you."

She peered back at her door. "312."

The man nodded and put the receiver back to his ear. Nella ran back into her room and picked up the phone halfway through the first ring.

"Frank?" she asked.

"Sorry, Nella, it's me."

"Sevita are you okay? Is Christine with you?"

"Yes, we're fine. But Frank isn't with us. He and all the rest of the people on the floor were taken away separately. I think he's upstairs but I can't find a soldier who can tell me. Are you all right? Are you infected? Someone said you found the broken vials."

"No, we didn't find anything. It was Stan Kembrey that figured out Dr. Pazzo had infected himself."

"The metal detector guy?"

"I think he's responsible for a lot more than the metal detector."

"You think they'd let me have an interview with him?"

"A phone interview maybe. We aren't going anywhere for at least a week."

"Us either. One of the soldiers said that the people who were on the courtroom floor were going to have to be in isolation at least a month. They had a greater chance of getting infected and they won't be symptomatic until then."

Nella sighed. "At least the interior phones are working."

"Yeah, outside lines are tied up but I should be able to talk to anyone inside. At least I'm where the action is." Sevita's voice broke and Nella was shocked to realize that her friend was truly scared.

"Hey, there's a guy down here, one of the techs. He thinks we caught it in time."

"Yeah?"

"He says Dr. Pazzo could have been infected in the time he had, but he probably isn't contagious yet." She heard Sevita blow out a shaky sigh.

"That's good. Christine will be so relieved." She paused for a minute. "Listen Nell, I don't want to hang up, but they're here to check our vitals and take blood tests and stuff."

"It's okay Sevita. I'm going to try to find Frank though, so if I don't answer for a while-" Nella trailed off, unable to speak past the panic choking her throat.

"Okay, Nella. I'm sure he's fine. I'll try to find out which room he's in too. If I hear anything, I'll call. Chris and I are in 517 if you need us. Talk to you later."

"Yeah, all right." Nella hung up the phone. She walked down to the elevator where there were two guards posted.

"Can I help you ma'am?" One of them shouted over his mask.

"One of my friends was on the floor of the courthouse. I'd like to call him. Could you find out which room he's in?"

The guard shifted his weight. "They're awfully busy up there ma'am. I can try to reach someone, but it will probably be a while before we hear back."

Nella summoned a charming smile. "That's

okay, I can try each room on the floor if you just tell me the floor number."

"Sure, I think they are up on seven."

She thanked the guard and tried to walk calmly back to her room. She noted the room numbers as she passed. 333 was the last number on this hall. She hoped the seventh floor had fewer. Nella closed the door to her room. She sat on her cot and held the heavy phone. What if she got Dr. Pazzo instead? She decided she didn't care. She dialed 701 and held her breath.

"Hello?" It was a woman's voice. Nella hoped it wasn't Dr. Schneider but she couldn't tell.

"I'm looking for Frank Courtlen. Do you know which room he's in? Can you see him?"

"No, they have us in separate cells."

"Cells?"

"They're all glassed in. I can't see down the hall, just the room across from me. Do you know what's happening?"

"They didn't tell you?"

"No. Court was going on as usual and all of a sudden a large group of soldiers burst in and started yelling. That defendant, Robert Pazzo flew past me and kissed the other defendant square on the mouth. And then all hell broke loose."

"Who did he kiss? Ann Connelly?"

"That sweet girl they found incompetent yesterday? No she wasn't there. That Schneider woman. Jake- that's the other bailiff and I, we jumped up to stop him but the soldiers already had their weapons out and they bundled us all into a bus, except for Pazzo, he went separate and brought us here. They told us someone would be by to talk to us, but it's been hours. What's going on? Is it a coup or something?"

Nella tried not to scare her as she explained,

but the woman was in tears by the time she finished. "I'm sorry," Nella said, "I just wanted to find my friend." She hung up. Then she remembered that she hadn't asked the woman what the room number across from her was. Nella swore. She walked to the nurses' station and scrounged for a pen and clipboard. She tried to avoid looking at the patient files that had been abandoned during the outbreak of the Plague. They still lay scattered on the desk and underfoot. The dusty footprints of scavenge teams and the soldiers here now obscured most of the information, but Nella felt like it was an invasion of privacy anyway. She found an old takeout menu in a drawer. She wrote down 701 in the wide margin and returned to her room. She tried 702. The other bailiff. She kept her answers perfunctory, trying to keep the man from panicking. He hadn't seen Frank since the bus either. Dr. Schneider's lawyer was across from him in 712. She thanked him and hung up. 703 was Judge Hawkins. He managed to flag down a soldier for her. He sounded sad and frightened and angry at the same time.

"We think we caught it in time," she offered.

"Really?" he asked, "How soon will we know?"

"I guess when Dr. Pazzo starts showing symptoms. I think they are going to let everyone down here go in a week if our tests are clear. We had far less risk of exposure. I know- I know that doesn't really help you, but I thought you might like to know."

"No, no, that's a big relief. I know I was reluctant to let you and Frank pursue this- I thought the military would handle it better. I just wanted to say that I don't think anyone but you two would have followed it this long or found it in time."

"I wish we'd found it sooner. I wish I hadn't been searching for an elaborate plot and just paid attention to what was staring me plain in the face."

"I guess I can say this now, because I don't think we're going to be seeing Robert Pazzo return to the trial, if there is a trial after this. He had most people fooled Dr. Rider. I confess, I watched that footage that Mr. Courtlen left with me. I wasn't supposed to, it could have tainted the case, but I was so worried about what you two were up against and whether I'd made the right decision, so I watched it. And I was convinced right along with you. I don't know how you figured it out. Maybe someday after this, when I'm retired or Mr. Courtlen's decided to get out of the lawyer trade, we'll all have a drink and you can tell me about it."

"That would be nice, Your Honor."

"Now though, you must be itching to talk to Frank. This fine young gentlemen tells me he is in 708. Don't be a stranger Dr. Rider. It's going to be a long month and I have a feeling we're all going to need your services up here before the end."

"I'll check in with you often, I promise."

Nella hung up and dialed Frank's room.

"Hello?" His voice was liquid warmth sliding into her chest.

"Frank," she said and then her voice failed.

"Nella? Is that you? Thank goodness. I've been trying to reach the prison for hours. Please tell me you wore masks- Dr. Pazzo has already released it. I don't know how, but he did. I'm at the hospital-"

"I know Frank. I'm just a few floors below you. Stan was the one that figured it out. The pens, they were just like the lock. There for show, so we wouldn't pay attention to what he was really doing. He infected himself. Did you shake his hand today? Did he cough on you?"

"No. He seemed nervous and I was still angry with him so I didn't try to get him to talk. It was my turn for opening statements anyway so I was standing for most of the session. When the soldiers came in he bolted across the room and kissed Dr. Schneider though. He must have wanted to make sure. How did you know I was here? Are they going to let you come upstairs if you wear a suit?"

"No, not yet anyway. I'm in quarantine too, at least for a week. They don't know if the cell block was contaminated."

"But you wore a mask, didn't you?"

"Yes, a whole biohazard suit. But they want to be sure. The rest of the court is here too, somewhere upstairs from me." Nella heard a hoarse yell through the receiver. "What's that? Is everything all right?"

"Yeah, it's Dr. Pazzo. He hasn't stopped screaming since they grabbed him. He's in the room next door right near me and Dr. Schneider. They must think we're the highest risk." She could hear Frank nervously tapping the phone cord.

"There's a guy here, a microbiologist. He thinks it's going to be okay. Maybe not for Dr. Schneider, but for everyone else. He doesn't think Dr. Pazzo is contagious yet."

"That's good news."

"Frank, I'll come visit you as soon as they let me. And we can talk as much as we want on the phone until then."

"Don't come up here. I don't want you to be exposed."

"I won't be, I'll wear a suit and all of the rooms are contained I think."

"Maybe- maybe you shouldn't come up here anyway." She heard another yell from Dr. Pazzo and Frank's breath shook in her ear. There was a soft thud as Frank's forehead gently struck the glass wall of his room.

"You aren't going to get it Frank. It's going to be a long couple of weeks because I'll miss you, but I'll talk to you or see you every day-"

"If I- I can't turn into that again. You can't see me that way."

"It's not going to happen. We caught it in time. You'll see, a month from now we'll be walking out of here together-"

Frank sobbed. "I have to go. There's tests. I have to go." He hung up.

Nella put the receiver back into its cradle. She curled up on the cot, her back to the bright afternoon and cried herself to sleep.

She woke to a knock on her door. It was Stan with a tray of food and a doctor in a biohazard suit.

"Sorry," Stan said, "I didn't want to wake you, but Dr. Corey needed to evaluate you."

Nella sat up. "Hi," she said to the blank mask. The eyepieces were opaque unlike hers had been, so she couldn't see the person inside. Dr. Corey pulled up the folding chair.

"Officer Kembrey has given me a rundown of events, so I will just need to ask a few question and take some blood samples." Nella was surprised to hear a woman's voice float out from the mask. She had expected a man. Stan backed out of the room and two more soldiers in plastic suits entered the room holding large guns. "I trust that won't be a problem?" Dr. Corey continued pointedly.

"Of course," said Nella, bewildered.

Dr. Corey started pulling supplies out of her suit pocket and laying them on the cot beside her. "Officer Kembrey tells me you and Mr. Courtlen first discovered Robert Pazzo's plan some time ago. Why didn't you notify authorities?"

"We only had hunches. And we were afraid if we reported it and Dr. Pazzo found out, he'd release the bacteria early and we wouldn't have a chance to find it."

"I see, and you thought you and Mr. Courtlen were qualified to find this bacteria? Mr. Courtlen has had no medical training and you-" she snapped her gloved fingers and one of the guards handed her a folder. She flipped through it. "You've had basic microbiology and some general biology courses in college and medical school?"

"It wasn't a matter of being qualified or not being qualified. Someone had to do something and we were the only ones that knew about it. We're what was available."

Dr. Corey opened an alcohol swab. The smell stung Nella's nose and made her feel chill before it even touched her. The doctor was so rough that Nella's arm was sore even before the needle. She gripped her wounded shoulder as Dr. Corey pulled on her arm.

"That's not true though. Various people knew

about the bacteria at different points in time, isn't that correct? The trial judges, the prosecutor, a prison official, even a reporter. Yet none of you contacted authorities."

The needle bit into her. Nella ignored it. "I told you. We had to keep it quiet so Dr. Pazzo didn't realize we were suspicious. We did the best we could, but we had to involve other people to move forward."

Dr. Corey switched vials and drew another. Nella wished she could see the woman's expression. After four vials, the doctor handed Nella cottonball and a bandage. Nella closed her elbow around the cottonball. Dr. Corey stood up. "I understand you were bitten on your trip to Dr. Carton's lab."

"Yes, but what does that have to do with-"

"I'll need to examine it. Please remove your blouse."

Nella glanced at the guards. "Very well, but do I have to do it in front of them?"

Dr. Corey waved her hand at the guards and they left, closing the door behind them. Nella slid out of her shirt.

"I understand you have more than a professional relationship with Mr. Courtlen." Dr. Corey probed Nella's shoulder with two rough fingers. Nella tried not to wince.

"Was that a question?"

"Have you had sexual relations with him?"

"I really don't think that's any-"

Dr. Corey blew an exasperated sigh through her mask. "Dr. Pazzo could have been infected anytime between Sunday night and today. Mr. Courtlen may have been infected during Monday or Tuesday's court session. Therefore, we need to know if you and he had intercourse between then and now to assess your risk."

Nella blushed. "Yes."

"Put your shirt back on please. Do you have any personal effects here?"

"No, why?" Nella pulled her shirt on again.

"Come with me please."

Dr. Corey led her into the hallway after pocketing the lab vials. She handed Nella a thin respirator mask. "Put this on please." She thumbed her radio as Nella obliged. "Would you please add one more to the meals for the seventh floor?" Dr. Corey said into it. Nella caught Stan's eye and the look he gave her was a mix of pity and fear. The guards grabbed her arms and propelled her forward to the elevator. Nella was too startled to struggle. Dr. Corey joined them and selected the floor button. Stan was yelling, "Wait, where are you-" as the silver door slid closed. Nella felt sweat stand out on her face and on her arms where the guards were holding her. She began to hyperventilate.

"It's okay, just breathe normally, the mask is just to block disease, not oxygen. Calm down and take slow breaths," One of the guards said beside her. Dr. Corey and the other guard ignored them. Nella tried to concentrate and slow down her breathing. "That's right," said the guard, "If you breathe so rapidly you'll get dizzy. Feel better?" Nella nodded. The elevator chimed and they walked down a long hallway. All the rooms were fronted with thick glass and Nella could see people sitting or sleeping against the far walls.

"Please," she said, "Is there a room near Mr. Courtlen." The friendly guard looked down at her and then at Dr. Corey.

"I don't care," said the doctor, "put her where you think she'll be the least trouble."

"Be nice now," said the guard, "and I'll put you across from him. That room is empty."

Nella nodded and the other guard released her

arm. The friendly guard led her gently down the hall. She could hear Dr. Pazzo yelling, but she couldn't make out what he was saying. The guard unlocked the glass door and held it open. She obediently walked inside. He closed the door and said, "You can take off the mask now if you want, you're safe in there. I know you missed dinner, I'll make sure they bring you something later."

"Thank you!" she called after him. Frank was on his cot, his back to her. His legs were too long to fit and they trailed off the end. She decided to let him sleep. She was relieved to be near him. She tried to pull her cot closer to the glass wall, but it had been bolted to the floor. Were they preparing for the day the patients went feral or was it just to prevent blocking the door? Nella lay on the floor next to the glass to be closer to Frank. She was asleep in moments.

DR. PAZZO SNAPS

The phone jarred her awake. She sat up. Frank was sitting cross legged across the way, watching her. He was holding the receiver to his ear. She reached for the phone.

"You can't hear much through these walls. Just Dr. Pazzo's yelling. What are you doing here?"

"The doctor- knew about us. I don't know how. Stan maybe. She said you might have been infected yesterday in court, so I could be infected because of last night."

"But I thought we caught it in time. I thought you said he wasn't contagious yet."

"I think they are just being cautious. At least I'm with you now."

Frank shook his head. She could see the lines on his face draw down in sharp angles. There were dark patches under his eyes and sweat marks on his shirt. "So now you can watch me turn back into one of those things. I can't do it, Nella. I'll die first."

"It's not going to happen. To either of us."

"If it does- will you find a way to- will you ask them to shoot me?"

Nella nodded, not trusting her voice. Frank cleared his throat. "You said Sevita is here with Christine?"

"Yes. Everyone who was in the courtroom or on the cell block is downstairs."

"She must be going crazy. She's in the middle of the biggest story, maybe of all time and she can't report it."

"Don't count on it. I bet she'll get some coverage somehow. Her camera guys are still with her. And if everything goes well, they'll be out in a week."

"And us?"

Nella shrugged. "A few more weeks? Until Dr. Pazzo gets sick maybe."

Frank groaned. "Have we even made it through one day yet?"

"It was early evening when I came upstairs. I wish there was a window."

He scratched his chin. "Well unless they start giving us toiletries we'll be able to measure by beard length. Or clothes deterioration." He grinned and Nella was relieved.

"I hope you know some good jokes," he said, "Or this is going to be a very long month."

"Let's plan our trip. When they bring us food, we can ask for paper and pens. We can make lists of what we need and where we'll stop."

Frank laughed. "I think we're both unemployed Nella. How are we going to buy a boat?"

Nella shrugged. "I have my ways. I've been saving for a while. Little things, matches and sterno, decent cloth, jewelry and several good pairs of shoes. Things people traded me for sessions. And there's-" Nella leaned her head against the glass and looked down the hallway. Empty. She put her hand in front of her face and whispered, "there's the guns and the car too."

"You'd really trade all that just to sail around the world with me?"

"In a heartbeat."

They stayed that way, talking in front of their glass walls until Nella drifted off again, listening to Frank making plans and trailing into sleep himself. When she woke up, the receiver had made an imprint on her cheek. Frank was rolling up his sleeve for a doctor in a plastic suit. A soldier knocked on the glass and Nella backed up, startled.

"I'm bringing you a meal and some new clothes.

After you put on the new stuff, put the old stuff into the bag. Make sure you take any possessions out of the pockets. Your old clothes will be burned."

Nella nodded. The soldier opened the door and another brought in the clothing and a tray of food. The doctor closed Frank's door and discarded her gloves. She walked over to Nella's room.

"We should probably get this all done at once."

Nella was not pleased to hear Dr. Corey's voice. Nella held out her arm and was silent while the doctor took her vials and then departed with the guards. She turned back to her cot and picked up the clothes. They looked like a prison uniform. She hoped they were warmer than they looked. She pulled off her shirt and then realized the wall behind her was glass. She held her shirt in front of her chest and peered down the hallway. The phone rang and she jumped.

"I'll watch for you. Hang up the phone. If someone is coming it'll ring." Frank waved at her.

"What about you?"

"I won't peek. Eyes on the hallway."

"Yes you will."

Frank grinned. "Yes. I will."

They measured the time that way, by meals and clothing changes. Sevita called them until it was time for her to go. She promised to visit and Nella told her not to, that they'd see her when they were released, so she said she'd call when she could. The hall was quiet, even Dr. Pazzo having quit his frustrated rage within a day. Only the soldiers and the doctor wandered by on occasion, faceless and silent in their suits. Nella tried to keep Frank's spirits up, but even she was struggling by the end of the second week. One day, during the third week Nella thought, a much older looking Judge Hawkins stopped in front of their rooms. He sat in the middle of the hallway so he could see them both. They were releasing the rest of the court, he said, all but Dr. Schneider, Dr. Pazzo and the two of them. They were highest risk. He said the military government was convening a hearing about the whole affair, but he promised to stand by the decision to keep the bacteria secret. He said he'd see them in a week, but he looked troubled as he walked away. Nella was becoming nervous, though she kept it quiet so that Frank wouldn't worry. There was even less bustle on the hall now. She thought most of the staff must have left with the rest of the people in quarantine. She began to feel forgotten and it frightened her. She spent hours watching the guard at the end of the hall, making sure he was still there and hadn't abandoned them.

The phone's harsh ring woke her one night. She looked across the hall, but Frank's light was off. It continued to ring, so she picked it up. "Hello?" she asked.

"You know, last time I saw symptoms every time I moved or spoke or tried to work out a problem. But I think it was just exhaustion. It was hard to convince myself I wasn't sick. Especially after performing for Gerta." His voice was slurred and depressed. If Nella didn't know better, she would have assumed he was drunk.

"I'm not here to make house calls Dr. Pazzo."

He laughed and Nella shuddered at the hollow sound trickling into her ear. "But don't you want to know why I did it Nella? Don't you want to hear the whole grand scheme? Every sordid little detail? That's what we always want in the end, isn't it? We don't want the villains to get away, because we want to know why they do what they do. It's like asking a magician how. But a good villain never tells."

"You don't need to tell me why, Dr. Pazzo."

"Because you know everything, right?" She could hear the sneer in his voice. "The great Nella Rider always knows. Except you can't help one poor, innocent girl. And you couldn't keep up with me either."

"No. It's not because I already know why you did this. I can take a guess, but I'm not even sure *you* entirely know why you did this. I don't want to know why, because I don't care. Your 'grand scheme' was just a mistake, Dr. Pazzo. You messed up. There was no master plan. Sure, you covered your tracks afterward and trapped Dr. Schneider into admitting what you already knew on camera. Maybe when you went after her you meant to keep the samples only as evidence. Maybe you thought it would help you find a cure for Ann. Maybe you wanted to destroy them but couldn't find the time because Ann needed to eat all the time and you couldn't risk being away from her for long. But you didn't *do* anything. You just sat in the lab and watched the world deteriorate around you. Watched Ann die. Tell me, Dr. Pazzo, how many times did you think about killing her and being done with it? How many times did you walk out of the lab intending never to come back? You don't love Ann. You never did. You may be overwhelmed with guilt by what your research did to her, but you don't love her, not if you could bring yourself to do what you've done."

She heard him sobbing into the phone and begin to pound on the glass wall. "You wanted me to undo what you did, so you wouldn't have to feel guilty any more. As if fixing one girl would make the world what it was. You show the world this penitent face, even I believed you for a while. But if you were really so remorseful, if you really felt the weight of the billions of deaths you are responsible for, you would have turned over the samples either when you were caught or to Frank when he was preparing your case or even when we returned with Dr. Schneider. We gave you what you wanted. All you had to do was give us the vials."

"I gave the world what it DESERVED!" His shout rang in her ear and she winced. Frank's light turned on and he pressed an ear against the glass. Dr. Pazzo continued shouting and she pulled the receiver a few inches from her ear. "I only did what the world would have done to me. What we already do to each other. No one wants the villain to escape Nella. I *told* you that. I *told* you we were all villains. That's all that's left."

She watched Frank jump as he heard Dr. Pazzo yelling her name. He looked up at her startled. Dr. Pazzo's voice dropped to almost a whisper and she pulled the phone back so she could hear. "But I knew how to take care of it. All those people going home from the court to their happy little undeserved lives. They're going to kiss their babies and make love to their spouses and shake hands with their friends. For a few weeks now, everything's been ordinary. But now, now they're going to start showing their true selves. We're all murderers anyway, Nella, even you." Nella shuddered thinking of Martin in the Cure camp.

"You failed, Dr. Pazzo. There's no one infected but you. We caught it in time."

Dr. Pazzo snarled and shrieked. "Liar! I can see Dr. Schneider across from me. She's slipping, Nella. She bangs her head on the glass and bites her own flesh. She's pulled almost all the hair out of her head. And then there's Frank next to me. You know, he thinks he's in love with you. I told him you'd never let a monster like him touch you." She heard a clunk as the receiver was dropped. Dr. Pazzo began banging on the glass wall. "Frank! Frank, are you still sane? Having any cravings yet?" he yelled through the glass. Frank's face was red but he didn't turn his head toward Dr. Pazzo's cell. He was watching her. Dr. Pazzo picked up the phone again.

"But I was wrong about that, wasn't I? You like that mangled behemoth don't you? But underneath that cool, polished face he's just like me Nella. He's angry at the whole world. If I hadn't done it, someone like Frank would have. Has he snapped yet? I assume it would be harder to resist the urge the second time. He already knows what it feels like to tear into a woman's fragile skin with his teeth. And he's wanted yours for such a long, long time . . . You're so soft and you smell so good, Dr. Rider. His jaw must ache just thinking about it. I wonder if he'll get to you before you get sick. You better hope that guard doesn't let him out Nella."

"He's not sick," Nella whispered, "You were too late. You didn't infect him."

Dr. Pazzo just laughed. Nella hung up the phone. She could still hear Dr. Pazzo laughing through the glass. She told herself he was mad, that he had sprung his trap too late. But dread began to creep up and gather in her chest.

The phone rang. She looked over and Frank tapped on the glass, the receiver in his hand. She picked up the phone.

"Did we miss something? Could he have infected someone else without us knowing? Or left a vial somewhere?"

"Nella, it's okay. We checked everything." She wanted to relax into the warm calm of his voice, but Dr. Pazzo had shaken her badly.

"We didn't check his lab."

"Other people did. Very thoroughly. If it had been there it would have been found. Think like a psychiatrist Nella. You told me he couldn't bear to have it out of his control, that he'd have to have it nearby where *he* could decide when and how to use it. He used it. He failed. It's over. The only people that may be sick are right here."

She sat on the cold floor in front of the glass. "Don't be sick, Frank."

He smiled at her. "What was it you said? 'The world will keep going' even if I am."

"What if I don't want it to?"

"Even if you don't want it to and even if Dr. Pazzo doesn't want it to."

DR. SCHNEIDER SNAPS

Another week crawled by. Nella told Frank every dirty joke she could remember. Frank made up a few more. They persuaded the guard to bring them dry erase markers and played hangman on the glass wall. Frank drew a sailing route on his. Nella was persuading him to add a stop on the coast of Africa when they heard a commotion. Nella leaned her head against the glass.

"What is it?" Frank asked.

"I don't know," Nella said into the receiver. "It's Dr. Schneider's cell I think."

The doctor hurried by with a first aid kit. "What-"

"Listen," said Nella pressing her other ear to the glass.

"How did this happen?" snapped Dr. Corey.

"I don't know," said the guard, "I heard a thump and came over and there she was on the floor."

"Did she say anything?"

"I couldn't understand her, it's like she was drunk."

There were a few moments of silence. Nella glanced at Frank. He had backed away from the glass and his face was ashen in the cold light of his room.

"Just a sprain," said Dr. Corey, "Dr. Schneider, I want you to take it easy now. Try not to move around too much."

Nella retreated from the glass. Frank had hung up the phone. He was pacing the small room at a frantic pace, his long hands raking his head over and over. Nella dialed his room. He didn't answer and she hung up so that he could have some peace. Dr. Pazzo began banging his head on the glass about half an hour later. She watched it shake with the impact. Frank curled up next to the glass and covered his ears with his hands. She sat down opposite of him, her heart a high tension wire thrumming between panic for Frank and worry at Pazzo's frantic bashing.

The banging continued into the night. Nella lay in the half dark, pressed against the glass, trying to see into Frank's dim room. They hadn't spoken since that morning. Dr. Schneider began yelling, a high shriek. Nella squeezed her eyes closed as Dr. Pazzo grunted and continued slamming himself against the glass. The phone rang.

"I can't do this Nella. I'm sorry."

"Yes you can Frank." She sat up. "It's okay. We knew this was going to happen. They were bound to get like this eventually. But we're not sick."

"I must be. If he infected Dr. Schneider then he must have infected me too."

"No, Frank, He kissed her, he put his mouth right on her. He didn't touch you."

Frank sobbed and she thought she could see him rocking back and forth in the corner.

"Turn the light on."

"What? Why?"

"I'm going to show you we're not sick. Turn on the light." Nella flipped hers on at the same time. "Good. Now take your marker and draw a line on the floor." Nella put the receiver down and streaked a line across the tile floor. She picked up the receiver. "Okay Frank, you first. Walk toe to toe down the line without falling or stepping off."

"It's not straight."

"It doesn't matter. If you're sick you'll fall over."

Frank walked slowly on the line. He picked up the receiver. Dr. Pazzo banged again and Dr. Schneider shrieked in response. Nella flinched.

"Now you do it," Frank said. She walked smoothly down the line.

"Okay, balance on one foot for as long as you can, say thirty seconds if you can. We'll do it together."

She put down the receiver and picked one foot off the floor. She watched Frank do the same. There was a loud crash from another cell and Nella jumped and ran to the glass. Dr. Schneider had ripped the cot out of the floor and was hurling it against the glass. Dr. Corey came running with one of the guards. Nella looked wide eyed at Frank. He watched the doctor enter the cell. Nella pressed her ear against the glass.

"Do it! Fucking give her the sedative Corey," the guard was shouting. Nella heard a shriek and Dr. Schneider came hurtling out of the room and toward Nella and Frank. Her mouth was streaming with blood and something poked out between her teeth. Most of her hair was gone, pulled out, leaving great purple scabs and she'd chewed most of the skin from her hands. She slammed against Nella's glass wall, her fingers scrabbling at the smooth door. Dr. Schneider screamed in rage and bashed her forehead against the glass. Nella could hear Frank yelling for help and pounding on the glass wall. A gloved hand pulled Dr. Schneider's forehead from the glass and another slid around her neck with a knife and made a bright bubbling line across her throat. The shrieking ended and what was left of Dr. Schneider slumped to the ground. Nella vomited in the corner. The soldier knocked on her wall. "You okay?" It was the friendly one. "Then get on the line and tell your friend to stop yelling or I'll have to assume he's sick."

Nella picked up the receiver with a shaky hand. "It's okay Frank, I'm okay."

He stopped pounding on the glass. The soldier

walked down to the last cell. His buddy stumbled out. "That bitch bit me," he said. The other soldier raised his gun.

"Dan, no, it's okay. It'll be okay, it barely broke through the suit." The wounded soldier held up his hands. Nella could see his arm dripping blood onto the floor. It sounded like a leaky faucet in the quiet, even through the glass.

"Sorry man, I have to. It's better this way. Trust me," said Dan and fired. He stepped farther into the cell. Nella heard a groan and then another shot. Dan walked out of the room and up to Dr. Pazzo's door. It was smeared with oil and feces and blood so that he couldn't see through it. Nella watched him take a deep breath. He flung open the door and fired. Nella was shaking. She whispered into the receiver, "I love you Frank."

She could see the sparkle of tears on his cheek. "I love you too," he said.

Dan was talking into his radio as he walked toward them. "I need a cleanup at St. Helena's, full biohazard suits." He stopped in front of Nella's cell and looked at her for a long minute. She shut her eyes. "I also need a new doctor down here. I have two quarantined that need to be cleared asap." He walked farther down the hall and disappeared into the elevator.

Nella heard Frank start breathing again. She cried until she fell asleep still holding the receiver.

THE MILITARY GOVERNOR

The cleanup took a while, but soon the hall was silent and clean, as if Dr. Pazzo and Dr. Schneider had never been there. Nella and Frank waited through another four days of the same routine, blood tests, meals and new hospital clothes. At last a doctor in normal scrubs walked up to them. "Where's your mask?" Frank asked. The doctor grinned.

"Don't need it. Will you open the door Dan?"

The soldier appeared and Nella was mildly surprised to see his face. He was middle aged and a great scar raked across his face and neck. He opened Frank's cell first.

"Dan? It was you?" Frank shook his hand and the larger man pulled him into a hug. Frank looked over at Nella. "Thank you for- for everything."

"I'm sorry I didn't say anything, but if I'd had to shoot you-" the soldier swiped at his eyes. He walked over to Nella's door. "I told Frank he should be more social and that he didn't need to hide you away." He swung the glass door open. "Yet here we are, meeting for the first time. Sort of." He stuck out his hand and Nella shook it. This was the large man that had helped defend Frank the night Terry had gotten nasty. "My wife was so upset when she heard you were in quarantine. She wasn't the only one. I'm so glad you and Frank are okay." He pulled her into a hug.

"Come on Dan, I've been waiting a month to kiss her," laughed Frank.

"You and everyone else," growled Dan and then released her.

The doctor cleared his throat. "You are healthy and free to go. I understand if you need a minute, but there're some people who are pretty anxious to see you downstairs." He clapped Dan on the back. "Let's give these folks some space."

They walked down the hall toward the elevator. Frank and Nella were alone on the floor. No glass wall to separate them, no doomsday hanging over them.

"You want to stay another night? I hear the food is first rate here."

Frank grinned and walked toward her. "Eh, I give it three stars. The beds are too hard. But the view is excellent."

"You peeked." She wrapped her arms around him.

"I did," he said.

"I missed you." Her chest was too tight and she felt her breath catch inside and swirl as gravity flipped.

Frank didn't stop to answer, kissing her mouth, her neck, her cheek. She could feel the hum in his chest sing it's old familiar, yearning tune as he hugged her.

The phone in Nella's room began ringing. Nella pulled back an inch. Frank reached behind her and pushed the glass door closed. "Don't even think about it," he said.

"It's probably Sevita," Nella said.

"I don't care if it's the Governor himself. It can wait," said Frank and kissed her shoulder, backing her into the glass.

"She'll just come up here if we don't go down." Nella pushed him gently away.

Frank laughed and gave in, letting her loose. "Okay, okay," he looked around the hallway and Nella watched a shudder ripple through him. He took her hand again. "Let's go home."

They stepped off of the elevator and it took Nella's eyes a moment to adjust to the bright summer light pouring into the windows. For a second all she saw was a shadow of Frank lost in a halo of sun. A great roar like an ocean wave and a sudden downpour of pattering rain hit her at the same time. She threw up an arm in front of her face and blinked. Her eyes adjusted and she saw the lobby filled with people applauding. Sevita was poking her cameraman. Frank nudged her with an elbow, "Look," he whispered, "It *was* the Governor."

Sure enough, the Military Governor surrounded by a cadre of grim looking soldiers stood in the center of the lobby. "Do you think we're getting arrested?" Nella asked.

"Good thing you know an excellent lawyer," Frank grinned, pulling her farther into the crowd. Cheers came from all sides and people reached out to touch her, to shake hands with Frank, to clap them both on the back.

They reached the center of the lobby, the crowd separating and making a ring around them and the Governor. "Dr. Rider, Mr. Courtlen," he said, "It's taken a while, and interviews with a surprising number of people, but I believe I have now heard almost the whole story regarding the New December Plague and your role in preventing it. As head of the provisional government, I cannot condone your decision not to notify the authorities. However, as someone who has lived through the same harrowing events over the last decade that the rest of you have," the Governor looked around at the crowd and Nella was pleased to see both Immunes and Cured comfortably mixed, "I can understand why you acted the way that you did and why you feared tipping your hand too early. Without the heroic actions of you and your friends, today would have dawned on a terrified and violent City. You have safeguarded one of the last Plague-free zones in the world. And for that, we honor and thank you." The Governor paused as an explosion of applause engulfed them. "There is nothing we can offer you that would even approach what we owe to you. But I understand from some of your friends-" the Governor nodded at Christine who was blushing in the back of the crowd, "You've been planning an exploring expedition to the lost parts of the world. And that you intend not to return. I can't allow it."

He stared intently at Frank. Nella felt Frank's hand tighten around hers. The Governor continued. "This City needs you. It needs to realize that we all need to work and live together, Immunes and Cured. And you exemplify that. So you must return. Therefore, I am appointing the two of you as ambassadors for us. To contact other surviving communities and to distribute the Cure to anyone that still needs it. To set up trade routes and peaceful interaction between us and, if that fails, to explore and rediscover the regions that have been lost to us.

In the harbor there is a sailboat, outfitted by the military and supplied with doses of the Cure, our own provisions from the Farm and a wide variety of trade goods provided by the people around you. You are free to leave when you choose and to return when you choose. But I and the people of the City, hope you will return quickly and often." The Governor shook their hands and departed, riding a whirlwind of cheers. The lobby slowly emptied after dozens of well wishes and hand shakes, until only Sevita and Christine remained behind.

Sevita hugged Nella. "I'm so glad you're okay," she said, "But I'm going to miss you. You have to come back and see the baby." Nella was surprised to see Sevita crying.

"You're getting soft," she said, "Don't worry, it will be a few days, we've got to pack after all."

Sevita shook her head and smiled. "No, we did that for you."

Nella laughed. "Here's your hat, what's your hurry?"

A step behind Sevita, Christine spoke up. "There *is* one more thing to do before you go." She handed a small envelope to Frank. "I thought I better pick it up from the jeweler, since you were-indisposed."

Frank grinned and thanked her. He glanced around. "Not here though. And definitely not in hospital pajamas."

"We thought you'd say that. And we thought you might be tired of hospital food," said Sevita, "so we'll meet you on the boat in an hour." Christine put her arm around Sevita's waist and gently pulled her away. They walked out of the hospital into the bright, bustling afternoon.

"What was that about?"

"You'll see," said Frank with a grin.

THE BOAT

Sevita and Christine drove her to the docks to meet Frank. Nella had the windows open, enjoying the first fresh air she'd breathed in months. The day was warm and bright and more people than normal wandered the streets on errands. Sevita drove slowly, afraid to hit anyone and unwilling to part with Nella any earlier than she had to. When they puttered past Dr. Carton's mansion, Nella sat up. The house was dark, as it had been when they had snuck in, but the front door was hanging open as well.

"Sevita, did Dr. Carton move?" Nella asked.

Sevita glanced back at her in the mirror. "Ms. Jacobsen and I decided he would be better off with someone to take care of him. I know that's your area Nella, but you were so wrapped up in this whole mess- he had a stroke. For now he's at the prison, just because the medical care there is better than the hospital's. He'll go with Ann to Harbor House when she goes."

Nella nodded and let Dr. Carton and the mansion drop out of her thoughts as it disappeared behind them.

She shifted the flimsy fabric of her dress over the jagged red scar on her shoulder. Nella hadn't worn a dress this impractical since college. Still, it felt nice, like she was floating in the warm breeze of the docks. Christine had insisted that she wear it, just for this once. The short sleeve kept slipping and exposing her old wound and Nella was self conscious. She heard Frank's quick, light step behind her and hurried to cover the scar again.

"Don't," he said and kissed the rough raised

skin. "You look beautiful."

Nella blushed and turned around. "It's a nice boat Frank."

He looked up at it, hung with little lanterns and flying a bright white flag. "It's more than I ever thought we'd be able to find."

Sevita appeared at the top of the ramp and waved.

Frank slid an arm around her waist and walked beside her. He was transformed; happy and easy and utterly beautiful. He looked down at her. "I didn't think I'd ever be standing here you know."

"Are you sure you want to go? It could be years before we come back."

He looked back toward the City and the black shell of the Barrier closing it in. "There's things I'll miss, but I'm sure. But if you aren't ready-"

"No, I'm ready," Nella said, "When I walked here from the university, the City seemed so big. And so empty. You'd think it would seem the same after a month locked in a room. But it doesn't. It feels tiny and vulnerable and ancient. Like there's too much shared memory to really start over. It's time to spread out. To be explorers again."

Christine and Sevita were waiting for them on the deck. An impossibly full table was sitting in the center, a lit lantern flickering just a little in the breeze. Sevita was busy filling glasses. "Welcome home," said Christine smiling.

Frank turned to face Nella. "So, is my boat nicer than the other guy's?"

"Definitely," laughed Nella.

"Do you think I have a chance?"

Nella looked at him, confused. "A chance at what?"

Frank reached into his pocket. "Sevita warned me that I'd better do this properly. So, almost-Dr.

Nella Rider," Frank knelt on the wooden deck and held out a glittering thing, but Nella's eyes were too blurry to see what it was, "will you marry me?"

"Oh! Yes." And she didn't know if the ship were rocking or she was as he lifted her off her feet to kiss her. "Yes, Frank Courtlen, esquire-"

"Esquire-as-was," he interrupted.

"As-was," she laughed, "I'll marry you. I never want to us to be apart again."

Ned Glist wiped his face as he left the hot parking lot and entered the cool cement prison. He walked up to the young guard slouching next to the metal detector.

"Look," he said gruffly, "I been all over town. Someone told me that Dr. Carton was here. I've got a delivery for him."

"Yeah, he's here, in the infirmary. Go down the hall and make a left after the door," said the guard.

"Well, don't you want to wand me or check it or anything?"

The guard shook his head. "No prisoners here anymore. Just waiting on orders for my next rotation. No need for security anymore. You can go."

Ned shrugged and loped down the blue hall. He wasn't a curious man and he didn't stop to gawk at the empty cells. It only took him a few minutes to find the infirmary where a lone nurse sat at a badly lit desk.

"Do you know where Dr. Carton is?" he asked.

"Sure, he's in the far bed. Are you family?"

"No, just delivering something that was commissioned for him."

"I see. I'm sorry, but I don't think he's going to be able to accept it. He hasn't been able to speak at all since his stroke and he seems not to be very aware of what's going on around him."

Ned puffed out his cheeks in a sigh. "Look, it's nothing big and I promised I'd deliver it. Do you think you could take it and keep it for him, just in case?"

"I don't see the harm," said the nurse, "what is it?"

"Just a fancy gold fountain pen. It was commissioned weeks ago by someone here actually." Ned pulled the shining pen out of his shirt pocket.

"That's a strange coincidence," said the nurse.

Ned shrugged and handed her the pen. "Say, do you mind signing for it? I just want to have proof that I delivered it in case someone asks."

The nurse smiled and took the delivery scrip. "Sure." She pawed around her desk for an ink pen but only found pencils. Shrugging, she used the gold fountain pen and signed her name. "That's funny," she said, shaking it, "no ink."

Ned squinted at the pen. "But I put the cartridge in myself, it was a special glass one instead of plastic."

"Eh," said the nurse, picking up a pencil and signing the scrip, "You know how these special pens are, sometimes takes a while for the nib to start working." She glanced over at Dr. Carton. "Between you and me, I doubt he'll ever get to use it anyway."

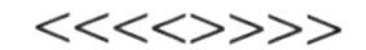

15884769R00233

Made in the USA
Middletown, DE
26 November 2014